A race against time.

Earth's survival at stake.

Four of the most unlikely heroes face a daunting task and should they fail...Earth will die. Every life on the planet depends on them and they in turn depend on the supreme kindness of an alien race. It's a story of love, hate, fear, determination and ultimate sacrifice.

The Messenger Within is a fast paced, insightful science fiction tale that takes the reader to Venus and returns with an extraordinary message and warning...

THE MESSENGER WITHIN

P G HARDING

StellarSky Publishing

StellarSky Publishing
PO Box 16008, 617 Belmont Street,
New Westminster, British Columbia, Canada, V3M 6W6

This book is a work of fiction. Any reference to historical events, real organizations, real people or real places are used fictitiously. Other names, characters, places and events are products of the Author's imagination and any resemblance to actual events or organizations or places or persons, living or dead, is entirely coincidental.

A CIP catalogue record for this book is available from Library and Archives Canada.

ISBN - 0994744501
ISBN 13 - 9780994744500
ISBN (ebook) - 978-0-9947445-1-7

ACKNOWLEDGEMENTS

It's been a very, very long journey and the following people kept me on my path and saw me safely to my destination. My dear thanks and love to all of them for their support and advice,

Noemia,
Amber,
Gordon,
Brian,
Pat,
Carrie,
Muriel,
Vic,
Craig,
Ceri,
Sarah

and finally, my wonderful wife,

Suzanne.

A life is not a life if not for love.

PG.

TABLE OF CONTENTS

Chapter 1

DISCOVERY

The sign at the side of the dark, quiet, two lane desert highway read, *Slow to 35 miles per hour.* Scott Benbow hardly noticed it. He had lost count of the number of times he had driven this road. He was commuting to work. For a brief second Scott took his foot off the accelerator, let the Lotus feel its way into the curve, then in a smooth continuous motion he pressed down on the gas pedal. The Lotus leapt forward, a Cheetah after prey, its claws dug into the pavement, holding the car at a seemingly impossible angle on the road. Scott was pushed back and sideways into the form fitting seat. He could feel the G forces tearing at his head, trying to shove him into the side windshield. *He loved that feeling!* In control, yet out of control. At the very edge. *Now he was alive!* The tires were still silent, not a whimper out of them. Scott pressed a little harder on the pedal. They began to sing a soft, high-pitched tune. Still the car was glued to the road, held there by ephemeral rails. His foot squeezed some more. The soft tune became a scream. The Cheetah was losing its grip, back-end first. Scott casually glanced down at the speedometer—ninety-five miles per hour. *Not Bad. A new record.* He held the car, almost on willpower alone, at that speed through the entire corner. By the time he reached the straight stretch the Lotus was two thirds into the oncoming lane. Scott was betting his life on the odds. He almost never saw a car on the road at six thirty in the morning.

He didn't have to get up at that time; most of the other guys got into work much later than Scott. But at the end of the thirty mile journey was one of the most impressive sights that he had ever seen.

He glanced at his watch, *I'm a bit late. Going to have to push it today.* He shoved the gas pedal of the Lotus almost to the floor and ran it full-out over the three-quarter mile straight-stretch that lay in front of him. The car was flying down the road at one-hundred-and-eighty miles per hour when he started over-braking in preparation for the next corner. Immediately the Lotus began to sway. Scott could feel the backend of the car losing its grip as it slid one way and then, countering his desperate correction, the other. *Going too fast!* Any further braking would send the car into an out of control, fish-tail slide. Contrary to all his instincts, Scott pulled his foot from the brake pedal and let the car continue its disastrous course toward the corner. His feet fired off a rapid tap dance as he double clutched, shifted down one gear and kicked the engine revs up past the red line. As soon as the clutch engaged the second time he eased his foot slightly off the pedal. The screaming car was now careening into the corner. The rear wheels were beginning to slide off the road. As Scott struggled frantically to keep the car on the pavement, he ever-so-delicately, ever-so-carefully released the gas pedal, letting the engine slow the car down. Meanwhile he held the shaking, shuddering, steering wheel tight as he could. The car had slid almost entirely into the oncoming lane but he was going to make it, he wasn't going to crash. Scott was thinking, *Boy that was clo...*, when he saw headlights right in front of him.

Right in front of him! No way could he get back into his lane. He'd flip the car if he twitched that wheel clockwise one more hair, and if that happened he was almost certainly dead—at this speed the Lotus would disintegrate. Scott had only one, minuscule, chance of survival—he released the wheel and let the massive momentum of the car take him straight out of the corner across the path of the oncoming vehicle onto a flat, one-hundred-foot wide, gravel embankment that followed the curve of the road and was often used as a parking area for sight-seeing. The other car was just a smudge in the corner of his eye as the front of the Lotus hit the gravel. He braced for a collision...nothing. The car had missed him! Now the Lotus was tearing through the gravel, on course for a fifty-foot drop into a dry river bed. Scott slammed on the brakes and whipped the wheel back towards the road as hard as he could—praying that the wheels would grab something solid. The car slid sideways toward the drop off. He wasn't going to make it. Not a chance. *Wait! Wait! A road!* Just over the edge of the embankment a road was angling its way down to the river bed. Scott could see that the car's momentum was taking him just past the beginning of that road, just past his salvation.

He pounded on the gas pedal as hard as he could and tried to steer the sliding, bouncing, out of control car towards the road. But the Lotus continued on its sideways route to the river bed. The back-left wheel was starting over the cliff when the front wheels stabbed themselves into the road. The car began to pull forward. The other rear wheel was almost over the edge. The car was starting to tilt. The front wheels were scraping and screaming at the road, rocks were kicking up—beating the heck out of the undercarriage; a cloud of dust and dirt swirled furiously around the car. Scott's entire body tensed as he involuntarily braced for the crash. Suddenly, miraculously, the car lurched forward; Scott felt a bump as the left-rear swung back and finally re-established itself with the ground. Then he was rattling down the rough gravel road. Scott stamped on the brakes and in a cloud of dust and rock, brought the poor Lotus to a stop. He took several deep breaths as he watched the dust slowly settle...once again the world was a quiet, peaceful place—in the distance a robin sang its morning song. Scott slapped his hands against the steering wheel and started to laugh. *This is the luckiest day of my life!* An instant later his mind returned to its original objective—he glanced at his watch. *I can still make it.*

Scott slammed the car into reverse and red-lined his way up the hill. There was no sign of the other car. With the Lotus still sliding backwards, he shifted into first gear and floored the gas pedal. Two big rooster tails of gravel, dirt and dust flew up behind the Lotus as Scott swung the car back to the pavement.

He was in a great mood. *What a rush!* He ripped along the road, not the least deterred by his incredibly close call. With the Lotus, his Cheetah, back in control he weaved his way, corner after corner towards his destination.

Then, with little warning, the road thrust its way out of the hills and opened into a flat, seemingly endless expanse of desert. Just that view on its own would be spectacular, but the array of radio telescopes that fanned out before him took his breath away. Here, every day, Scott would pull the car over and soak up the view one more time. The road, slightly elevated from the desert floor, provided Scott with an unobstructed view of each row of antennae as they fell away from him. The array was a good half-mile from his viewpoint, yet in the clear desert air it seemed to Scott that he could reach out and touch it.

His wake-up call was carefully timed so that he would arrive just as the sun rose. There, in the twilight of dawn, he would sit for a few minutes, his expectation building, eyes ready to reap the reward of his early morning trip. Then, as the first fine rays of light climbed over the hills behind him, as if by magic, the tips of the massive structures began to glow. The raw, hard contrast between the dim shadows of the untouched desert and the brilliant reflected radiance was absolutely stunning. As the sun rose, it seemed as if the whole structure grew out of the desert sands like huge metal petals unfolding to the sky. It was spectacular and surreal. It was a landscape from a Science Fiction film. *Extremely fitting given the purpose of this place,* thought Scott.

The antenna array, the largest and most modern of its kind, had been specifically built for the purpose of searching for faint radio signals emanating from space. Not for radio signals from stars or black holes or other nonsentient signals, but for intelligent signals, ones which would prove the existence of life beyond Earth.

Ten rows of thirty antennas—three hundred silent soldiers, each a hundred feet high, facing the heavens, stood on guard straining to hear a hello from the cosmos. It was an incredible, awe inspiring sight. These special flat panel photon receivers which collected radio wave energy packets were the result of years of research, a thousand times more sensitive than any of their predecessors; they were mankind's hope of finally finding other intelligent life in the Universe.

"Morning guys. What's on the menu for today?" As he sat at his desk, Scott's thoughts were broken by Graham Billings. Graham, a dark-haired, slim, five-foot-nine, twenty-four year old, was one of Scott's partners at the Search for Extra-Terrestrial Intelligence Institute or as it was commonly known, SETI. Graham was a good guy, sharp, quick witted and definitely a believer—Scott categorized everybody into two groups, believers and nonbelievers—in Alien life. To Scott and people like Graham it was obvious, a no-brainer. The sheer numbers of planets in the galaxy, let alone the universe made it impossible to refute life on other worlds. It was just a matter of finding them. Had they traveled to earth? Well that was another question. The "traveled to earth" people were a subculture of the believer group. He was sitting on the fence with regards to that, didn't know which way to topple.

"The same old crap." That was Scott's other partner, Blair Cunningham. Short, round and at the age of twenty the youngest of the team, Blair was a definite nonbeliever. Well actually, a "didn't give a damn," subset of the nonbeliever category. Scott didn't know why he was even here. It couldn't be the pay—it wasn't great. It wasn't the work because Blair made it plain that he hated it. "Boring, repetitive, mind-numbing, brain-sucking, drain-the-life-out-of-me garbage." he said, over and over again.

"Well, what the hell are you doing here then?" Scott had asked.

"Okay, I admit it, I'm the laziest son of a bitch around, can't be bothered to look for another job."

"Well then shut up about it will ya?"

"I gotta admit another thing...I'm a natural born complainer. The only time I feel good is when I'm complaining about something. If I wasn't complaining about this awful job, I'd be complaining about something else—probably you. So be happy that I'm able to completely focus on bitching about this god-damn, awful, boring, life-sucking, brain-diddling, job!!!"

"Fine. Have it your way. I give up." Scott had exclaimed in mock frustration.

Strangely enough, Scott didn't mind Blair. At least he was honest about it all, and Scott must admit that even for him, sometimes the work was boring. At the very least, the stuff that came out of Blair's mouth kept them entertained.

Their job, every day, was to point the antenna array at some tiny part of the universe and leave it there while the ultra-sensitive receivers scanned through the radio band straining to find some kind of signal that just might be intelligent. Although software could help to identify signals that were possibly sentient, Scott didn't completely trust it. He used the program to help him—he always looked at those signals first. But he would run through the whole band anyway, just in case—you never knew—it would be a real shame if, just because the team was lazy, they missed the biggest discovery the world had ever known. To Scott it just wasn't worth it, and because Scott was the team leader, that's what they did. Of course Blair hated it, and every day Scott had to listen to a morning stream of invectives, along with some pleading. Today was no different.

"Oh man, we're not going to run through the whole band again are we? Christ! You're killing me! Why don't you stake me out in the sun and just get it over with? I hear the Indians used to dig a hole in the sand in the desert, right in an ant hill, put their enemies in the hole, filled it in—right up to their necks and let the ants eat them alive. That would be a more merciful end than what you're putting me through today. God-damn useless job. Boring, stupid, waste-of-time job."

Then came the pleading, "Hey, who's going to know that we didn't check the whole spectrum? The chances of us finding the 'big one' are so slim that we could do this for the rest of our lives, our children's lives, their children's lives, so on and so on and still not find anything. Hell!

We've got a better chance of winning the lottery. Let's just skip it today. Why not?" Blair's pudgy face screwed itself up into what he thought was a good imitation of a tortured saint; unfortunately it more closely resembled a tired Saint Bernard, "Okay, I don't normally beg, but I'm begging you!"

"Blair, you begged me yesterday. As a matter of fact you begged me the day before yesterday and the day before that and the week before that...I'm pretty sure you have begged me every day since you started working here."

"Okay but this is a new improved kind of begging—I'm going to start crying as well."

"Well it won't work, so don't bother. Besides it will just put Graham off his lunch."

"Damn rights it will." Graham said with a grin. "If you keep whining, I'll try that ant hill idea, see how well you like it."

"Okay then, I'll just go and surf some porn—let me know when you're done."

"You do that and you will be looking for that new job you're too lazy to find," Scott replied angrily, "Tell you what, just for that comment, I'm giving you a little extra today. You can do some surfing alright. You can surf the whole spectrum at these coordinates while Graham and I work on next week's plan." As he spoke, Scott punched up today's plan on the computer, scribbled down the coordinates on a piece of paper and handed it to a dismayed Blair. "Let me know when you're done."

Blair shut up. He knew that he had gone too far this time. He wasn't going to mess with Scott. A well-built six-foot-two, Scott could do some serious damage if he wanted to.

A depressed Blair dragged his sorry ass off to what he called "the hole." It was a windowless, merciless room filled with electronic equipment, computers and screens. The dreary hum of air conditioning and equipment fans greeted him as he entered. Blair didn't know which was worse, the lack of sunlight or the God-awful sound of those fans. Besides that, you had to wear a jacket or you'd freeze your ass off.

"Stuck in here all day." Blair cursed under his breath. Just about everything he needed to do could be done from the main office but Scott thought that working in "the hole" was much better for concentration—there were no distractions. He sure was right about that. It was pure torture.

Blair's hands rummaged through all his pockets looking for the co-ordinates but to no avail. *Damn. I left them in the office.* He checked all his pockets again. Nothing. An embarrassed, determined thought soon surfaced, *I'm sure as hell not going back there to get them.* An instant later, Blair's face wiggled itself into a comical look of confused concentration as he tried to mentally reinstate the missing coordinates. With eyes glazed over and pursed brow, his mind searched frantically for the missing numbers. But for a long period of time his brain remained frustratingly blank. Then he remembered a trick he had heard of before—visualize the paper and read the numbers back as if he were staring down at them. Blair's expression changed again, his pursed brow became more pronounced, the eyes shifted to narrow slits and, with lips protruding slightly, his mouth followed suit. While he applied a level of concentration that was totally foreign to his underutilized mind, his nearly shut eyes attempted to read a non-existent paper in front of him. *Nothing.* He took a breath and tried again. Then, a small miracle, *Yeah.... Yeah.... I got it!* Round, overfed fingers hastily punched out the coordinates on a keyboard.

Sadly, the most impressive part of his job Blair never got to see—watching the whole radio array track to the new coordinates in the desert. Like gigantic robots in a slow motion ballet, the whole network of antennas, all three hundred, on cue, moved precisely to the new focus.

"What the hell are you doing?" Scott said as he burst into the room.

"Huh? What?" shouted Blair as he almost jumped out of his chair. "Jeeze, you scared the crap out of me!"

"Blair, the antenna array is practically pointing at the horizon. You're sure as hell going to find intelligent life down here. You've screwed up the coordinates again."

"Sorry, I thought I knew them. Let me get them, they're on my desk."

Scott watched as Blair ran out of the room. The array was pointing about five degrees above the horizon, nowhere near where it was supposed to be. He sat down fuming, they had lost almost an hour—it took twenty-five minutes to move those antennas to the wrong coordinates, and now it was going to take even longer to get them back to the right ones. He impatiently looked at his watch and then glanced at the spectrum monitor, started to look away...felt a slight sensation, a disquiet—something wasn't quite right. He looked back. Nothing there. Blair had started the spectrum scan, so it was running through the frequency band. Probably wasn't anything, or perhaps Blair had managed to pickup one of the local TV stations, a radio station, a cell phone call, a satellite signal or something else, who knows?

A debate started in his mind—should he check? Just to be sure? It's a pain in the ass, he'd have to run through the entire scan, demodulate each suspected signal, look for nonrepetitive indications and check that it wasn't indeed from Earth. Even if it was a real signal, he sure as hell wouldn't be able to understand it, unless of course the alien race just so happened to use ITU or ANSII telecommunication standards. So it was a ton of work to ensure that the signal wasn't a nonsentient object or some weird aberration of interstellar noise. Without a doubt, the team was looking at a day's worth of work just to review these few moments of received signal. But Scott prided himself on his thoroughness. Once that scan was started, he felt obliged to complete it. Otherwise someone else, maybe even his team, was going to have to do it again at some time anyway. Also, there was always a very, very, very minute chance that he would miss the one opportunity to claim that he was the first person to discover intelligence on another planet. It was something he had dreamed about all his life. It drove him to do what he was doing now. It was what kept him sane during all these failures, kept him determined to never quit, kept him from becoming another Blair.

Okay—first thing—find out where in the sky Blair actually pointed the array. Maybe after that I won't feel compelled to do anything further.

"I've got it," Blair said as he charged back into the room and quickly sat at the control console. He was reaching for the keyboard when to his surprise, Scott's hand suddenly shot out and stopped him.

"Don't do anything," he said quietly. So quiet that Blair immediately looked at him, startled. He knew that Scott had an inverse personality—the quieter he became, the more pissed off he was. He was very quiet.

"You really screwed up this time—you've started the scan. While I was sitting here I thought I saw an energy spike on the monitor. Now we have to review it. It's going to cost us lots of time. Don't know what I'm going to tell the boss."

"Aw no, no we don't, let's just pretend it didn't happen."

"Be quiet." Those soft words held Blair in stasis. His voice dropped even lower. "Just do as I say. Check out those coordinates that you entered. I want to know where you pointed the array. Let me know when you're done."

Scott left the room. He could feel his whole chest getting tight—it was the sensation that he experienced every time he had to control his emotions. He needed time to relax.

Blair typed in the co-ordinates into a computer near-by. He wasn't the kind of guy who could take a lot of stress. It was the biggest reason he hadn't quit this job ages ago—*No Stress*. But, like the loser he was, he managed to create his own. The coordinate location popped up on the computer, "Bloody hell! I must have typed them wrong." He tried again. Same thing. Again. Same thing.

Scott was standing outside the building, in the shade, looking over the desert. Not at the antenna array, just the desert. The morning air was already heating, distant objects were beginning to shimmer. The warm air, touched him, soothed him. The desert was such a peaceful place.

That's where Blair found him.

"Look, I'm really sorry. I know I blew it big time."

"Yeah, well, too late now. Let's fix it and move on."

"Just what I was hoping. Only one problem."

"What?"

"The coordinates I calculated don't make sense."

"Why?"

"Well, the array seems to be focused on Venus." Blair saw an angry look of disbelief on Scott's face and desperately fired off an anxious, high pitched reply. "I checked it ten times!! Couldn't believe it myself. Can you come and double-check for me?"

A sense of excitement began to build in Scott. If the array was really pointed at Venus he knew what that meant. *Wait a minute,* he thought. *He's probably got it wrong.*

He replied, calm as always, "You bet I'm going to check it. You know why? Because I'm sure that I saw an energy spike out of the corner of my eye while I was waiting for you and if that's true and the array is pointing at Venus then you know what that means. Venus is too close for any kind of serious interstellar noise, unlikely you would pick up any nonsentient type of signals. Maybe, just maybe, the scan detected a lightning strike but otherwise...."

"Yeah. We hit the mother lode!"

"Don't get too excited, first thing—we go back and double-check everything, review the whole scan and secondly...."

"What?"

"We tell absolutely no one. Not until we are completely certain. Now go get Graham. We have a ton of work to do."

Chapter 2

KURT

It was one of the driest, hottest summers on record. A time of concern for adults but for the Summertime Gang, it was paradise. Almost every day they would meander their way to the lake—stopping here and there, poking at a dead raccoon, throwing rocks at a can, giving each other wedgies, chasing a rabbit into the bush. Summer was coming to an end. Soon it would be back to school. But no one mentioned it. They were clinging to summer, determined to keep it for their own.

The gang had a secret spot at the lake. In fact, it was almost another lake in itself. At the far end of the big lake, a half mile from where all the cottages, houses and mansions stood, was a small, overgrown creek. If one waded through the shallow water of the stream, shoved his way through countless reeds and ducked a thousand branches, after about a hundred yards, he would find a quiet, isolated pool surrounded by tall trees and dense underbrush. It wasn't big, but big enough for the Summertime Gang. A quarter mile at its largest extent, it had an irregular shape that provided little hidden bays and nooks. Full of turtles, frogs and fish, isolated and secret, for seven young boys, it was magic. They all had sworn never to speak of it to anyone outside of the gang.

Wayne, who had found this place first, discovered a much easier way to get in and out of what turned out to be private property. Actually there were several ways, but the best was a mile long, winding, steep gravel road, partially overgrown, that took them up to the highway.

They didn't know who owned the property surrounding the pond but in the three summers that they had taken it as their own, they had never seen a soul. Almost every day, weather permitting, they would approach the entrance to the lane from the highway, post a sentry on either side of the passage and on a special "safe" signal from the lookouts, dive under the gate, past the "NO TRESPASSING" sign, onto the forest path.

Once at the lake an almost infinite variety of adventures awaited them. They fished, they swam, they polled their rickety raft around the shallow pond, they dove from rocks and tree limbs into the sweet water, they captured turtles and frogs, they hunted squirrels and rabbits, they built tree forts, they fought ancient battles with sticks for swords, they captained a pirate ship or just basked in the sun. As far as the Summertime Gang was concerned, their world existed only within this enchanted land of magic and fantasy.

It was late afternoon. The gang, in damp shorts, with towels and T-shirts in hand, were trudging up the steep, narrow dirt lane which ran up to the highway. They were walking along a straight stretch, a few hundred yards long—they were spread out across and down the dry, dusty track, almost like a platoon on a mission—each boy taking his own route. Sycamore trees, thick with leaves waving gently in the breeze, lined both sides of the path. The beautiful trees provided welcome shade from another hot, hot day. Birds, perhaps hundreds of them, sat hidden in the branches, whistling and twittering in an incessant backdrop of pleasant, peaceful chatter.

Up front was Kellen "Skinny" Mickleson. He was a black kid with endless energy whose father had made it big in the stock market. He was quick witted—there was always a joke on his lips and a smirk on his hard, angular face. He had stopped to kick at a dry, rotted log at the edge of the road. Each swing of his boot produced a spray of jagged bits of wood and dust.

"Cool. Have a look at this!" he shouted. "Tons of ants. Wow!"

Mike Newbury and Lyndon Niven rushed up to see the panicking ants swarming out of their tunnels—determined to protect their home. Mike, another rich boy whose forty year old dad had already retired, was average height with reddish-brown hair and regular facial features that most of the time held a happy, satisfied expression. Lyndon came from the other end of the financial spectrum. His father had left his mother years ago and hadn't made a single support payment. His mother worked as a clerk at an insurance company in downtown Boston, and they lived in a small run down apartment an hours bus ride from the city center, but during the summers he stayed with his Aunt and her husband in a small home about a mile from the lake. He had met the rest of the guys three summers ago and had fit in. Lyndon was slightly chubby, had brown hair and a round face with a flat nose. A small scar over his right eye contributed to a boxer like appearance—one who had seen one punch too many. With a permanent worry frown tucked between his blue eyes, Lyndon provided a stark contrast to the countenance of his best buddy Mike.

Wayne Dockerty, tallest of the bunch and unspoken leader of the gang walked with Kurt who fancied himself as second in command. Fair, good looking, smart and rich, even at the age of just thirteen Wayne was already on the fast track to success. Kurt, who was short for his age but strong and stocky, with dark hair, a mean bull-dog face and a temperament to match, couldn't make any claims to the same. Kurt's father worked at the slaughter-house just up the road—killing and cleaning. Every night he came home smelling of blood, guts and booze. His mother...well she was pretty much useless. Scared and submissive, she did nothing to prevent the almost daily beatings that Kurt received from his abusive father; the one time she had tried to interfere she had taken a good pounding herself. Kurt was the tough boy of the gang, the enforcer. He kept the rest of the local yokels away from the rich kids. He did a good job, even if he did say so himself—certainly none of the gang had the guts to complain to his face, and so far as he was concerned that was good enough.

Just behind Wayne and Kurt, Gunnar Lindquist had stopped for a moment and was staring up into the trees, looking at who knows what. He was so quiet that they often forgot that he was there. Gunny, as they called him, was a recent immigrant from Sweden. His family, who were already prominent in the community, had brought a ton of money with them. He was almost as tall as Wayne with blond hair, blue eyes and a strange sharply pinched face—his nose, chin and forehead tapered too quickly towards the center of his head. In a bizarre fashion it looked almost as if someone had started to sharpen his skull into a blade and then changed their minds.

It was sure hot. They had just pulled themselves out of the cool waters of the lake but already Whalen Stipple, bringing up the rear as usual, was complaining about the heat. Whalen was another rich kid and a big boy. Not tall—he was average height for his age—just big. Whalen was heavy-boned and unfortunately had an innate tendency to pack on the pounds which, when combined with a natural laziness, caused him to amass some serious weight in his short life. Those extra pounds were an advantage in the cold water of the lake where he could outlast everyone but it was a definite disadvantage on this uphill climb. His features, which might have been handsome, had been somewhat softened by an extra layer of fat that left him looking like a youthful Friar Tuck.

"Why do we have to go this way? It's too steep! Let's go through old man Ryker's place."

"Christ Whalen, we'll walk an extra mile going that way." replied Wayne.

"But it's not so steep. I don't want to go this way. It's too steep and it's so stinkin hot. I'm already sweating my ass off."

"And that's sure a big ass!" shouted Kellen.

"Screw-you Kellen! Come back here, and I'll wipe my big ass on your face!"

"Come on Whale." Kellen turned and slapped his skinny butt. "Come up here and catch me."

"Don't call me that you jerk!"

Whalen reached down and picked up a nice sized rock and chucked it at Kellen. The rock, a good fifty yards from its target, wobbled its way uphill and like its' master gave up about halfway, splattering and clattering with a little puff of dust onto the ground. The whole lane erupted into laughter. Whalen, mad, a little humiliated and very glad that his impulsive rock hadn't reached its destination swore a blue streak at the lot of them.

Someone shouted, "Dirt-lump fight!"

The platoon scattered in all directions, off to the sides of the road, kicking at caked mud, long since dried, each of them building up a miniature ammunition dump of nice, throwing sized, hard packed lumps of dirt.

"Every man for himself!"

The air filled with missiles, yells of pain, cries of sadistic delight, curses and laughter.

"No fair!" screamed Lyndon, ducking dirt bullets as a well-armed Kurt charged in his direction. Lyndon, who was feverishly replenishing his stock, was trying to invoke a "no fly zone."

Kurt was still coming. Lyndon tried one more time, "NO FAIR!", but Kurt was still coming. Lyndon managed a weak, errant throw with his one and only missile and then turned and ran for the trees. Several of the bombs whizzed by, self-destructing in a cloud of grey-brown smoke as they struck the undergrowth near the trees. He was close to safety. Close to the trees. A triumphant giggle bubbled out of his lips which was cut short by a yell of pain as Kurt's final shot struck the back of Lyndon's right thigh. Two more limp-hop strides took Lyndon into the trees.

"Ha! Gotch ya!" It was Kurt's turn to be triumphant. His sadistically gleeful, chiding voice chased Lyndon into the woods, "Where you going? Come back! Chicken! Hee! Hee! Come back! Don't run away.

Chicken! Chicken! Chicken!" Kurt's attempt at coercion had no effect on Lyndon. He continued dogging through the trees, still whimpering and moaning from the point-blank, direct-hit on his leg.

Kurt swung happily back to the road and began a pan of the situation, looking for weakness, looking for his next victim. There was Whalen. He had trundled up the road, heat and sweat forgotten, determined to get in on the action. His ample back was towards Kurt, just begging for a big bruise. Kurt, practically drooling in anticipation, started quietly moving in his direction—he wanted to be really close when he drilled Whalen. He wanted to hear the thud and the scream of pain. He wanted to watch Whalen squirm and wiggle as he suffered. Kurt was so excited he could hardly breathe. Ten feet. Another stride. Seven feet. One last stride. Arm back. Adrenalin exploded into his body and shot towards his arm.

"KURT!" The voice was loud. It was Wayne and he was close. Very close. Instinct told him to move, to turn toward the voice. Quick as lightening he swiveled...started to crouch...but too late! A big, size of your fist, dirt bomb hit him in the center of his bare chest, exactly over his heart. There was a brief moment of nothing...then pain sizzled its way to his brain. Damn it hurt. HURT! HURT! He doubled over. But kept silent. He wasn't going to give anyone the pleasure that he had so anticipated a few seconds ago. Pain fueled anger made its appearance, quickly spreading and growing. He wanted revenge. Kurt straightened up, brought his already loaded arm into position. When he took another hit. This time on his throwing arm. Right on the biceps. Numbness and then more pain. The dirt lump dropped from his hand. His arm, numb and weak, was useless. He was done for. In terrible pain, but refusing to show it like the rest of the wimps, he stuck a crooked smile on his face, raised his hands and said, "Okay, I give."

His attacker, his best buddy, Wayne, looked at him, hesitated, his eyes widened...suddenly laughter exploded out of him, and boiled up the lane. The combatants paused. Eyes looked to Wayne, and then traveled to Kurt. The rest of the gang, wary of Kurt's temper, struggled to hold back their laughter. Then, the normally quiet Gunny surprised them all and said with his Swedish accent,

"Holly fewuck Kurt! Yoouo lewke like yoouo were newuuked!"

That was too much for the rest of them, the dam had been broken. Faces stretched tight by suppressed laughter burst open, spewing spit and sound into the air.

Kurt looked down at his chest. It was covered in a spray of dirt centered at his heart and radiating outward and upward. He touched his chin, lips, nose and forehead and became aware, finally, for the reason of their mirth. He was covered in the stuff. Dirt and grit, previously masked by pain, became the center of his attention. He wiped his lips and started spitting the crap out of his mouth, then wiped again, then spit again and again. His repeated actions started a new round of laughter.

"Very funny," Kurt said.

Wayne, noticing the red welt forming on Kurt's chest and feeling guilty for being the cause of his friend's pain and embarrassment said, "Are you okay?"

"I'm fine."

"It was just...well...you were such an easy target."

Kurt refused to give Wayne and the gang any further pleasure at his expense, "I'm fine." was his monotone response.

Wayne continued, "Wow, you're tough man." The welt was starting to grow. "Look at that bruise. I'm really sorry, didn't think it would be that bad."

"It's okay."

The whole crew had gathered around, "oohing" and "aahing" at the war wound. The attention and respect that comes with suffering in silence was making its mark. Kurt was starting to feel better. But, the undercurrent of jealousy and resentment that Kurt had always felt towards his friend, the rich boy, had risen to a new level. Thoughts of revenge were simmering and waiting...waiting to go to a full boil.

———

It was the end of August, and two weeks after the "dirt bomb" incident the dreaded word, *School*, had finally forced its way into their thoughts and out of their lips. For the modern day Tom Sawyers, the sense of loss was pervasive. This was the last hour of their last day. Would another summer like this come again? Next year, some of them would be fourteen. These halcyon days of play and pretend would be left behind as time pressed them toward adulthood.

The Summertime Gang was slowly, silently working their way back up the hill. This time they had a guest. Wayne had brought his dog, Hero, with him. Hero was a beautiful, black and white, four year old Boarder Collie who was so full of life and happiness that none of the Summertime Gang could remain solemn for long. As they trudged up the tedious hill, Hero kept them entertained, running from one to the other, chasing squirrels, birds and any other wildlife he could find, barking and jumping with his shiny, gleaming coat shimmering in the air. They all had a good laugh as they watched him fruitlessly try to capture a brilliant yellow butterfly, winking in and out of the dappled sunlight, as it flitted its way across the road—fifteen feet above the ground.

Kurt, off to the side and away from the group, noticed a stick, around four feet long, at the side of the road. He bent down and picked it up. It was a nice hefty stick—reasonably straight. The base where it had been snapped off was jagged, nasty-sharp and as thick as the handle of a tennis racket. The other end tapered down to the size of his thumb. In-between, a few tattered branches still remained. He held the fat end and took a couple of swings in the air. There wasn't much bend to it—it wouldn't make a good switch. He was about to toss it away when he noticed the dog, now making a charge up the hill to the front of the pack and...had a thought. With a quick, easy, motion he lifted his knee in the air and snapped the stick in half across it. He kept the thick half and flung the other into the woods. His stick now had two ragged, sharp ends. As Kurt walked up the road, he slowly pealed back the one remaining little offshoot branch, watching as the pathetic limb struggled to remain with its parent...bending at the join to an impossible angle...

then with a sound like a sucking sigh, tearing away—taking a bit of soft, smooth bark with it.

Once it was gone, he picked at the wound in the supple green bark, working his thumbnail underneath the skin. When he got enough of a purchase, he brutally pinched the bark between his thumbnail and forefinger, then pulled hard down the shaft of the wood. The soft skin of the young sapling ripped in a jagged V down the length of the branch with a sickly, squelchy, sucking sound. Little drops of moisture, the saplings blood, oozed out of the wound. Kurt looked up from his dissection—they were approaching the busy highway, he couldn't see it yet, they were still down the hill a bit but he could hear the quiet hiss of motors and wheels, almost like a wind rustling through distant trees. It was growing louder as they approached. Kurt looked for Hero. He was back with his master, fifteen feet in front of Kurt. Kurt subtly increased his pace and turned his attention back to the stick. The remaining skin, now horrifically damaged, peeled away easily. Soon he had a sickly white-grey, slimy, two-foot long weapon. He held the thick end and looked at the ragged point at the other. His eyes swung up to Wayne and Hero. They were only ten feet away now. The highway was close. Trees still blocked the view but the noise was no longer a sweet wind in the distance, it was a rumbling, roaring, hissing monster daring Kurt to come on. He looked at Hero again. He was such a healthy, happy dog. Kurt took the stick and stabbed it into the gravel at the edge of the road. Bent over, he dragged it through the dirt watching the ragged point rip open the soil, expecting to see blood pour out of the gash. He stood straight and looked at the dog again. Hero had rushed over to Whalen, tail wagging, barking. With a big grin on his face, Whalen reached down and patted the bobbing head. Hero responded to the loving attention by rising on his hind legs, placing forepaws on Whalen's chest and giving him a big, wet, doggy kiss on the face. Whalen let out with a "Yuck!" and leaned back—trying to escape the well-meaning dog slobber. Laughing, the Summertime Gang stopped to observe the struggle—it seemed that Hero was winning. Kurt took one extra step and slid up beside Wayne.

"Wayne! Get your friggen dog off of me!" yelled Whalen.

Wayne, between gasps of laughter said, "Hero! Come on boy! Come here!" and then "Good boy" as the dog bounded back toward Wayne and Kurt. Hero, happy in his innocence, launched himself at Wayne, attempting the same tactic that he had used so successfully on Whalen. Wayne, smiling, easily dodged Hero's advances. Undeterred, the dog continued on to Kurt and brushed against his leg – Hero's joyful head was turned up to Kurt and seemed full of unconditional love. An unexpected, warm, wonderful thought flashed into Kurt's mind, *beautiful.*

Hero sailed past, stamped all four paws into the soil of the path, and in a smooth, incredibly coordinated motion swung back towards the two boys. Suddenly he spied the stick hanging loose in Kurt's right hand. Seeing a new opportunity for play, he made a leap toward the stick. Kurt pulled his hand back and up. In an instant he and the dog were in a game of "get the stick" with Kurt moving the stick this way and that, up and down, round and round. The dog was barking, jumping, following the stick—always a jaw snap away from success. Kurt was smiling and laughing—everything but the moment forgotten.

A few happy minutes later, Hero had turned back to Wayne. Kurt, still warm inside, looked down at the stick, once murderous, now...unnecessary. He lifted his arm, about to toss the weapon into the trees.

"The bruise is almost gone."

That soft, ethereal voice held the stick motionless above his head for an endless moment, a moment around which his entire world revolved.

Then the arm dropped back to his side and remained inert for some time. Finally, Kurt, dazed and confused, slowly turned his head to Wayne. Wayne was watching Hero gallop off towards Mike who was closing in on the gate and the highway.

"Yes it is almost gone," Kurt said.

"What?"

"The bruise."

"Huh? Wha.... Oh!" Wayne looked at Kurt's bare chest and said, "Yeah it is, isn't it? It took a long time to heal." A look of care and concern crossed Wayne's face. He said, "I still feel bad about it. I'm glad it's almost gone."

"Almost gone...yes...almost gone," was Kurt's toneless, distracted reply.

The highway beckoned once again. Harsh, hating sounds of engines under stress tore apart the peace of the woods. Kurt raised his arm for a second time—lazy almost—and flicked the stick up into the air. The stick performed a slow motion, half-revolution and was caught as it descended toward Earth. Kurt, whistling an unrecognizable tune, strode forward, past Wayne. As if on cue, the rest of the gang moved toward the road.

Hero had now passed Mike and was on a course for the highway. Wayne, with just a touch of concern in his voice called, "Hero! Hero! Here boy!" Hero, playfully disobedient, continued on. In an instant he was under the gate. Wayne, his concern now self-evident, put full power into his voice and called again, "Hero! HERO! COME HERE NOW!" The dog, at the edge of the road, stopped and turned back to Wayne.

Mike, the sentry for the day, ducked under the gate, crouched in the brush and looked down the highway in both directions. On his signal, the Summertime Gang made their last rush for the road.

Kurt, Wayne and Hero left their domain together and started walking down the road, towards home. On the opposite side of the highway, an old, dark-green pickup truck, with broken muffler belching harsh sound and smoke, was approaching. Then, just as Wayne turned to take one last look at their sanctuary, Kurt silently waggled the stick at Hero and moved ahead of Wayne. Hero bounded forward, eyes alert, watching the stick. The truck was coming quickly. The rattling, ragged noise became loud and menacing. It would soon be on them. Kurt looked down at the wonderful collie jumping and bouncing beside him. His face glazed over and then...hardened. The stick, pointed and jagged, sticky with tree blood, rose, almost by itself, above Kurt's head.

Abruptly, Wayne turned back to the road and immediately saw the danger. He screamed, "KURT! KURT! WHAT ARE YOU DOING?"

Kurt's face, a mask of pale, uncaring marble, swiveled toward the voice. Wayne let out a yell of fear and horror, "KURT DON'T! DON'T!" But the marble mask swung back toward the highway. He hesitated...no...paused. As the truck reached a screaming crescendo of hatred, the stick dropped behind Kurt's ear and shot forward, up into the air. Hero, tense with excitement, saw the pale white object flash upward into the sky. Like a defense missile system, he locked onto his target—completely focused—determined to capture this errant prey. He lunged out onto the highway. In an instant he was traveling at full speed. Head up, Hero followed the slowly rotating stick, flickering though sun and shadow, as it rose in a gentle arc over the road.

"NO! HERO! NO!" Kurt was dimly aware that others had joined Wayne's cry. In the blur of peripheral vision, the shapes of the Summertime Gang were converging on him. But Kurt's eyes were frozen on the scene, his macabre creation, unfolding in non-time before him.

Hero, who had just crossed the center line, finally became aware of the danger roaring toward him. He stretched out, thrusting front legs forward, throwing all his might into his rear legs. Front paws touched down so briefly that he looked to float. Rear paws struck the pavement again with gigantic power. The speed of this animal was awesome, incredible. He was going to make it! Was it possible? Could he? Could he do it?

The pickup, with its broken muffler spewing murderous, gleeful noise passed under the arc of the stick. It was then that the front right wheel struck Hero as he stretched out for one last lunge to safety. It trapped him, its tread clawing at the velvet fur of the dog, slamming Hero down into the pavement. The wheel passed precisely over the midsection of the dog. In a flash the truck bounced over Hero like he was a speed bump—front wheel first then the back. The dog's ribs and internal organs must have been pulverized, yet, as if a miracle had occurred, Hero jumped up and ran off the road into a deep, dry ditch.

The boys, now gathered around Wayne, sprinted to the other side of the road. Except Kurt. He stood calm, quiet. He heard Kellen exclaim, “He looks okay! Did you see how quick he got up? He’s going to be alright!”

Later in life, Kurt would see this many times during his four year military draft in the Middle East—the land of eternal war—he would see that humans as well as animals, could perform remarkable feats of strength in the throws of death. It was as if one last extreme, pointless effort could make everything good again.

But now, at the age of twelve, Kurt was surprised. Maybe the dog was okay. Curious, he started to saunter over to the ditch. As he did, Kurt noticed that the pickup had slowed, then stopped. It sat there, two hundred yards away, in the middle of the road, unmoving. Through the back window, Kurt could see eyes in the rear view mirror. Pained and uncertain the eyes held still for a few Kurt strides, then morph’d into resolute, cold, uncaring glass. The idling engine belched to life, brake lights winked out, gears engaged, the rusted muffler let out a wicked howl and Kurt’s unwilling accomplice set off down the road, leaving behind a trail of dust and destruction.

The other boys were almost at the ditch. Kurt had to stop in the middle of the road to avoid a speeding car that whizzed by without the slightest hesitation.

“He’ll be alright,” cried Mike. “He’s gotta be alright!”

Wayne was the first to reach the ditch. A soft moan filled the temporary quiet of the road. It was Wayne. Then, “No! No! Poor Hero!”

Sounds of sickened horror and revulsion joined Wayne’s voice as the rest of them arrived. Hero was laying at the bottom of the channel. He was trying to pull himself further away from the road, away from his attacker. Front paws scratched at the dirt, one rear leg moved spasmodically, the other was still. Behind him was a growing puddle of urine and blood. Frothy, crimson-red blood bubbled out of his mouth and nose. The dog’s high-pitched, almost alien cries and whimpers tortured their ears. Lyndon thrust his hands against his head and turned away. Whalen’s suddenly pale cheeks puffed outward as he dropped to his knees and released today’s lunch. Wayne leapt down into the trench and stood above Hero, uncertain of what to do. He looked up at the gang and said, "Go get help!" There was no movement. Only stunned, ghastly stares. "GET HELP!"

Finally, Kellen sprinted down the highway towards the nearest house.

Wayne kneeled down, one leg in the puddle of guts and blood and stroked Hero's head and face. The dog tried to turn its face toward him but it was too much. The head dropped back into the dirt. Wayne reached down and gently lifted Hero to his lap, placed his head against Hero's and started to cry. Kurt stood over the pathetic scene, not sad or sick or triumphant or gleeful, just...satisfied.

Abruptly, the dogs shaking, shuddering, scratching motions stopped. His tormented cries softened, then diminished to a grating wheeze, then stopped altogether—one more horrible, desperate gasp came, then... nothing. He had died. Wayne let out a gut-wrenching sob. It was echoed by others. The entire Summertime Gang were crying and bawling... except Kurt.

After a time, Wayne became aware of a shadow, stretching down into the ditch, touching himself and Hero. He looked up and into the sun. The shape, ugly even in silhouette, brought rage to his heart. He shouted, "You Bastard!" and flew up the slope with both fists flying.

Kurt, not at all surprised, blocked the uncontrolled swings, and with a precise, merciless, vengeful punch to the chest, exactly over the heart, sent Wayne backwards into the bloody pool at the bottom of the ditch. Wayne lay there beside Hero, gasping for breath—weak and emotionally destroyed. He raised himself up onto an elbow and pushed out a hoarse cry,

"Why? Why did you do it? He never hurt you!"

"Hey, it wasn't me. It was that dumb dog of yours. He should have stopped when you called him. Wasn't my fault that your dog is...I mean... was...stupid. That's your fault, not mine. Should have trained him better."

"You bastard! You knew! You knew he would run out onto the road! You killed him!"

"Not my fault. Yours."

"Bastard! Psychopath!"

It was then that it happened. That word, *psychopath*, sizzled in his brain. At that precise moment he knew. He understood that he was different and...better. He understood that he could stand there in the face of all this mess and remain unemotional and remain uncaring. He was able to think clearly with these kids bawling, with the dog screeching and dying—with Wayne trying to beat the shit out of him. He was stronger, smarter, better. They were no match for him, no match for a *psychopath.*

He looked down at Wayne and said, smug and confident, "You're right, I'm a psychopath."

Chapter 3

EXTRAORDINARY-ORDINARY MAN

Bill Cummings dropped into the ultra comfortable, forest green low-backed leather chair. Air whooshed as the chair molded itself around his tired body. One or two others in the lounge took stock of the newcomer and quickly returned to their drinks and quiet conversations—there wasn't anything special about Bill. In fact, he fit right in with the somewhat elegant ambiance of the club. His moderate length hair, grey-green eyes, narrow nose and short-cut, grey-white beard, carefully trimmed to fill out his thin face, gave him a sophisticated college professor look. Brown shoes, neatly creased beige pants and a dark-brown, short-sleeved shirt created a casual but tasteful image that helped to enhance the illusion.

Basking in the glow of luxurious comfort his right hand reached for the menu on the small circular mahogany table in front of him. As he perused the bar menu his left hand touched the armrest; fingers absentmindedly stroked the leather, feeling the smooth ridges and wrinkles in the material. Those subtle messages worked their way to his brain. He looked down and realized with a start that the wrinkles in the leather were echoed by other wrinkles, wrinkles of age crisscrossing his hand. An amused thought, one that only surfaces in those who have begun the downward slope of life, poked its way out, *I'm getting old. Too old for this crap.*

Mercifully, the thought dimmed quickly, and with fingers still following their rhythmic, comforting motion, Bill scanned the bar, eyes casually stopping briefly at each person. His mind started up the usual game. A dedicated observer, enhanced by many years of experience, he took in each figure and began to build a profile—personality, occupation, married or single, gay or straight, successful or unsuccessful—anything and everything that he could possibly deduce without moving from his chair. So as not to stare, he would follow a seemingly random pattern of observation, eyes a few seconds here, a few seconds there. Over time, he would build an inventory of attributes—age, gender (which sometimes wasn't as obvious as one might expect), happy, sad, angry, aggressive, submissive, intelligent (or not). Once he had his inventory, a process of deduction began.

He picked out a man and woman sitting in a quiet alcove to the left of him. They were easy to read. Some might think that they were new lovers reveling in their companionship in that romantic little corner of the club but no—Bill could see immediately that the typical lovers intensity was missing. Words were sparingly exchanged. Eyes looked anywhere but at the other's face. A quick glance verified wedding rings. A married couple whose time was perhaps coming to an end. Was this a last gasp? A last stab at love? The woman, whose face years ago, Bill imagined, had once been filled with happiness, now struggled to push out a sad, half-smile. The husband, if you could still call him that, stared about the room with a look of grim determination set deep into his face. Bill had seen it many times before—he was a man desperately trying to find some comforting words, but all that came to him was last night's Celtics score, the stock market figures or an in-depth review of his company's latest budget numbers. He could feel the melancholy of a lost relationship oozing out of their souls. There was a price to playing the game. Sometimes it struck too close to home.

And there was something else, something that scared him, really scared him—at times it seemed that he was too good. He knew things, felt things, that no amount of deduction could have produced. It would start with an interest, an interest in a particular person. He would feel drawn to them for no obvious reason. They could be a child, a man, a woman—good looking, ugly, it wouldn't matter. He would start, unconsciously, uncontrollably, to focus exclusively on that person. Then slowly, subtly, sound and light dimmed, all around, everywhere, except...except on this one person...until he and the subject were alone in a tunnel with walls dark and blurred, connected by glowing, gleaming light. Once started, he couldn't stop. He was in a trance of heightened acute awareness where everything about that person—hair, skin, eyes, mouth, clothes, posture, movement, breath, words—even, he could have sworn...heart beat...became interwoven—interwoven into his being. Body motions were anticipated and mimicked, words from an unknown conversation formed in his mouth, strange names touched his mind. Happiness, sadness, anger, boredom surged through his body. Nothing was his. He was a stranger in a strange body. It was horrifying and enticing, deceitful and voyeuristic, repulsive and addictive, wrong and right.

How long? How long did it last? Time became meaningless. Then, slowly, silently, the tunnel which centered on the heart of his alter ego, unable to bear the weight of the world around it...collapsed...shrank to a pinpoint and popped out of existence, leaving Bill in total sensory deprivation—no light, no sound, no feeling. For an infinite second he was suspended—trapped in some kind of horrible, dimensionless, netherworld. Then as air gasped into his lungs, light and sound, rescuers of his sanity, ripped and tore their way to his perception. Finally, to his great relief, similar to someone who has just barely escaped a terrible car crash, he would be left in a state of exhaustion, with hands shaking and body coated in cold sweat.

Bill didn't know what to make of these bizarre events. What were they? Some sort of extra-sensory perception? Over active imagination? A psychotic episode? He didn't know, and he didn't want to know. One was as bad as the other. Bill had never told anyone about them. It was too personal, too intimate and, most importantly...too weird. Thankfully they were rare occurrences—only five in the last ten years. The last one was three years ago. The memory was becoming dim and hazy—he rarely thought about it now.

Now there's the opposite end of the spectrum, Bill thought. A young couple, center right, safely out in the middle of the room. Without doubt, a first date. All the signs were there: man—over eager, nervous, extremely attentive, woman—cautious, smiling timidly, laughing with just a slight sense of *not true*. Bill's eyes swung through the rest of the room. Not that many people, it was a quiet night. But there were enough "subjects" to keep him busy for the rest of the evening. It was a game that produced endless hours of entertainment, and even with the few scares that he had, he never tired of it and yes, he was good at it. Which was just as well...his profession required it.

Bill, a reporter with thirty years' experience, had used his talent a thousand times to get what he needed. Sometimes he used it to evaluate a statement postulated as true but verified only after a face to face meeting. Sometimes he used it to effect control—once you knew a man's soul his life was for the taking. Sometimes he used it to get himself out of trouble. He followed the three K's—Know your enemy, Know your friend, Know your acquaintance. Much power could be found in those three K's.

A new subject entered the bar, one that required very little analysis. A lanky, six foot, big-boned man was stopped by the door, his long nosed, horse like face, staring this way and that. His clothes hung on him loose, waiting for the extra pounds required to fill their interior. It was the same old outfit—plaid shirt, blue jeans and brown loafers. Bill had known Ken Ferguson for fifteen years, well...maybe it was longer than that, and had never seen him wear anything else.

Ken, a technician at the Jet Propulsion Labs, also known as JPL, had been a good source of information in the past so when Bill got the phone call, he didn't hesitate to haul out his wallet and buy a plane ticket to Florida. As usual, Ken wouldn't tell him anything over the phone. "Look," he said, "I'm sticking my neck a way out this time." Of course he always said this; it was his precursor to the money negotiations. It was followed by, "I'm in big doo-doo with my bookie," another standard phrase.

Ken's wide spaced eyes swiveled towards him. Bill waited for the long, slow strides to reach him. With a reluctant heave, he pushed his old bones up from the seat, reached out and shook Ken's hand. The palm was moist. That was unusual for Ken. Ken's eyes were nervously darting about the room. His face was tense.

"Good to see you Ken."

"Yah, you too." Ken looked around some more. "I don't like this place."

"You chose it."

"Yah, I know. I still don't like it. Let's get out-a-here."

They stepped into a soft, delicate evening; just a touch of deep blue lingered in the sky. Sweet, moist, ocean air cooled Bill's skin. As they walked, the bar with its single, lonely neon light tucked away in the darkness of the dim lane dwindled behind them.

"You're looking nervous Ken. Is it your bookie or something else?"

"I'm onto something big this time. If I get seen with a reporter from the Times, I won't just get fired; I'll go to the slammer. They take a dim view of someone blabbing out top secret information—specially to the press."

"Relax, no one's going to find out,"

Bill waited for the story.

It didn't come,

"Well? What is it?"

"We got a deal on the money?"

"Yes. But only if it's as good as you say it is."

"Don't worry that's not a problem."

Twenty minutes and a thousand unconscious steps later, Bill said, "You're sure about this? This guy's at JPL?"

"Ya."

"And he's meeting with the engineers working on the new rocket engine."

"Ya."

"How strange...how very strange."

"When do I get my money?"

"As soon as I check this guy out."

"I need that money now man!"

"Christ, take a pill will you! If you're right, you'll get it in a couple of days."

The next day, after a few of hours of research, Bill was pretty sure that Ken was onto something. All the information Ken had given him checked out. There was only one item left on his checklist—a face--to-face meeting. With Ken's unenthusiastic help, he found out where the mystery man would be the next day and waited.

The weather had turned during the night. Yesterday's sun had been replaced by seamless grey. Bill was standing across the street from the JPL building. It was another of those modern skyscrapers—no imagination to them at all—acres of grey concrete, energy efficient, practical, cost effective and uglier than sin. The rain, pounding down, had started two hours ago and showed no sign of quitting. Bill, umbrella to the rain, spotted his target on the other side of the street and with a speed that was surprising for his age, splashed across the road—dodging several cars on the way.

"Excuse me. Excuse me. It's Mr. McArthur? Mr. James McArthur?" Slightly startled, the figure turned towards Bill.

"Pardon? Uh.... Oh.... Yes it is."

"Could I...." James McArthur now faced Bill. Bill stopped, confused. Something wasn't right. It was the face. It seemed so....

He started again, "Could I have a few minutes of...." Bill's voice trailed off. A sensation was starting. A....

Sensation....

He was sliding, out of control...into.... *No!* A trance! This had never happened before. He was not playing the game! *How?* Fear, blunted by confusion, tried to push its way through his body. His peripheral vision darkened, sound decreased to a low, disturbing hiss. The tunnel was forming! This man's face, now magnified, glowed sharp and harsh—then blurred—then leapt forward in stark, severe, painful clarity—then shimmered—then cleared again. The face was moving in and out of focus. Bill had never felt this, seen this, in any of his previous experiences.

Suddenly, the face was changing...another man—similar yet different. It changed again...and again... and again...and again.... Some were men, some were women—different ages—young, old, in-between, indiscriminate. It was speeding up, like a film on fast forward—accelerating, faster and faster, face after face. *What was happening?* ***What...was...happening?***

Suddenly, the film stopped.

Frozen on a single frame.

Another face...half man...half animal stared at him. Thoughts and sensations came in disjointed bursts...confusion, hatred, fear. There was hair everywhere—beady eyes with intelligence gleaming, unblinking. Lips pulled back, huge teeth revealed, breath of rotted meat. Teeth grew larger...mouth approached...larger and larger. He was going to be eaten! He tried to raise non-existent hands to protect himself. He was going to die! Fear and anger, not his, smothered his mind. Then, a powerful, all encompassing "***DREAD!***" struck him, threw him backward, "***DREAD! DREAD! DREAD!***"

He was on the verge of being swallowed by this horror. What was left of his sanity was slipping away, perhaps forever. The person called Bill was almost gone. He had been replaced by a mindless energy called ***DREAD.***

Then,

Something...,
Some...thing...,
Change...Changing...,

Wha...Whaaat?

The view of the face! It was shrinking! He was leaving! He was escaping this horrible place! The tunnel was collapsing, inward on itself, centered on the right eye of the monster. Gradually darkness slid over jaw, ear, lips, teeth, eye, nose until only one milky, black-red eye remained. It hovered there, fighting dissolution, still eating at his sanity, until finally, with one last frightening whisper, "*DREAD!*", it was gone.

He floated in blissful darkness and silence, no longer afraid of the absence of life, wanting only to linger, hidden from that face, hidden from DREAD.

But, a sound rippled to his brain.

It said,

"Whhhaaaat'sssss... maaaaatter... himmmmmm?"
"Doooonnn't... knnnnow... sssssss... Sieeeeezzzzzure?"

Comforting darkness began to slip away. Light was breaking its way through to his stunned and exhausted mind. Blurred images leaned over him on all sides. He moved his head to the left and felt a hard, wet surface below him. He noticed his umbrella angled at the feet of a passerby.

Bill was lying on his back on the concrete sidewalk. He turned his head back toward the sky and became aware of drops of harsh rain stinging his face. A much clearer voice said,

"Is he hurt? Did he fall?"

Another voice, a familiar voice, said, "Yes, but I caught him before he hit the ground."

"Let's get him out of the rain."

Hands lifted and carried him to some dry place. They gently lowered him to the ground. A rolled-up jacket was pushed under his head and neck. Embarrassment replaced dazed fear. He turned onto his side and with a weak, wobbly right arm, pushed himself into a sitting position. He took a couple of sucks of air and said,

"I'm okay."

The familiar voice said, "An ambulance is on its way."

Bill, weak but determined, rose to his feet. "No, that's not necessary. I'm fine."

"You're sure?"

Bill turned slowly toward that voice—afraid of what he might see. But, it was nothing, just an average face, almost too average. A shiver gripped his body. Remnants of the hallucination still waggled at his psyche. He fought it and looked closer at his subject. *What could have caused that vision?* He looked ordinary—mildly pleasant actually. Nothing special or strange in any way. Sandy-brown, moderately short hair, blue eyes very evenly spaced, average nose, average lips, average jaw, average height—around five-foot-ten, average build. Face rounded but not too much. Everything average...and yet...something else was there. He could still feel it—no, couldn't be, it must be his imagination. But yes, there was something, he did feel it, something extraordinary about this man...but it was inside...hidden away somehow. The words *Extraordinary*, *Ordinary* flashed into his mind.

"Yes, I'm sure, thank you."

"You were starting to ask me something before...before your, mishap."

"I was?"

"Yes, you stated my name and started to say something."

"Really? I'm sorry I don't remember," lied Bill. All he wanted to do was to get out of there—get away from this guy...away from *memory*.

"You're sure you are okay?"

"Yes, thank you for your help. I'm sorry to have troubled you." Bill turned and almost lost his balance. He took a much more cautious next step, very aware that the Extraordinary-Ordinary man's eyes were on him, watching....

An hour later, after a donut and a long, very tall coffee, Bill pulled out his cell phone and made a call. It was answered.

"It's Kurt, who's...oh it's you. How's my intrepid snoop?" Kurt continued on, not waiting for a reply. Bill knew that Kurt didn't care how he was. "I take it you have some information for me. I'm in a hurry so don't waste time."

"Okay, well...my source was correct. This guy, James McArthur, is at JPL. I just met him today on his way into the JPL office here in Miami."

"And who is James McArthur?"

"To start with he's considered brilliant. He's a Canadian, graduated top of his class from the University of Alberta in...guess what department?"

"Don't play games!"

"Archeology."

"He's an Archeologist?"

"Yes and not just any Archeologist, he's considered one of the best."

"What the hell is an Archeologist doing at JPL?" Kurt queried.

"Meeting with the Engineers working on the new rocket engine."

"What?"

"You heard me. But it gets even better. James McArthur is also a full time member of SETI."

"SETI? Really," replied Kurt. He paused. And then said, "Okay, so what we have here is an Archeologist who is somehow involved with SETI and somehow involved with JPL. You'd almost think...." Kurt stopped.

"Exactly." Bill filled the thoughtful silence. "Oh, and there's something else."

"What?"

"There's something weird about him."

"Yeah?"

"He gives me the creeps." Bill immediately regretted the statement—Kurt wouldn't understand. As a matter of fact, Bill didn't understand either.

"He gives you the creeps," echoed Kurt in a flat voice.

"Yes."

"Very informative. Perhaps you could elaborate."

"I can't," Bill cringed, knowing what was coming next.

"Well then I don't want to bloody-well hear it! Don't waste my time with some boogeyman fairy tale!"

"Sorry...it's just...."

"I don't want to hear it!"

"Yeah.... Okay...." Bill was about to blither on when he heard a distinct click. Kurt had hung up.

Later that night Bill was sitting in that same leather chair in that same bar, drink in hand, thinking about what happened. He still couldn't explain it. He never had an experience like that before. *All those faces! And the last one! Horrible!* A shiver of disgust charged through him. Bill raised a shaking hand up to his head and ran it through his silver-grey hair. The other hand brought a glass filled with fifteen year old scotch to his lips. A moment later Bill looked down at his glass. It was empty. *What did it all mean? How was it related to James McArthur? Was it just a crazy hallucination? It had to be!* Still there was something about James McArthur that went deep. He had sensed it, felt it, even after his vision. It was as if the sum of all those ordinary parts had combined to produce something extraordinary.

Extraordinary... Extraordinary... Extra... Ordinary... Extra...

Ordinary

The words bounced around his mind—back and forth—back and forth—back and forth. *Extraordinary... Ordinary... Extraordinary... Extraordinary... Ordinary.* What a strange epithet—an oxymoron certainly. But...yes...that described him, it felt exactly right....

The Extraordinary-Ordinary man.

James McArthur watched with concern as the stranger walked away. He didn't know what to make of the encounter. He was sure the man had called his name. Impulsively James started after him but a sudden internal alarm bell caused him to look at his watch. *Late again!* In a flash he stopped, turned and rushed toward the large glass doors etched with the letters JPL.

It seemed he was always in a hurry these days. At least his mind was. He couldn't stop thinking about "It." "It" was constantly in his head—a part of his psyche. His nightly sleep had been reduced to a few hours and even then he dozed in fits and starts...never complete, never satisfying. Yet somehow he felt more alive than ever, as if he was in a state of Zen excitement—completely focused, able to perform great feats of energy—never tiring. He knew that if he kept on like this he would collapse from exhaustion. He was a star gone supernova, burning bright, thoughtlessly using every last spark of energy. He had to slow down, get some rest.

But "It" would quickly envelop his thoughts, turning his mind back, back to the primary purpose.

Ever since he was a child of ten, James had two seemingly unrelated interests, Archeology and Extraterrestrial life. But to James, they weren't unrelated at all. When he was just five years old he watched the old classic movie, Close Encounters of the Third Kind. Like the guy in the movie who couldn't keep the desert mountain out of his mind—even going to the extent of building the image out of mashed potatoes—James's young mind was completely fascinated by these strange beings from another planet. As a child of five, he believed that alien races existed. Why not? His mom and dad tried to convince him that aliens were just pretend, like the Boogeyman. But he wasn't buying it. He was pretty certain that there was a Boogeyman and if there was a Boogeyman then there certainly should be aliens. When he got a little older he learned that there was something called Science. Science said that there was no proof that aliens existed. But on TV he saw people who said they had been taken by aliens, or saw space ships from other planets, or were convinced beings from outer-space built the pyramids. These people seemed pretty sure of themselves. James didn't know what to think but he wanted to find out who was right. By the age of ten he had become interested in those ancient ruins that might have been built by aliens—the pyramids in Egypt, the Aztec temples, the stone circles, the lost city of Atlantis. That's when he first heard the term Archeology. To James, Archeology was the link between science and his aliens. Perhaps he could use Archeology to prove the existence of life beyond earth.

He threw himself at Archeology. Absorbing everything he possibly could. He joined SETI under the student program. High school became difficult. He had no interest in any other studies. Every school year-end, when the threat of failure loomed large, he would cram his brains out and squeak through. It was only when his chances of entering an Archeology program at University had shrunk to almost zero that he finally put in a consistent, determined effort. Grades that once scraped the bottom of the "C's" soared to "A's" and "B's." He surprised everyone—his teachers, his friends, his parents and most of all, himself. At University he continued his new-found success. He built a reputation for brilliant, original work and four years later graduated at the top of his class.

After University, James traveled the globe, visiting those ancient ruins, looking for evidence of any kind of alien interference. He found nothing. In fact he seemed to be single handedly refuting every theory of Alien construction ever suggested. He was becoming convinced that Aliens had never traveled to Earth. Perhaps Aliens didn't exist at all. Perhaps life beyond Earth didn't exist. Perhaps, as once was said, the human race was a "Fluke of the Universe." His life's work—his life's hope—was slipping away.

Then came a phone call. One that he would never forget.

"James, it's Allan, Allan Hume. How's it going buddy?" Allan was your down-home, real friendly type. Impossible to dislike. He was also a very respected senior analyst at SETI.

"Listen, we got something interestin', reeaaall interestin', goin on down here."

"Really? What's up?" James wasn't getting too excited. Allan always sounded this way—loud, happy and animated. Allan could put drama into a description of frying an egg.

To be absolutely certain that James heard him, Alan doubled his decibels. "First off, you've got to keep this completely quiet! No one else can be told."

James jerked the phone back from an ear that had just been assaulted—he turned the volume down and replied, "Of course."

"Well, if what we found is correct, we may be shutting down the old biz."

"What?? Why??"

"Cause we won't need to look for any more life on other planets. We will have found it."

There was dead air on the line for a long time. Denial was the first response.

"Allan, don't joke with me, you know how seriously I take this work."

"Hey! I'm not fool'n ya buddy! This is the real stuff, the whole enchilada, the big time! The fat lady has sung!"

NO! Could this be it?

A thought surged through James's body, *Allan is not the kind of guy to pull this kind of joke.* With that reflection, all time seemed to stop. He felt an incredible sensation...breath stopped, heart pounding, ears buzzing, body tingling, head light. For a long, almost infinite moment his mind transcended beyond his body to a place of calm, warmth and glory...then was harshly yanked back by doubt and denial.

"Come on. You're full of it! Someone has put you up to this!!"

For once, perhaps because of the true drama of the moment, Allan lowered his voice and said with utter conviction, "It's true."

"No, it can't be."

Again, complete calm. "It's true."

"I just can't believe it, it's so hard to believe after dreaming about it constantly for the last twenty years," James said.

Allan replied with a voice filled with happiness and conviction, "There is no question about it, absolutely for sure, we are receiving a radio signal from Venus that has intelligent purpose. We have eliminated all possible interference from earth or anywhere else. A nonsentient radio source could not generate this signal. We don't know the meaning; we have some guesses but nothing concrete so far."

"Okay, give me the story and you better not be kidding."

"Hey! This is completely legit buddy!" Allan was back to his usual self. "There was a bit of a screw-up at the new radio telescope array. Someone pointed it at Venus. Luckily, someone noticed an energy blip before they redirected the array. It's a very, very low power signal—a complete fluke that it was found. Who would have thought it. Right under our noses. It's still hard to believe, but it's transmitting right now.

We've eliminated all possible interference sources. It's a low frequency signal—in the six hundred Kilohertz range, same band as AM radio, very, very weak. The power is so low, only the new SETI site could have picked it up. What a fluke. I'm still amazed that we found it."

"Have you tried to return communication?"

"Yes, but no noticeable change in the signal."

"Do we know anything about that region of Venus?"

"Well that's kind of why I'm calling you, buddy."

"Why?" James held his breath; he desperately wanted to be a part of this.

"We looked back at some of the scans of the previous Venus probes and found something that was missed the first time." Allan paused, perhaps to add further emphasis on what was already a humdinger of a story or perhaps because he too was struggling to determine if he was in a dream world—still mentally pinching himself.

"What?"

"It looks like there may be some kind of structure—almost certainly a partial structure, near that radio source. It's very, very faint on the pictures we have. We need someone who is used to piecing together something from almost nothing, someone who has spent years determining how structures were built, someone who might be able to find similarities to other structures...say...like a renowned Archeologist...say like a James McArthur...." Another pause. "So get your butt down here!"

A huge smile lit up his face, "I'm on my way." That feeling of warmth and joy was back...perhaps forever.

Chapter 4

MATT

It was a warm, sweet summer day. One of those precious days where everything is perfect. Not a cloud in the sky, the temperature from early morning onward so ideal that you could step out of the house naked and not feel even the slightest difference. A breeze, just enough to gently stir the leaves of the trees, whispered through the city. It touched the skin like a ghostly lover's imperceptible caress... there, yet not. Air so pleasant and clean it seems to have been transported from an untouched mountain forest. The soft summer sounds, birds chirping and singing, insects buzzing from bush to flower, all saying, "this is life," all saying, "I am life." What a day! So subtle, so sweet, so beautiful...so sublime. A day that calls to you, that urges, "touch me, feel me, take me into your soul for I may never come again." Yes, on a day like this it is not hard to imagine the spirit of every living thing bowed in homage.

The whole city seemed as if at peace. Perhaps in a soft slumber, napping in the sun. The sensation was overwhelming. Only an unfeeling, soulless monster could deny this languid summer day.

"What the! I don't believe it!!"

Matt was brutally wrenched out of his peaceful, happy dream world. As if he were dragged out of a warm, soft bed into sub-zero temperatures, he felt a huge shiver run through his body. Back to the horror of his real life. Back to life with his dad...Kurt.

He turned from the sunny view of Boston Harbor. The office was located on one of the highest floors of the Hancock Tower and had an unobstructed, one-hundred-and-eighty degree view of the Charles river, the city, the airport, the harbor and just about everything else.

It took all the courage he had to face his dad when he was angry. Kurt was a short, squat, bulldog of a man, massively built. Arms bigger than most people's legs. He never worked out, yet, somehow, even at the age of fifty-two he hadn't put any fat on...well maybe the tiniest of a beer belly but you'd have to look really hard to see it. *Must be some weird genetic fluke going on there*, thought Matt.

Kurt had a face only a mother could love. However, in this case, Matt was pretty sure the "love" part didn't apply. He never met his grandmother and Kurt never talked about her. *She must have run like hell after giving birth to him*, Matt surmised. Kurt had a wide, fleshy face with short-cropped jet-black hair, dark-brown, intense, loveless eyes, a pudgy nose and a lower lip that tended to drag downward at the corners leaving his face in a perpetual lolling snarl.

Matt on the other hand hadn't received any of the physical genetic bonus that had somehow been over-liberally applied to his dad. He got the short stature all right—five-foot-three, just like his dad—but ended up with his mother's skinny genes. Strangely enough, even at the age of twenty-six, he could put weight on at the drop of a hat—but it went straight to his gut and stayed there. Short, skinny, toothpick arms and legs, a big beer gut and his dads, "*good looks.*" It was quite a combination. Once, when he was looking at himself naked in the mirror, something he tried to avoid if at all possible, it suddenly dawned on him—*he was the skinny, fat man. A circus freak. Yes Sir. Step right up! See the Skinny, Fat man!* If it wasn't so pathetic, it would actually be funny.

"Sorry Dad. What's the matter?" Matt asked with a slight quaver in his voice.

"Christ! How many times have I told you not to call me "Dad" in the office?" Kurt bellowed back. Matt had once again managed to make whatever was wrong, worse.

"It's unprofessional calling me 'Dad' and it makes you look like an office boy, bonehead! You need every ounce of respect you can get from the employees of this company. Continually emphasizing that you are the Senior Executive VP because I'm your 'DAD' doesn't help one bit!" Kurt's face was starting to go red. A very bad sign.

"Call me Kurt!" he yelled. "I should make you call me Mr. Dragonovich like everybody else but because I'm a good '*DAD*,' I'm trying to raise your credibility in the eyes of this company and its board by allowing you to be the only person to call me by my first name."

"Sorry, Kurt. I wasn't thinking." Matt's face crumpled into its usual sad, pained expression. It was an expression cultivated and grown over the years by Kurt's verbal and physical abuse. Matt's features provided just a hint of the churning, tortured, lost soul that existed within. No face, no matter how horribly disfigured could truly represent the mess that was his soul, Matt had thought many times.

"So...what's wrong?" asked Matt again, now on full alert.

"That bloody Darren Hubert. Screwed up First National Oil's budget again. After I had already caught one mistake. He's scaring the shit out of me. I swear I gotta do his job and mine. There's no way I'm going to have any mistakes in that budget when I go to the board."

Darren was the Chief Financial Officer of First National Oil, one of the many companies that Kurt owned.

Like a balloon suddenly losing air, the tension in Matt's entire body slipped away. Relief quickly followed. His perpetual grimace relaxed slightly. Not his fault, someone else's ass was going to fry. He didn't care, so long as it wasn't him. Matt wasn't sure he could take anymore destruction today.

"I want you to take this budget to Darren and tell him that this is his last chance. No more screw-ups."

"Yes Sir." Matt hustled out of the room. Off to poor Darren. Matt was betting he wasn't going to be around much longer. He was going to either quit or be fired. Matt guessed he'd quit. Most people couldn't take the pressure.

Once they were in the bad books, it was almost impossible to get out. Even Senior Executives, who had taken a lot of abuse on the way up the ladder, couldn't handle Kurt. Kurt had a favorite saying, "I'm tough but fair." Well it required a mammoth mental stretch to believe the fair part. In fact, you'd have to be an idiot to believe the fair part. There was nothing fair about Kurt. He'd rip your face off if you made a mistake and success achieved no response from him at all. When Kurt was in a good mood, he'd let out a secret or two to Matt, "Matt, if you really want to be a successful businessman, you have to keep everyone scared to death of you. It's absolutely the best way to be sure they work their guts out. I don't care if they burnout. If they do, I just fire'em and find another one to fill the boots. It's a real fallacy thinking that someone is irreplaceable. There's always another one around the corner; as a matter of fact there's usually a line of them; they can't wait to move up the ladder, stab a few guys on the way up if necessary. I love those guys! Why? Because I can control them. And I can control them because I know them better than they know themselves. Why? (Kurt loved to ask himself questions) Because I'm just like them, except I'm worse than them, ten times worse than them. I'll work them into the ground, keep them scared—never having time to think or plot. I use 'em up and spit 'em out. It's beautiful."

Of course this was no surprise to Matt. He'd seen it put into practice many times. Like everything else about his dad, he hated it. Like everything else, he said nothing. Like everything else, he hated himself for saying nothing. Who did he hate more? Himself or his dad? He knew he was gutless, he knew he was a coward; he knew he should get out of this mess, away from his father. He knew, he knew, he knew, he did nothing.

As he walked, Matt could feel himself slipping down the deep, dark shaft of depression. The toilet had been flushed. He was spiraling down with the big globs of smelly, putrid excrement. He'd been there many times before. A shock of imagined pain pulled his lips back tight across his face. He pressed both hands on either side of his head, squeezed hard and thought, *Shut it out! Shut it out! Shut it out!* Like a mantra he repeated this over and over. He called it "mind over mind." It was the conscious, sane part of him trying to shove the conscious, insane part into a special hidden place, a "protect me from myself" vault that he had created.

"Matt? Are you okay?" Greta Steel, a director of something or other—Matt could never remember what—had just rounded the hallway corner and had caught him in mid-squeeze.

Embarrassed hands jerked down from his head to his sides. He could feel a flush of blood leap to his face. Head down, eyes glancing sideways at her, he mumbled a quick reply. "Oh, just a headache. I'll be fine."

As he passed, she said, "Must be a really bad one. I have some prescription pain killers if you want."

Matt apologetically waved his hand and picked up the pace, "No. No, that's fine. I've got my own stuff." He was aware of a quizzical expression swiveling, and then following him as he darted down the hall. He was sure she must have been thinking, *there's something wrong with that guy.* He followed that up with another thought, *and she'd be right.* He could feel the depression closing about him. He fought again to push it through the special doorway...push it into his bulging mental vault of horrors.

Lost in his internal struggle, he aimlessly wandered through the office. Head down, barely aware of life beyond his pain, he ignored anyone who passed. Sadness and self-loathing, depression's brutal partners, held him almost incapacitated. The elevator to his left opened—dark, inviting, somehow soothing to his battered soul. As the single occupant stepped out, he stepped in...and squeezed himself as far into the back corner as he could. The doors closed. In the dim light Matt stood motionless. The elevator descended, stopping here and there. Vague bodies entered with voices disjointed...and paid the insignificant figure at the back no mind. A thought shimmered its way into his numb brain, *Was he real?*

The door slid open again; more silhouetted, faceless figures entered the elevator. A wall of bodies now surrounded him. A quiet cacophony of babble filled the space. No one looked at him. No one seemed aware that he was there. The thought came again—stronger this time, *Was he real?*

Perhaps not. Perhaps he was a ghost, trapped between life and death. Trapped....

Trapped....

Trapped by his fear....

Yes, that was it....

He was a living ghost....

Trapped in a life he hated.

Doomed to cycle between light and dark,

Doomed to cycle between life and death, catching only snippets of happiness as life's doors snapped shut before he could step through.

The elevator reached the ground floor. Bright daylight found its way to the corner of the dark elevator, found its way to his eyes, then to his frazzled, tortured brain. It was the happy daylight that had caressed his sight and mind in his father's office—it seemed, so long ago. The world outside this cold, heartless building was still suspended in the bliss of a perfect day. It was his hope.

Step by step his mood began to change. The mind monsters were returning to the vault. He was beginning to slip back into his dream world, his world of fantasy. He spent as much time as he could there. Living the life he really wanted...or at least the one that he thought he really wanted; that kind of changed on a regular basis, sort of like the flavor of the day.

He began to think of the empire that his dad had built. He thought of what he would do when it was finally his, when the old man was gone—he prayed it was soon.

He had to admit that "Kurt" had created an incredibly intricate and secretive business conglomerate. He had holdings in many different companies: high-tech, oil and gas, military applications, weapons—Kurt was a strong supporter of the NRA. Although no one knew it, Matt was sure that Kurt controlled some of the largest oil companies in the world. He also had a big stake in the power utilities in the United States, Canada and Europe.

Of course, it was illegal to control so many similar companies but Kurt had created a pyramid of shell companies so deep that it would take an army of accountants to work it out. Internally there was no single person who came even close to knowing it all. It was like a gigantic picture puzzle with the pieces scattered all over the world and hundreds of people holding only a small part of a small section of the puzzle—with none of them aware that they were spun into a worldwide web of deceit and deception.

Only Matt had pieced some of it together and then only because of his close association with his dad. *I'm smarter than he thinks...he lets out more than he should*, thought Matt. Over many years, Matt had slowly grasped the magnitude of this masterpiece of business. His father's method was brilliant. He was a master at controlling people and therefore a master at controlling companies, and Kurt was the best Matt had ever seen. Instinctively, Kurt knew what buttons to push, how to force someone to do his bidding—cheat shareholders, lie to the auditors, bend the law, break the law, do anything he wanted. There were many methods to achieve this; a pat on the back sometimes was enough, maybe a good word or two—" Well done Joe!", perhaps a pot of gold at the end of the rainbow, a threat, some blackmail, physical harm—pain was always a good one. The real trick was knowing which one to apply. Everyone had their button and Kurt always found it.

How wealthy was Kurt? Matt didn't know but guessed it was gigantic, enormous, humungous. Certainly bigger than the gross national products of some countries. But he didn't flaunt it. No sir, he did the opposite. And that was part of the master plan. Stay low, keep a low profile, stay out of the news; Kurt Dragonovich, a small time player in the oil and energy business. He deliberately ran the business from Boston, away from the oil boys in Texas. First National oil wasn't even on the radar of the major players. A lot of them wouldn't even have heard of it or Kurt. Yet many of them were in his power.

Kurt never touched the companies he controlled directly. There were always intermediaries, sometimes many levels of them, buried in holding companies galore. Only one person in each pyramid would know Kurt. Always by another name and never by sight. Kurt would research every executive who could possibly have an impact on their company. He would do this surreptitiously. No one in the company would ever know. He'd read everything he could about each person. Sometimes he'd employ a private detective to dig up more dirt. Often he would have a spy or two within the company, recruited and paid for by a third party.

The Internet could often provide detailed info on individuals. Kurt loved the Internet; it was a wonderful medium for a crook. You could hide in the anonymous World Wide Web. Kurt had several Internet Service Providers in his control and had the technical capability to take advantage of them. He made sure that he had the passwords to key routers and servers in their network. Once he was in, he could disguise emails and messages so that they looked to come from some other source or appeared not to have a source at all. He could gain access to servers in companies that he controlled, send out email memos and never be traced. Kurt could hack into the hard drives on the office desk tops or even laptops when they were plugged into the corporate net. He was fond of telling Matt that thanks to the Internet he could control his empire from anywhere in the world with a cheap laptop. If he didn't want to ever leave his office or his house he didn't have to; he could order food, clothes, furniture, electronics, everything he could possibly want from the Internet and have it delivered to his door.

If Kurt suspected someone of doing anything that could interfere with his agenda or needed a little more dirt on a particular executive victim, he would have his spies set up hidden web cams in the appropriate offices and locations. Once connected he could personally keep an eye on things. *Very voyeuristic. Kind of fun actually*, thought Matt.

Wireless was proving to be very handy. Kurt was able to hack any of the standard encryption methods commonly employed by wireless users. He could see everything they were doing, get personal info, bank account and credit card numbers, passwords, social security numbers. Very handy info to have if you needed to do a little more "research" on one of the subjects.

Yes, *Dad* had built a fabulous organization. So much time and effort had gone into its creation.

When I get my hands on this empire, the first thing I'm going to do is sell every friggin part of it, thought Matt with a warm sense of satisfaction. *The old man will turn in his grave forever. His precious empire, so carefully built over a lifetime, gone in a brief few months. Then I'm gonna party! Party big time! Spend! Spend! Spend!*

Matt popped out of his daydream and found himself standing in the sunshine half a block from the entrance to the building. As luck would have it, there was poor Darren just leaving the building—probably running from his own scary monsters.

He let out a shout, "Hey! Hey! Darren! You're in big trouble man." Matt was feeling much better now. Time to shock the heck out of Darren.

Twenty minutes later, a peaceful Matt was whistling a horribly off-key tune as he sauntered down a corridor towards his office. He was off in "lala" land again. He glanced down at his watch. *Hey! It's five past six. Quitten time. My how time flies when you're havin fun.* He stopped, reversed course and headed toward the parking lot and the Ferrari. *The weather is still nice, it will be great to get outside, catch the evening sunset.* His cell phone started to ring. He pulled it out of his pocket, slightly irritated. That changed very quickly. *Damn! It's him! What's he want now?* For a brief moment he considered ignoring the call but he knew the old man would just keep phoning and if he left it for too long Matt would have a lot of explaining to do. It wasn't worth it. He was trapped. "Hello?"

"I need to talk to you right away, there's a little job for you to do. Come to my office."

Matt felt his whole body sag as the fleeting joy and happiness of the past few moments was torn from his body. Kurt called him any time he wanted, day and night. He was never free of him. He thought, *I hate cell phones. The phone companies just love to tell you how the cell phone "frees you," allows you to have more time, more time on the beach, at home with the family, blah, blah, blah. What a pile of crap. It chains you to your desk, twenty-four hours a day, seven days a week. You can't escape. That phone can ring anytime, don't answer it and you're in the bad books with the boss. The next thing you know, it's, "gee Joe, you're just not a good fit, you'd be better off doing something else...."* With Matt it was worse, his dad owned him body and soul. He didn't have the guts to ever say no. The cell phone was a tether, a tether from hell...with the devil at the other end.

Matt stood for a moment at the doorway; the urge to go the other way was strong. But fear of reprisal was stronger. He took a deep breath and stepped through.

A black, angry head turned toward him,

"What took you so long? If you walked any slower, you'd be going backwards. Sometimes I think you do it just to piss me off." Kurt growled.

"Umm...err...no...no...not at all.... I'm sorry...sorry Kurt...I was lost in thought."

"You're going to be lost all right...lost without a dime if you don't smarten up. Now listen carefully. I've got something important for you to do and I don't want you to screw it up. Okay? Okay???"

Matt stood silent, uncertain...no, scared, was a better description.

"Come on. Say something. Christ!" Kurt knew that the nastier he became, the more Matt's brain turned to mush. Kurt also knew that he regularly needed to do a "destroy and rebuild" on Matt's psyche. Destroy any self-confidence then rebuild and reinforce Matt's total dependence on Kurt. It worked well, it worked very well. If Kurt was honest with himself, which he wasn't, he'd admit that this was one of the ways he got his jollies.

"Okay dad...OH! No! I mean Kurt!"

Kurt chose to ignore that. "Listen, I've been hearing some rumors... little whispers about something to do with SETI."

"SET who? Who is SET?"

"I said SETI!"

"Oh...yeah...sorry.... Umm...who is SETI?"

"The search for extraterrestrial life guys."

"Oh, those goofs."

"They are only goofs if they don't find anything. If they find something then they are *geniuses.*"

"What? They have found something?"

"That's what I need you to find out."

"But why do we care?"

"You mean, why do I care." Kurt carried on, not waiting for an answer. "Because, something that big could provide business opportunities—money will be spent, maybe a lot of money, maybe shit-loads of money."

"Oh...yeah...makes sense."

"Yeah, no kidding bright boy," Kurt rolled his eyes.

"I don't have any good contacts in that area. I do know that SETI is at JPL right now. Which is what got me onto this. SETI at JPL makes you think that something big might have happened. Use Dean Sullivan to help you. He's very good at getting contacts."

"Okay, no problem." Matt knew Dean Sullivan, he was Kurt's best private detective.

"Don't get involved directly; I don't want our name implicated. You manage it, let Dean do the rest."

"Yes, you bet."

"Oh, and Matt."

"Yes?"

"You call me *DAD* in the office one more time and I'm going to slap you silly." Kurt didn't raise his voice, he didn't have to—he knew Matt would know he meant it.

Chapter 5

SCOTT

All his life Scott Benbow had been waiting, hoping for this moment. Proof that life existed beyond this tiny ball of rock, water and air. Now here it was, right before him. This was his opportunity. He had found it. It was his discovery. His determination, his diligence found it. He wasn't going to let it go now. If the SETI big-shots thought that they could give him a happy slap on the back and with a "Good job Scott," send him on his way, sweep him under the carpet, kick him out the door...they didn't know Scott Benbow.

Scott Benbow was one of the most single minded, determined persons ever to walk this earth....

Or at least that was what he told himself every day for the last twenty years. Each morning before he got up, he lay silent in his bed while he prepared himself for the days events. In his mind he would repeat these words:

I am the most single minded, determined person to ever walk this earth,
I am the most single minded, determined person to ever walk this earth,
I am the most single minded, determined person to ever walk this earth.

I shall hold every minute of the day precious, no moment wasted,
I shall hold every minute of the day precious, no moment wasted,
I shall hold every minute of the day precious, no moment wasted.

I will constantly strive to improve myself, physically and mentally,
I will constantly strive to improve myself, physically and mentally,
I will constantly strive to improve myself, physically and mentally.

Scott was an only child. His father had a decent job as a salesman for a successful furniture store. His mother worked a low paying job as a waitress. As a family, all was well; they had enough money for a house, two decent cars, some nice electronics and a trip or two a year.

It was a good life but Scott had always battled with his father. If his father said one thing, he'd do the other. He couldn't understand it, he loved his dad, he was a good father, a loving father, but for some reason, unknown to Scott, he just couldn't follow; he had to lead. The harder his dad pushed the harder he resisted. And so, every time he was told to do homework, he'd refuse; he'd argue, he'd complain, he'd whine, he'd stall. This lead to some major fights and arguments and ultimately to punishment of some kind. But it didn't deter Scott; he'd do as little work as possible, bring home passing marks and then use those as a excuse next time he was told to study. He'd say, "Leave me alone. I'm getting okay marks. I'm passing." His dad would reply, "You can do much better than that, Scott. You're very smart. Don't waste your talent." Then the arguments would start again.

Just after Scott's sixteenth birthday he and his dad had a huge fight, about school work again, with Scott threatening to leave home, telling his father that he hated him and wishing he would just go away and die. As was typical with his father, when the battle reached its peak, he'd just stop speaking, no further yelling, no further demands, no further threats. His face would change from anger to sorrow, and then in a quiet voice punishment would be dispensed. This time it seemed to Scott that he saw a tear in his father's eye as he grounded Scott for two weeks. Scott spent the rest of that day in his room without videos, games, TV or computer. All he had was text books, which he threw all over the room. To this day he still remembered, at that exact moment, how much he hated his father, how much he wished he would die. It took until the next day before sanity returned and he apologized for what he had said. But it was too late. A week later everything changed; his comfortable, spoilt life, was turned upside down. That's when he learnt his father was dying from cancer.

At the reading of his will, the lawyer gave Scott a letter from his dad. It was a long, rambling letter that talked about the great times they had and how much he loved him. He asked Scott to watch over his mother. He remembered all of it but the last paragraph he knew word for word. Scott's father said, "I'm not afraid to die but I regret very much that I can't be by your side to guide you and to support you and your mother. This is the last time I will be able to say this, and I know you won't like it but this is my job as a father, it's my duty, so I will say it anyway; Scott, you're one of the smartest people I've ever known. You could have any career you want. And you're throwing it away. You're only a year away from graduating from high school. You need great marks to get into a good University, not okay marks, not sort of good marks...great marks. Even you can't get those by doing nothing. You have to challenge yourself. You have to get out of your comfort zone. Set goals for yourself, set high goals, ones that almost no one else can achieve. Then you'll be great. Maybe the best. But if you continue to hang out with your friends, watch TV and movies, play video games, you're not going to make it. If you don't make an effort you'll regret it for the rest of your life. It will haunt you. You will always wonder how good you could have become. The time is now. This is your chance. Take it."

It was that day, that very day, that Scott started his ritual. He had not missed a day since, for twenty years, not even when he was sick. And he had held himself to that daily promise as best he could. It was something he was proud of. At university he was the hardest worker, in sports and fitness he'd push himself so hard that sometimes he'd vomit, recover and then start again.

Scott was forced to put his new found determination and dedication to the test immediately. They had some savings and his father had a small life insurance policy, just enough to pay for his funeral, but the house still had a large mortgage and the cars were not fully paid for either. They weren't going to be able to make it financially unless Scott found a job. So Scott started working, almost full time. He worked so hard that even his mother periodically told him to take a break. But he reaped the benefits of all that effort. His marks skyrocketed. Each success drove him to try even harder, his confidence soared, an eagle above the clouds, looking down upon a past that was now insignificant, straining to reach heights that a few months before were beyond aspirations, beyond dreams.

Scott barged his way into Phil Black's office. A big, six-foot-two, very physically fit person, Scott could be extremely intimidating if he wanted. He was at his best now. Phil, Scott's boss, felt it immediately.

Scott already had a game plan when he stormed into Phil's office. He knew what he was going to do. He had to play it carefully but if he did it right, he'd get what he wanted. He charged into the office with a carefully planned, grim look on his face. He didn't say a word, just waited. Phil looked tense. *He's not surprised—he knows I know. Let the game begin!*

"What can I do for you Scott?" asked Phil. There was a touch of a waver in his voice.

Scott had a big featured, somewhat round, smooth countenance that gave him a pleasant, easygoing demeanor. That was on most days. Today, the face had changed. Hard angles replaced the gentle, happy curves. The short black hair, combined with heavy, now pursed, eyebrows gave him a military, "I'm going into battle," look. His eyes, which were very dark, almost black, seemed to be drilling right through Phil. The nose, perfectly shaped and proportioned for that face, now was hawkish, the tip being pulled downward by lips, once full, now tightly pursed. And what happened to that jaw? It used to be masculine and strong yet rounded enough to be a pleasant prominent feature. Now it was thrust forward and more hard angles appeared where none were before.

Phil couldn't resist the urge to push his chair back, away from Scott. He'd been dreading this moment for weeks. He knew that he should have done the dirty work ages ago but kept finding excuses, something else was always a higher priority. Now it was going to be a lot worse.

"I've just heard a rumor," said Scott.

"Oh?"

"I'm thinking you know all about this Phil. Frankly, I'm very disappointed that you didn't have the guts to tell me yourself. Why'd I have to find out from some schmuck in Tony's group? What were you thinking? It was bound to get out." Scott kept his tone smooth and quiet. It was a trademark of his. Everyone knew about it: the quieter he became, the angrier he was. It was a useful quality; he could be very professional and still scare the bejesus out of people.

"Come on Phil, do the right thing here. Tell me."

"Okay, okay, look I'm sorry; it's just been so busy here since the discovery."

"You know that's a load of garbage. What's more important than this? Are you telling me that I'm not important? That I count so little that you can choose to ignore something that has an enormous impact to my team and myself? A life-changing event for my entire group? That's not important?"

"No, no that's not what I mean! I'm really sorry. I...I just..."

"I don't need any more excuses. Tell me and get this over with."

"Of course. Okay." Phil paused; he could feel himself starting to sweat. He really, really hated this.

"Spit it out Phil, it's not going to be any easier five minutes from now." Scott could see that Phil was already broken, a bead of sweat was on his brow and he was no longer keeping eye contact. Scott was in complete control; Phil was going to look for any way to get out of this.

"Well? Well?"

"Umm, yeah, it's a bit difficult.... After we found the Venus signal...."

"We? We? We found the Venus signal? Phil?"

"Yeah, sorry...sorry I meant you; you found the signal, you and your team."

"That's the first thing that you've said that's made sense so far. Come on, stop stalling."

"Umm...yeah...sorry...." The sweat was pouring off him now; Phil could feel his shirt starting to glue itself to him. A rapidly growing sweat stream was exploring its way down his temple.

"Okay...." Phil paused again; he made a very audible swallowing sound and spewed the bad news out as fast as he could go. "Now that a sentient signal has been found, you and your team are no longer required. SETI is going to pour all its financial resources into the Venus work. All other projects will be terminated for the foreseeable future. I'm afraid that we have to let you go."

As prepared as Scott was, he still felt anger as the words blew past Phil's trembling lips. To Scott's surprise, some of the anger crept into his voice.

"What a callous, cold-blooded statement that is. Considering that I'm the one that made the discovery. What do you think the public will say if this got out? SETI fires the guy who made the greatest discovery this world has ever seen?"

"This can't get out to the public! Not yet!"

"It will eventually and when it does its going to look really bad. A lot of people are going to be asking questions, wondering if there is some kind of plot, perhaps the whole Venus thing is made up, an excuse to get some more attention and budget dollars. Who knows what they will think. Some people didn't believe that there had been a landing on the moon. They thought that it was made up."

Phil paused, he began to see a way out, a glimmer of hope, get bloody Scott off his back for now. "You know, that's a good point, a very good point, Scott. Look, let me go to the Senior Administrator, Jack Anderson. I know he wouldn't want any negative publicity. Perhaps we could relocate the team, move you into a new department, you could review some of the Venus signals, gather more data, err...something like that. I can't promise you anything yet but I'll do my best to present this new position."

"How about we both present this to Jack? I think I might be able to provide a little more emphasis, add my point of view, that sort of thing."

"Well, of course, yes...good idea."

"When?"

"Huh? What do you mean?"

"When are we going to Jack?"

"Oh, I don't know he's pretty busy, maybe in a couple of weeks."

"How about this afternoon? I happen to know Jack is around and doesn't have any meetings booked at three p.m.."

"Oh. Really?"

"Yes, really."

"Oh...okay...yeah...I guess so...." Phil's voice trailed off to a whisper.

"Don't worry, I have it all in hand, you just do the basic intro, I'll do the rest."

"Okay, yeah...sure, why not?" Phil's voice, still soft and uncertain, held no conviction. He felt an overwhelming urge to get Scott out of the office. He put as much strength as he could to his voice and said, "That's great. Thanks."

As he left the office, Scott thought, *Game, set and match. There's nothing better than beating the heck out of somebody and then having them thank you for it. I'm back in business. Phase one is complete. On to phase two.*

Scott had not been surprised when he heard the rumor three weeks ago. It had been four long months since he had found the Venus transmission. He knew that things were happening fast. He had expected that, as the hero, he would be included in the SETI plans. For the first couple of weeks he kept waiting to get called into Phil's office for the good news. It didn't happen. Phil kept stalling. As much as possible he avoided

Scott. Scott's team continued the same old work, pointing the telescope array at some part of the universe, looking for intelligent signals, pointing the telescope array, looking for intelligent signals. Over and over again, day after day. It didn't take long for Scott to realize that something was wrong. He wasn't the great hero that he had hoped to be. He got a couple of weeks of smiles, handshakes, back pats, "Well done!", "Way to go!" and many more of the banal, painfully patronizing comments. Then even that started to tail off. Meanwhile he could sense that a lot of action was happening in the background. But he wasn't included. It was like being in the eye of a hurricane. Motion all around him, but nothing happening to him. It was frustrating as hell. What was worse, he decided that he shouldn't say anything or indicate in any way that he was unhappy. He needed time to work out a plan, to find out what was going on.

The day that he had barged into Phil's office, Scott had already booked a three p.m. meeting in Phil's name with Jack. His plan had been ready for several weeks. All he needed was a time when Jack would be available. That had proven to be more difficult than expected. The discovery had created chaos in SETI. They weren't prepared for a signal so close to earth. It produced many more possibilities than would some transmission from hundreds of light years out. Jack was working fifteen hour days, seven days a week. He was hardly ever around and never available. So Scott had a dilemma. How could he keep tabs on Jack's schedule without it getting back to Phil? Once Phil had agreed to see Jack, he wanted to strike quickly. He didn't want to give Phil an opportunity to change his mind. He decided to take a bit of a chance, a little minor hacking...well, not really hacking—Scott installed a key-logger on his own computer. The key-logger tracked all the key strokes made on the keyboard. Then he called IT and told them that he had a problem with his calendar. When the IT guy came to fix it, the key-logger recorded the administrator login and password. After that he had access to Jack's calendar and everyone else's for that matter. Amazingly easy.

What he hadn't anticipated, the really good part, was all the extra info he now had access to. Jack's calendar entries almost always had some basic description of the planned meeting. Often there was a lot of detail. It became apparent that Jack liked to keep good notes. Scott was now privy to the most highly confidential SETI plans. Before he walked into Phil's office he already knew exactly what SETI was up to—and it was much, much more than he expected.

As he and Phil approached Jack's office, Scott mentally ran over the phase two game plan one more time. His approach with Jack had to be completely different from his aggressive, bullying manner with Phil. That would get him nowhere with Jack. First off, Jack was a much tougher personality. Secondly, he wasn't carrying the, "I'm going to let you go and haven't told you," guilt that Phil had. Finally, he had to be careful with the pecking order. Jack was the kind of manager that expected the chain of command to be followed. You didn't go over your manager's head—unless, of course, you wanted to get fired. It had to look like Scott had Phil's complete approval. Which was what phase one was all about. He could feel the butterflies in his stomach.

At the age of sixty-three, Jack was at the end of a successful career. An ex-NASA scientist and administrator, Jack was pleased to have been offered the Senior Administrator position at SETI a little over a year ago. It was a good fit. NASA and SETI regularly collaborated on projects. With a very limited budget, SETI often relied on some temporary help from NASA.

Jack was in a great mood. It was starting to look like accepting this position was the best decision of his entire life. He had really lucked out. If he played the politics correctly, he was going to be a key figure in the biggest event this world had ever seen. Hell! He might even be "the" figure. In charge of the whole project. It was possible, he was perfectly positioned, NASA and SETI experience, well respected, etc. etc. He made a quick note on his PC—*work up a resume promoting my capabilities.*

"Come on in gentlemen. How are you doing Scott? Sorry I haven't had much time to come by since the big event." Jack Anderson had a friendly way about him that had a very deliberate tendency to put you off your guard—a well-liked, innocent uncle, that nobody pays much mind to. That kindly, happy manner hid a razor sharp intellect.

His appearance dovetailed nicely with the *Uncle* facade. Grey hair, a fair number of wrinkles, especially around the brown-green eyes, height around five-foot-ten...well, actually more like five-foot-nine now. He didn't like to admit it but he was aging faster than he would have liked. His eyes were starting to go—he was going in for cataract surgery in a week and a half. His knees would ache after relatively short walks; he was starting to avoid stairs. It didn't help that he had packed on some pretty serious pounds—he had moved into the *pudgy* category. On every visit to his Doctor he got the, "you've got to take better care of yourself," lecture. Each time, he'd start in on a new diet and exercise program but he could never stick with it, he was just too busy—work was a wonderful excuse for a lack of willpower.

Contrary to most scientists, Jack was also a good manager. He was well organized and an okay judge of character. Scott was counting on the "okay" part, really hoping that the epithet wasn't more like, "good or great."

"I'm not clear on why we are meeting. I was kind of surprised to see the two of you booked into my calendar." Actually Jack was very surprised, he had expected that Scott would have been long gone by now. He had given Phil explicit instructions to terminate the group. As a matter of fact, now that he thought about it, he was getting a bit angry.

"Well...why are we meeting?" Jack repeated.

There was no reply.

"*Crap!*" Scott thought. Not at all what he wanted. He wanted Phil to do the intro. He wanted it to look like Phil was fully behind the idea and was driving the bus.

"I know what you are thinking," Scott said. "I shouldn't be here... well, when Phil told me that my group was to be terminated, I asked him for a little time to prepare a presentation justifying our continued employment with SETI."

Phil joined in. "Right, I know I should have told you but you were so busy, I didn't want to bother you with a fairly low level issue. At least not until I had heard Scott's side of it."

"Really? So you and Scott have had this little confab and you are completely onboard and agree whole heartedly with whatever idea Scott has for salvaging his job with SETI? I just want to be sure before spending any more time with this. I need to know that you are a hundred percent behind this...this plan." Jack put extra emphasis on those last two words.

There was a pause, dead silence.

Scott casually looked over at Phil, heart in his mouth.

More silence.

Then finally, "Of course...of course, I wouldn't bring it to you if I didn't believe in it," Phil's voice contained the tiniest of a quaver. Scott prayed that Jack hadn't noticed. He looked closely at Phil's face. *Damn! There's a bead of sweat forming on his temple.*

"With your permission Jack, I'd like to go over what I presented to Phil." With a calm, smooth motion, Scott stood and moved slightly further away from Phil.

"Yes." Jack's critical eyes studied Scott for a moment and then, "Yes that's fine, Scott, thank you."

Scott fired off the start of a well thought-out speech, rehearsed many times, "Okay, I think you would agree that I have a very hard working, diligent team. It was my team that brought you proof of intelligent life on Venus."

"Yes, I agree, but your team made a mistake, that's what resulted in the find," Jack retorted.

"That's true. However, we stayed with it. Once I saw an energy spike, we worked our tails off to check and double check the entire spectrum. I could have told the team to refocus the array and get back to business but we stuck with it.

Even if we hadn't found the Venus transmission, I would have had a very good argument that our team should stay, just based on our experience and performance. We are one of the most capable teams that you have. We have met our objectives every year."

"Phil, is that true?" asked Jack.

"Yes it is, Sir," Phil replied. He took a shallow, nervous breath and started in on what he thought was the critical part of their argument. "There is also the matter of public perception. How will this look when it gets out? We would have let go the team that helped prove the existence of life beyond earth. At the very least it would seem uncaring and callous. At worst it would be highly suspicious—what are we hiding? I think it would be a very bad PR move."

Scott let that sink in for a few moments and then jumped back into the fray. "Jack, you don't know much about me. Let me tell you a little bit about myself. Since I was sixteen years old, I've known what I wanted to do. I've wanted to be part of the search for extraterrestrial life. I've wanted to know that there is something beyond this planet. I've wanted to know that there is something that is bigger than us. I wanted to know that humans, animals, fish, birds, trees, flowers, hell...grass even...I...I... needed to know that all life wasn't a fluke of the universe. That there was some bigger picture beyond Earth. I needed this for me; I needed a purpose, a goal. I chose this grand search, this noble endeavor as my reason for being. I made it my lifelong quest, my holy grail.

Many times I thought it a fruitless pursuit but I never gave up, I persevered. When my team made that mistake, that ultimate serendipity, I could have ignored it, gone back to the proper coordinates as fast as I possibly could. Let's face it, it would have been better for me—once I started down this path, no matter what happened I would have to admit to a pretty big mistake—I could have easily hid it by getting back to the proper coordinates. What were the chances that I would find something? As someone said to me; I would have a better chance of winning the lottery. I did it because I'm thorough and determined—I never give up. Why am I telling you this? Because I think....no...I KNOW...that I am an asset to you and to SETI. You couldn't have a more determined, dedicated person working for you. That alone should convince you to keep me here, but I also have credentials. Credentials that I worked long and hard for, slaved for, killed myself for...more that you could possibly know...." Scott could feel pride welling up within him, "I have a bachelor's degree in Astronomy from Yale. I finished first in my class. I also have a master's degree in Electrical Engineering from MIT. I was second in my class. At MIT I majored in Telecommunications. I am ideally suited to continue this cause. Surely there is a place for me and for my team."

Scott's eyes poured over Jack's face, looking...looking for a sign...of weakening...was there? Possibly.

"What if I told you that all the search teams are going to have to go?" Jack asked quietly.

Ah! This is what I have been waiting for, thought Scott. "Why is that? Surely you still need teams to go through all the data that has been gathered so far? It's an enormous amount—the signal has been transmitting twenty-four hours a day since I and my team found it. The signal doesn't seem to be repetitive—it all has to be analyzed. After all this, how could you possibly consider dropping it? It doesn't make sense."

"Well there's more to it than you know," Jack replied emphatically.

There was silence—a long, long pause. Scott could see that Jack was hesitant; churning something in his mind...he was weakening. This was his chance.

Scott broke the silence. "Let me tell you what I think is going on... it's just a guess...but logic tells me that it makes sense." Scott barged on, not waiting for an answer. "I think you are shutting down all non-essential groups and departments because you are going to run out of money. And you are going to run out of money because you are going to plan, design and build a mission to Venus. You don't need to interpret all that transmission data because you are going to the source. You are going to get it from the Venusian's themselves."

Dead silence.

So silent and prolonged that Scott could hear Jack and Phil's breathing... each breath suspended...suspended in the air. He could have sworn he could hear the beating of their hearts. No...no...he was wrong...it was the beating of his own heart. It was a drumbeat, the drumbeat of a warrior, the heartbeat of a champion....

He had won!!

Chapter 6

EVIDENCE

James McArthur paused to stare out the window of the borrowed office at the SETI complex.

It was a lovely, peaceful view. A small garden area provided a welcome visual break from the dreary technical document that he was reading. A lot had happened since that wonderful day—the day that changed his life forever—the day he got the call from Wayne Hume. Looking out over the idyllic garden setting, he thought back to when he first arrived at the SETI offices. It seemed a million years ago. At first things had not gone very well, not well at all....

The first few weeks at SETI had been very exciting. Looking for additional evidence of structures on the Venus surface, he reviewed every possible image ever taken of the planet. He examined. He evaluated. He assessed. He studied. For hours and hours, over and over again. But as the weeks went on, nothing more had been found. Only two very tantalizing images from the Venus Orbiter had shown any signs of alien intelligence. The images were very faint—even after further digital enhancement—which explained why the shapes on the surface of Venus hadn't been seen during the first review; the digital enhancement technology didn't exist when the orbiter first took the images. If you looked at the original pictures, there was nothing there. Even now, after James had looked at them over and over again, till he was sick of it, he still could only piece together one elementary shape. Too geometrical by far to be anything natural, it had to be Alien made, but no matter how hard he tried, he couldn't predict, estimate or even guess at the purpose of this structure.

He was getting worried. His sole purpose—his "*raison d'etre*"—was to provide an analysis of this structure. He had been working on the problem for two months now and still couldn't give SETI any more information than he had after the first two weeks—there was one structure in the shape of a perfect square, that was it. Four faint, insignificant lines. No other buildings, structures, shapes, or whatever you wanted to call them, had been found anywhere else on the surface of Venus. SETI was going to become impatient with him...turf him out of the project... the end of his career as an alien hunter, gone from the biggest event the world had ever seen. He couldn't let it happen. He had to solve this problem. He had been working non-stop for as many hours as he possibly could—hardly sleeping or eating. He still had plenty of energy but he was losing hope.

Then one particularly difficult day, after a week of depressing failures, as he was staring at those elusive pictures for the thousandth time, the data Engineer, Kevin Rix tore into the room—literally blowing papers off the shelf near the door.

"James! James! I've got something!" he shouted.

As James turned towards him, Kevin, slightly out of control, tripped over some books that had been perilously stacked just to the right of the door. Now completely out of control, he careened into the bookshelf next to the desk, knocking several books, two pens, a can of Chef Boyardee (along with its spoon) and a multitude of papers into the air. Unable to get his hands properly in front of him, he bounced off the bookshelf. His new trajectory vector was aimed precisely at James sitting at the desk. Kevin, frantic to stay on his feet, thrust out his right hand in the hope that he would steady himself on the desk. The plan would have succeeded...except that James's face was in the way. In a split second, with no time for either of them to react, Kevin executed a perfect football running back stiff-arm to his face. James felt his head snap back. Meanwhile his chair decided to go in the opposite direction, the rollers on the smooth floor singing as the chair disappeared from under him. On his way down, his back hit the desk, throwing him forward slightly and causing him to land on the floor in a sitting position. Kevin now had another new trajectory, which mercifully allowed him to just miss the two thousand dollar ultra-high-res screen on the desk. He caught the edge of the table surface with his right hip, performed a ballerina-like pivot as he fell and landed with a thud squarely on his ass. Through the whole, amazingly bizarre episode Kevin had kept a steadfast grip on the papers that he clutched in his left hand.

Kevin and James were now sitting on the floor facing each other. James's face, neck, shoulders, back and rear were all starting to report damage. Kevin on the other hand seemed not to notice that anything was in the least bit odd—as if it was perfectly normal to be sitting on the floor in the office with papers lazily drifting towards their new home on the ground and with a can of soup, slightly dented, wobbling towards the wall and with the chair on its back in the doorway—its rollers still spinning. He watched the can make one last sorrowful rotation before coming to rest and then without any explanation, excuse, "*Gee, I'm sorry*", or anything, Kevin shoved out his left hand and said with the brightest eyes James had ever seen. "You have got to see this!!"

Kevin or Kevie as most people called him was a very young, brilliant engineer and mathematician. He had been assigned to look for any additional methods of dragging further information from the Venus images. Along with James, Kevie had been reviewing every image ever taken of Venus—trying various different imaging enhancements, messing with some new transforms of his own, doing anything he could to pull up more detail—hoping to find some new structure. Like James he was becoming worried, he hadn't been able to make one bit of difference. Nothing he tried worked—until now.

Kevie could hardly get the words out fast enough. "Last night, just before I went to bed, I had a brainwave, I thought that if I combined a Fourier transform with that new transform I built, I just might be able to get a little more detail," he stopped to suck in some air. "You're not going to believe it! Look! Look at what I got!"

James was looking all right...he was beginning to feel that warm glow again; he could feel the joy building...the square structure now had some companions. There was a triangle, a circle and a rectangle. They were so precise that undoubtedly they had been created by some kind of intelligence.

Kevie said breathlessly, "I tell you what I think, I think that the reason we couldn't see these structures before is because they are buried—there's only a small ridge left on the surface, it was too fine to be found with the other techniques."

"Fantastic! Absolutely Fantastic!" replied James. A thousand thoughts filled his mind all at once. Some of them made it to his mouth, "Let's calculate the dimensions of these objects. You should run your new transform on all our images. How long would that take to do? Can you estimate how high these ridges are? How far apart are they? Why are they all geometric? This is incredible! Let's get working!"

Then he looked around the room, his mood dropped a bit. "But first, we'll clean this mess up."

Two days later James was sitting in front of a large group of people, probably one hundred or so, about to present his findings. The place was full of SETI, JPL and NASA management types. There was also a smattering of federal bureaucrats. He was ecstatic. The last two days had flown by. He had a theory. Everything fell into place once the new structures were visible.

Jack Anderson stood up. He was to do the introductions. "Everyone. Could I have your attention please. As you know the purpose of this meeting is to review the current status of the Venus investigation. First off, I want to make this very CLEAR. None of the information that you will hear today can leave the room. This is absolutely confidential." Jack paused long enough to ensure that his statement had full impact and then continued, "We have made some progress with both the signal from Venus and the apparent structure at the transmitting site. First, I'd like to have James McArthur present the detailed structure analysis results. James is a renowned Archeologist and a longtime member of SETI, James...."

James stood up. The entire room became silent and so did James. He wasn't used to talking in front of such a large and important audience. Those one hundred pairs of eyes, intently staring directly at him, waiting for him to speak, shocked him. Suddenly, his mind felt like a water-filled sponge slopping back and forth inside his skull. Out of the corner of his eye, he was vaguely aware that Jack was starting to squirm. Finally, words began to form in his brain—they staggered their way to his mouth.

"Thank you.... Thank you. Thank you Jack. Well Ladies and err... Gentlemen, I'm sure some of you are wondering why it's taken so long to...to get any more information about the structure...."

Once he had forced a few words out, he relaxed. Very quickly he was more than relaxed. He was so enthralled with his theory and its implications that he forgot entirely that he was presenting to some of the sharpest minds and most influential people in space science. James gave a quick summary of what he and Kevin had found and the reasons behind the delay. To lighten things up a bit, he described how Kevin had told James about his discovery, "Kevin needs to work a bit on his presentation skills...."

He was just wrapping up the findings, about to get to the really good part, the part that had totally occupied his mind for the last twenty-four hours, when there was a question from the audience:

"Do you have any theories about the purpose of these structures?"

"Funny you should ask that, I was just about...."

"Thanks James, I'll carry on from here," interrupted Jack.

"Oh? oh! okay...yeah...no problem," answered James. He sat down. *What's Jack up to?*

Jack said, "I'd like to say that what I'm about to tell you is still very preliminary and NOT a final conclusion. Also, there is something that James forgot to mention. It's regarding the dimensions of these structures."

Forgot to mention? I didn't forget to mention anything. He didn't give me a chance to finish. What the heck is going on???

"They are enormous, many miles on an edge. As James said, we are also speculating that these structures are mostly below the surface...."

"How large?" someone called out from the crowd.

"Well, as an example, the square object, which incidentally is, within the accuracy of our measurements, is a perfect square—it's over forty-eight miles on a side. That's an incredibly large building. In fact, impossibly large by Human standards. As I was about to say, these structures are mostly below the surface, which leads us to speculate that what we are seeing may only be some kind of foundation which is now partially buried beneath the soil. The atmosphere of Venus is so harsh, as you know the surface temperature is nine hundred degrees—it's possible the buildings themselves have been destroyed, leaving only the subsurface material—the foundations." Jack paused. He wanted them to chew on that for a moment.

Someone asked, "How could there be any life on Venus? I mean how could anything survive those conditions? It doesn't make sense."

"I agree. It doesn't make sense. But the signal is there. Without doubt, there is, or was, some form of intelligent life on that planet. Possibly this alien race didn't originate on Venus. I don't know. We don't know. We just don't have enough information at this time," Jack said.

"I also said that we were going to talk about the transmission signal that we have been monitoring. We now feel that the signal is very weak because the antenna structure and the antenna are no longer there—possibly for the same reason that the buildings are gone; they've been destroyed."

"How could we receive any transmission if there is no antenna?" The question came from one of the bureaucrats.

"An amplifier can still radiate a signal without an antenna. It's just that the subsequent signal will be very weak...which is what we have here. In this case it's likely that there is a powerful amplifier attached to a length of transmission cable which has been cut off at the surface. The signal would radiate out the end of the cable. It's only because of the SETI antenna array, the most sensitive of its kind in the world and new signal processing techniques that we have been able to detect the transmission. Five years ago...no...not even five years ago, we would have been unable to detect this signal."

Jack continued, "So, I'm pretty sure this is clear to you all now...." A sudden sarcastic thought surfaced, *Actually I'm not so sure—with the feds here*, "But just to summarize, our current guess is that this site has been abandoned."

"If that's true why are we still receiving a signal?"

"Good question. We think that it's an automated signal, possibly it's been running for years. At this moment we just don't know," replied Jack.

"Is it repetitive?" That came from one of the NASA guys.

"Not so we can tell. But we really still don't know what we are dealing with. We really don't even know if we have demodulated it properly. We don't know what kind of race created this place, how they communicated, what language they used—or even if you could call it a language. We just know what it is not—it's not a naturally generated signal."

A series of questions leaped from the audience. "What's the spatial relationship of each building...err foundation? Where are they located? How far apart? Where do we think the antenna is with respect to the foundations?"

"They are clustered together; none of them are more than five miles from the edge of its neighbor. The transmitting antenna would have been located somewhat in the middle of the group. However, at this moment I don't want to discuss the exact sizes and locations of each structure."

A number of other questions started to bubble up from the group but Jack cut them all off with, "We have a lot more work to do. We will keep you updated. Thank you everyone."

Jack had just returned to his office when James stomped in. "What the heck was that all about? Why did you cut me off? Why did you skip the most important part?"

"Because I had a change of heart...changed my mind."

"Why? Why? The theory, my theory, was the key element to the whole presentation. It's going to cause a huge sensation."

"That's exactly why I didn't want to say anything. Listen James, I know how important this is to you, how hard you have worked, but you and the rest of the team have only had one day—twenty-four short hours—to think about the theory. That's nowhere near long enough. Think about the audience you were talking to today. They have a lot of influence, they will ultimately determine the path that we will take, how much money will get spent, where and when we will spend it. It's really important that we get our facts straight, make sure any theory we present is well thought out and is as accurate as it can possibly be. We make a mistake with these guys and our credibility is gone. After that, they won't listen to anything we say and we won't get a dime out of them."

"I see. Yeah. You have a point."

"Finally, and just as important, there were a hundred people in the audience today. What do you think the chances are that whatever we told them would stay in that room? I can tell you—next to none. I told them that all this was confidential but I did that to cover my ass. I know that what we said today is going to get out, others will hear about it. Eventually someone in the press will hear some rumors and start snooping. That theory of yours is too fresh, too important to let it get out to the public at this time. Once the public has it, the politicians have it. If the politicians have it, all our control is gone. Obviously the President and some key others know already. I am providing daily updates to them but they are as concerned about secrecy as we are. When we are ready, we will present our theories, our recommendations and a concrete plan to the President and senior staff. We will tussle it out with them, make some compromises and with a little luck we will get, not what we want, but at least what we need. If we don't play this game, the general public and the politicians will get to make the decisions—as I said, our control will be gone."

"You're right. Sorry I don't normally think about those sorts of things."

"I understand. Dealing with bureaucrats and politicians is pretty much the most important part of my job. I wish it wasn't. So get back to work James! We've got lots to do."

Chapter 7
INVITATION

It was exactly three weeks to the day since Jack and James had presented their initial findings. As usual, Jack was in a meeting. It was the most important meeting of his long career. He was at the White House meeting with the President and his Senior Technical Advisors.

This was it. After twenty-one days of non-stop day and night work Jack's team had solidified the theory and built a plan. He was now going to present the plan as a series of recommendations. Jack had really pressed his guys hard—there was no time to spare; the rumors were starting to spread. Internally people were starting to speculate—guessing what was happening, making their own theories, some of them pretty bizarre—"the aliens are already here!" was the latest one he had heard. The longer they postponed announcing their plan, the worse it was going to get. It was a bad situation. He had to move quickly.

As he prepared, self-doubt assailed him. Was he up to it? The plan was so important. He was absolutely certain that the recommendations, if accepted, would affect the course of human history; it was very controversial. He had to be absolutely convincing; this was the biggest sales job he had ever had to do. No one could be immune to this pressure. He hadn't slept in two days.

The President entered the room, *Here we go!*

"Mr. President, thank you for taking the time to hear the recommendations regarding the Venus *Adventure*." Jack stopped and allowed that final word to sink in, "I call it an adventure because, in my opinion, should you accept the proposed recommendations, you will be endorsing and supporting the greatest adventure mankind has ever attempted."

"As you know, we have found four structures. Actually, I'll call them objects...four objects near the transmission site. They are of enormous size. There is a perfect square—it's slightly over forty-eight miles on each side; there is a circle that has a radius of fifteen miles; there is an equilateral triangle—each edge is almost five miles long—and finally, there is a rectangle whose sides are a half mile on the short side and almost one and a half miles on the long side. They are dispersed roughly equally around the source of the transmissions that we have been monitoring for the last three months.

Since I talked to you last, we have found something interesting about these objects. Each one of them has a component that forms part of a geometric progression—a geometric progression with π as the common ratio. The progression starts with the rectangle. If you draw a line across the rectangle from one corner to the other and then measure that line, it turns out that it is the first term of the progression. Take the length of that line, multiply by π and you have length of the edge of the equilateral triangle. If you take that length, multiply by π again, you have the radius of the circle. Finally if you take the radius of the circle and multiply by π, you get the length of the side of the square." Jack paused to catch his breath.

"Initially, we thought that these objects were the remains of buildings; thought that they were foundations partially buried below the surface. However, we have now changed our minds about that. We think...."

"Sorry Jack, sorry to interrupt but I'd like to take you back to your statement about the geometric progression. Are you sure that this is correct?" asked the President.

"Yes, very sure. Obviously we were surprised when we saw this, so we checked and rechecked," Jack replied.

"What practical purpose could something like that serve?" queried the President.

"That's exactly what we asked ourselves...and I believe we have the answer," replied Jack, "Let me explain it to you as it was explained to me."

These were James's words, almost verbatim, "As you know, we have concluded a thorough search of all the Venus images ever taken. We have not found any evidence of any other structures anywhere else. We also have been monitoring the entire planet for further transmissions from other locations. We have found nothing."

Jack took a moment to catch the eye of every person in the room. He turned back to the President.

"Don't you think it's strange that the only objects that we can see on the entire planet are at exactly the same location as the transmitting signal? Yes it could be a fluke, just pure chance, but how lucky can you get? Maybe...maybe it's not a coincidence...maybe we were meant to find this...maybe all of this is intentional. What if, we, the human race on planet Earth, are being monitored? Monitored. Watched. Watched for a particular moment in time when we have achieved a certain level of technical capability. Say a level of competence that would allow us to travel to Venus," He paused and involuntarily held his breath as he felt the tension of the most important moment of his life, *then*,

"Mr. President, we believe that this signal is an invitation."

"An invitation? Oh! My God!"

"Yes, we believe that the large objects were put there to convince us that the transmission we have detected was not an accident. What's the best way to do that if you don't know how to communicate with the other race? Create something simple. Something that could have no other purpose. Add some simple mathematical construct that again makes no sense for any logical purpose, except to show intelligence."

"Why haven't they replied to our attempts to communicate?"

"We don't know that they haven't. We know so little about that transmission."

"What about the planet? Surely it can't support life now. I thought we were speculating that the alien race had abandoned Venus."

"We don't know that. Possibly they are underground. Possibly they can survive, perhaps even thrive in that environment. Over the last fifty years we have discovered many species on earth that exist in environments that are incredibly hostile to human life. We now believe they are still there. They want us to travel to Venus. Mr. President, I am absolutely convinced of this. Nothing else makes sense to me."

"Why haven't they traveled to earth to contact us?"

"We don't know that answer. Maybe they have traveled to earth but chose not to make direct contact. As you know, we have had numerous unexplained umm...situations in the past. Perhaps some of them were real after all."

"Maybe they can't travel in space. Perhaps their bodies can't take weightlessness."

"Possibly this is a test, a test to see if we are ready, a test to see if we have the will and the courage to make this voyage. Let's face it, the manned trips to the moon will seem like a walk to the corner store compared to this endeavor."

"Well...." The President paused, looked around the room at the rest of the silent, stunned group. He turned back to Jack. "Okay, let's assume for the moment that you are correct. Please give me your recommendations."

"Yes Sir. We believe that the invitation should be accepted."

"I knew that was coming. Why?"

"Because we may never be able to communicate with them unless we do. It's possible that the signal from Venus may never be understood. We just don't know enough about this race. Well actually, we know nothing about them except that they are capable of some simple math, they can make some very large, simple shapes and they can send a radio frequency signal of some kind. That's it. That's all that we know. It's not enough.

Not enough by far." Jack said, "Look at how we learn languages—say you were dropped into Outer Mongolia. You would learn their language by interacting with them—pointing, hand signals, images scratched out in the dirt, words repeated over and over again. You could reach out and touch the Mongolians, you would be face to face with them, you would be able to watch their reactions and modify your assumptions based on those reactions."

The President replied, "Well that's true, but what about dead languages? We didn't have to reach out and touch an ancient Egyptian. We couldn't—they were all dead." Soft chuckles filled the air.

Jack said, "That's a very good question. With the ancient Egyptians we had one very important asset. We knew they were human. We have a common understanding of what it means to be human. How we think, how we communicate. We know the range of human vocalization—sounds we can make and sounds we can't. We understand emotions—anger, happiness, sadness, love. We intimately know their environment—air, water, animals, birds, bees, trees, plants. We know sensations—touch, smell, taste. We understand their desires and needs—hunger, sex, a warm place to sleep, the determination to always improve—to do better. All this provides a huge advantage. It's almost trivial learning a human written language—so long as you have enough of the symbols and lots of time, eventually you will figure it out."

"In this case, as I said, we are working from almost nothing. We can't even tell if they have replied to our signals so there isn't any give and take—we can't send a basic signal, wait for their reply, we send another one, they reply again, etc., etc.

I haven't even talked about the complexities of telecommunications, the methods of sending radio wave signals. There are many different ways of modulating a radio signal; some of those ways allow a signal to travel further than others. It's very likely that there are methods that we haven't discovered. Perhaps this Alien race is using one we have never considered. Perhaps we couldn't understand the technology even if they told us—it could be too far advanced for us at this time.

After you have demodulated the signal, you then have to interpret what remains—the information part—but, for example, if it's a digital signal, in our world, there are many layers, many choices that are made before you get to the true information. That information is riding on top of a stack of digital conversions and encapsulations that are intended to ensure that the information gets to the far end as quickly and as accurately as possible, or as cheaply as possible, or some combination of the two. But we don't know anything about how the alien race is doing this. We have no point of reference from which to even start. All we could do is begin guessing, but how would we know that we have guessed right? We don't know how they communicate. So we're back to where we started, needing to understand how they communicate. We've gone in a complete circle. It's a chicken and egg scenario.

Mr. President, we see no other choice, not if we want to take the next great step in the history of mankind—to communicate with another race of beings. Think of what that means. The opportunities to learn will be endless. Perhaps they are far ahead of us in technology, medicine, science. We would learn what their culture is like, how they communicate, what their desires are. For the human race, it will be a collective mind expanding event on a galactic scale. Without a doubt we will be changed in some way for all time. I...I...feel changed already, knowing that we are part of a cosmos that includes other, sentient life. How can we not take up this challenge? How can we not take this next grand step on our path to the future?

We have received an invitation—not just an invitation to travel to another planet but an invitation to learn, to grow, to evolve. We have no choice, we must accept the challenge. To ignore this invitation, is to refute the most human of all our qualities—the desire to explore and learn. We have no choice, we must accept the challenge."

Jack was finished. He had done his best. Was it enough?

He watched the President's face intently, afraid to blink should he miss some subtle change in his expression. The fate of all humanity was resting on this man's shoulders.

Would he accept the challenge?

The tension was unbearable. Jack could feel himself starting to crack. The seemingly endless hard work, the stress of the last few days, the lack of sleep was culminating in this one short, yet infinite moment in time. He was a star gone supernova, now collapsing to a black hole, about to become infinitesimally small. ***SAY SOMETHING!***

"There would be a massive cost, so massive it could bankrupt us."

"Mr. President, it would be worth it, worth every penny. However, the United States doesn't have to bear this burden all on its own. Certainly many, many countries will want to participate. What politician would want it to be said that they denied their countrymen the pride of membership in this club, the pride of participation in this great adventure?"

Silence once again descended upon the room—an oppressive silence that threatened to crush Jack, threatened to crush his spirit, threatened to crush his life's crowning glory, threatened to crush mankind's hope—his chest was so tight he could hardly breathe. He knew he had to keep silent. He knew he had to wait. It was unbearable.

The President, looked about the room, his face was grim, he shook his head, "It's a big risk...a huge risk...we haven't come close to space flight on this scale. And when we get to Venus, to put someone on the ground, in that environment...it's almost suicide. But.... We have to try. Jack's right, we have to try."

Chapter 8
ATTACK

James was working late again at JPL. He had traveled from the SETI headquarters to work with some of the Jet Propulsion Lab people.

He was studying, cramming actually....

After the revelations regarding the "*Invitation*" James had experienced a big letdown—a depression like he had never known—he realized that his job was complete. He had done his part; others would take up the cause and he would be left behind. A quintessential scholar, he wasn't good at looking to the future; he had been intent on solving the problem. He hadn't even thought of what would happen afterwards; it was a shock to put two and two together. After Jack's meeting with the President, Jack had said to the whole team:

"You all have worked so hard. It's time to take a break, relax, and prepare for the next round. I want everyone to take two weeks off."

Turned out that was a big mistake for James. That's when he started thinking about the future and realized that he didn't have one.

He spent the rest of the two weeks utterly depressed—hardly ever left his apartment. Watched useless, mindless TV day and night. At the end of the worst holiday of his life, he was preparing to go into the office and pack up his things when his cell phone rang. It was Jack.

"James, where are you?"

"On my way to the office."

"Good. Come see me right away when you get in."

What's that about I wonder? Probably wants to say goodbye.

An hour later James entered Jack's office.

"Well, I've got something to tell you and to be honest I'm not sure how you are going to take it," Jack said.

Here it comes. No surprise really. James felt his soul sink—sink right through his feet and out of his body. "Oh?" said James despondently.

"Please sit down."

"Uh...sure...thanks."

"We have a problem. We are starting to think about who we need to send to Venus. We are developing a list of requirements: how many people should go, the personality types, the fitness levels, technical capability and so on. There's not going to be much room in the Venus ship, so we have to be deadly efficient with the numbers. The people we take will have to be multifunctional, capable of doing many different tasks. We've got most of that worked out," Jack said.

"The problem is that we have to be prepared for a lot of eventualities, including that the site, contrary to our current beliefs, has been abandoned. If that's true, then we have some different challenges and there would be a need for people with different capabilities...and in this case we may need an Archeologist." Jack stated this very casually. It took a moment for the meaning to sink in to James's miserable mind.

He said, incredulous, "What? Did you say you would need an Archeologist on the mission team???"

"Yes, that's correct. I'd like to know if you would consider taking this on. Of course you will have to pass the physical and a number of very serious competence tests. As I said you will have to take on many other duties besides Archeology."

"Oh! Oh! Well! I need time to think about this. I really, really want to stay with the project but I never thought about being on the mission team. I mean...gee...I'm not an astronaut! Never even thought about being one. Wow. This is quite a shock."

"I understand. Of course. Look, take some time to think about it. Remember as well, I'm not offering the position. I'm offering the opportunity for you to prove that you can do the job. There will be a lot of testing. Tons of work. I know you can handle that part. Anyway, think it over. Let's talk later in the week."

James hardly slept for the next two days. He knew that the mission would be very risky. They might not survive. "It's a one way ticket," he'd heard someone say. He vacillated for two straight days—"Okay I'll do it" then "No, not a good idea," then back to "I'll go," then "No," then "Yes," back and forth, back and forth. It was driving him nuts.

It was the thought of making a personal sacrifice for a cause that would truly affect the entire human race that made the difference. If he didn't make it back, if he died out there, at least he died for a cause like no other in the history of man. He thought about all those people who had, in war, made the final sacrifice for their country. How could he refuse this calling when so many others before him had accepted the challenge, had held back their fear, had done their duty? They had sacrificed for their country. His sacrifice would be for all of mankind.

He called Jack right away with his decision.

The very next day, Jack sent him on his way to JPL, "We have some people at JPL right now reviewing a new rocket system that's being designed. It's a good opportunity for you to get involved straightaway. You can attend some of those meetings. The rest of the time, you will be studying this." He handed James a large capacity USB flash drive. "These cover some of the basics—astronomy, physics, engineering, computer science, aerodynamics." I realize you know some of this from your time with SETI, so you should be able to work through it pretty quickly. We don't expect you to be an expert in any of these subjects but you need to have a good grasp of the fundamentals. And some of the testing will include topics from this drive. So study it well. I'll get in touch with you when we are ready to start the tests."

Jack started to turn away and then remembered, "By the way, you have to pass a very comprehensive physical. Do you have any major medical problems that I should know about? If you have, it's best to let me know now. It would be a shame to put a lot of time into this only to find out that some physical problem prevents you from being accepted."

James didn't have to think very hard about that one. He had been lucky. Couldn't remember the last time he even had a cold. "None that I know of. I've been pretty healthy. I do need to start working out more. I get a bit lazy."

"Join the club. Okay, that's great. I'll have someone contact you about some exercise routines that you can start. Make time for them. It's going to be important. I'll see if I can arrange for the basic physical tests as soon as possible—blood tests and so on. And, you know, look for any major issues that you may not know about."

It was after 1 a.m. when James left the JPL complex. As he stepped out of the air-conditioned building, he was hit with a waft of clean, warm, sweet air. It was a shock. After working for sixteen hours non-stop in that building, he'd forgotten what the real world was like. He took a deep breath of air, smelt the fragrant scent of a nearby lilac bush. *Wonderful!* He looked up. It was a perfectly clear night. The stars were all about him. They sang to him. *At this exact moment, I'm as content and happy as I could possibly be.* He turned and started toward his car. He glanced up and stopped dead in his tracks. *There it is. Right over the car. Venus!*

It was then that the full impact of what he was about to do hit him. He had been so concerned with preparing for the exams that he really hadn't considered, truly considered, what was about to happen. When he saw Venus, suspended in the night sky, hovering over the car, it suddenly came to him; *I could be going there. There! That tiny white light over the car. It's so small. So small. So far away.* Loneliness, fear and excitement joined to form a kaleidoscope of pulsating emotions. It felt so, so...*so alien.* A shudder ran through him. He began to feel sick. *What have I done??*

He stood there, trance-like, staring at Venus in the empty parking lot in the dead of night. He was frozen, unable to move, locked in some strange emotional stasis. Then, suddenly, the sensation withdrew leaving him stunned and overwhelmed. Caressed by the cold, uncaring light of Venus, he dropped to his knees on the pavement and cried.

James drove home, feeling better, a little more in control, when he remembered that he had forgotten a document he needed for an early morning meeting. He was very tempted to leave it, go home and get some sleep, but he couldn't; he needed that document. Cursing under his breath, he slammed on the brakes, made a quick U-turn and headed back to the office.

Twenty minutes later he was back at the complex. As he rounded the hallway corner he saw that the light in his office was on and thought, *that's funny, I don't remember leaving a light on....* He opened the door, stopped short, surprised.

Someone was standing over James's desk with his back to the door. They started to turn.... James said, "What? Who ar...." Suddenly he sensed a movement then heard a whisper of a sound behind him—he started to turn his head, but the lights in the room went out. Temporarily blinded, he was violently shoved from behind. As he fell, he thought, *there's at least two of them.* His left arm hit something on the way down, he felt a sharp pain near his elbow. Off-balance, unable to get his left arm out in front of him, he hit the floor of the office hard. He gasped as all his weight landed on his right hand, arm and shoulder. More pain! As he smacked the ground, he felt a body, on its way out the door, pass him. Mindlessly outraged by this violation, he reached out with his damaged right hand and grabbed the intruder's leg. James heard a surprised grunt and a soft impact. Someone yelled "Watch out you moron!" Then came a series of yells and bangs. James realized that he had tripped the first guy right into the second one—they were both going down, banging off the bookshelves, walls and door as they went.

James jumped to his feet. He could dimly see two bodies on the floor in the doorway—one guy partially on top of the other. They were cursing and struggling to get to their feet. The guy that James had tripped now had his feet under him and was halfway up—with his back to James. Using both hands, James pushed him as hard as he could. The intruder, now jet propelled, flew head first through the doorway into the hall. James had bought himself a microsecond or two. He yelled as loud as he could, "Help! Help!!" Simultaneously he leapt over the second guy, through the door...and felt a powerful tug on his leg. He landed in the hallway; face down, one guy in front of him, one behind. Now they were all struggling to their feet. It was a race; the first one up had the advantage. The guy James had pushed was almost standing. In desperation, James reached out, grabbed his jacket and started pulling himself up with both hands. The jacket's seams stretched, ripped and tore but somehow the fabric held long enough for James to gain his feet. In an instant they were both standing. James saw the guy draw back his hand and start to swing at his head. Still holding on with both hands, James ducked as far as possible and lifted his left shoulder as high as it could go. The blow glanced off James's shoulder and barely caught the top of his head. The man threw a blow from the other side next. James ducked again. He heard a sound behind him, turned his head and saw a fist coming his way. Still holding onto the first guy with one hand, James reached back, took one shot to the face, grabbed the second guy by the jacket, then using the intruder's momentum and with a mighty heave, threw him around in front of him. The two guys were now facing him and he had each of them by their jackets. He was dimly aware that he was sustaining damage from both sides. Still hanging onto the two of them, James pushed with both legs, driving the pair into the wall behind. He could hear both of them grunt; one of them went limp—the wind had been knocked out of him. He released that arm and started to swing at the other guy. But, before he could land his punch, something hard, something really hard, hit the side of his head. He staggered and literally saw stars. Abruptly, James felt warm liquid running down the side of his face. *Blood.* He started to lose his grip on the jacket. He hung on. He was hit again—the jacket slipped out of his fingers, he started to pass out, fought it. He was hit again, this time he got his left hand up, partially deflected it, lost his balance and started to go down. As he slipped to the floor he was kicked hard in the stomach, then in the head. *More blood.* He got his arm up. The next one hit him in the shoulder. He tried to stand. A big mistake! He opened his privates to a direct blow. His whole body went limp. As James collapsed onto the ground, he was overwhelmed with pain and sickness. He could feel himself starting to barf, tried to hold it back and was vaguely aware of another kick, somewhere in the chest. He curled up—trying to protect himself, in complete agony... helpless...he waited...*would they finish him off?* Moments passed. Nothing. Nothing...no sound—only his wheezing, moaning, sickly, erratic breath. *Were they gone?* James attempted to move, attempted to twitch his head to see down the hallway but started to gag...tried to hold it back...then let go.

The next day, in the hospital, James stared at himself in the mirror and was shocked—it was worse than he expected. His face looked like it had been run over by a steam roller. The left side was one gigantic bruise, starting at the hair line on his forehead and ending at his jaw. His eye was so completely swollen that he couldn't see out of it at all. The other side wasn't too bad—he'd only received one good punch but it was enough to cause some swelling. His head was almost completely bandaged, hiding around forty stitches in two different locations. His left elbow and right shoulder were sore but not too bad. Of course, his nether region wasn't too happy either. Sitting down had become a painful venture. Even so the doctor had told him that he had been very lucky, nothing broken, no concussion. They surmised that he'd been hit by a heavy wooden club. The doctor wanted to keep him in the hospital for a couple more days for "observation" but James had said, "I'm sorry, to be honest, I can't stand hospitals. They make me feel sicker than I already am. Besides, I need to get back to the office—find out if anything has been taken and I have a ton of work to do. I really can't afford to fall behind. Thank you for all your good work but if I could just have a prescription for some pain killers, I'll be on my way." The doctor didn't push it; there wasn't a compelling reason to keep him in the hospital, nothing was broken, his swollen eye would get better in a few days, it would look pretty awful while it healed but that was about it.

He had spent some time being quizzed by the police. He couldn't tell them much. Both attackers had stockings or something like stockings on their heads. It was dark; he couldn't even tell what they were wearing. About all he could say was that they were taller than him, one maybe around six feet, the other maybe six-foot-two. They were very fit, solid muscle everywhere. They had said nothing except when they bounced into each other. Even the animalistic grunting and yelling that comes with a desperate fight was kept to a minimum. It was James who made most of the noise. Although he wasn't any kind of an expert, it seemed to him that they were professional—not some kids on a break-and-enter whim looking for some extra change.

He was very worried about his office. Did they take anything? He had a lot of info lying around—enough for a reasonably intelligent person to work out what they were up to. Luckily, he had his laptop in the car—everything was on the laptop hard drive: e-mails, minutes of meetings, diagrams, detailed specifications. Would have taken no brainpower at all to determine their plans.

When the police started asking questions about what was in the office, JPL security, who at Jack's request had been with James ever since they found him struggling to stand in a pool of his own blood and vomit, jumped in with, "I'm sorry but the information in that office is top secret." The cops weren't at all pleased with that response and they weren't too subtle about their displeasure, "Well, if that's the way you want it. There's nothing more we can do." They got up and left the hospital room. It was the last time James saw any of the local police regarding the event.

It was quite different with JPL security, however. "We're going to do some investigation on our own. We can't find any evidence of forced entry. We also can't find any unaccounted for security card entries in the log for that period of time. Everyone that came or went has been checked. That points to some insider work—either someone knew how to diddle the security system or it's one of our "accounted for" people. Perhaps someone let those guys in. In any event, security at the building is going to be seriously beefed up."

By eleven a.m., with a big sigh of relief, he was out of there. He hadn't been kidding about hating hospitals but more than that, he was very, very worried about falling behind with his studies. He knew that the intensive part of his preparation was about to start. Jack had told him that he would call him in a few days to make arrangements to bring him to NASA.

He went straight to the office, well not that straight, his head was aching horribly. He needed those pain killers.

The office wasn't as bad as he had imagined. Most of the fighting had taken place in the hallway. The bookshelves on either side of the door were in disarray. One shelf was cracked, *that must have been what I hit on the way down*, he thought. Of course, there were books and papers scattered all around the entrance to the office. But on his desk everything looked perfectly normal. Nothing disturbed. He tried to remember exactly where the papers were before he had left the building that previous evening. He couldn't find anything changed.

He called Jack to give him the good news, "Looks like we lucked out. I can't find anything important missing or disturbed."

"That's great. How are you feeling?" Jack had asked. However, Jack pretty much knew how he was feeling; he was just being polite. He had a long talk with the examining physician. He heard one really interesting comment, "Well, your guy is a lot tougher than he looks. Those two hits on the head would have cracked most people's skulls. I mean not even a concussion. Pretty amazing. Also, he is in much better shape than he thinks—the basic work-up showed that he has a remarkable respiratory system and a very strong heart. His resting heart rate is forty. You don't normally get that except in world-class athletes like long distance runners, Triathletes, Tour de France cyclists. The strange thing was that James seemed genuinely surprised. Said he didn't do much exercise."

But Jack wasn't surprised at all. James had finished his preliminary physical at NASA and Jack had the results. He knew more than the doctor. He knew that James's lung capacity was twice normal and his physical strength was much higher than expected. Preliminary indications were that he was a very, very fit person. Who would have thought it. Jack mentally shook his head. James was full of surprises. He was an enigma. Everything about him screamed out "average," yet when you scraped off the surface dirt, you found gold. What was it someone had called him? The Extraordinary-Ordinary Man.

A quick smile crossed Jack's face as he thought, *How true. How very true.*

Chapter 9
BETRAYAL

He was running, running as fast as he could...in the woods, something behind him, something big, something monstrous, he had to get out of there! He looked behind him. Looked for what? What? What was it?? He was scared, more scared than he had ever been, he looked forward again, never breaking stride..........but he wasn't in the woods anymore, it was a new landscape, a strange landscape, weird...alien, a landscape on another planet, but he felt he knew it, felt comfortable. But it was still behind him!! He was still running...heart beating so fast! Is it possible for a heart to beat so, so fast? A sound, loud, very loud.... It's coming, it's coming!! That sound...that sound...familiar...familiar.... Familiar....

He woke almost screaming, his heart pounding, racing. Groggy, not sure where he was, or what was happening. He thought, *I'm having a heart attack!* His heart rate climbed another notch. *What? What's going on?* Gradually, awareness crawled into his consciousness. *That sound. It's the alarm clock!* Half blind, he stretched out his hand, swiped at the clock, missed, tried again, and knocked the clock off the nightstand, *Christ!* He did a half roll off the bed, onto his knees. As he grabbed the clock, a rage started to take him. He was within a hair of ripping the clock's power cord out of the wall when he found the "off" button.

Matt leaned weakly on the side of the bed. He was covered in sweat, his heart still going a good one hundred and fifty beats a minute, the nightmare still fresh in his mind. It was an awful feeling, sitting on the floor, the unseen monster of his dream still lurking about. He looked at the time—four thirty a.m., *I must be crazy doing this. Just to impress my dad.*

Early last night, he had received the results of the "research" that his dad had asked him to do at JPL. It was amazing, incredible, remarkable...wonderful! He had told Dean Sullivan to keep his mouth shut, not a word to his dad. Matt was going to do this personally. He was going to show his dad that he wasn't a screw-up, that he could do something right. He had tried many times before but every time...failure. His dad always found something to pick on, something to beat him up about. He shoved that thought down. This was so big. He was bound to be impressed. This time he was bringing information that was going to blow this world apart!

He had set the clock for four thirty a.m. so he could be in the office when his dad got there at six. He knew Kurt would be there. Kurt hardly ever left his office. He was the ultimate workaholic. To Kurt, this was normal. He expected all his minions to do the same—*especially his son.* Matt decided that he was going to show him that he could do it. Work just as hard. Go toe to toe with him. *Yes Sir. The workaholic's marathon. Let's see who can work the longest and hardest. The guy with the most hours when he dies.... Wins!*

He checked the clock again. *Well I've got lots of time, an hour and a half.* He had a nice breakfast, flipped on the TV—watched the news. He carefully picked his suit. *Dress for success you know.* Then changed his mind, tried on another one, went back to the first one, *humm, which tie?* Finally, fully dressed, he thought, *looking pretty damn good today. It's going to be a great day! Whoo Whee!!*

He looked at his watch. A look of horror crossed his face. *That can't be right!* He ran into the kitchen and verified the time with the clock on the wall. *Hell! I'm late, I'm late!* The blood pressure began to rise—just a little. *I'll be okay. I'm just fifteen minutes behind. I'll make it up on the freeway.*

Matt arrived at six twenty five. He might have made up the time but, *Damn! Just his luck!* That very day road repairs had started on the route he had picked. He lost another ten minutes. He wasn't feeling so confident anymore. Still, as soon as he thought of the news he was bringing, he ramped up again. *It was a doozer! A double doozer! The doozer extraordinaire!!!*

He walked into his dad's office at precisely six-thirty, feeling very smug. Kurt casually swung his head in Matt's direction. Matt thought, *Look at him. He's trying his best not to appear surprised.*

"Well, good morning," Kurt said.

Matt strode, almost strutted, over to the desk and sat down at the chair closest to Kurt, "Have I got a story for you!" he blurted.

"Really?" Kurt replied. There was just a slight sarcastic tone in his voice.

"Yeah, Dean Sullivan finished his mission."

"Go on."

He couldn't hold it in any longer, he said in a high pitched, excited voice, "We've made contact with an alien race. Can you believe that? Can you???" He watched his dad's face. He expected some sort of surprise or shock. Nothing. It was like he had told him it was raining.

"Really."

"Yes...umm...yes...you know.... It really looks like something has happened," replied Matt, disheartened.

Kurt scowled at Matt, "What do you mean, 'Looks like?' Do we know or don't we?"

"Sorry...yeh...yes. Yes we know. Umm...Dean and one of his guys broke into JPL, got a lot of info. I...I've got photos of it all!" He handed over a file to Kurt. The file shook ever so slightly. With just a hint of a smile, Kurt reached out, steadied it in Matt's hand, and then took it.

"So that's it?"

"Yes, yes that's it."

"Really, nothing else? No other problems?"

Matt's mind went numb. *He knows! He knows! Damn Dean!, Bloody Dean! He's told him the whole story! The bastard!*

"Oh well.........yeah...umm, there was...ummmmm...a slight problem, I wasn't going to worry you with it. Everything worked out in the end." Matt tried to put a tone of confidence in his voice but Kurt has having none of it.

"I'm glad you're concerned about my "worries". Why don't you let me decide if it's anything to worry about," Kurt replied sarcastically.

"Well...you know...it was...well.... A guy caught them when they were in JPL. Not a big problem though." Matt tried to make it sound like it was nothing. "They got away okay.... Ummm.... Err.... Had a bit of a fight though...didn't hurt the guy too much. Dean checked."

"Oh, that's alright then."

"Yeah." Matt's confidence got a boost. "That's the problem with those space geeks; you never know when they are going to be in the office. Who would have expected some dork to be coming into the office at two-thirty a.m.?"

"**NO EXCUSE**!!"

"Sorry...I...d...d...don't understand." Matt could feel his insides starting to squirm.

"I said, That's **NO EXCUSE**!"

"Oh. Yeah. I see where you're coming from. That stupid Dean Sullivan! He...."

"I don't mean Dean! You idiot! You're the stupid one! I didn't delegate the job to Dean! I delegated it to you! It's your job to make sure there are no screw-ups! It's your job to ensure Dean is doing the right thing, has the right guys! It's your responsibility! You answer to me! After all this time, you still don't know the first thing about management! The buck stops there!" Kurt shoved an angry, thick forefinger at Matt.

"I asked **YOU** to take care of this! But I bet **YOU** didn't do the first thing...anything...to make sure Dean was on track. Did Dean check what this guys work hours were? I'm betting that the only thing you did was to lift that lazy arm of yours, pick up the cell phone, dial Dean's number and tell him to find out what was going on! Geeee! I hope moving your lazy-assed fingers over the keypad wasn't too much for you!"

He sneered, "Did you need to take a nap after? **CHRIST!!**"

Kurt was almost screaming now. It wasn't make-believe this time; he was mad, really mad. Every muscle in his powerful body was ready to explode—explode right out of his skin. The pent up energy in those muscles begged for release.

"When you take responsibility for something, you ask questions, you make sure that whoever is going to do the job fully understands what is necessary, you ask him how he is going to do it, you follow up, you get him to give you reports! **CHRIST! THIS IS BASIC STUFF!!!**" Now he was screaming.

He paused to gather another lungful of air and then, "**So tell me!**"

Matt could hardly breathe now, "uhh...uhh...uhh...tell...uhh.... What?"

"Tell me if I'm right!"

"Oh. Oh..... Y...y...yeah....uhh...uhh...*Dad*...NO! NO! NO! I'm sorry, so sorry Kurt! Please!...it's my fault, it's my fault!"

Kurt thought, *Damn it, I hate it when he whines like that! DAMN IT!*

"Come over here."

"Look!.... Uhh...uhh.... Please.... I'm sorry...sorry...sorry.... Sorry!"

"I don't give a damn that you're sorry!!! Get...over...here!!!"

Matt ever so slowly, ever so carefully, stood...then took the few steps to his dad who was now standing by his desk.

Kurt watched with disgust as his son walked toward him. *Although it could hardly be called walking*, Kurt thought, *Some kind of crawling, slithering, dog-like wallowing.... How could anybody at the age of twenty-six be such a coward! Pathetic!*

Head down, Matt had almost reached the desk when Kurt struck. Lightning quick, before Matt could even flinch, Kurt's chunky palm whipped out and landed on Matt's cheek with a hard smack. In an instant, the whole side of Matt's face was red.

"I warned you!! You knew!! I'm going to beat that word out of you!!!" He lifted his hand again, it began a repeated, rhythmically brutal dance on Matt's face, "Don't...call...me.... Dad!"

Chapter 10
THE PLAN

Jack stood in front of another large audience. He was particularly aware of a core group of fifty-two eager faces, fifty-two Astronauts, situated in the center of the room, staring intently at him. The entire Venus mission team was here: Astronauts, Designers, Engineers, Mission Specialists, Support Staff. He had cracked the joke that he hauled out for special occasions. It was always guaranteed to get a good laugh. This time he only got a smattering of chuckles and a laugh or two. Not much. They were tense—but it didn't bother him. *Hell, I'd be tense if I was them.* He was in another great mood. His politicking had worked. He was in charge of the entire Venus project. A special appointment. He was reporting directly to the President of the United States. *Fantastic!!*

"So let's get down to business," Jack said, "You all know why you are here. There are fifty-two of you remaining. You have all passed the most rigorous of competency testing. You are the elite. You are the final lucky few who have been chosen to participate in this...this magnificent quest. Thousands, perhaps hundreds of thousands would like to be sitting in your place in this room today."

Jack scanned the room. "You can be very proud...feel that pride, remember that pride. You're here from many countries—from all around the world. I know that the people of your country are proud of you. Hold your head high. Be proud...but be proud because you represent all the nations of Earth, all peoples of Earth. To whomever, whatever, we meet on Venus, we are a single...nation. The nation of Earth. It is a wonderful feeling, a wonderful idea, to be a single people with a single goal. Let this thought be with you always."

Jack paused. "Much is expected of you...much is expected of all of us," A confident smile settled on his face. "I know that you will do your duty. You will not fail. I thank you for making this sacrifice."

He said, "We are now starting the next phase of the project. Each one of you will have some role to play. What that role will be has yet to be determined."

"There will be three teams," said Jack. "First there is the mission team itself. There will be twelve of you. Your task is clear. You will travel to Venus, make contact with the Alien race and return home safely."

"Second, there will be a backup team—another twelve—an exact copy, if you will, of the mission team—a one-for-one pairing." He stated. "You will train and work as if you were selected to go to Venus. Each backup person will provide detailed, intimate support to their counterpart, their partner, during the trip. Your job will be as important...no.... no...your duty will be more vital than the mission team. You will be your partner's twin, you will know them as well as you know yourself, you will be their emotional lifeline, their family—their mother, their father, sister, brother... wife or husband (a few laughs). It will be your job to ensure that whatever they require is provided. Their needs will take precedence over your own. You will be available twenty-four hours a day, seven days a week. Should something go wrong, a million miles from Earth, you will be their hope, their courage. You will share their fears. You will not falter. When they need you most, you will be there to comfort them and give them the will to go on. They will never give up because you will never give up."

Jack said, "For the rest of you, the remaining twenty-eight, the third team.... you... you will have the most important duty of all. You will transport all the necessary material to the moon. On the moon, you will build the craft that will carry these twelve souls to Venus and back. Fail in your task and the mission fails. A single bolt, rivet or screw put wrong and no one comes back. Their lives are in your hands. You will be tireless in your endeavor. You will check and double check and triple check each step that you complete. You will use whoever else you need to ensure that your task is completed properly. The rest of the support team is at your beck and call. Everyone, including myself, answers to you. We are at your service twenty-four hours a day, seven days a week."

Jack stretched out his hands to the audience. "Those of us who remain behind carry the crew to their destiny. Clasp your hands tight, let nothing slip through your fingers. Their destiny is your destiny. When they come back safe, they will owe their lives to you. You will be able to proudly say, "I took them to Venus and brought them home."

"Finally, I am going to make a pledge. A promise.... A sacred promise to you." Here he paused, took a deep breath, recognized the importance of what he was about to say, recognized the responsibility.... And accepted it.

"I, Jack Anderson, promise to do everything in my power to ensure this mission's ultimate success...If I have but one single ounce of life...a single breath left in me, I will give it freely to this mission...."

Jack smiled as he said, "Now Ladies and Gentlemen, in return I have a request of you. Please stand and repeat this pledge with me. Pledge your lives to this task. Promise to never give up, to never quit until it is successfully completed."

James, sitting near the back of the audience was stunned, overwhelmed. He had expected to hear some dreary management, organizational speech. Not something like this. He felt reborn. The cause...his cause... mankind's cause, reaffirmed. He no longer felt afraid. He was proud to be a part of this noble endeavor. He would never give up.

Scott Benbow was there as well. He understood this speech. He understood it to a depth that, he was sure, no one else could comprehend. He had lived it. The dedication, the determination, the will, the honor...

the pledge...he lived it every day. It was his pledge to himself. Now he was going to pledge to a higher cause. Suddenly it became clear to him, *this is evolution...my evolution, the next natural step in my growth as a human being. It feels...it feels...Wonderful!!*

After the pledge, after the spontaneous yell that ripped through the entire room, Jack continued on with a review of the current mission's status. James knew this part well. It had been six months since his "incident" at JPL. He had passed all the testing and was now a member of the preliminary mission planning team.

They had been very lucky. The Mars project, started during the George W. Bush era, many years ago, had been delayed numerous times. Jack had called it the "binary project": "on" one moment, "off" the next. However, each time it was "on" some progress had been made. The Earth orbiting space station had been completed. The moon station was very close to completion. Most of the Mars orbiter ship design had been done. Thanks to all these delays, the Venus mission would be able to use most of the Mars development—they would take up where the Mars mission had left off. Thus the Venus mission was able to considerably shorten the preparation time. Many, many years had been shaved off the project.

The final work had already started on the moon station. There wasn't much to do. It was essentially complete. For the last two years it had been running on backup power. All that remained was final testing and the delivery of supplies and tools.

The Venus space ship would consist of two sections. The first section, the Orbiter, would move the team from the Moon to Venus and back. They could use the old Mars design—only the engines needed to be changed as there was now a more efficient propulsion system that required less fuel.

The second section, the Lander, would shuttle the team down to Venus and back to the Orbiter. The Venus atmosphere was nothing like Mars. It was a harsh, deadly environment that would not allow the use of the Mars prototype. The temperature was almost nine hundred degrees Fahrenheit and the pressure at the surface was equivalent to ninety-one Earth atmospheres. Consequently, the Venus project required a completely new Lander. There was a big question mark stamped on the Lander plans. A design like this had never been attempted. Until very recently, to withstand the Venus surface pressure, the Lander would have been built like a diving bell. Diving bells were heavy, too heavy to allow the Lander to lift off a planet with almost the same gravity as Earth; however, a new composite material that was lightweight yet extremely strong had given the Venus Lander new life.

But to meet the launch date, they had only eighteen months to complete the design, build and test the prototype, and then manufacture the Lander. James remembered Jack saying, “It can be done. We’re sure it can be done.” His voice had been confident but his body language had said otherwise—Jack wasn’t sure it could be done.

The Venus ship would be manufactured in several stages to minimize the time, effort and cost. First, all the individual parts for the ship would be built on Earth. Then they would be transported to the Earth Orbiting Space Station. This would require many, many space shuttle trips. Once at the space station, the parts, equipment and supplies would be held in a special “space warehouse” until there was enough material to fill the Moon shuttle. The Moon shuttle was a much larger, medium distance ship, intended to carry large volumes of equipment to the moon. Finally, the individual pieces would be assembled on the Moon.

Everything was prefabricated and tested on Earth, then disassembled in preparation for shipment. Each piece was carefully designed to meet the weight constraints required for transport and assembly on the moon. They also must fit into the Earth orbit shuttles. It was a very, very complicated business.

Jack had just finished the review. He stepped off the stage and was immediately surrounded by a gaggle of fervent team members, all of whom wanted to have their opinions heard. He didn't have time for it and with his patented "Uncle Jack" smile, he politely excused himself. As he stepped through the crowd, he caught sight of Scott. He raised his hand, got Scott's attention and motioned him over. Jack swung his head in the direction where he had last seen.... Yes, there he was. He called out "James! James!"

"James, I'd like you to meet Scott Benbow. Scott was the team lead of the group that found the Venus transmission."

A huge smile leapt to his face as James vigorously shook Scott's hand. "If it wasn't for you, we wouldn't be here today. Many thanks and congratulations."

Jack said, "As you can surmise, like yourself, Scott has also been named to the Venus Mission team. You two are the only SETI personnel in the Venus Astronaut program."

"I expect that we will be seeing each other quite a bit," Scott said.

"More than you think," Jack interjected, "I'd like you and James to work together on a bit of a special project."

"Oh really?"

"Yes, we need two members of the mission team to work closely with the Venus suit designers. As you know these suits are going to be very special. They have to handle the extreme atmospherics of Venus. There has been considerable work done with high-pressure underwater suits intended for deep sea diving and with a surface pressure of ninety-one atmospheres, which is equivalent to the pressure found thirty-two hundred feet below the surface of the ocean, we need that same attribute for Venus. Of course, in addition, we need suits capable of withstanding temperatures approaching nine-hundred degrees Fahrenheit. They must also be able to survive a very corrosive and caustic environment. A very big challenge. However, given the vast improvements in material science and engineering, it's one I feel the designers are up to."

"When do we start?" asked Scott.

"Immediately—there is no time to lose. I picked you two because I know you can handle the extra work-load. You have a meeting this afternoon at one p.m. with the design team. I'll email you the details."

As Jack hustled away, James turned to Scott, "I've heard a little about the proposed design of these space...err...Venus suits. They are more like body armor, reminiscent of the armor that the medieval Knights used to wear—supposed to be lightweight with interlocking solid, double walled pieces and some kind of super insulation in between. I'm wondering about the "lightweight" part—with the rigors of the Venus atmosphere, I can't imagine that they really are. Anyhow, it should be very interesting."

"Yes it should be," Scott was less enthusiastic. Always cautious, he wondered if there was another motive for the assignment.

It was just about lunchtime. Scott suggested that they go grab a bite to eat.

As they walked the hallway, they talked about their backgrounds. James's sincerity and enthusiasm was very apparent. Scott began to realize that there was a massive intellect behind that very average demeanor. He had a good feeling about this guy. There was something about him. Something sensed—not proven...not yet...something about both of them. A common bond. He suspected that it was a bond that went deep. It was very, very rare that he had this thought, *I believe this is someone I can trust.* A couple of days later, he bumped into a SETI friend of his and mentioned that he had met James. His friend said, "Oh! The Extraordinary-Ordinary man."

"What??" Scott replied.

"The Extraordinary-Ordinary man. That's what everybody calls him. Of course he doesn't know that. I don't know who coined the phrase but it sure fits him."

Scott couldn't have agreed more.

The next few weeks were a bit of a shock for Scott. He felt like he had jumped off a bridge into some very cold, very fast moving water. Even for Scott, a hard worker by any measurement, the load was extreme. It was taking some getting used to. Not that he couldn't handle it. He just had to be even more careful with his time. He had to be deadly efficient and very well organized. *There's so much to learn.* The final duty selections were being made now. It was a tough time and he was worried. Scott wondered why Jack had assigned the two of them to the Venus suit design. Did Jack already know? Perhaps they weren't going on the Venus mission. That would give them extra time to assist with the prototype testing. *God! He had come so far!* To miss the final step, to slip at the very last moment would be so hard to take. He had resolved to do his absolute best no matter what task he was given but like everyone else on the mission team, he wanted the grand prize. He wanted the ultimate glory. He thought of the poor athlete who, within sight of the winner's tape, falters, too weak to make those last painful steps to glory, then watches the champion pass him by. How painful that would be. Far more painful than any physical injury. It didn't matter how dangerous the voyage would be. He had found these beings from another planet. He was in the right place at the right time. Destiny was with him. He couldn't falter now.

Chapter 11

THE SUIT

Six months later, Scott and James were standing in one of the many prototype labs at NASA staring at the new Venus suit. A lot had happened during those six months. Both Scott and James were feeling very smug. They had been assigned to the Venus mission team. Every Astronaut on the team would participate in all three phases of the Spacecraft manufacture. Scott and James would fly Earth to Space Station shuttles and move equipment to the space station. They would pilot the moon shuttle, help unload cargo on the moon and of course help build the ship. It was good training, especially for the Venus mission team and their backups. Just like the hard working, solitary farmer, once in space they would have to be a jack-of-all-trades. He remembered the old saying, *You can fix just about anything with some bale wire and electricians tape.* He really hoped that maxim was true.

The project was going very well. It was slightly ahead of schedule. It seemed as if the resources of the entire planet were focused on Venus.

And there it was, the Venus suit, the fruit of many thousands of man-hours—designed, redesigned, tested, redesigned, retested....

It was a disappointment.

The suit was enormous—not tall, but wide. It looked like metallic sumo wrestler. The boots added about four inches to its height, so that wasn't too bad but the legs, arms, body and head were, to put it politely, "super-sized." The first thought that rushed through Scott's mind was, *it's gigantic.* The design engineers and developers were proudly showing off their creation to upper management. Scott leaned over to James and whispered in his ear with a perfectly straight face,

"I thought we were going to Venus—not duke it out with Godzilla."

James struggled to keep from laughing out loud. A grin was attempting to twitch itself onto his face. He quickly countered, "I hope they told the Lander designers—they are going to need a larger door."

Even Scott couldn't completely hold back a laugh. It slipped out as a combination burp, barf and chuckle. He quickly covered himself by bending over and coughing. James obligingly gave him a hard smack on the back. *Actually a little too hard,* Scott thought. He glared back at James. James's grin was fully established now. As James turned back to the demonstration, he discovered Jack glaring at him—James's grin disappeared. Now it was Scott's turn to smile, he thought, *Funny how fear could take a grin off twice as fast as it went on.* The suit was so big and heavy that all of the joints required motor-drives to assist the Astronaut. That meant a larger fuel cell had to be attached to the back. Venus's gravity was almost as much as Earth's. Scott thought, *this thing is going to be incredibly heavy.*

He glanced back at Jack. Jack was definitely looking unhappy. He was thinking the same as James and Scott—it wasn't going to be practical. There's that old saying, "*what looks good on paper may not work in practice.*" They could certainly put a picture of the Venus suit next to that one. Scott decided to chance one more comment to James. In his best southern drawl he whispered, "Ah doooo balieve it's back to the draawin board."

Three months later, they were back in the same lab. The Venus suit was looking much fitter. It had been put on some kind of weight loss program. The senior engineer, Dave Bollard, was going over the suit specifics with James and Scott. Some pretty serious trade-offs had been made. The armor itself, made of a complex combination of titanium, fiber and carbon was designed to be very lightweight, yet extremely heat resistant and very, very strong. It had been slimmed down considerably so the puncture risk had gone up. Dave was very positive about the pressure resistance though, "There is no question that we can survive ninety-one atmospheres—there's no chance of a crush."

James, already feeling a little concerned, was not impressed by the use of the term "crush."

Dave continued, "Should the outer shell be penetrated, in the Venus atmosphere, you have thirty minutes before you start to boil in your suit."

Boil? Boil!!

Scott asked, "Why is that? We still have the second skin, same thickness. Isn't that what it's for?"

"Well, no, the second skin reduces the chances of a compete rupture."

"What happens if there is a complete rupture?" Scott queried.

"Ever seen a lobster dropped in boiling water?"

"I get your point."

"Thought you would. As you know, the suit is made up of three layers: the outer skin, a layer of insulation, and the inner skin. So to answer your question a little further, if the outer shell is breached, the insulation is also breached. The insulation can't stop the flow of hot gases by itself. It will slow them, that's why you have thirty minutes. Once that heat reaches the inner skin, it will be transmitted through the inner skin to your body in about three minutes. Those shells or skins are extremely strong and will not break down under stress or heat but they will transmit heat. That's the purpose of the insulation. To work properly, the three layers must be unbroken. Ever heard the word "synergy"?"

"Yeah, that's where the sum is greater than the parts," replied Scott.

"That's exactly what's happening here. On their own, each layer is completely useless on Venus. Together they are satisfactory."

"Satisfactory? That doesn't sound very comforting," said James.

"That's intentional. I don't ever want you to feel comfortable in this suit. I don't ever want you to be complacent. You get complacent and you will make a mistake. Make a mistake in this suit and you're likely to die."

"Well that's pretty clear." A glum James looked over at Scott and then back to Dave.

"Now let me tell you about the other limitations," said Dave.

"There's more?" the pitch of James's voice climbed a bit.

"I'm afraid so. We couldn't lower the weight of the suit as much as we wanted. If I put you in this suit right now, you wouldn't be able to move it. So we have added lightweight, very efficient motor-drives to the ankle, knee and hip joints. They are pressure actuated. In other words, as you move your leg, a microprocessor will sense the pressure and determine how much motor-drive force is required. Increase your leg pressure and the motor-drive will provide more torque. Electricity is supplied by the ultra-light fuel cell on your back. You can actually move rather quickly in these. At full force, you can travel about ten miles per hour. Of course you will rapidly drain your fuel cell if you do this continuously."

"How long could I go at full speed?" asked Scott.

"Thirty minutes."

"And after that?"

"You ain't going nowhere. You will have drained your fuel cell. Without the fuel cell your cooling system will fail. If there is no one else to help you, your suit will slowly heat up and in about an hour, you're back to the lobster scenario...remember what I said about complacency?"

"How long could I go at a normal clip?" Scott asked.

"If you call a normal clip one to two miles per hour, then eight hours. You have a heads-up readout on your helmet mask. Among other things it gives you the fuel status," Dave took a quick break to allow them to absorb these details. He continued, "There's still more. Actually I'm surprised you haven't asked me this. It's the joints—where the arm meets the elbow, hand meets wrist, etc. Obviously, that's not a continuous surface. The surfaces that meet at each joint overlap such that there is never an occasion when there is a break in the Armor. However, because these sections must move independently, there is an opportunity for hot gases to seep under the overlap. We have sealed these with a flexible, somewhat rubbery substance. They are capable of withstanding the Venus temperature and pressure. We call them the vapor rings. They will seal and keep out any gases for eight hours, the same length of time as your fuel cell will run. After that, the seal will start to degenerate or break down. You have maybe twenty minutes once that starts to happen. This is a cumulative problem. So after every Venus trip, you will have to replace those seals. Part of your job here, now, is to work with us to develop a training plan. Everyone on the Venus mission has to know how to replace these and they have to know it very well. A mistake and... well, you know the story. I'd suggest that you follow the old parachute rule—pack your own chute."

"Done!" said James emphatically.

"There's one more layer in the suit that we haven't talked about."

"What? Another one?"

"Yep, it's your internal environmental control. It's a suit that fits next to your skin. It provides some moderate temperature control and collects excess water—if you know what I mean. It also has the capability to hold a "number two." I don't recommend that you try it though. It wasn't designed for comfort—not like Huggies diapers. Don't sweat, piss or "number two" too much. There's a limit to how much this suit can take. There are two tubes that you can suck into your mouth, one for water, one for a glucose solution. Again, just to be clear, if you have a full breach, this suit isn't going to do a damn thing for you, besides melt to your skin.

Okay, now that I've scared the poop out of you, let me give you the pep talk. An enormous amount of time has gone into this design. It's been tested over and over again. I'm very confident that it will work "as advertised." Your job is to verify that supposition. I fully expect that we will be doing some fine-tuning and that's it. Nothing more than that.

Finally, once in the suit, you have an enormous amount of information and warnings at your disposal. The really important ones have an audible warning as well as a heads-up display. For example, inside your suit you have several hundred temperature sensors. Any sudden increases in temp anywhere in the suit and you will have an alarm. That alarm will also be transmitted to the Lander, forwarded onto the Orbiter and subsequently sent to Mission control on Earth—so will any other critical alarms.

You need a second person to help you into your suit. There are many lock-down points. Should any of them get missed, you will have an audible alarm as well as a notification in the heads-up display. You have indicators and alarms for fuel and oxygen. Your suit tracks the accumulated time on the vapor rings and gives you an alarm when there are only two hours left. It gives you another alarm when one hour is left. After that it will drive you nuts...don't let it get to that point." He paused for emphasis. Then, "I'm done for now. Suffice it to say that we have thought of, and done, everything humanly possible to ensure that you survive your walk on Venus. You have a very detailed DVD pack documenting all the features and limitations of the suit. Read it today and tonight. Tomorrow we start in earnest."

The next few days flew by. James had a good laugh when Scott, a very big person by astronaut standards, had trouble getting into his suit. You couldn't "pull" these suits on. They were rigid, heavy, armor. They came in three pieces—the waist, legs and feet, the torso (including the arms) and the headgear. To get into the leg portion, you had to climb a ladder-like device, and lower yourself into the contraption. As Scott went through the procedure for the first time, the unit came loose—just as Scott was getting his legs lined up. He had one leg in and one out when it started to twist. James watched with amusement as Scott, supported only by his arms, tried to get the second leg in. With a look of intense concentration, Scott performed a strange kind of dance routine with his suit—his body twisting as he followed that recalcitrant leg hole.

At the last moment, when James thought that Scott had no chance of success, and with amazing grace for a big man, he lined himself up and dropped into the suit. James was just about to applaud when he realized that Scott, in his desperation to get into the suit, had ever so slightly lost his balance. For a brief moment, he did a remarkable imitation of the leaning tower of Pisa—frozen in time at an impossible angle. Then, with amazing grace for a big man, he toppled over.

On the fifth day, Dave gathered the two together and said, "Okay, you're finally proficient with the basics of the suit—getting in and out, performing simple movements." Dave stopped and looked at them both to ensure they were listening closely.

"Now here's where you earn that big salary of yours," he said.

"We need to do some final stress testing. That means we need to test the suit at the pressure and temperature of Venus. We are going to do this in three stages. First we are going to verify the suits pressure capability. The easiest way to do this is to drop you into the sea. We have found an area where the sea bed is three thousand, two hundred and seventy-three feet below the surface. That's the depth we need to achieve ninety-one atmospheres of pressure. So, for a short time, you are going to become deep-sea divers. Don't worry; we aren't going to let you drop like a rock. We will take you down slowly. You will be stopping at intervals to verify the integrity of the suit. Once on the bottom we want you to do some tests. You will pick up some objects, move to a bin, and drop them in. Your movement won't be indicative of motion on Venus—you will be moving in a liquid here, not a gas. So this is not intended for you to practice moving, it's to check to see that we don't get any leaks when you are in motion."

"What happens if something goes wrong? Say we do get a leak?" Scott queried.

"I was just getting to that. First off, you are going to be tethered to a submersible at all times. Second, it will be no more than fifteen feet above you. Any problems and the submersible team will reel in your tether and get you to safety. Any other questions?"

"No." replied Scott and James in perfect unison.

"Okay, now the second phase.... Oh, I almost forgot. You will be setting a record. No diver has ever gone this deep before."

"Wow. There's a lot of side benefits to this job!" exclaimed James.

Scott looked at him and shook his head in mock disgust.

"Back to the second phase. We have a nice, large oven waiting for you. We will crank up the temperature. Again in increments—testing as we go. Once at nine hundred degrees Fahrenheit, you will perform similar movement related tasks. Any questions?"

Nothing, dead silence.

"Okay, good. Finally, phase three—the big test. We can use that same oven, it has been very specially designed—enormously thick walls—we will turn up the heat and the pressure to Venus levels. The same tests will be performed. Any questions?"

Nothing, dead silence.

"Guys.... I know what you're thinking...first prototype...there's always some problem. You can stop worrying. As I said before, this suit has been tested nine ways to Sunday. The suits you are going to wear have been in the bake-pressure chamber many times. We have mechanically moved them during these tests. We know they are safe. What we are looking for now is some minor issues—mostly with the vapor rings—for example, do they show any signs of exceptional wear after eight hours of moving around?"

"We're going to be in these things for eight hours?? You didn't say that!" James voice was an octave higher than normal.

"Like I said...this is where you earn your salary."

It was a beautiful day off the coast of southern California.

Dave exclaimed, "Calm seas, perfect weather for the test, boys."

Dave, James and Scott were standing on the deck of a moderate sized, specially modified freighter. Just off to the right of them, the submersible was being lowered to the water. There was calm, practiced activity everywhere. James and Scott were looking and feeling a bit grim. Both of them were completely focused on the task ahead. While James was running through the final prep checklist, Scott was mentally reviewing the emergency procedures. They had been through a lot during their training at NASA. They were both confident of their abilities. Still this was the biggest test of their short Astronaut careers. They were about to do what no one else had ever done. Although Dave and his team practically glowed with confidence and pride, James and Scott did not feel complacent. Dave had done his job well.

"Okay, as we discussed, once the submersible is lowered to the water, you will get into the suits, the attendants will attach the tethers, you will do your final checks and wait for the signal to enter the water. These suits have enough weight to offset buoyancy, so you don't need any additional weight to help you sink. As a matter of fact, if you weren't tethered, you'd hit bottom in a hurry." Dave was now serious. His earlier jocularity was gone. It was all business now.

To help smooth out his nerves, James said, "I'll race you to the bottom, Scott."

"Okay, tell you what, I'll give you a head start. Try not to make too big of a dent in the ocean floor."

"The submersible is down, time to get into the suits," Dave called out.

Twenty minutes later, after going through all the checks, they were ready. Scott could feel the tension building. *Butterfly time.* He knew James was feeling the same.

On his helmet headset, James heard Dave say, "Gentlemen, enter the water."

The radio system was specially modified for the underwater test. The signal traveled from the freighter via a cable to the submersible and then to the tethers attached to each Astronaut. It was a four way system. Scott and James could talk to themselves, the submersible or the surface ship.

James felt his heart rate climb. *This is it.* He watched the water approach as he was lowered by his tether. He looked over at Scott, descending at the same rate as he. James fired off a quick "thumbs up."

His "hands" were actually mechanical attachments to the suit. His real hands were protected inside the arm. He controlled the mechanical fingers via a series of sensors attached to his own fingers. He had been quite surprised the first time he operated his "fingers." They were dexterous. After a bit of practice, he could pick up a dime off a table.

James looked down; his feet were now in the water. He checked his heads-up display. *Water temperature sixty-three degrees.* He saw the most important indicator and felt a slight qualm, *Pressure one atmosphere.* The water was slowly rising. At his knees...now his waist...chest.... When it reached his mask, hard as he tried not to, he could feel fear rise with the water. *Anything goes wrong and this suit is a tomb*—the thought wriggled out of his subconscious, a slimy, insidious snake, intending to do harm. He wasn't claustrophobic...but now...*Chest...is...tight....* His breathing was accelerating—becoming fast, shallow, desperate sips of air. The urge to get out of the suit was welling, surging through him. It wasn't a thought, it wasn't a feeling. His whole conscious being was engulfed, swallowed by primordial horror. From somewhere deep within, a thought—a mental scream—squeezed its way through, sending horrendous shivers into his body, *I'm...panicking!* Then a psychic bomb exploded in his mind. He was gone. Gone. No longer human, just a bit of cosmic goo, a blob of screaming fear. His arms and legs mindlessly going everywhere at once. He started clawing at the fasteners; he was trying to get out of the suit but it wasn't possible when the suit was under pressure. He fought the panic, tried to stay in control, tried to regulate his breathing but it wasn't working. By now he was fifteen feet below the surface. It seemed to him that he could feel the pressure of the water on his suit, straining to get in. Sweat was pouring off him. Panic hit him again and he violently reached for the tether above him in an effort to pull himself up out of the water. He missed it and thrashed around, twisting and turning in an attempt to get at the tether. He was sinking faster now; soon he wouldn't be able to pull himself up. He thrust his head upward, looking for the surface and impossibly, started trying to swim, legs and arms moving at a frantic pace.

"James. James?" It was Dave.

"James. Your heart rate is too high. You alright there?"

That simple, wonderful, little human noise brought him back. Saved him. Saved his career. He fought the panic, tried to focus on his breathing.

"James! Please Reply!"

He took a couple of long breaths, composed himself and put every ounce of calm he could into his voice, "Yeah, yeah, I'm fine, thanks."

"Good. Yup, your heart rate is coming down, you had me a little worried there."

"Just a bit of last minute nerves. I'm fine now, real fine." The shakes were gone, breathing normal. His confidence was climbing, building.

James was at least thirty feet under the surface now. He was soaked in sweat but at least he was in control. To stay sane, he needed to be completely focused on his tasks. He couldn't have another panic attack or he was done. Dave would surely haul him back to the surface.

"Time for your first report gentlemen," said Dave.

He heard Scott's voice, calm as ever, "Everything normal. No problems."

It was James's turn, "Same here. All readings are normal."

Scott gazed about him as they descended. There was not much to see. It was murky. Visibility only about two hundred feet. He had been staring off into the distance when he caught a movement out of the corner of his eye. It was in James's direction. He looked over just as he heard Dave call out. James's arms and legs were jerking about. He immediately knew what was happening. He waited, watched...prayed. James's entire career was thrashing, spasming in front of Scott. He liked James, liked him a lot. If James could get himself under control, he would say nothing. He knew that he was taking a chance. Should James panic in some other situation, it could cost both their lives. But Scott had a feeling about him. It was a feeling that he had since they met. It was a weird, subliminal sensation, not something he had ever felt before, a feeling that James was needed. No...no, it was more than that.... Required...yes required. He was required. That he somehow played an important role in this adventure.

Dave called out again. There was a pause, a long pause. Finally James answered. Simultaneously the spastic movements stopped. He was back in control.

He understood what James had gone through. Scott had felt something similar himself. Dangling below the submersible in the dim, dappled light produced a very strange sensation which increased as total darkness descended. *I feel completely weightless. This is truly like being in space. This is space without stars, sun, earth, moon...without anything....*

Suddenly, without warning, the submersible lights flashed on, seemingly brighter than day.

"Hey, how about a little warning next time you want to blind us?" Scott shouted.

The submersible pilot, Cameron Schilling replied apologetically, "Sorry, I should have switched them on a lot sooner. Wasn't paying attention."

Damn. Things aren't starting out very well, Scott thought.

Other than to provide some comfort in the almost total darkness, they were well below a thousand feet now, the illumination didn't provide any useful purpose. There wasn't anything to see—a periodic fish drifting through the murky waters, that was it. But it was good to have the lights on.

"Readings are normal," he called out.

"Same here," James echoed.

"I know it's a little late asking this Dave but what's the upper end pressure tolerance on these babies?" Scott asked.

"It's slightly over one-hundred atmospheres."

"Hell! That's only about ten percent tolerance."

"Yeah, that's what happens when you have to carry these things to Venus. Everyone gets bent out of shape about the size and weight. Seems to me, someone gave me a hard time about the first prototype—said it looked like the Pillsbury dough boy. After that comment you're lucky you got ten percent."

"Okay, okay, you're right. I'll shut up. That's the problem with you engineers, you're too sensitive. You'd think you gave birth to the thing."

"Talk to my wife. She says I've spent more time on this than with our first born."

"How old is your first born?"

"Nineteen."

"Oh man. You are in big trouble."

Scott checked the pressure reading again. *Eighty atmospheres. We're getting close.*

He heard someone clear their throat. It was Cameron. "Okay boys, we're near the bottom. I'm going to slow the descent. Stay alert."

"Roger," replied James and Scott in unison.

James was feeling pretty good. The remainder of the descent had gone well—there had been no further sensations of panic. He was comfortable, confident and, most importantly, in complete and total control of his thoughts and emotions. After that terrible, horrible, experience, James now realized that it wasn't the fear of death that was the worst part of the ordeal—it was the clear and certain knowledge that he was losing control of his mind, that his sanity, his capability for rational thought was being destroyed...by himself. He never, ever, wanted to feel like that again.

It was time to review the mobility tasks that they were to perform. James selected them on the heads-up display. He could scroll through menus with a rotary dial near the thumb of his right hand and a button near his first index finger allowed him to select different items. They were going to be down here for seven hours. They had larger oxygen packs installed for this test – these special packs would provide ten hours of air. Surprisingly, they weren't as big as he expected; there had been a number of improvements that allowed the size of the units to be reduced, including a clever way to recycle unused oxygen. Human lungs aren't completely efficient; some oxygen is exhaled with each breath. There was a filter on the pack that captured ninety-nine-point-nine percent of the exhaled oxygen and reintroduced it to the air supply. James felt very comfortable. Even with the descent and ascent, they had plenty of spare air.

"There's the bottom boys." It was Cameron again. "I'm going to hover around fifteen feet above you. Your tethers will be extended so that you can move about. Remember, watch you don't catch them on anything."

James felt a slight bump as his feet hit the bottom. He looked down. A puff of disturbed sediment rose up around his feet. *Who knows how long that soil has been here, quiet, untouched. Hundreds, maybe thousands of years.* As James surveyed the area, Cameron flipped on the full battery of lights. They were standing in a hazy circle of light, about one-hundred feet in radius. It was desolate. Just a few rocks and muck. Some sea life still existed at this depth; he saw a fish swim idly by and thought, *Probably blind, no need for eyes here.* The area had been carefully chosen—exactly the right depth to give ninety-one atmospheres of pressure—reasonably flat but with enough terrain changes to give the suit a good workout when they walked. NASA had dropped a number of objects of different size and weight in the region, some regular shapes—square, rectangular, spherical—and some irregular. None of the items were heavy enough to overtax either the astronauts or the servo motors in the legs of the suit. Several baskets were strewn about. They would put the various objects into the baskets and when they were done, they would take them out and put them back where they were found. They would keep repeating this procedure until the time was up. An unexpected thought popped into James's mind, *Who would have predicted that Astronaut'ing could be so boring?* He immediately recognized the irony, a short while ago he was a screaming nut case and now he was bored.

James started to work. Special techniques were required to do virtually anything in the Venus suits. Many movements were restricted because the armor of the suit had to overlap. The bending angles were reduced at the wrists, elbows, knees and ankles—so you couldn't lean over and touch your toes. Picking anything small off the bottom of the sea floor would have been impossible had Dave and his gang not thought up the magic extending hand trick. Each mechanical hand could be extended from the arm by eighteen inches. By carefully bending at the waist, hips and knees and extending the hand, James could pick up an object the size of a dime right by his feet. At the insertion point between the hand and the arm was another vapor ring that had to be replaced after every trip.

They had been working for some time when Scott looked at the clock on his heads-up display, *two hours left—Good. Can't wait to get back to the surface. The cold beers are going to be on me.*

Cameron and his copilot, Dwight Moss, were jabbering about the upcoming Lakers game when an audible alarm fired off. Dwight's head snapped toward the sound. He cursed, "Christ! Scared the shit out of me, man!"

Cameron, who was concentrating on piloting the submersible in a current that was starting to increase in strength, without turning his head said, "What is it?"

"Just a sec, let me turn this audible off, it's driving me nuts." Dwight reached over, flicked a switch and looked at the alarm indicator, "Okay, oh yeah, I forgot about this bloody thing."

"What?"

"You know how we were having trouble with the oxygen meter yesterday?"

"Yeah."

"Well, I thought I fixed it but this morning it started acting up again. It keeps showing a low oxygen level even though the tanks are full. Didn't have time to repair it. I should have disabled the alarm."

"You sure it's broke?"

"Yeah. Do you think I'm a complete dufus? I checked the tanks this morning; there's enough air in this sucker to run for fifteen hours at this depth."

"Okay."

"Anyway, like I was saying before I was so rudely interrupted, I think they give Jakeem way too much leeway when he's shoving some poor shmuck right out from under the hoop."

"BS! Everybody does it. He's just bigger...."

Scott dropped another block into the basket. He was feeling good, they only had one more hour to go. Suddenly, out of the corner of his eye, he saw the submersible, which had been hanging oppressively close above them for six hours now, start to drift to his right.

"Hey Cameron, did you decide to take a bathroom break?"

No answer.

"Cameron? Hey! Wake up in there!"

No answer.

The submersible, caught in an increasing current, picked up speed, continuing its course off to the right of Scott. Scott looked down, saw the slack of the tether line.... *No! No slack*! He was pulled off his feet. Simultaneously, he heard James shout something to someone, another voice, probably Dave's, was shouting unintelligible commands. Scott didn't care.

He was fighting for his life.

The tether line, as it was being sucked up by the submersible had tucked under a large rock. Instead of going upward with the submersible, Scott was dragged downward into the sea floor muck, head and back first. He was wallowing, sliding, bouncing along with a great trail of sea gunk billowing up from the floor behind him. He couldn't see but knew he was about to go head first into the boulder. He'd be jammed against the boulder with the whole weight of the submersible pulling on him. *How strong is the tether? He couldn't remember.... The emergency release!* The tether was attached at the back of his shoulders. It was held there by a harness that connected on his front at waist level. There was an emergency release located at that point. He grabbed it and twisted. Nothing! Again! Nothing! There was too much pressure on the tether. He tried to roll onto his stomach to get his hand on the tether. He couldn't; his backpack, with the oxygen tank and the fuel cell attached, was digging a groove in the sea goo. He was stuck face up. With a great heave, he reached as far as he could behind him, grabbed at the tether line. *Missed!*

Again!

Missed!

Again!

Missed!

He just kept swinging his body and arm toward the tether, clutching, squeezing the mechanical hand uselessly over and over again. A horrific thought zinged through his mind, *I'm going to hit the rock! There's no escape!* He tried to look forward by twisting his head as far as possible backward—he got just a glimpse. It was close. He started to brace for the collision. Suddenly he felt a push on his feet. The pressure on the tether momentarily went slack. His other hand was still on the emergency release; he twisted it and felt an immediate reduction in his speed. *I'm disconnected!* The thought was still joyously echoing in his mind when he clobbered the boulder with his head and shoulders.

James had been working steadily—into a rhythm, oblivious to the fact that he was on the ocean bottom in ninety-one atmospheres of pressure. He had a task and some goals. He was doing well. His troubles from earlier in the day forgotten.

Then a vague sensation began to irk him. Something was not right....

Through the top of his visor he saw motion...*the submersible was moving away!* He felt a tug, *the tether!* In an instant he was being dragged off the ocean floor. He yelled out to Scott to warn him but, *too late.* Scott was being dragged all right...but along the ocean bed. He took a second look, saw the problem, recognized what was about to happen. He reached to release his tether. Stopped. *If I let go of the tether, I'll never be able to reach Scott in time.* For a brief, brief moment he was lost. There was no solution. He was being pulled up and away from the sea bed, away from Scott. He could do nothing to help. Then it came to him. The thought and motion were almost simultaneous. He rolled, twisted himself onto his stomach—facing the tether and the submersible. As best he could in the clumsy, awkward, god-damned suit, he put himself into a dive. With arms and head down, he surfed his way towards Scott. If he could reach Scott he could push him and momentarily reduce the pressure on the tether. The tethers were about the same length and connected at the same point on the sub. He should be able to reach him but will it be in time? He was moving in the right direction. A quick mental calculation, *Close, so close!* The boulder was closing in on Scott. James was almost there. He visually checked the distance again and realized that he was not going to make it. Abruptly something from the heavens spoke to him. A flash of brilliance. James threw his arm out as far as it could go; simultaneously he hit the button to extend the hand another eighteen inches. He made contact!

He lost sight of Scott. The push had caused James to roll upwards and as he started to rise he struck the top of the boulder. A shudder ran through the whole suit. Then he was past the rock. The sub was dragging him off to who knows where. He reached for the tether release, twisted it. Enormous relief flowed through him as he felt the suit start to slow. He looked back toward Scott, hoping, praying, that he wasn't going to see a train wreck. At first he couldn't see anything; the water was so murky from his collision with the mud caked boulder. He held his breath. Then...something. Something on the bottom. *There! There he is! He made it!* More sediment drifted in front of him. He lost sight of Scott. James was slowly sinking to the sea bottom about twenty feet from the boulder. He made another quick mental calculation, *I'm close, I'll be there in about a minute.*

That's when he saw it.

His heart sank.

The ring of light, that beacon of safety was moving toward him...sliding past him...and was gone. He stood in almost complete darkness. Horrified, shocked, James turned to see an aquatic sunset, as beautiful as it was terrifying. Weak rays of light were sifting through murky water, fanning out above him, sparkling and twinkling as the ghostly glow enveloped tiny particles suspended in the deep, deep water. The top of a small ridge was softly silhouetted as the submersible drifted past the shelf and down into the depths. The last image he saw, perfectly fitting for this strange, surreal world—a fish, an underwater cowboy—swimming towards the sunset of the deep. Then nothingness. Complete and total blackness. Incredible blackness. What was that term? *Utter Blackness.* Now he truly understood what that meant. It wasn't just a term—it was a feeling, a physical sensation, a sickness...it was the blackness of despair and horror burnt into his soul.

Chapter 12

SHANNON

Bostonians are some of the best jaywalkers in the world. Most people in other cities treat jaywalking simply as a way to cross the street quickly. Sometimes it takes courage, sometimes desperation, sometimes complete, absolute stupidity. But always the method is the same: look for an opening, then run like hell out into the middle of the road. Have another look...if all is well, reduce speed and try to look cool over the last half of the route. Otherwise...to hell with looking cool. Of course, in reality, it's just another way human beings choose to chance death for no particular reason at all.

But in Boston, jaywalking is different. Jaywalking is an art. Jaywalking is a sport. It's a sport and an art. It's the concrete jungle version of Olympic high diving. Beautiful, graceful and dangerous. When an accomplished Bostonian jaywalks, he glides out into the street, into the traffic. He never breaks stride, never acknowledges the danger, never notices the wheels spinning within inches of his body, within inches of his life. He is going for a stroll, eyes forward, head steady. An observer would think he was in a park, walking along the water's edge with not a care in the world. To flinch at the sound of a horn, the squeal of brakes or the gasp of a passerby is to be defeated, is to be shamed. While anyone else at an intersection crosswalk would wait the few seconds for that little striding white man to give permission, the Bostonian seizes the opportunity to once again prove his death defying skill. He steps so casually and so gracefully into the street that many a tourist has followed, a stride or two behind, thinking it was their turn. Some have not lived to see the other side of the road.

Of course, Matt knew this and as he would tell it, was a master of the art. But on this fateful day, as he walked back from another lovely lunch at his favorite restaurant on Newbury Street in the Back Bay area, as luck would have it, he was in the middle of a really good fantasy.

Matt had attended the Boston Bruins game the night before. Sitting in his father's private box, he had been treated to another painful, awful Boston loss. If it wasn't for the fact that the tickets were free, he'd have demanded his money back. So here he was, walking back from lunch to the Hancock tower, starting down Dartmouth Street, thinking *if only I could play hockey, I would have ripped through that whole New York Islander team.*

Just like that, he was there, on the ice, starting a magnificent end-to-end rush.

He screamed up the ice—as he reached his own blue line an Islander forward dove toward him. Matt gave him a head fake, a little shoulder shrug, bounced the puck off the boards and slid around the other side of the outwitted moron. He left him behind, still trying to pick his shorts up off the ice.

He crossed the alley between Newbury and Boylston Street.

He was at the centerline now...another Islander was desperately trying to catch up to him. Unable to match his blazing speed, the bastard dove and swung his stick at his skates, hoping to trip him. So obvious! Matt effortlessly hopped over the stick and picked-up speed.

Halfway to Boylston, he stepped around a lost tourist consulting a map.

He was moving in on the defenseman, New York's last stand before the goalie. Matt could see a look of fear on his face. With a laugh, he moved inward towards the center of the ice, crossing in front of the forlorn player. At the last moment, as the dumb jerk moved to cut Matt off, Matt ever so lightly tapped the puck between the defenseman's stick and skates, then cut sharply back to the outside of the rink. The defenseman slid helplessly by his prey. Out of control, he smacked into his own partner, knocking both of them on their asses. Without breaking stride, Matt cut back again to the center of the ice, picked up the puck and descended on the net. He could hear the crowd gasp with excitement as they sensed the outcome of this incredible end-to-end rush.

It was then that he made his mistake. If it hadn't been that he was just about to come to the glorious end of a glorious fantasy, he would never have been fooled. *Just his luck!* Matt reached the intersection of Boylston and Dartmouth, as he, the great hero, made his last move on the goalie. The man beside him stepped out into the street. Matt, a little slow to react, stepped out two strides behind him.

The goalie is down! He shoots.... He scor....

The sound of a horn and the squeal of tires and brakes stopped the great hockey player in his tracks. He turned to face a truck grill about as high as a skyscraper, sliding, screaming toward him. Matt thrust his adrenalin packed legs backward as hard as they could go. The truck missed him by inches—he could feel the wind of the slipstream tug at his hair as he landed on his feet in the parking lane.

He was starting to congratulate himself on his lightning fast reflexes when he looked up to see a bicycle helmet attached to a pair of the most beautiful eyes he had ever seen flying directly toward his chest. He felt an enormous impact. Matt flew backward; hit his head on the pavement. He saw stars, then felt a strange numbness, followed by horrible pain in his chest. *I can't breathe! I can't breathe!* As he lay there on the pavement, writhing in pain, struggling to get a single sip of air, a face descended toward him. It was those startlingly beautiful eyes, wide open, unblinking.

"Hold on, don't move. Let me look you over...I think you're okay," said the eyes, "You've had the wind knocked out of you. Your air will come back so don't worry, stay calm. You've also hit your head. You'll have a bump for a while."

Matt's reply consisted of more writhing and rolling—along with some wheezy grunts. All he could manage was a thought.... *I wonder if she's single?*

Matt was sitting at a table in one of his favorite restaurants, the same one, as it turned out, that he had been in prior to his *hockey adventure* (as he liked to call it). He was nervous, more nervous than he was willing to admit. He could feel a little moisture in the armpits—always a bad sign. He had arrived early. He couldn't help it. He had spent what seemed like forever thinking about this, this...*Rendezvous.* He couldn't get it, or actually her, out of his mind.

It had been a week since she dove head-first into his chest and...into his heart, like a human cupid's arrow. As he had lain, then sat and finally stood on that street, with the angel next to him, his mind had been racing. Should I ask her out? Would she go out with an idiot that just about got himself killed by a truck? Dare I ask? Dare I? He was standing at a merry-go-round, watching his thoughts fly by, over and over, unable to make a decision.

He was shy, way too shy to ask women out on a date. He just couldn't get the courage to do it. Truth be said, the only relationships he had with women, if you could call them relationships, had been with hookers. And only when he was really, really in need. Strangely enough, what drove him to the ladies of the night wasn't the need for sex as much as it was the need for soft, delicious female companionship. It was their touch, their voice, their thoughts, their compassion that he needed. When he went to a woman, he wanted to be held, he wanted to be cuddled, he wanted someone to tell him he was alright, wanted someone to tell him he was good, wanted someone to laugh at his jokes, wanted someone to listen to his day at work, wanted someone to tussle his hair, wanted someone to caress him—wanted someone to just be there. Most of all, he wanted what he couldn't pay for, no matter how much money he had—he wanted someone to tell him she loved him.

So that day, that fateful day, as he stood there, his mind a whirl of conflicting thoughts, he was cognizant of one predominate feeling, *You have to try. Don't you let her go!*

The small crowd that had gathered, over time, slowly dispersed. The last person said, "Hope you'll be alright," and then was gone. They were by themselves. Just him and *her.*

She said, "I was distracted. There was...well...a nice dress in the window of the store." She pointed to a shop Matt had never noticed before. "I turned my head back and there you were—I tried to avoid...but hit a hole in the road and it sent me over the handlebars of the bike. I'm really, really sorry, Please forgive me."

"Oh! Oh! no! It's not your fault! My fault! My mistake! Wasn't paying the least bit of attention."

"I wasn't paying attention either. If I had, I would have had time to stop."

"No that's not right. It was my fault. If I hadn't stepped off the street when the light was red, you'd still be flying along on your bike to...to where...ever. I'm the one who should apologize."

He said those words with such emphasis, such sincerity, that she laughed out loud and replied, "Okay kind Sir, I accept your apology." As she spoke, she gave a little curtsy as if she was the fair maiden and he was the brave knight. Matt's heart shook at the sight of this wonderful, beautiful woman bowed before him. *I love her! I don't even know her name but I love her!... Ask her name! Ask her out!*

"Well, umm...I think I'm alright now...yeah...well...." Matt was looking off into space. A massive inner struggle was swallowing, consuming him. He was being eaten by himself.

"Oh that's good," was the reply.

"Yeah.... I'm...umm...much better...now.... I suppose." *Ask her out!*

"Good................ .... well........."

"Yeah..." He started nervously inspecting his shoes, then kicked at a hunk of paper lying on the ground. He could feel her eyes on him. Matt's hands were shaking and he was starting to sweat. *Ask her out!*

He couldn't! He couldn't!

"Well, well...I...I...guess I'll see you sometime."

As he turned to go, he felt his whole body shrink, curl up, like a dying old man. He was a gutless, useless, spineless piece of turd. He deserved the life he had. It was his fault. Trapped in a life of loneliness by his own fear. He started walking down the street, unaware of where he was going, wallowing in self-loathing.

"Hey! Wait a minute."

Matt stopped, looked back. She walked up to him, face intent but serene.

"Look...I know you think it's your fault but I still feel guilty. How about I take you to lunch sometime? It's the least I could do. What do you think?"

The heavens opened, sweet music sang to his soul! "Oh, sure. Sure! Yeah...." He hesitated, not sure what to say next.

"Perhaps you could tell me your name."

"Oh. Of course. I'm Matt Dragonovich."

"Well, my name is Shannon Jones."

Now here he was, at his favorite restaurant waiting for Shannon. He had done almost nothing at work the whole week. His old man had been even more of a jerk than usual but it had meant nothing. All he thought of was *Shannon*. He had rehearsed over and over again what he would say. Especially the really important part, the asking for another date part. Just thinking of that got him tense.

He wondered about her accent, he thought it sounded Australian but he wasn't sure, he was terrible with accents.

Just then, *she* came in. A sweet dream had entered the room. *Wow! I can't believe how good looking she is. She's even better than I remember.* All the male heads turned, human flowers following the sun, as she entered the room. Matt looked at her with love-filled eyes. A slim, sleek, five-foot-two, absolutely and without a doubt, perfect body strode towards him. "A body to die for" he had heard a buddy of his say one time. There was no better description than that. She had a body to die for.

Her blond hair suited her face so well that he couldn't imagine it ever changed. And that face! That face! The face of an angel! She was absolutely striking—her face gently rounded, with a narrow straight nose—just long enough to be exceptional, a delicate jaw, culminated by those incredible, unbelievable, green-grey eyes. As she moved toward his table, Matt was filled with pride that she had come to see him.

He had heard the term, "she took his breath away." He had never experienced such a thing. But now, he realized with a start, that he had stopped breathing. When he took his next breath, he drew into his body her scent. A subtle, sweet, glorious smell enveloped his lungs...then poured through him. Every sense in his body climbed to a higher plane as she sat down. He was in an unknown emotional realm, a place he had never been before. Matt could swear that he felt his aura, his life energy, tentatively reach out and touch hers. He could feel that energy, his and hers, gently mingle, then intertwine—intertwine in a soft, slow dance.

"Sorry I'm late."

Matt glanced at his watch, "Actually you're not. You're right on time."

"Oh, wonderful!"

———

Matt suddenly caught himself—he had been sitting there staring at her, silent, trapped in the pool of her eyes, mesmerized. Without thought, he blurted out, "This is a very appropriate place for you."

"Oh? Why?"

"Well...because.... Because, Boston, well actually Massachusetts...is renowned for their...well, their witches."

"Their witches?"

"Yes...you know...Salem...witch hunt." *Oh no! What am I saying??* He carried on, caught by his own words, "When I look at you I feel... feel... bewitched."

Shannon, not sure where this had been going, suspecting that she was about to be insulted, laughed. It was a melodic, bubbly, happy laugh—it was the most wonderful sound Matt had ever heard.

"Thank you," she replied still smiling.

She was used to compliments. She knew the affect that she had on men. Sometimes it was wanted. Most of the time it was not. She had long since given up on the classic, good-looking man. They all had huge egos, spent more time looking in the mirror than she did and had a much higher propensity (or perhaps opportunity was a better word) to "wander." She knew men and she knew that they just had no willpower when it came to sex. Regrettably, the good-looking guys had it handed to them. Most of the time they accepted gleefully, whether single or not. The average looking man was usually more interesting and certainly more appreciative of female attention. Matt was a bit below average on looks but he had what her mother called an "interesting" face. Shannon sensed that under that sad demeanor there was a happy person that wanted out. She was curious...what was he really like? She would not admit or conceivably did not know that the manner of their meeting had awakened her maternal instinct. He needed her help then. Did he still need it? With a little care and tending, could Matt's "happy" embryo be given birth? She hated the word molded, but certainly some men could be encouraged to fulfill their potential. Time would tell about Matt. Truth be known, it was why she was here.

"This seems a very lovely restaurant," she said.

That voice! How wonderful! Soft and sultry, her accent gave just a hint of mystery and a quiet sophistication, "Your accent, are you from Australia?" Matt asked.

"Actually, no. I'm from Auckland, New Zealand," Shannon replied, a little subdued.

Matt, whose every sense was tuned to the maximum and focused precisely at this incredible blond beauty, immediately knew he had said something wrong. "Oh. I'm so sorry. I...I didn't mean...."

"It's okay. We New Zealanders get tired of being mistaken for Australians. People forget we exist. We are a small country but proud all the same."

The meal was terrific. Matt had chosen well. The owner, Salvatore, who knew Matt on a first name basis, came by to chat. Matt was one of his best customers, so Salvatore, as only a restaurateur could, was at his obsequious best—ingratiating and fawning—congratulating Matt on his choice of the Insalada di Pomidori, the wine, his tie, anything he could think of. Also, Salvatore, being Italian and a man of the world, truly understood and believed in "amore." He knew immediately the purpose of this meeting of two souls. He would do his best to help his friend and to give love a chance to grow.

As he walked back to the office Matt was ecstatic. He couldn't be in a better mood. *It had gone so well!* He had asked her out on another date and she had accepted. He couldn't believe his luck. Something wonderful had happened and it wasn't in a daydream. It was real! So real!

He knew more about her now. She was a little younger than he. She was well educated with a bachelor's degree in Biology. She'd been in Boston about a year, working for that environmentalist organization,

Greenpeace. That came as a bit of a surprise. His first thought had been, *The old man, Kurt, isn't going to like that. She works for the archenemy of the oil companies.* His second, smug and perhaps very dangerous thought was, *Good. I'll rub his nose in it.*

He'd just got into the building when his cell phone rang. It was Kurt.

"Hi. Come to the office, I've got some interesting news," he said.

A few minutes later, without knocking, Matt sauntered into the office. Kurt looked up, a brief scowl crossed his countenance; he hated it when Matt didn't knock. But he quickly forgot about it. He couldn't be in a better mood!

"Well, BEI has won the communications bid for the Venus project!" Kurt exclaimed.

"Oh, good," replied a non-committal Matt. BEI, Best Electronics Inc, was another of Kurt's shell companies. In reality he couldn't care less about how BEI did but to keep his old man happy he had to say something positive.

It didn't fool Kurt, his mood dipped, his black brows pursed and he scornfully shook his head, "It's better than good, in fact, a lot better than good, you idiot."

For a moment his sleep deprived eyes bored a hole in Matt—it could have gone very badly, but then...inexplicably...almost miraculously... Kurt's mood brightened and even seemed to climb higher.

"It's fantastic. Incredible.... Superb! Stupendous!" Kurt paused for a moment—his lips quivered as they searched for another superlative adjective. They quickly gave up and he gleefully said, "As a matter of fact, I'm not sure if there is a word to describe how good it is!"

Matt hadn't seen Kurt like this before. Kurt had become obsessed with the Venus Mission—he researched the entire project, engaged technical experts, intercepted emails, bugged offices. He knew as much and sometimes more about the project than the senior people at NASA. Then he started purchasing controlling interest in any company that he thought would have an opportunity to profit from the venture. He was like a contestant who has won ten minutes of free shopping in a store—excitedly grabbing up everything he could, as fast as he could. Now he was reaping the benefits of those incredibly long workdays. He had already won several key contracts—constructing the hulls of both the Orbiter and the Lander, manufacturing some of the engine components and the most profitable one of all, the rocket fuel. A vast amount of rocket fuel was going to be consumed on the mission. Fuel was needed for all the trips from earth to the Space Station, for the round trips from the Space Station to the moon and finally for the Venus mission itself. Now he had this new communication contract as well.

"I don't think you know what this means.... No, I *know* you don't know what this means." Kurt stopped to see if Matt would contradict him. Of course he didn't.

"It means that I now have a front row seat to the entire mission—I'm going to have my boys add a couple of little "extras"—just for my own enjoyment and edification. I'm going to have a backdoor built into the communication system so that I can monitor every conversation and capture all data transmissions coming from either the Lander or the Orbiter. I'll get the transmissions as soon as NASA!"

He paused for just a second, his face convoluted into happy turmoil, then, "No! Wait! I can have better than that! I'll have a delay feature built in. So if I wish I can delay any transmission sent to any of the components in the network. Say from the Lander to the Orbiter or more importantly from the Orbiter to Earth or vice versa. That way I can see the data, review it and if necessary, act on it before anyone knows anything about it!"

He paused again, Kurt's bulldog face grew thoughtful and then lit up with glee, "Hey! Hey! Why not the full meal deal? Why not prevent communication all together if necessary? Yeah! Yeah! That's it! I love it!" Kurt was completely beside himself. He was practically giggling.

An incredulous Matt was starting to think the old man had finally lost it. *Off to the loony bin. I'm in charge now. Yahoo!*

"I don't get it. Why would you waste your time with that junk? I mean, who cares? You'll find out soon enough from the news. Or go to the NASA website, they'll have all that info." Flush with his recent success in love, Matt pushed the envelope a little too much. Show an inch too much neck and Kurt would chop it off.

A huge scowl descended over Kurt's face, "Well...because...moron! Because dumbo! Because idiot! It gives me the opportunity to decide what happens on Venus. Think, if you ARE capable of thinking, what I'll be privy to. This isn't a trip to the park. We are going to be meeting an Alien race! Think of the information that will be gathered there. Maybe this race is far more advanced than we are. Maybe they know how to cure the common cold. Maybe they know how to exceed the speed of light. Maybe they can get that goofy cold fusion to work. Maybe they know how to make gold from lead. All that information will be relayed back to Mission Control through my.... MY communication system! Now here is the most important ***maybe*** of all...maybe I won't want some of that info to get back to Earth, at least not right away, not until I have taken advantage of it! Make sense now, dumbo???"

"Yes," replied a humbled and frightened Matt. He knew he'd gone too far, knew he had to get out of there before things got worse. He turned to leave.

"Oh, Matt."

Matt's head swung reluctantly back towards his dad, followed even more reluctantly by his body, "Y.... Y.... Yes?"

"I know what you were thinking...you were thinking that I had lost it, didn't know what I was talking about...don't bother to answer...I know you wouldn't admit it...DON'T EVER THINK THAT! UNDERSTAND!"

"Yes. Yes. Sorry...I understand...Sor...ry."

Matt almost ran out of the room. He left behind a gleeful, smirking Kurt. He couldn't be in a better mood.

Chapter 13

TRAPPED

James stood on the ocean floor, over half a mile from the surface, in absolute darkness. Somewhere nearby, maybe twenty feet or so, was Scott. Was Scott OK? He didn't know. As James stood there, that feeling of panic, his old friend from earlier in the day, was beginning its funeral march.

He stopped his mind, put it on hold and remained in that state...a calm began to warm his entire body. But it was so dark. The weight of all that cold water above him seemed to be squeezing the suit into his body. Panic pushed itself forward again. He could feel uncontrolled fear swarming through his body. His legs and arms started to shake. His mind felt numb. He struggled to ward it off; he struggled to gain back that feeling of calm. He fought. He fought the greatest battle of his life. Fear and panic surged and ebbed. Back and forth. Back and forth. Endless, vital, life-giving moments were slipping by.

His sanity was almost gone. This time there wouldn't be a wonderful human voice to save him. He was alone. Just him and fear. He started to scream. It was a scream of absolute terror. As it echoed through his suit, his own horrified voice scratched at some tiny, sane place in his mind, which roared back in outrage. In an instant, his scream turned to a yell of anger. Anger at his fear. Anger that he was going to die down here without having done a thing to save himself. Anger that he was going to let Scott down. He had to stop this. *He had to win!* With that thought, his anger surged, became rage and then burst like a bubble—leaving a residue of calm. He stood there in the total darkness, soaked with cold sweat, and let that sweet feeling of calm envelop him. More precious moments slipped by but it didn't matter. He needed this time to gather his strength, gather his confidence, gather his courage. He cleared his mind until only a single thought remained,

I'm okay.

He felt pride, almost happiness. He had done it. Conquered fear.

He stood there, in the dark, calm. As calm as he had ever been. He began to think about their situation, what they had, what they could do,

This unit has a spotlight, not intended for ocean work, not very bright.... How long will it last? It will cause a drain on the fuel cell and I need the fuel cell for the servomotors that help move the suits legs. If I lose that I can't move.

So as not to waste a single electron, he left the light off and turned on his heads-up display. He checked the remaining power on the fuel cell. *Not much, maybe two hours, one hundred and twenty minutes, given normal movement and operating conditions. Let's see if there is anything in the database about the power utilization of the light...should be....*

The Venus suit contained a very large data base, stored in a form of non-volatile memory. Gigabytes of information. Everything about the suit was stored there, *or should be....* The tricky part was finding the info you needed and, in this case, in a big, big hurry.

After a couple of tries he found the info on the spotlight. He also had access to a fully functional, very high powered, computer. He could pull up various types of keyboards that were designed for his limited movement environment and could use the fingers on each hand to perform different functions. James picked the math keyboard, which could do some very complicated math—integration, differentiation even partial differentiation if he wanted (he couldn't think why he would ever need it). In this case it was pretty simple math. He just needed to work out what percentage of power the spotlight would consume—then use that to calculate the time-drain on the fuel cell. After a few seconds he had the answer—he was going to lose ten minutes of fuel cell operation because of the light. It wasn't much compared to the energy loss of the servo motors but if you were still below the surface at one hundred and ten minutes, it was going to matter big time. The best he could do was conserve as much as possible, shut it off at every opportunity.

He switched on the light and turned toward where he hoped Scott was. Almost simultaneously, he saw a light appear in that direction. That was Scott. Very relieved, James started to walk towards the light. Suddenly he thought, *how are we going to communicate?* The tethers were gone. They had relied on the tether to the submersible for their suit-to-suit communications. He walked toward Scott as he struggled with the problem. Scott came up close and it appeared to James that they were going to bump into each other so James took a step back. James could see Scott's face through the visor and saw him shake his head in the universal symbol for "No." Scott reached out with both hands, took James by the shoulders and pulled so that both visors were touching. Then James understood. The visors would transmit sound through the common touch point.

So there they were, over half a mile below the surface, headlamps throwing a small sphere of light into a curtain of absolute darkness, two strange metallic creatures locked in an embrace and kissing. James couldn't help himself, he started laughing, laughing so hard the visor defogger fan started running.

Then he heard Scott. He sounded like he was at the far end of a very long, narrow pipe.

"So, I see we are in a bit of trouble."

"Yeah, you could say that."

"I think I have you to thank for my escape," Scott stated with a warmth in his voice that was lost while traveling through the thick glass. He struggled to sound casual. No one had ever saved his life before.

"Yes, that's true," replied James, "What do you think happened to the submersible?"

"I have no idea but it must be something very serious; they didn't reply to any of our calls," replied Scott.

"Perhaps there was a problem with the communication system."

"I don't think so. We could still hear Dave and to hear Dave the signal had to travel through the submersible. So the communication link to the submersible was working. I think something terrible has happened."

James stated the obvious, "So we're stuck here...on our own."

"Yes."

"What about a rescue from above?"

"How will they get down to us? They don't have another submersible. Nobody ever thought about this contingency. How ironic! Our safety device, the submersible, almost killed us," exclaimed Scott.

"I think we can pretty much forget getting any help from up top, at least not in time. In a couple of days they might be in a position to drag our dead bodies out of the ocean. Alright, don't really want to think about that...."

"What's the plan then?" James asked.

"First, let's go to the ridge where we last saw the submersible. We need to rule out that they are hovering on the other side, with some sort of engine problem," replied Scott.

"Okay, and if they aren't there?"

"One thing at a time. Stay close and watch your footing! A mistake now and that could be it."

They started in the direction of the submersible. It turned out that it wasn't that far to the ridge. Maybe one hundred feet. Scott was in the lead. Suddenly he stopped and raised his hand in warning. James moved carefully up beside him. He looked down. It was a sheer drop. At least for as far as their weak lights would go. Nothing but blackness. No sign of the submersible. Scott stepped back from the brink and motioned to James. They pushed their helmets together. "Well that settles that. Who knows where they are. Now what?" queried Scott.

"Good question." James stopped for a moment. There was something tickling his memory.

"Hey! Hey! Wait a minute. I remember looking at the ocean bottom contours. There is a sharp rise to the west of us. Do we have the contour map loaded in the database?" asked James.

"Should do, we have everything else."

A couple minutes of searching produced results. James had been correct. The test site that NASA had chosen was on a shelf about a quarter mile wide. The ridge to the west rose, almost vertically, to within three hundred feet of the surface.

Scott said, with just a hint of excitement in his voice, "Okay, perhaps we have a chance. If we can find a way to climb this underwater cliff, that is."

"Did you do the power calculation?"

"Yip, about one hundred and ten minutes with the light on, right?"

"Yes, correct. The biggest problem is that the lights are not strong and the visibility is bad. Not a good combination—we can only see about twenty feet in any direction."

"It's going to be very hard to find our way with twenty feet of visibility," said Scott, "Let's assess the situation, we've got about one hundred minutes of continuous leg motion before the fuel cell packs it in. We've got about three hours or one hundred and sixty minutes of air. Those are the critical parameters."

"Yes. That might be enough time to get us up to the top of the ridge. But what do we do when we get there? We are still three hundred feet below the surface."

"A bit of a problem alright. There's only one way we get to the surface. We have to be lighter."

"Right and we want to be as light as possible now, to save energy on the climb. Hold it! What if we could shed enough weight to float to the surface from here?" queried James.

"I thought of that," replied Scott, "There's almost nothing we can unload now that will cause any major change in our weight. We could get rid of the fuel cell and oxygen tanks, then we'd probably rise to the surface but we would be dead when we got there. However, that gives me an idea. How about we climb to the top of the ridge and then unload the fuel cell, blow the remaining compressed air into our suits? It might be enough to get us to the surface and the air in our suits might provide enough breathing time until we are rescued."

"That could work. Let me see if I can calculate if there will be enough positive buoyancy," James said.

"Don't bother."

"Why?"

"Let me ask you this. Can you think of any other way out of our predicament?"

"Uhhh, well.... No."

"Then it doesn't really matter does it? You standing here trying to figure out if we will make it to the surface will just waste time and frankly I'd rather not know. Yah know what I mean?"

"Yes, unfortunately I do."

"Now let's see if we can find our way up. We know where the down-escalator is, take a right angle and we should find the up-escalator."

They started off towards the hoped-for underwater cliff. It wasn't easy. The beam of their headlamps was so short that they could not use a distant visual reference to keep them in a straight line. When they reached an object, little hillock or boulder, one of them would go round the obstruction, line himself up with the light behind and estimate the direction. The person behind would follow and provide a second direction estimate. They prayed that the technique would prevent them from going in a circle, or worse yet following a parallel course to the ridge.

James was timing the trip. He expected that at a two mile per hour rate, they should reach the cliff in about seven minutes. Trouble was he didn't know if they were going two miles per hour. The sea muck was thick and they had to stop periodically to check their bearings. James was guessing that they might be averaging only one mile per hour. He was giving the total trip fifteen minutes. If they went beyond that, they were lost. He didn't want to think about it. He concentrated on walking, checking the fuel cell consumption, the air consumption...anything to keep his mind off the impending disaster.

Scott had done the math as well. But he was thinking a little further ahead. Fifteen minutes was not much time, but given their air supply and fuel cell restrictions, fifteen minutes could be too much. *How much time did that leave them to get to the surface?* The limits of available air and fuel were starting to converge. At first, it seemed reasonable that they would run out of fuel before their air supply failed. Now, because of the time they had spent discussing their plan, because of the delays caused by obstacles, because of even further stops to discuss the route, they were now gobbling up their air at a greater rate than the fuel. He expected that this trend would continue. They would have to stop to check their route and to take rest breaks. He had no illusions about this climb that they had optimistically planned. It was going to be tough. Likely to be the toughest thing he had ever done. But the air...*the air was going to be the problem.* They were going to have to take some chances. Climb without taking many breaks and without taking proper time to evaluate the route.

Something rose up in front of him, a dark shape on the fringe of the light-beam. It was a rock-face. He took one more step, then another, one more; he looked up, then looked to the right, then looked to the left. As far as his wretched light would go, the cliff continued upward and to either side. *This has to be it. This better be it!* He stopped and waited for James to come up beside him. They stuck their visors together.

"The rock is sheer directly in front of us. No way to get up from here. We have to go either left or right—impossible to know which will be the best route. Let's pick a direction and just start walking parallel to the rock face—you can decide James," stated Scott.

"Okay, umm.... Let's go left; I think that the surface support ship was positioned a bit to the north of us which is a left turn when we face the cliff," James replied.

"Done...."

They started walking, their tiny lights insignificant against the dark, grey-black mass looming beside them.

Chapter 14

FAILSAFE

Several weeks after Kurt had told Matt his plans for the Venus mission, just by fluke, it happened once in a while, a parcel was delivered to Matt's desk that should have gone to his dad's. Matt, not paying any attention, opened it. It contained some schematics and attached to them was a hand written note. It simply said *Here it is.* Below that was a meaningless jumble of letters and numbers. But Matt knew what that was.

It was Kurt's secret code. Matt had stumbled across this code a couple of years before when he was looking for something on Kurt's laptop. Of course he wasn't supposed to touch the laptop but he had screwed up and accidentally copied Kurt in an email. In it, Matt had made a not-so-nice comment about his old man. He had been trying to look cool with some of his co-workers. As usual he blew it, did a "reply all" before he checked to see who was on the CC list. Lucky for him, that day, Kurt was out of office at a "meeting" for the afternoon. Matt knew the meeting involved a woman who was trying to work her way up the ladder. Matt guessed that Kurt wouldn't take his laptop. He slid into the office and sure enough, there it was. Matt had cracked his dad's password algorithm ages ago. Kurt used a sequence of twelve passwords—one per month. They hadn't changed since Matt had figured it out several years before.

After a couple of nervous minutes he found the email and deleted it. Matt was a click away from log-out when he noticed a weird application running on the desktop. Curiosity beckoned. Just for the heck of it, he opened the application. It was very strange—just two blank windows—nothing else—no text describing what to do with the windows or any other symbols or buttons of any kind. That was just too tempting for Matt. He had to know its purpose. He checked the time and decided that it would be at least an hour before his dad would be back. Matt dove into the computer and began looking for a read-me or help-file that would describe this application. After about twenty minutes of frantic searching (he really wasn't that confident of the timing of his dad's return—perhaps the "meeting" wouldn't go that well) Matt found a document that described the application in detail. Kurt had built a coder/decoder on his laptop. He could create or decode soft copies of any of his encrypted messages—emails, word docs, whatever. The two blank windows were for coding or decoding messages; one for coding and one for decoding. The document also contained the entire coding algorithm. Matt printed the entire read-me file. After that, as a matter of course, Matt decoded everything he came across. That was how he had been able to learn so much about Kurt's business. *I'm not as stupid as he thinks I am! I'm not!!*

So, on this day, just as a matter of course, he decoded it. It said "*Orbiter failsafe device, log in "failsafe", pwd "doomsday"*". What was this? He looked back at the schematics. None of it made sense to him. He looked back at the message, Failsafe*? No! It couldn't be!* Matt stared at the schematics again. Then back to that simple word, "*failsafe.*" A look of fear touched his face and then hardened into grim determination. He left his office with the schematics and walked as calmly as he could over to the copy machine—made a couple of copies for each page. With hands shaking, he grabbed his copies and started back to his office.

"Matt. Matt?"

Matt felt an electric shock run through his body—his arms and hands jerked spasmodically causing the folder with its copies to flutter open. A page started on its way to the floor. He made a swipe at it and by luck got it by the corner. Quickly, he stuffed it into the folder, then turned slowly and looked back; it was one of the secretaries from the floor.

“Did you leave these?”

“What? Let me see.... Oh! Yes those are my originals....” He looked closely at her face. Her expression was non-committal, “Thanks,” he said.

He walked back to his office. Thoughts were coming so fast that they were stacking up on top of each other. He had to get the package to his dad’s office and quick! He could be expecting it at any moment. At this exact instant he might be saying, *Where the hell are my schematics?* Matt had ripped the envelope almost in half when he opened it but he was so lucky. It was a standard manila office envelope. It had a standard typed label. He could easily reproduce it. Then he had to take it to his dad’s secretary and when she wasn’t looking, dump it under some of the new mail. Shouldn’t be hard but you never knew....

Fifteen minutes later he had recreated the envelope and sealed the papers inside. He tucked the envelope into the inside pocket of his jacket and then race-walked to the Kurt’s office at the end of the hall. As he approached Gina’s desk, he forced himself to slow down. To Matt, keyed up as he was, it felt like a funeral march. *That’s what it will be if I get caught!* The thought didn’t help one bit. He started to shake. Matt took a couple of deep breaths to steady himself.

“Hi Gina. How’s it going?” Matt had stopped right by her in-basket. She received all Kurt’s mail, sorted it and put it in his in-basket on his desk. Matt leaned over her desk, the envelope inside his jacket felt ominously heavy.

“Oh fine, I suppose Matt. Your dad’s got me multi-tasking again. Don’t know which end is up.”

“Oh dear, I’m sorry to hear that. How are the kids?”

“What? Whose kids? Oh mine? Yeah they’re fine. Nice of you to ask.”

“How old is the youngest now?”

“Well....” The phone rang. It was very conveniently located on the other side of her desk. As she rotated her chair she said, “Sorry, I’ve got to take this.”

Matt's hand dove into his jacket. He was starting to pull out the document when without any warning at all, his dad plowed through his office door.

"Gina, I nee.... Hey what are you doing here?"

With his hand still stuck in his jacket, Matt replied, "Me? Me?"

"Ya! You! Who do you think I'm talking to?"

As nonchalantly as he could, Matt took his hand out of his jacket, "Oh!...sorry...umm...yeah.... You just surprised me, that's all. I was going to ask Gina if you were free, wanted to see what was going on with the new project."

"What new project?"

"Well...you know...the new one." Kurt kept everything so secret that even his secretary didn't know much. Matt had to be very careful what he said in front of her. He had screwed up more than once before and each time his da...Kurt had screamed at him for hours.

"Yes, I understand, well come on in. I've got a couple of minutes."

Matt's heart stopped. He could have sworn it did. "Uhnn...sure... thanks."

"Just a minute.... Gina, bring in the Nexall contract when you're done there."

Matt entered the office in front of Kurt. He was sure his dad would see the skin on the back of his neck writhing in horror. He sat down in front of Kurt's desk. It was, like his office, gigantic. The desk was filled with flat panel screens, some as large as twenty-eight inches. He was monitoring every stock market in the world, monitoring his own businesses, spying on some of his employees, spying on competitors and now he was spying on the space agency. Nothing scared him. He did whatever he thought was required to continue to grow his empire.

Matt also knew that, should his dad feel it necessary, if he was threatened, he would get rid of anyone that got in his way. Murder if necessary. Matt's own life was worthless if Kurt thought Matt was a danger. Matt was convinced of it. Which didn't help matters now. He was shaking so bad that he didn't dare show his hands above the table.

"Okay shoot, what do you want to know?" Kurt asked Matt.

"Well...umm...you know...jus...."

"Sorry to interrupt Mr. Dragonovich. Here is the Nexall contract and the latest mail," Gina walked in quickly, handed the contract to Kurt and dropped the mail into his in-basket.

Oh no! Oh no! The mail! Matt squeezed a look at his watch. It was just after five p.m. Gina was finished work for the day. This was the last mail for Kurt's desk. He didn't dare leave it until tomorrow. He had to get it into that pile now. *How am I going to do that? The in-basket is on the other side of this friggin monster of a desk!* Gina walked out and closed the door.

Matt stared off into space. Kurt waited...nothing; waited some more...still nothing, *what an airhead!*

"Matt! What the hell do you want?"

"Oh. Yeah...umm...." He got up, started pacing—hands clasped tightly together behind his back.

"Well...I was just wondering...what was happening...umm...you know...with the Venus project.... Umm...did you get any other contracts?"

Kurt had just about lost all patience with Matt, "No, not yet. Will you bloody-well sit down! You're driving me nuts!"

"Oh, sure...sorry...." He sat down at the chair nearest the in-basket. The in-basket sat on the edge of the mahogany desk right in front of Matt.

Matt leaned forward, as if to get more intimate with his dad. He put his arm an inch from the in-basket and with the best conspiratorial voice that he could produce, Matt said, "I heard a rumor that maybe the Aliens are already here. Can you believe that?" With the exclamation, as if to emphasize his statement, Matt swung his arm up and somehow, accidentally, smacked the in-basket so hard it fell off the table, out of Kurt's sight. He screamed, "Damn! Damn! Sorry Kurt!"

Simultaneously, he got out of his chair, fell to his knees, stabbed his hand into his jacket, grabbed the document and started to pull it out. *It's stuck! It's stuck!* Kurt was coming around the desk, swearing. Matt could practically hear the steam coming out of his ears. *He's going to see!* Matt had no choice; he ripped as hard as he could. It popped out like a rotten cork in a wine bottle. He dropped it on the floor with the others and proceeded to pick up all the mail. He had one brief moment to view the envelope, *Not too bad. Just crumpled a bit, should be okay.* Then,

Oh! Man! I need a drink!

Chapter 15
THE CLIFF

Scott looked at the time; five minutes had passed since they had found the underwater cliff. They hadn't seen anything useful; the rock beside them was almost sheer; there was nothing that even Scott could justify as an opportunity to start the climb. He was getting desperate; they were running out of time.

Abruptly, he saw James wave. He was pointing upward at the rock face. About fifteen feet above them, the smooth surface broke into what looked to be the start of a chimney. To a rock climber, a chimney was his best friend. A chimney was a big, long, three-sided groove in the rock that could make a climb easy. If the climber were lucky, the chimney would be big enough to allow him to get inside and yet still allow him to reach each sidewall. If he could do that, he could use his arms and legs as levers against the sides. He didn't necessarily need hand or footholds; the pressure of his arms and legs would be enough to carry him up the rock face.

Scott hoped for more than that. *These suits aren't designed for that kind of rock climbing. Not enough flexibility.* They needed foot and handholds. However, the first challenge was getting to the start of the chimney. It was fifteen feet up. He could see a couple of spots that might provide hand and footholds. He moved up to the cliff, squatted as best he could, and with all his strength and the help of the servomotors, he jumped. He got one mechanical hand on a small outcrop and hung on. There was a small rock below and to the right that might be good enough for a foothold. Unfortunately, with his visor jammed against the rock face, he couldn't see it. He waved his foot around aimlessly; looking for the thinnest of ridges. He was about to give up when he felt James take his foot and set it onto the foothold. He found a new hold, then another. Finally he was at the base of the chimney where there was a slight outcrop big enough to stand on. He looked down. He could hardly see James in the murky water. To help James, Scott dropped to his hands and knees, then to his stomach and reached down as far as he could go. James leapt, got hold of the first outcrop and with amazing agility for a guy in a massive space suit, swung his other arm up toward Scott's outstretched hand. With Scott's support, James got hold of the ledge and pulled himself up. They stood there for a brief moment and then simultaneously, they both looked up. Nothing needed to be said. It was time to go.

At first the climbing had been difficult. Not a lot of handholds. The chimney was quite narrow in spots so they had to squeeze carefully through the rock on either side. But now they were making progress. The climbing started to get easier; there were more handholds and the rock was a little less shear. The gloom and fear that Scott had felt at the start of the climb was transitioning to hope and confidence. They had a chance! But they still had to be very careful. Now that there were larger flat surfaces, the mud was starting to get very thick. They tried to push most of it off any perch that they needed but it was still very slippery.

As he climbed, Scott checked the pressure; *Fifty atmospheres.* They were more than halfway up. He looked at the air and fuel cell readings. His mood started to wither; it was going to be tight. If they took too long to get to the top of the cliff there wasn't going to be any air left to breathe let alone blow into the suit. A thought began to grow in his mind, a scary, frightening thought; he shoved it down and continued on.

They were about one thousand feet from the surface. James was above Scott. They had reached a tough spot, an impasse. The chimney was blocked. Sometime, perhaps thousands of years ago, a huge rock had fallen, and then been trapped in the chimney. Their only way up was gone. Scott checked both sides of the chimney; the cliff was vertical, not a handhold or gripping point anywhere within sight. He looked at the blockage. It leaned out from the sides of the precipice a good ten feet. Smooth on the bottom. There was nothing that could be used for support. There might be some handholds on the other side of the outcrop but they couldn't see past the edge of the underside of this massive cork plugging their route to salvation. James started to descend to where Scott was located; there was room at this point in the chimney to stand side-by-side. He pressed his helmet up against Scott's.

"We're stuck."

"That's an understatement. Tell me something I don't know."

"I've seen how rock climbers do this. They rope themselves to the bottom of the outcrop with pitons and work their way out to the edge. They can then reach up and feel for a handhold. When they find one, they pull themselves over the obstacle."

"Well that's just great. But there are two problems. We don't have rope and we don't have pitons. Where are you going with this?" Scott asked.

"Well, you are going to be my rope and pitons."

"How's that?"

"You climb until you are just below the outcrop. I go as high as I can above you. Then you take my foot and raise it till I can touch the underside of the rock. I'll use my hands against the bottom of the boulder to slowly work my upper body out to the edge. At the same time, with one hand, you push my foot further out toward the edge. We have some buoyancy; we don't weigh what we would on land. With a little luck, you should have the strength to hold yourself on the cliff with your feet and one hand and with the other hand support me."

"Brilliant! It just might work."

"Once I'm out there I'll feel around above me, see if there is a spot that I can use to pull myself up."

Suddenly a thought came to Scott. "One problem. Once you start to pull yourself up, I won't be able to hold your foot. You will be dangling fifteen hundred feet above the shelf. There will be no way back. It's a one way ticket."

"Well...let me ask you the same question you asked me.... Can you think of any other way out of our predicament?"

"Ha-ha! Okay! Smart ass! But I want to change things slightly; I'll go out to the edge."

"Won't work. You're much taller and heavier. I won't be able to get you far enough out, even if I'm strong enough to hold you out there. Plus, you're the workout boy. Big muscles and all that. This is where all that sweating and muscle straining finally pays off; show the world how you can hold up bubble boy here with one hand."

"Trouble is, the world ain't watching." Scott stopped to consider the options and realized there weren't any. "Okay, you made your point. Times a wasting. Let's do it."

With James in the lead, they started to climb. James went as far as he could and then stopped. Slightly below James, Scott took hold of James's inside foot. James started doing a strange crablike, upside down crawl where each hand slowly dragged his torso toward the edge of the outcrop. Meanwhile Scott started moving the hand that was holding James's foot away from the rock face, away from safety. Scott could feel the strain of the weight on his shoulder, biceps and forearm. For the moment, it felt okay. He knew it was going to get worse as he stretched out his arm. He'd done this kind of strength test before, you'd feel fine at first but you get weak very quickly. It was going to be tough, very tough. Unexpectedly, a thought roared through his mind, *I WILL NOT LET JAMES GO! NO MATTER WHAT! I'D RATHER DIE!*

James was half way out. Scott could feel the tension increasing in his whole arm and shoulder. He shut his mind down, ignored the pain. His entire being, his psyche, his flesh had but one purpose—to hold on at all cost. Scott no longer looked at James. He didn't care where he was. He would hold on until James no longer needed him—nothing would stop him....

Scott had now reached his arm as far as it would go. The sweat was pouring off him; his hand, wrist, forearm, biceps, shoulder, back—his entire body was shaking. He was strained to the limit. The pain was building...building...and building. He couldn't ignore it any longer. It filled his mind. *I'm starting to lose it! NO! NO! Concentrate!*

Through the tremendous pain, Scott became aware that James was no longer moving. He was still...still for too long. Scott slowly, excruciatingly, with every ounce of strength, turned his head and looked up at James and saw that he could not reach the edge. They had both extended their mechanical hands as far as they could go. Scott couldn't stretch any further. *Wait! There is one thing....* Without thinking, without the least fear or concern, Scott released his handhold on the cliff face. Freed from his bond to the rock, he teetered outward—balanced only by the grip of his feet he provided the last few inches that James needed. He could see James reaching over the outcrop, scrabbling with his hand, looking for any perch that could allow him that last pull to freedom. Suddenly, he felt himself starting to lean out further from the rock; he was losing his balance. *It's now or never. HOLD ON! HOLD ON! HOLD ON!*

Then he was drifting, drifting downward.

James struggled to climb over the outcrop. As he got to his feet, a jubilant smile leapt across his face. It had been a close thing. He almost hadn't made it. The rock had been smooth everywhere except for one small spot where a chip had broken off the boulder, probably when it fell and became lodged in the chimney—there was just enough of a dip to allow his mechanical fingers to grip and pull himself up so he could reach with the other hand to the top of the boulder. After that it was just a matter of a lot of wriggling.

Still smiling he turned and looked for Scott. The boulder blocked his view so he had to step closer to the edge than he would have liked. But Scott wasn't there. Shocked, James looked off to his left and, just barely within eyesight he could see Scott in the water, no longer on the cliff, sinking. He could see that Scott was attempting to swim back to the wall. Then he was gone.

James stood there...and waited. He no longer cared about the remaining journey. He no longer cared about his air supply, his fuel reserves. He knew he should save himself and continue up the cliff but all he wanted now, at this moment, was to see his friend again. To see him alive one more time. There was a chance that Scott could make it back to the rock wall—so long as there was no current that would pull him away. How far down he would sink and how long it would take him to get back up and whether they would still be able to reach the surface before they would run out of air, James didn't know.

He waited. He waited. Eyes fixed to the very edge of the light. For a long time there was nothing and then....

Something different at the edge of his view.

It's a hand! Looking, searching, for its next grip. Slowly, painfully, Scott's form grew out of the depths.

Scott had reached the bottom of the outcrop for the second time today. He was stuck. In their hurry to get James over the boulder they hadn't thought that Scott would not be able to get around the rock by himself. He was trapped. He looked to the edge of that bloody rock. He should have been surprised by what he saw but by now, he knew James, he knew what he would do, what he could do—James was hanging by his arms from the top of the rock. He was waiting for Scott to leap to him. He was waiting for Scott to use him as a ladder. As Scott's powerful legs bent, as his legs prepared for that gigantic leap, a single brilliant thought ran through him, *How can I fail with a comrade such as this! I have been blessed!*

A short while later, Scott checked the readings on the heads-up display. They were seven hundred feet below the surface. But as he had been dreading, they weren't going to make it to the top of the shelf—to the three-hundred-foot level. He stopped James.

"We're going to have to go from here."

"I know."

Scott said, "This is it my friend. There is no way to know how buoyant we will be, how quickly we will rise to the surface or if we will rise at all."

"I know."

"Okay, here's the procedure. You blow the air into your suit. When you are done, give me the thumbs up. I'll remove the tanks and the fuel cell. If it works as we hope, you will have to hold onto me to prevent yourself from rising. Then, we run through the same routine with me."

"You bet.... Scott.... Scott?"

"Yes?"

"Umm, listen...well...I have to say.... If we don't make it.... I am honored to have known you.... Thank you for what you did for me back there...."

"Well we are going to make it. Don't you for one second think that we aren't! Fate will not let us down now. Not after what we have been through.

NOW! ARE YOU READY?"

"YES! YES!"

"LET'S DO IT! GO! GO! GO!"

A few minutes later, two of the strangest objects ever to rise from the depths of the sea bobbed to the surface. Their appendages waved back and forth at the surface ship a quarter mile away. They had been under the surface for ten hours, three minutes and twenty-three seconds.

Dave Bollard and the entire surface team had been struggling to find a solution for those ten hours. They had no idea what had happened. They couldn't reach the submersible or the Astronauts. Emergency equipment was on its way from the mainland but time was running out, they had little hope that anyone could be saved. While they waited, Dave had every available person on the entire ship watching the smooth, calm waters for any sign of life.

"Dave! Dave! There's something off the starboard bow. I think it's them...it's the Astronauts!

Chapter 16

LOVE, HATE AND FEAR

He felt a tug on the top button of his shirt. A door was being opened. A door not to his heart, for that had swung wide many months ago when he had first met Shannon. It was a door to something that was beyond his experience. He was stepping through a portal where love and sensual excitement coexisted. A place almost more powerful than life itself.

The tug had moved down one button. His skin, where now cool air touched, tingled and warmed as Shannon's breath flowed out, fanned out, exploring, caressing, touching. A flush of blood rushed to greet this most wanted guest, tracing each breath's pattern, echoing its touch. Breath and skin were locked in a soft, subtle, wonderful dance. In the pitch dark, blacker than black, sight became superfluous, unnecessary, unwanted.

Another button pulled away from its cloth. The breath became a kiss. A kiss over his heart. So close! So close, he could feel his heart leap forward to mingle with her caress, its beat racing as if repeated tries could pound its way through the flesh to her lips. He ran his hands over her naked back. *So Smooth! So Warm!* Love flashed through his entire being, love for this beautiful, wonderful woman who was giving herself to him. Flesh to flesh wasn't enough. He wanted to crush her against him. To somehow pull her into his soul.

The final button said goodbye. Her hands ran up his skin. Gently she pulled his shirt away from his shoulders, down his arms. Her hands followed and met his. Fingers intertwined, she leaned forward and up, her lips just barely brushing his. Matt felt her nipples, hard with excitement, sway against his chest. Another touch, lip to lip. Then another and another...another...another. Passion outstripped sensuality. He reached down, grabbed her soft buttocks and pulled her in and up to him. The gentle kisses had become fierce, desperate stabs of love and passion. Their bodies, still uncertain of each other, touched here and there, foot against foot, leg against leg, stomach to stomach...hands everywhere. Her breath, slow, smooth and comforting before, had transformed into sharp hard puffs, sudden uncontrolled inhale and irregular gasps. Now her mouth was against his belly. A soft moan pushed its way from his lips. The gentle tugs against his shirt buttons were now brutal hard pulls on his pant belt, his pant button, his zipper. Matt was enveloped, then held in a warm, wet, ultimate embrace. He reached down with both hands, felt her silky hair, ran his fingers over her head, then leaned forward, grasped her by the shoulders and pulled that incredible face back to his. He kissed her again and again. He held her face in his hands, explored every curve with the very tips of his fingers, kissed her brow, her cheeks, her nose and back to those wet, sweet lips. "I love you so, so much Shannon! I will die for you! Die for you!"

"Yes... Yes. I love you Matt. umm...umm...." Her kisses came hard and fast.

Funny how, when you love someone, the best part of sex comes after. When you are lying close, touching, hugging. Hell! Even sleeping is just so much better! Matt started to look over at her again, for about the thousandth time, just to confirm it wasn't another daydream, when the cell phone rang.

"Shannon, where are my pants? My phone is in the pocket."

"Over here on my side." She reached down, fumbled about and brought the phone up. As she checked the caller id she said, "It's that jerk father of yours."

"Aw, no," replied Matt as he took the phone.

"Hello?"

"It's me. I need you in the office, now."

Matt looked at the clock, a victim of their love, which was sitting a little askew on the side table. It was ten p.m. *Christ!*

"Now?"

"Yes! Now, Dumbo! Why do you think I said now?? Did you think I said 'now' but meant tomorrow?"

"No. Of course not. I'll be right there." Matt hung up, "Damn! Damn! Damn!"

"Tell that jerk to screw-off!" Shannon exclaimed. "Matt you have to do something about him."

"I know. I know. I...just.... Well...he's my father."

"I don't get it. He treats you like dirt."

"I don't get it either. I don't know why I'm like this. I don't know why...I'm scared of him. I hate him and yet somehow...still love him." He paused. Sadness and pain filled the silence. "Well, perhaps love is the wrong word...." He stopped again. His face, already miserable, grew solemn. Then, a whisper slipped from his lips,

"Need. Yes that's it. The word is need. I still need him. He's my father. It means something but... now...now...."

Thoughts that he had kept hidden in a prison of fear and shame, were trying to break out. He struggled to stop them, but the pressure was too great. He had to share this horror with someone. He couldn't keep it inside any longer, "There's something else."

"What?"

"Well...I...I...think he's done something, or rather, I think he might do something."

"Tell me."

"I'm not sure I should. It could be...." A sigh escaped him, "could be dangerous. He doesn't know about you. I don't want him to know. He'd have a fit if he knew that you worked for Greenpeace. I'm not sure what he'd do but I'm scared he'd make me leave you."

"Leave me? Leave me??? Come on Matt! You don't have to do anything you don't want to. He doesn't own you."

"You don't understand. He'll check up on you, look into your past, try to dig up some dirt and then use it against you or against us."

"Let him! I've got nothing to hide!"

"You see! You don't have a clue what he's like! If he can't find anything, he'll make it up. He could get you fired. He could have one of his guys plant something, make it look like you're stealing!" he cried.

"And then there's the money. He might disown me, leave me with nothing. I.... I will inherit his empire someday. I told you, it's worth an unbelievable fortune."

"Who gives a damn about the money? You don't need it. We don't need it. I don't care about money. Do you? I hope not!"

Eyes downcast, Matt said nothing. Emotion flooded into Shannon's voice. It began to crack. "Maybe I made a mistake. Maybe I'm with the wrong person."

Tears began to well in her eyes. A single drop formed, hung there for a moment, then slid onto her smooth, beautiful skin. It began a heartbreaking dance down her cheek. Matt had never seen her face like this before, contorted with sadness, anger and perhaps...perhaps fear...perhaps fear of a lost love. It tore his guts out. He felt physically sick. He could see his whole life with this wonderful person, like that single drop of water, sliding away, evaporating.

Her expression shifted to one of solemn resolve. She reached up to wipe away the tear, to wipe away their relationship, to wipe away Matt. His hand shot out and took hers before it could destroy his life.

With a voice shimmering with sorrow, he cried, "No! No!"

He took her hand and held it in both of his. He raised it to his lips and kissed her fingers over and over while he rocked back and forth in pain.

"You don't understand. I.... I'm useless! If he fired me. I'd... I'd never get another job. I'm no good. He only keeps me around because I'm his son. I'm a VP because I'm his son. He's told me that if I wasn't his son he wouldn't even keep me as a janitor. And he's right. I'm a complete screw-up. I'm sorry. So sorry! I never wanted to tell you this. I wanted you to be proud of me." He dropped his head into his hands and sobbed.

"Matt! Matt! Listen to me!" Shannon took his hands away from his face and looked into his eyes, "You can do it. Your dad has done a number on you since you were a little boy. You're not stupid and you're not a screw-up. You are an intelligent man. You will find a job. I don't care about the money. We will survive, no matter what."

"I... don't know."

"Matt! Look at me! Look at me! WE WILL SURVIVE!"

"But you don't understand my father. He hates to lose. I don't know what he'd do if he found out about you. He might.... He might even have someone hurt you! You just don't understand. He's a monster! Every time I see him, I get the shakes. And now...now.... I've found something out, something horrible."

"What Matt? What's horrible?"

"I should...shouldn't tell you. If I'm right about this, anybody who finds out is in big, big trouble. Honestly, I think my dad would kill anyone who knew."

"Look, if this is as bad as you say it is, do you think he is going to let me go? I'm your girlfriend. He's going to assume that you told me anyway."

"I can't let him find out about you."

"Tell me what you are talking about!!!"

Matt still hesitated, still hoped for a way to avoid the whole mess, but it was too late, he'd gone too far.

"Okay...okay...here it is. You know how Dad is heavily into the NASA Venus program."

"Yes."

"Well, by accident I found something out." He stopped again, struggled with words, "Umm."

"Matt! Tell me!"

"I think he has had someone build a fail-safe into the Venus Renaissance."

"A fail-safe? What's a fail-safe?"

"A fail-safe is a device used to prevent an object, usually a rocket, from going out-of-control. If the rocket goes out-of-control, the fail-safe is used to destroy it. You can activate it remotely or sometimes it's a self-destruct mechanism—the machine determines that it's out-of-control and destroys itself."

"Okay, yeah, so? That's a good thing isn't it? You don't want a rocket going out-of-control."

"But there are people on this ship. The ship is destroyed, they are destroyed. And certainly this is not something that my dad should have access to. Why would he want it? There's only one reason—to destroy the ship if he feels it's necessary. Can you believe it? It's just so...horrible!! We're in big trouble. I've hardly been able to sleep since I found out. Every time he calls me into his office, I think it's because he knows...he knows that I know!

"Okay. It's okay Matt. Let's figure this out. Tell me everything...."

Chapter 17

MOON STATION

Scott Benbow leaned on the ledge and took a sip of his coffee. It was hot! Too hot! *Bastard! I just burned my tongue!* With no place to spit, he had to slop it round his mouth, while trying to suck in as much cool air as possible. All he achieved was more burnt mouth. He was standing there, mentally cursing the coffee machine, when he looked up through the tripled-paned plexiglas at the view outside. He stared at the sight before him, his burnt mouth forgotten; Jack's speech from eighteen months ago, a thousand years in Astronaut time, flashed into his mind.

"That view is absolutely remarkable," said a voice behind him.

Scott, slightly startled, turned, "Oh. Hi, Jack. How was the trip?"

"Not so good. A few of our, hurrumm, dignitaries had difficulties. Pretty much as expected. A good number of them couldn't take the weightlessness. They are resting, nicely sedated in the infirmary."

Jack continued, "So are you ready for the song and dance, the dog and pony show or...." He quickly looked around and lowered his voice, "The waste of time. Sometimes I really hate my job. But it has to be done. The politicians have to see how their money was spent."

Scott didn't reply. He knew that Jack was venting and didn't expect an answer. Scott had arrived at the moon station on the previous shuttle. This was Scott's penultimate trip, his second to last. He was here to perform some pre-launch system checks and to help Jack. Then it was back to Earth for a series of final meetings and a two-week holiday. Then came the ultimate trip, the final trip to the Moon. From there they would lift off to Venus. *The Ultimate, Ultimate trip! I don't think there is a word in the English language for that journey.*

He was ready. He was prepared—as prepared as he could be. Scott was confident; he knew his tasks inside out and backwards. But for all that, sometimes, he couldn't prevent a small seed of fear from growing, its black shoots winding through his heart and mind, tugging at his confidence, pulling at his courage. Each time he had to stop, rip that seed from the soil of his psyche and crush it to a pulp. He knew that everyone else on the team felt the same. How could you not? You wouldn't be human. Out of all of them, James seemed to be the most relaxed. He talked, walked, breathed...did everything with a calm intensity. Scott didn't see the far away looks that he periodically caught on the faces of all the others. Somehow, the submersible disaster had cleansed James. He had faced his fear, faced his terror. He had battled those monsters and won.

Scott was sure of this. Scott had to be sure—it was his job now. He had been chosen to be the leader of Venus Mission team.

It was a controversial decision that Jack Anderson had to defend vigorously. There were many, many other Astronauts with more experience but Jack believed with every ounce of his heart that Scott was the right person. Sure he was young but Jack knew Scott's history. He understood the willpower required to achieve his goals. He knew what it took to fight day and night to become this confident, utterly determined person. Scott didn't have the direct experience of some of the more senior Astronauts but he had the experience of the street. He had struggled against incredible odds and won. His actions during the submersible affair proved that he was a very capable leader even under extreme stress. All the training and testing during the program had put Scott at the top of the class. He was above almost everyone—including the most experienced astronauts in every metric: physical, IQ, leadership, organization, decision-making, psychological stability. Only one person exceeded him in any of the categories—James McArthur. James's IQ was almost off the scale and in some physical characteristics he was superior to Scott. But James didn't have the necessary leadership skills.

The submersible affair had been a very sad business. After a day of searching, they found the sub about a mile deep on a small ledge just below where the testing had taken place. The submersible could easily handle the pressure one mile below the surface but it hadn't mattered; both men were dead; they had run out of oxygen. The investigation revealed, as it often does in these circumstances, a confluence of problems; the odds that all of them would happen at the same time were minuscule, yet through a horrible coincidence, they had coalesced to produce a tragedy. The submersible had a broken oxygen gauge that the team failed to repair before descending. They also failed to report the incident. During the descent, the oxygen tank developed a leak. The team chose to ignore an alarm that they should have known was an independent oxygen warning—it measured the oxygen level in the submersible, not the level in the tanks. Finally, the surface team were only monitoring the Astronauts, so they were unaware of any problems on the submersible. It had been a complete catastrophe.

The rest of the suit testing had gone without a hitch. A few more modifications had been made but the suit itself was a total success. Although not every astronaut would be required to use them, they all had very thorough suit training; they could get in and out of them in their sleep.

The Lander was ready. It had been a challenge to complete its construction in the given time period but they had done it. The Lander team had killed themselves on the project. When they started missing some of the milestones, more resources, from all over the world, had been allocated to the team.

The Orbiter was ready. It was called Renaissance. There was a lot of disagreement about the name. There's that old saying, *you can't please all the people all of the time*, but in this case it should be, *you can't please the entire planet at all.* There were all sorts of names that were considered better by someone, somewhere—Seeker, Explorer, Adventurer, Alien hunter, Inquisitive, Voyager, Surveyor, Fortune, Enterprise, Humanity and so on. Some of them had already been used before. It didn't matter; someone wanted to use it again. The cynics had their own list—The Please help us!, Budget Buster, The Bankruptcy, Destroyer, The Inquisition, The Rape and Pillage and a thousand others. To Scott the name, Renaissance, meaning rebirth and renewal, was perfect. This ship represented a new beginning. A new age was coming. Scott could see it already, every country wanted to participate in some way in the grand adventure. For the first time in history all countries, all peoples, had a single purpose—there was no doubt a renaissance was underway; when that ship took off, the entire world would collectively hold its breath.

Scott and Jack walked down the corridor and entered the meeting room where the "survivors" of the trip were waiting. Some of them were still looking a little green. Jack started off the tour with a preamble, "How is everybody making out with the lower gravity?"

"It's taking some getting used to," said one of the greener guys.

"Yes, I understand. You have to hold back your legs when you walk. The best term I can think of is, "Walk Softly". However, for those of you that can't—all the ceilings are twelve-foot high. You don't have to worry about bumping your head." Jack said.

"As I'm sure most of you know, the moon station has been a work in progress for eleven years now. You are standing in the main building complex. The entire Moon Station is located inside a ten million year old crater that is twenty miles across and has sides as high as one thousand feet. The main building complex is buried in the side of the crater. The launch pads are two miles away, pretty much on a line from here to the center of the crater. They are reached via a tunnel that runs below the crater surface. We have chosen this location because the high sides of the crater give us some protection from asteroids. During your...."

"Excuse me Jack. Why is everything buried underground? Surely, that's very costly. Why not just build on the surface?"

"Good question. We did it for three reasons. First, as I stated we are concerned about asteroids. In particular, we are concerned about small particles traveling at very high speeds penetrating exposed building walls. By burrowing into the crater's sides, we limit the number of exposed walls. Second, heaven forbid, we are protected in case of some kind of launch explosion. Third, the tunnel to the launch site allows a pressurized air environment right to the space ships. Once the external hulls were complete, the Astronauts no longer required space suits. This increased our construction efficiency tremendously. As a matter of fact, it's the only reason we were able to build the ships in a short eighteen months. Any other questions?"

"Why aren't you concerned about larger asteroids?"

"Because there is no way to protect ourselves from an asteroid that is, say, the size of the one that caused this crater. Any other questions?"

There were none.

"As I was saying, during the tour today, we will take you to the Moon Control center and then out to the Orbiter. Now before I say anything further, let me give you a view of the launch area."

Jack had picked this room for a very particular reason. It was the only location that had windows from floor to ceiling. He dimmed the interior lights and signaled Scott to flick the switch that operated the blast covers. The covers rolled away to reveal an eerie, futuristic view that had only ever been seen before in science fiction movies.

In a thousand-foot deep crater, crystal clear in the non-existent Moon atmosphere, stood the Venus Orbiter and Lander. The crater was located on the dark side of the moon, so only the light from the Station, uninhibited by any atmosphere, lit up the crater basin. The effect was remarkable. The crater was dappled with sharp bright light and the hardest of black shadows. The far crater wall, a thousand feet high, hovered ominously over the space ships. Even the slightest pebble, a mile away, was easily distinguishable. It was a holographic scene where every object seemed to push forward towards the viewers, filling their eyes, their minds, their hearts.

Slightly to the left of their viewpoint stood the Lander. Almost directly in front was the Orbiter. To the right were four more launch pads. Even further to the right, perhaps a mile away, was what looked to be a tall spire. Taller than anything else in the crater, the spire was illuminated by several floodlights so that it glowed a silvery white from top to bottom. It looked like a white-hot needle pointing up into the dark. NO! Not into the Dark! It was pointing to a blue-white orb dangling above the hard, pitiless crags of the crater. It was pointing to the Earth!

No human could be immune to the emotional effect of this spectacular vista.

The entire room was silent. Then somebody began to applaud. It rippled through the room, infectious. It spread to every person. Sounds of approval—yelling, clapping, hooting—became a roar so loud it seemed that the reverberation could burst through the walls, into the crater, into space and shoot off toward Earth.

Scott was not surprised by the reaction. He knew how he had felt the first time he looked upon man's creation on this lonely ball of rock. He remembered the strong emotions.

Jack waited for the applause to subside. He couldn't help but feel proud of what they had accomplished. With a grin as wide as a house, Jack began again.

"Now let me tell you a little about the Space Craft. It is the greatest engineering accomplishment in the history of Mankind. You may be surprised to see that it is still in two pieces, the Renaissance Orbiter and the Renaissance Lander. They will be launched independently. Once in Moon orbit they will be attached. The reason for this is twofold; to reduce the size of the fuel tanks on the Orbiter and to perform a final engine test on the Lander. Both units will be refueled in Moon orbit. Now...."

"Excuse me Jack?"

"Yes?"

"What is the tall spire for?"

"It's a memorial to the Astronauts who lost their lives while building this marvel of human endeavor. The height of the spire is equal to the total length of the Renaissance. As you know, twelve people, twelve men and women, have lost their lives. It is an odd coincidence that this is the exact number of Astronauts who will be traveling to Venus. The spire stands beside the destroyed lift-off platform where ten of our brave people died."

"How did it happen?"

"The shuttle came in too quickly and hit the platform with such a force that it completely destroyed the platform and the shuttle. After that tragic event, we redesigned the platforms. You will notice that the platforms are quite high. They are seventy feet above the surface and continue another fifty feet under the surface. They operate like gigantic shock absorbers. When the ship lands, there are huge hydraulic cylinders that compress and therefore absorb the excess speed of the Space Ship. The top part of the platform can also move twenty feet horizontally in any direction. That way we can absorb, should the ship have some drift, a horizontal velocity vector. Finally, on lift-off, there are rockets on the platform that help push the ship into space. This platform design has kept the fuel tanks on the Moon Shuttles as small as possible." Jack said.

"Now let me tell you about the orbiter...."

Scott tuned out. Of course, he knew all of this. The Orbiter was long, thin and heavy. It could never lift off from Earth. It had to be built either on the moon or in space. Designed to carry twelve inhabitants for a period of just over two years, the Orbiter had to be large enough for the Astronauts, all the support and test equipment, food, water, a water treatment system, as well as a mini agricultural system for carbon dioxide filtering and oxygen production called Environmental Vegetation.

The main body of the Orbiter was one hundred and fifty feet long but was only a little over twenty feet wide. It was narrow for two reasons:

First and foremost, the diameter allowed prefabricated pieces of the outer shell to be carried in the Space Station Shuttles. When the pieces arrived on the moon, they could be put together like a giant toy Mechano set. The Renaissance construction was intended to be as simple as possible. In the case of the outer shell, each piece interlocked with its neighbor such that when the pieces were lined up, inserted, then twisted slightly, a rivet and pin system, using compressed air, was driven into the shell automatically. No tools required. All the Astronauts had to do was inspect the fit using a specially designed tester.

Secondly, a narrow diameter design allowed the internal air-lock bulkheads to be easily constructed and prefabricated on Earth. The bulkheads were intended to provide containment for three equally spaced Environmental sections. The orbiter had been cleverly designed such that, in case of a hull breach, each section could stand on its own. There was food, water, an environmental system (including the Environmental Vegetation) and emergency sleeping facilities in each section. All facets of the Orbiter could be controlled from each Environmental area which included operation of the engines, stabilization jets, external cameras, all communications equipment and test equipment. The control wiring for each section ran independently through the hull. Only a catastrophic hull breach would sever control to the Engine and the stabilization jets. As one engineer put it, *if you have a catastrophic hull breach, you won't need the engines anyway.*

The nose of the Orbiter tapered slightly to a flat end approximately fifteen feet in diameter, which gave it a rather unattractive telephone-pole look. This was where the Lander would be attached. Once in Venus orbit, the Astronauts would enter the Lander through the nose of the Orbiter. The Lander added another seventy-five feet to the total length of the spacecraft, while the engines, which were located at the tail end of the Orbiter, added another twenty feet. Finally, the fuel tanks, attached to the sides of the Orbiter, were disposable; there was enough fuel to lift the ship off the Moon but the remaining fuel, already in its tanks, was to be picked up in Moon orbit.

The Lander, like the Venus suits, had been specially designed to withstand the very harsh Venus environment. It was almost as heavy as the Orbiter and because the gravity on Venus was very nearly as strong as Earth's, the weight had posed a very big problem for the designers. Launching the Lander from Venus would be impossible; there would not be enough fuel. To overcome the problem, the designers reduced the size of the Lander and built it in two pieces. The lower piece would remain on Venus. The upper piece, very much smaller, would be launched to rendezvous with the Orbiter. These tradeoffs meant that only six of the Venus team could travel to the surface.

Once on the surface they had enough supplies to last a month; if they were to stay longer, they would need the assistance of the alien race. For travel on the surface, the Venus Lander also carried two, three-man vehicles, which were driven by electric motors located on all four wheels and powered by both solar panels and fuel cells. They too had been very carefully designed to withstand the pressure, temperature and corrosive atmosphere of Venus.

"I'm sure that you have noticed that there is a critical piece missing," said Jack, "It's the living and exercise quarters for the crew—the physical shape of the living quarters negated any chance that it could be constructed and launched from the Moon. It had to be built in Moon Orbit. It is a gigantic six-hundred-and-ninety-one-foot circumference cylindrical hoop that will circle the Orbiter at the first airlock. It will be attached to the main portion of the vessel by three, ten-foot diameter spokes—the Orbiter's diameter is expanded at this point to allow the connection. The expanded shell is part of the living quarter's prefabrication—it gets installed with the spokes, and each spoke is one hundred feet long. The inside of the hoop, the living and exercise area, is fifteen feet in diameter. As with the main body, it too is broken into three compartments with one spoke serving each subdivision. The sections also have a separate environmental control, which is provided by one of the systems on the main body of the Orbiter. Once installed on the Orbiter, the entire ship will start rotating, thereby causing a type of pseudo-gravity in the living quarters."

"What's the total length of the Renaissance?"

"The living quarters insert adds another fourteen feet, so the total length is two-hundred-and-fifty-nine feet."

"How will you land something as ungainly as this when it comes back to earth?"

"It wasn't designed to land. The ship will be parked in Moon orbit and the Astronauts will be off-loaded from there."

"Why not Earth Orbit?"

"There's enough space junk in Earth Orbit already. And it's our intention, should funding be available, to keep the Renaissance for a Mars trip. Or perhaps we will need it to return to Venus. Who knows?"

"What about the air-locks? Won't it be difficult moving through the ship if you have to open and close the air-locks each time?"

"The air-locks remain open unless triggered by a sudden decrease in air pressure or an alarm from the temperature sensors or smoke detectors, at which point they will automatically close." Jack quickly looked around the room; it was time to wrap this up. He asked,

"Any other questions?" None came. "Okay let's start the tour."

An hour later, after the Mission Control tour, they were on their way to the Orbiter on the monorail system that ran underground between the building complex and the launch pads. At the Orbiter launch pad, they disembarked from the monorail and entered an elevator that took them to the top of the ship via the gantry.

Someone from the European delegation with a tone of disappointment said, "No windows in the elevator."

Jack replied, "We didn't think it was worth the extra expense just to provide the Astronauts with a view." There were a few chuckles. "However, this gives me a chance to say that the gantry you are in serves three purposes: first, as a crane during construction; second, to physically support the Renaissance prior to lift-off; and third, access to the space vehicle. You should also know that there are three separate entrances to the ship, one for each environmental section. They are located near each air-lock. Today we are going to the top section, where the primary control room is located."

As they approached the top air-lock, Jack said, "Okay, here we are. Because it's pretty tight quarters in the ship, I'm going to break you into three groups. Scott will take the first group in. The rest of us will remain here."

Scott brought the first group through the airlock door. One at a time, they climbed a temporarily installed ladder up to the main deck and found themselves standing in a bright, no nonsense, room full of equipment.

"No room for a picture of the wife and kids?" someone joked. It was very congested. Every inch of space had been accounted for.

"Well, certainly not in the control room but there is plenty of room in the crew quarters. Although, in this case, there won't be any pictures of the wife and kids. NASA decided that, due to the length of the trip and the obvious danger, everybody would be single. I think it was a very wise decision," replied Scott.

"I've heard some expert's estimate that you only have a ten percent chance of coming back."

"I heard that also and frankly, I was very angry when I heard it. This ship has an enormous number of built-in safeguards, the Lander and the Venus suits have been thoroughly tested and this crew is the cream of the crop in the Astronaut program—they are extremely intelligent, resourceful people. I have complete and total confidence in every single one of them. Without a second thought, I would put my life in any one of their hands," Scott said.

"And you may have to."

"That's my point. That's why they are on the team."

"Why are there only four seats here?"

"Only the pilots and copilots are required during takeoff. The rest of the team will sit in the middle section of the craft."

"There are no windows."

"Correct, with all the external cameras, we don't need them. The cameras we have can look at both visible and non-visible light. They are much better than our eyes and it's much safer as well. We have cameras located such that we can see every part of the ship without ever having to take a space walk. It's the same for the Lander as well."

"What about food? Why not grow your own? You have plants for the environmental system."

"Well it was very tempting, particularly for the Astronauts. We argued vigorously for fresh veggies but in the end, NASA believed that a full-blown agricultural food farm would be just too difficult. The space and plant management required was prohibitive. We can pack an awful lot of dried food into a small space and vitamin tablets take even less room. The Environmental Vegetation has been genetically designed to maximize carbon dioxide take-up and oxygen production; they aren't edible. NASA has gone to a lot of effort to emphasize and reemphasize the "not edible" statement. They didn't want some desperate Astronaut, after many, many months without "greens", taking a bite out of the Environmental system."

"However, there is a very serious side to the Environmental plant system. We can only survive for six weeks without the vegetation. So to be safe, NASA has included a Horticulturist as part of the team. Now let me show you some of the features of the ship."

Scott ran through a number of the design benefits and features of the spacecraft; the seats could be removed and folded into a remarkably small storage area; there was a cable system, with handgrips, that ran the length of the ship. As the central portion of the ship was weightless, the Astronauts could hold the handgrip, activate the cable from a button on the handle and it would pull them to their destination. So that they could travel in either direction, the Astronaut-hauler, as it was called, ran up and down the main isle-way and was carefully designed such that, in an emergency, the air-locks could still be closed without damaging the mechanism.

Besides the very specialized Venus suits which were located in the Lander, there were two other different types of space suits on-board; one for space walks, which would be required for the in-space completion of the Renaissance and may be needed for any emergency external repairs during the flight, and another special emergency suit, only intended to be used for short durations inside the Orbiter during a hull breach—they were located throughout the spacecraft and had a twenty minute air supply.

Finally, they all had a good laugh at the toilet and shower facilities that had to withstand the rigors of weightlessness. As Scott said, "It really puts an Astronaut off his grub if a turd happens to go floating by."

Chapter 18

THE LAST HURRAH

Scott stared down into the eyes of the woman in his arms. She felt good, nestled in tight to his chest...*actually a little too good*, Scott thought as he stepped back just a hair. He applied a touch of pressure to her right hand with his left, slid his right hand along her back toward the left side of her waist; he started to lift her right hand just the slightest; he immediately felt her respond, *Wow! She sure can follow. Is there anything this woman can't do well?* In an instant Penny McFadden was spinning in front of him, a soft, happy smile on her face. Then she was back in his arms, facing him. He brought her back at a more appropriate distance. At five-foot-ten Penny was the only female Astronaut on the team tall enough to not look silly up close to the six-foot-two Scott. She was not bad looking. As a matter of fact, he suddenly realized, she was pretty damn good looking. This was the first time they had been together in a social setting. Scott just hadn't looked at her this way before. After almost eighteen months, he had finally looked at her as a woman, not as a Biologist and a member of his crew.

All Scott's senses were under attack. Her dark hair, which she always wore tied up, Scott suddenly realized, in a really ugly bun, now temporarily released from its prison, reveled in its freedom, swaying and caressing her oval face. With each breath, he drew a wonderful, cloying perfume into his body. Her dark-brown eyes floated below him; the precisely applied makeup had turned them from no-nonsense, matter-of-fact, work-a-day orbs to soul grabbing magnets. Her high cheekbones, small nose and delicate mouth had been all tastefully painted—if there was one adjective to describe Penny tonight it was tasteful...or perhaps it was classy...no, no.... *Sophisticated! That was it! Sophisticated!* If all this wasn't enough, the warmth of her body, so close to his, was turning his legs into jelly. Powerful emotions tugged at him, confused him. He was the Captain of this crew of Astronauts. A relationship of any kind, even of the most temporary kind, with this woman was absolutely inappropriate, and given where they were going, where any distraction could have a high cost, it could also be dangerous. They had to remain entirely professional. Scott was going to make sure of that. He gave her a little more distance on the dance floor.

Penny McFadden, the daughter of an Australian Aborigine mother and a British father, had a Ph.D. in biology as well as a medical degree. She was going to be a key member of the Lander team. It would be Penny's job to evaluate any Alien life forms and determine if there were any microbes that could harm humans. It was going to be a very stressful and difficult job. Although NASA had included various types of test equipment on the Lander to help her, there was really no way of knowing if the tests missed a particularly virulent bug. NASA and Scott were going to have to rely on her judgment. The rules were strict—no personal relationships of any kind during the mission. NASA psychologists had spent many hours evaluating the group, hoping to weed out any possible "problem situations" as they called it.

As the song ended, Scott felt a hand touch his shoulder.

"Mind if I cut in?" It was one of the technicians from the Lander team. He'd been loitering around Penny all night.

"Not at all."

A very much-relieved Scott strode off the dance floor towards Adam Coleman.

Tonight was the "Last Hurrah" as someone had called it. They had two weeks before they went airborne. *Or a better yet, space borne.* Two weeks off, then they were on their way to the Moon and then on to Venus.

NASA, after some reluctance had given permission for tonight's party. All of the Venus project team had been invited—Astronauts, Engineers, Technicians and Administrators from JPL, NASA and SETI. It was shaping up to be a hum-dinger of a party! There must have been four or five hundred people in attendance. The stress and strain of the last eighteen months was being unleashed in this room tonight.

"Hey, you're a pretty good dancer!" shouted Adam over the music.

"Actually it was Penny, I just followed along."

"Ha-ha!.... Boy! She sure looks good tonight."

"Oh really? I hadn't noticed."

Adam was a Geologist and Copilot of the Lander. Like everyone else on the team, he was a very cool customer. Adam could be locked in a death struggle and still manage to crack a joke. And that was the one trait that Scott was a little concerned about; he had a tendency to be a bit mischievous. Other than that, Scott really felt comfortable with Adam; he was a superb pilot and geologist and a very good listener—a total team player—he was willing to give his opinion but didn't push it.

Adam was five-foot eleven with sand-brown hair, blue eyes, a bit of a narrow chin and a smallish nose. Adam was one of those people who should have been rather good looking but somehow the parts didn't quite come together. His eyes were just a tad too wide spaced, his nose a little too small, his chin just ever so slightly pointy. He wasn't ugly by any means; he just didn't make the "Handsome" grade. He wore a mustache that Scott surmised was to enhance his manliness. Unfortunately, it was small and somewhat delicate. Brodie Cavanaugh, the pilot of the Orbiter, with his usual tact had said, "It makes you look like a fag." Adam had responded with, "You lookin for a date, Brodie?" That was another of Adam's attributes. He was definitely a "sticks and stones can break my bones but names can't hurt me" guy. Nothing bothered him. You could insult him forever to no effect.

"Hey, you know, I think it's time for my announcement." Adam stated.

"What announcement?" replied Scott.

"You just wait and see," Adam said with a smirk. He walked toward the stage. On the way, he stopped to talk to Pascal, the Venus communications specialist. Scott couldn't hear what they were saying but both of them had huge grins stuck to their faces. Adam continued to the stage while Pascal walked over to a table that held a laptop and projector. Adam climbed the two steps to the top of the platform and tapped the microphone that was standing at center-front on the podium. A muted thump-thump filled the room. There was a lectern next to the Microphone that held a control panel; Adam punched a button on the panel and a huge screen at the back of the stage descended.

"Excuse me, LADIES AND GENTLEMEN!"

"MAY I HAVE YOUR ATTENTION PLEASE!" Adam, having had perhaps a drink too many, didn't need to scream into the microphone but his ear-splitting cry did have the effect of attracting everyone's attention. Instantly the room became quiet.

"I think most of you know my good friend, Brodie Cavanaugh, the brave pilot of the Renaissance Orbiter. What most of you probably don't know is that Brodie has discovered a special potion—an elixir of youth! He's been trying to keep it secret, even from his good friends. The selfish bastard wants it only for himself! Now you might say to yourself, no that can't be true, there's no such thing as a fountain of youth—you can't make yourself younger!"

Adam stopped and stared, a bit wobbly-eyed, at the audience—looking for disbelief. Then, "But I say to you that it is true! I have proof! Let me show you some pictures that I took of Brodie, just recently over a period of two weeks. As you will see, something magical happened!" A huge smile spread over his face and he turned toward Pascal, "Pascal if you would, please sir!" Pascal punched a key on the laptop.

An enormous, close-up picture of Brodie's face jumped onto the white screen behind Adam. "Roll it Pascal!" cried Adam.

The audience was treated to an unusual form of time lapse filming. Adam had surreptitiously photographed Brodie's face and head from approximately the same position for fourteen days in a row.

The first gigantic picture showed Brodie up close and a little too personal. No face could have stood up to scrutiny on that huge screen. It was particularly cruel to a countenance that had seen more than its fair share of "trouble" over the years. Every scar, pit and blemish stood out like craters on the Moon. A few forlorn hairs that were unfortunately missed during his morning shave protruded from his face—reminiscent of giant forgotten redwoods still standing in a logging clear-cut. The whole room shouted with laughter.

Brodie, who was in his late forties, still considered himself a ladies man. Certainly, he did attract the women but Scott sure couldn't figure out how. Brodie had jet-black hair that was slowly being overwhelmed with grey, brown eyes and a bit of a pudgy nose, which had been broken at sometime in the past, probably by some woman's unhappy boyfriend or husband. That nose gave him a funny, disconcerting visage—pointing in one direction while the rest of him looked in another, somewhat like a Picasso painting. Clean-cut with a wide jaw and a scar or two, he undoubtedly had, what could only be called, an ultra-rugged look. Scott surmised that women must have thought he had "Character." Brodie was about six-foot tall, unusually stocky for that height and, as with all the crew, was in great shape. A while back, the guys had held an informal arm-wrestling contest. The odds had been on either Scott or Brodie winning. Scott had trouble with Brodie. It had been a best two out of three and he had needed all three tries to beat him. Brodie was bloody strong. Scott could still remember his arm completely drained of energy, shaking and shivering when he lifted it in victory. But he wasn't the one who won. Once again, it was the Extraordinary-Ordinary Man, James, who surprised everybody. Scott had faced him in the final and lost in two straight; James's strength was frightening—incredible power that seemed to come from nowhere. James was the most surprised of all. He had said, "You were still tired from the Brodie match." That was certainly true but Scott had a feeling that no matter how strong he had been, James would have been a little stronger.

The first picture of Brodie showed a definitely forty something guy with a fair amount of grey woven into the jet-black hair. The side-burns were almost completely grey. The second picture sprang up on the screen. It looked mostly the same... except there was...something different. The angle of the photo had changed a little but that wasn't it. There was something else. The next picture followed. Wait! Wait! Brodie looked a little younger! What the heck? The subsequent picture solved the puzzle. His hair was getting darker. The rest of the pictures followed. The Brodie transformation was remarkable. He was reverse-aging.

Adam had looped the pictures so that they were repeated over and over again, getting faster and faster each time. As the photo-series sped up, the metamorphosis became more apparent. A huge roar of laughter filled the room. Abruptly, Adam held up his hand for quiet.

He said, "Pascal and I spent many hours trying to work out how he had done this. We wanted the secret elixir too! After all, we all want to stay young. But to our disappointment, we found that its magic is temporary and only works on old geezers like Brodie. But, because we love him and he's going on a long trip where he will certainly require additional quantity, we have, at great personal expense purchased more of the wonderful, magical potion for him. Brodie! Please come up and accept a full case of hair dye!"

Everyone started laughing again, a few started clapping. Someone at the back started chanting "Brodie! Brodie!" The rest of the crowd picked it up, "BRODIE! BRODIE! BRODIE!...."

Brodie whose ego was being severely pummeled wasn't at all pleased, but that bastard Adam had trapped him.

As he dragged his ass up the stairs to the stage, amidst the laughs and chants, with a wiry smile he turned to the audience and gave them the finger, which unfortunately had the unintended effect of causing the laughter and chanting to double in volume. He reached the lectern and roughly took the box from Adam, who by now was almost doubled up with laughter. With one hand Brodie gave him a not so gentle shove and pushed him out of the way of the microphone.

"Well, I'd just like to thank Adam and Pascal for their considerate concern for my well-being. I gotta say that I don't know how that sneaky bastard took those pictures." With a sour look he turned his now overly scrutinized face toward each of his tormentors and then said, "Someday, I hope to repay both of them in equal kind for this wonderful gift." He threw one final glare at Adam and Pascal and with as much dignity as he could muster, walked off the stage. He left behind Adam, who was now sitting on the stage floor, tears rolling down his face, shaking his head while struggling to catch his breath between laughs. The unfortunate Brodie spent the rest of the evening warding off "his friends" who kept trying to run their hands through his hair.

Still smiling, Pascal Beauchamp walked over to say hello to Scott. Pascal was a true electronics genius. He was part of the Venus mission team and had primary responsibility for communications and electronics. Pascal loved to talk about his hometown, Entrecasteaux, in Provence; he spoke with such passion that you'd swear that the village and the surrounding woods, hills and vineyards were the best in all of France.

"So, did you enjoy our little presentation?" asked Pascal.

"Very funny. Poor Brodie's ego has been brutalized. You know he is going to retaliate. I would suggest that you and Adam find some way to kiss and makeup before we get underway. I won't have any fooling around once we are gone. Understand?"

"Of course, no problem, boss."

Scott glanced over at Adam who was still giggling away on the stage, "Talk to Adam tomorrow—not tonight. I don't think he's going to remember much of this evening."

"Sure."

"Pascal! Pascal! How are you this evening? You're looking fine. Very fine, I must say." A cute blonde, Scott had seen her around but couldn't remember her name, was doing her boozy best to snuggle up to Pascal.

Pascal with his usual charm gave her a little French, “Ah! Mademoiselle! Vous êtes très belle ce soir!”

“Oh! Pascal! I just love it when you speak French. It’s such a lovely romantic language and it sounds so wonderful coming from you!”

“Well, let’s find a quiet spot and I’ll give you some lessons.”

With a sideways look and smile to Scott, he wrapped his arm around her shoulders and walked away. Scott noticed several unhappy female heads turn and follow them. Pascal was definitely the looker on the male side of the crew. He had that dark Mediterranean visage but with a little softer, more rounded shape that gave him a delicate yet masculine appearance. The women loved it. It was another case of the eighty-twenty rule—twenty percent of the men attracted eighty percent of the women. Actually, with Pascal it was worse. He attracted ninety-five percent of the women. Some of the guys hung around Pascal just so they could have a chance at his “leftovers”. Scott couldn’t help but feel slightly envious. *Oh well, there’s always trade-offs.* Pascal usually has at least one jealous woman pissed off at him. And sometimes more. *I wouldn’t wish that on my worst enemy.*

He turned to see Peyton Billingsworth, the Lander pilot, talking intently to several people in a corner of the huge hall. Along with Brodie, Peyton had many years of experience and could lay claim to the Mission Leader position that Scott held. But unlike Brodie, Scott didn’t feel any resentment from Peyton. He had accepted his place in the world. Around five-foot-ten with light-blond hair, hard grey-green eyes and a small mouth, he had an intense stare that gave him a stern look which he used to his benefit when necessary but otherwise he was deceptively easygoing. A natural leader, Peyton always let everyone have their say but when the chips were down, he would make the tough decision. Scott knew he could count on Peyton’s advice and help.

Peyton glanced toward Scott, saw him and waved. He turned back to the group he was with, excused himself and then walked over to Scott.

“Hi, Scott. How’s it going?”

“Fine, and you, Peyton?”

"I'm having a great time. Looks like everyone is here." He scanned the room and locked onto several women who were dancing together to the music that has just started up, "Hey! Maybe we should help out the ladies!"

Scott followed Peyton's eyes; there, on the dance floor was Akemi Matsushita, one of two medical specialists assigned to the mission. She was swaying in a smooth rhythm to the music, gracefully moving from one foot to the other, a happy twinkle in her eyes. Akemi was Japanese and at four-foot-eleven the smallest person on the team. She had been born in the USA but moved with her family to Japan when she was seven years old. An expert surgeon, the team would rely on her calm character and those graceful, steady hands in times of emergency. She was dancing with two other team members: Natasha Petrov and Crystin Ackerman.

Natasha, a very tough Russian Cosmonaut and the Orbiter co-pilot, had dark hair and a round Slavic face. At five-foot-one she was the second shortest person on the team. Very cool under pressure, Natasha was a person that you wanted around when there was big trouble. Perhaps self-evident from the way she bounced around the dance floor, she had a happy, confident, gregarious personality.

Crystin Ackerman was the second copilot of the Orbiter. She was a British Astronaut on loan from the European Space Agency. Crystin danced with quick, sharp and precise movements—her whole body etching out a new complex shape with each beat of the music. Blonde with blue eyes, very slim but strong, she was beautiful in a regular sort of way; you could say she had "classic" good looks. When she first arrived at the NASA space program, she had attracted a lot of attention from just about every single guy and a few married ones as well. She kept them all at arm's length. Most people learned very quickly not to jest with Crystin. If you did, you'd spend the next half an hour trying to explain what exactly you meant. She was very professional and absolutely no-nonsense—she told it like it was, no matter how harsh. Even Adam, who had his face ripped off a couple of times when he had gone a little too far, had finally caught on.

Scott looked back at Peyton, leaned down to his ear and yelled over the music, “Yeah! Great idea! Let’s do it!” The music had just changed to a rippin’, hoppin’ tune with a heavy beat. With Scott in the lead, the two men worked their way through the throng of gyrating dancers to the group. Natasha who immediately saw the makings of a dance line slipped behind Scott and put her hands on his waist. Peyton jumped in after her. The other two women quickly linked up behind Peyton.

Someone screamed, “HEY! WAIT FOR ME!”

Scott could feel the back end of the “soul train” take a sudden right turn as a very happy Adam made a poor docking maneuver. Laughter rippled along the line. Scott began searching for the rest of the team. There was Pascal. With a new lady of course. As the line wiggled by, Pascal casually disconnected from his current attraction and reconnected to the back end of the dancing line of Astronauts. *Who’s next?*

Off to the left was Donatella Mancini, the mission’s Linguist, standing in a large group of people. Scott yelled out, “DONATELLA!” Donatella swung around, laid out a huge smile and started snapping her fingers and shaking her black-brown hair back and forth to the music; like magic, the beat rippled its way down her buxom body—at her shoulders, then her chest, waist, hips and legs. As the line passed her, she held up her left hand and high-five’d each person. When she reached the end of the line, with her left hand she deftly grabbed Pascal’s waist and let his momentum pull her around, perfectly in time to the music.

Scott saw his next victim; it was Brodie, in a corner, still sulking from his beating. As the gliding, musical snake wove by, Brodie, with a broad smile, shook off his brooding lethargy and jumped aboard.

Ahead was Henrich. Henrich Sauber was the team Horticulturist, their brainy boy, the German chess champion. A quiet, gentle person, five-foot-nine, blond with blue eyes, he was everything the Nazis with their warped logic had tried to cultivate and yet he was not. Henrich stepped away from the boyfriend he had brought to the party and with a twirl, he glued himself to the back of the line.

Scott pushed his way through the crowd. It parted and there in front of him was Penny, standing as if she was waiting for her limo, one hand on her hip, tapping her foot to the beat, the soft smile still caressing her face.

"What took you so long?" she asked as Scott passed her.

Scott looked back, did a quick count. *Hey! I'm one short! Who is it?* He searched the faces. *Of course! It's James.* James, a little out of his element, had been hovering around the edge of the action like an outer planet in a galaxy. Scott had seen him earlier near the back of the room. He spotted James and turned the laughing, giggling, dancing, tripping and sometimes staggering (thanks to Adam) Astronaut chain in his direction. As they approached, James started trying to dance to the music. It was an awkward, spastic, out of control, waltzing kind of motion. *Okay, he can't dance,* thought Scott.

Brodie yelled out, "Get him to the back of the line before he hurts himself!"

Amidst the yowls, catcalls, laughter and general screaming, Scott brought the ship around and pointed her toward the center of the room. When he reached the middle of the hall he made a sharp turn, came up behind James and locked onto his waist. The whole room was now focused on the rotating circle of Astronauts; everyone cheering, laughing, yelling, clapping. It was then that Scott looked around him and thought,

The Last Hurrah.

Chapter 19
REFLECTION

James strolled home from a day in the park—his last day in a park, his last day on earth for two years. It was early evening. He had lost track of time, and before he knew it, it was dark. A clear, clear night stood above him. As he often did now, he stopped and searched for Venus. In an instant, he was transported to the planet. It was a harsh, harsh world. How could life exist there? These beings must be completely different from humans. Perhaps not even carbon and water based creatures. He thought with a grin, *Will we even recognize them? Maybe we will accidentally step on them. Start an inter-planetary war!*

He wondered how he would feel when he saw them. How would he react? Would they be incredibly ugly or unbelievably beautiful? Will they have hands? Or a mouth? Eyes? One would think that they should have appendages of some kind and a way of seeing. Is it possible for any species to advance without these basic requirements that we humans take for granted? What about the sci-fi specials? The blobs of goo or the invisible beings of pure energy? Perhaps that's what they would be like. Possibly, we won't be able to approach them; they will be caustic to the touch or spit sulfuric acid. Maybe they will be so advanced that we won't have any commonality at all. They could look at us and say, "How can we communicate with an ant?"

He remembered his pet Iguana, Augustus. James had a mirror next to Augustus's enclosure. The other Iguana in the mirror had fascinated

Augustus. Each day he performed the same ritual. He would hiss at it, thrust himself against the glass and wobble his head back and forth. Everyday, his alter ego would do exactly the same. It was quite amusing...at least until James had a thought. *He is never going to understand that this is his reflection. It is beyond his comprehension.* James realized that the Iguana's brain didn't have the capacity to ever understand the concept of a mirror. *Surely, it must be the same for humans. There must be some level of knowledge that is beyond our comprehension. Perhaps the universe is our mirror. We will stare at it forever and never understand. No matter how hard we try.*

The aliens could be beyond our comprehension. Perhaps we will never be able to communicate with them. They could exist on some other dimensional plane. Possibly their existence is multi-dimensional. They could live in six dimensions, ten, a hundred or a thousand. Conceivably we will only see the part of them that exists in our three dimensions. We would never realize that we are only seeing a small part of a complex Alien entity. Perhaps to communicate with them we would have to exist across all their dimensions. It was a frightening, humbling thought. *We humans have such egos. We just naturally think that we have the capacity to understand everything.*

Scott stopped to peer into the Butcher shop window. *No, no I think seafood. Yes...Seafood Fettuccini with a light cream sauce for the main course.*

Tomorrow was his last day on Earth for two years and he was out shopping for fresh vegetables and seafood. His friends told him that he was crazy to waste his time cooking. Why not go out with them to a really good restaurant? They didn't understand...he was saying goodbye....

This was his way of saying goodbye to Mother Earth.

He couldn't wait to get started. As soon as he entered the house, he turned on his favorite classical music and started to prepare the meal. A friend had lent him a house on the California coast, right on the ocean. The view was magnificent.

The seafood selection had been superb. Scott was to fly out of California. As a precaution, the Astronauts were split into three teams of four. Each group would fly on a different shuttle. They would all meet on the Moon over the next three days.

As he looked down at his choice of tiger prawns, sea scallops and salmon, the dulcet sound of violins, violas and cellos filled the air. He loved the sound of the stringed instruments. They were his favorite. The music they produced was sophisticated, yet earthy. When played correctly an orchestra of stringed instruments could bring nature to life—a deer striding through a forest, flowers gently blowing in the wind, the sun rising over an ancient valley, waves lapping against a distant shore. The sounds of those instruments were the sounds of Mother Earth.

Tonight it was an imaginary cloud of big, round, fluffy, golden, bumble bees; all buzzing to a perfect tune. He could see them, a tight packed cluster...like a school of fish...moving in unison...changing shape...swaying precisely in time to the music. He stood stock still, his body forgotten; only sweet sound mattered, each note filling his existence. Wonderful music. *So Wonderful!* It was music perfectly in tune with Nature.

This was his last day...his last day on Earth for two years...perhaps forever....

Suddenly, he turned on his heal and strode to the nearest window and flung it open as far as it would go. He leaned out and sucked in a massive lungful of air. It wasn't enough. Scott moved swiftly from room to room, opening every window in the house. Each time he took the biggest breath he could and held it for as long as he could. Then he closed his eyes and stepped inside his body. He could feel sweet air on his face, in his nose, in his mouth. It roared to his lungs, surged into his body and with each magical pulse of his heart, was swept to every cell in his body.

This was his last day...his last day on Earth for two years...perhaps forever....

He started to prepare the meal. Each touch, each smell, each movement he gathered to his mind, as if it was his first time, as if it was his last time. He moved in slow motion, pausing to touch or smell or taste. He dipped his finger into the cream, gazed at its pure whiteness, pinched it between his thumb and finger, felt its texture, lifted it to his nose, then touched it to his tongue. He let each sense soak through his body.

Then he raised his knife, lowered it, and cut into the salmon. The smell of the sea wafted up to him. He turned and looked out at the waves pounding onto the shore. The last of the sun was catching the frothing tops, turning them a golden white. He wondered, *Why do humans have such a strong reverence for the Ocean? It must be primordial. It must be our genetic memory from the time when we rose, not yet human, from the sea.*

This was his last day...his last day on Earth for two years...perhaps forever....

Someone had asked, *Why cook? Why is it so important? Why do this on your last day?* Food was the primal essence of Mother Earth. Food was about renewal. Food was about a beginning and an end. Every single life, any life—a plant, a tree, an animal, a human—was born as a miracle, grew, then passed on. The next new life took what the previous had given up. By cooking and partaking of this last meal, Scott intended to reaffirm his participation in the cycle of life. He was a warrior in an ancient culture, making a sacrifice to Mother Earth. *I have supped of life and shall promise to do everything in my power to return to you and complete my part.*

This was his last day...his last day on Earth for two years...perhaps forever....

Scott took one last taste of the apple torte. He held it in his mouth, let it melt there, then as slowly as he possibly could...swallowed. He was done.

This was his last day...his last day on Earth for two years...perhaps forever....

It was just past midnight. The moon was almost full; it coated the ocean and beach in a soft, silvery glow. Light and shadow seemed to blend together. The world had become a living, two dimensional, black and white painting.

This was his last day...his last day on Earth for two years...perhaps forever....

A figure entered the painting, standing at the edge of the surf, naked, bathed in the moon's reflected, silver-grey, light. A powerful, masculine figure, etched in moonlight, stretched out his arms and hands to the sky, to the moon, to the stars...to Venus.

This was his last day...his last day on Earth for two years...perhaps forever....

Chapter 20
WARNING

"That little pecker-head is up to something."

A brutal, drunken head swung toward it's wife, "Julie, bring that little pecker-head to me.... NOW!"

The little boy, barely seven, stood shaking and cowering, almost crying, in the filthy bathroom next to the dirty, scum ridden, boozy kitchen where the horror had bellowed its command. He bit his lip as hard as he could in an attempt to stop the tears. Even at that young age, he knew that tears would only make it worse. His face, twitching back the liquid, briefly contorted with sadness—sadder than sad, then took on a new shape as one tooth sunk deep into his lip—it was a pain riddled, snarling, defiant look of a bulldog on death's door. He held that façade only for a moment, then his whole face started to tremble uncontrollably—two short moans, like gunshots, escaped his lips as his slim body began its own spastic shaking. He grasped the dirt-caked rim of the sink to steady himself. He was defenseless. He was fighting fear. He was fighting sadness. He was fighting the desperate sorrow that a child feels when the ones that should love him most have abandoned him, have left him alone in the world. Only for him, it was worse; they were still here, waiting to hurt him, wanting to hurt him, wanting to feed off his pain.

His mother stumbled into the bathroom and said with words slurred by a fifth of crappy gin, "Git out here."

He didn't move. As the tears started to fall, he just said, "No Mama, No Mama."

"You little puke! Git out here." She stuck her fingers in his hair and pulled. His Mama dragged the little body, head first, into the kitchen. He stood there, head down, watching the teardrops falling silently through the air then splattering, with a soft, little, "tick" sound, on the chipped, worn-out, muck-muted tiles.

"What's that in your hand? I saw something in your hand. Bring it here." Those harsh, hating, horrid words from his father, stuck him as hard as any physical blow. He slowly, miserably, extended his hand.

"Not that hand, pecker-head, the one behind your back."

He drew his trembling hand out from behind his back and there, shinning bright, like a beacon in the dark, was....

A single red rose.

A beautiful, ruby red rose. It was perfect in every aspect. It was perfect in every way. It was perhaps the most wonderful thing that had entered this shambles of a house in many, many years.

His mother drew in a sharp breath and softly said, "Oh...it's beautiful."

Kurt, his high-pitched voice wavering with misery, said, "I got it for you Mama. I wanted it to be a surprise, Mama."

His mother's alcohol driven anger melted away and left a residue of sorrow and sadness—tears began to form in her eyes, "Oh thank you, Kurt. It's...it's lovely." She reached out to hug him. Then,

"Don't you touch that pecker-head." The brutal head, which a moment ago had been confused and unable to find an excuse to have "a bit o' fun," turned back to the little boy as a great gory grin swam across his face. He said, "I bet the pecker-head stole it."

"No. No, I didn't!"

"You little pecker-head, you stole it didn't you?"

"No. N...."

A hand snapped out and hit Kurt hard on the side of the head. As Kurt fell to the floor the rose flew from his hand and landed at the feet of his mother. She bent down, picked it up and stared at the beauty of its innocence in this house of horror—she recognized that innocence—it was the same innocence that had once belonged, and should still have belonged...to her son. Then, as the brute was rising from its chair, planning its next blow, she moved in front of Kurt and yelled, "Leave him alone!"

"To hell with you, bitch."

She took a hard right hand directly in the face, flew backward into the kitchen cabinet and slid to the ground. She sat with her back against the cabinet, chin tucked tightly into her chest, unconscious, with ruby red blood dripping onto her dress, settling all around the ruby red rose that she still clutched to her heart.

The brutal head swung back to the little boy and said, "Your turn pecker-head...."

Then the dream changed—as it always did—he was happily, contentedly, swinging a heavy wooden baseball bat; each swing picked up strength and momentum as it smacked an object.... With each smack the feeling of contentment changed slightly, contentment became nasty satisfaction, then gloating glee, his heart rate increased, his excitement grew...until his testosterone and adrenaline combined to become something...*exceptional....*

Smack!

So satisfying, that sound, after all these years. He thought he could do it all day.

Smack!

That sound reminded him of hitting a baseball. Well, perhaps this was a deeper, heavier sound—more of a smacking-thud—still, he'd always loved the sound of a bat making direct, full contact with a fast moving ball. Wait.... What was that? A groan?

Smack!

It felt good to swing those arms—muscles held back for so long were now fulfilling their need.

Smack!

Yes, there it was again. Definitely a groan. He wasn't swinging hard enough. He raised the bat high over his head, held it there until he felt a whoosh of energy and rage shoot into his arms and then drove the bat downward with all his might.

Smack!

Ahh! That felt good! He did it again.

Smack!

And again.

Smack!

Over and over again.

Smack!
    Smack!
    Smack!

Until there was nothing left to smack.

The seventeen-year-old Kurt, gazed down at what had been a brutal head but was now only refuse—mashed in skull, brain parts, blood and gore. Then he looked over at his mother, lying a dozen feet away, at the entrance of the kitchen. He could still recognize her face. On the counter next to him was a single, ruby red rose. He picked it up, walked to her, placed it in her dead hand and then, as gently as he could, moved it over her heart.

The dream changed again—as it always did—he was standing in his kitchen with that long deceased, bitch of a wife of his. Matt, barely a year old, was sleeping in his room on the floor above. Kurt was listening, for the thousandth time that morning, to her complaining about his not doing this, complaining about his not doing that, complaining that he was never around, complaining that he never spent money on the baby or on the family. After she finished that tirade, she moved on to old hurts—past offences that she somehow dragged out of her memory—some of them from years before. Kurt didn't remember most of them and, as a matter of fact, probably wouldn't have remembered them the day after they happened. But somehow she stored them away in her "angry closet" and yarded them out and put them on display every time she had a fight with Kurt. Amazingly, they weren't even the same ones. Each time, she managed to find a specific set of related offenses that had occurred over the years, perhaps modified slightly to suit the current circumstances, and shot them back at Kurt as hate-filled, verbal arrows. So, here he was, for the thousandth time, listening to the same old shit. He could feel the same old tension building, the same old anger growing, the same old muscles needing release....

The dream changed again—but not as it always did—changed to something new, something disturbing...he had his hands around his son's throat, around Matt's throat. Kurt was screaming, "Pecker-head! Pecker-head!"

He awoke from the dream—as he always did—clear headed and fully alert. So alert that it seemed to him, sometimes, that he had been awake all the time, that the events in his dream were real and had just taken place. Once in a while, pretty rarely now, but still, once in a while, he found himself looking for blood on his hands and clothes. Kurt turned to the clock on the bedside table and, yes, sure enough; it was four-thirty in the morning. He didn't know why he had even bothered to check—he'd been waking up from this dream every morning at precisely four-thirty since he was seventeen. Kurt didn't need an alarm clock—his dream was his alarm.

A*larm....*

A feeling whispered to him—an irritation tickled his brain. He couldn't quite get his head wrapped around it but something...*Alarm...Alarm... Warning.... Yes.... Warning....*

With that thought, the last events of the dream popped back into his mind. Not his usual ending. Matt wasn't normally in his dream. Matter of fact, he'd never been in his dream before. *Never in my dream....*

Matt had been different lately—something wasn't right about him. Kurt had been too busy recently to put any thought to it but it now seemed to him that his dream, his subconscious, was warning him.

Kurt thought a little more, ran his mind back over the recent "Matt" events. Yes...there did seem to be something wrong. Matt's moods were not the same as before. He was either very nervous, very confident or just too happy. Not at all like Matt. Kurt worked hard to keep Matt under his complete control. Destroy all self-confidence, destroy all happiness, destroy all that was good about his life. Keep Matt totally dependent on him. Yes, something was not right about Matt and Kurt didn't know what it was. That was bad. To have someone this close to him acting out of character was bad, very bad.

He picked up the phone and dialed a number. An extremely groggy voice answered, "Hello?" then became angry, "Who is this?"

"Kurt."

The tone of the voice changed immediately, it became almost obsequious, "Oh.... Yah.... Sorry. What's up?"

"I need you to check-up on someone...I want you to watch that son of mine," he paused for a moment and then said,

"That little pecker-head is up to something."

Chapter 21
LIFT-OFF

Scott sat in the Commander's seat on the Renaissance Orbiter, running through last minute checks with Moon Mission Control. The pre-lift-off procedures were progressing as planned. From one of his half-dozen monitors he could see the status levels change as the rest of the team ran through their checklists. He scanned the last monitor on his left. *Everything going fine on the Lander*, he thought. The Lander would lift-off six hours after the Orbiter and then the two ships would rendezvous at the Moon orbiting space station where there was already a contingent of Astronauts waiting to assist with the final construction. He mentally ran through the order of work:

1. Separate the Orbiter at the second air-lock section.
2. Install the crew quarters.
3. Dock the Lander with the Orbiter.
4. Replace the fuel tanks.
5. Leave moon orbit—On to Venus!

The first monitor to his right displayed the vital stats of all eleven of his crew, five of whom were on the Lander. He had access to heart rate, blood pressure, breathing rate and most interesting of all, several key brain wave measures that gave him an indication of the individual's mental stability. The brain wave measures were able to predict trouble or problems much sooner than the more primitive heart rate and blood pressure indicators. It was a very new technology that had been developed over the last two years and it needed to be fine-tuned to each individual. The Astronauts weren't very happy about it. It was too personal; most of them felt it was some kind of weird invasion of privacy and there were claims that it didn't work, but so far, Scott hadn't seen anything to confirm that supposition. Still he was going to be cautious. He wouldn't be hauling out the tranquilizers at the first sign of trouble.

Brodie, who was piloting the Orbiter, sat beside Scott. During any takeoff or docking procedures, Brodie was in charge. This was the only time that Scott followed orders from someone else. But it didn't bother him at all. Brodie was an incredible Astronaut who had amazing will power when he needed it—his legs could be on fire and he would still maintain his concentration on the tasks at hand. Behind Scott and Brodie sat the only other Astronauts on the primary control deck—the two Orbiter co-pilots, Natasha and Crystin.

Below them, on the next deck were Henrich (Horticulturist), Akemi (Surgeon), Pascal (Electronics and Communications). They were not involved in the takeoff or docking activities. As Brodie had described it, they were, 'As useless as tits on a bull.'

The rest of the team were on the Lander. Although the Moon's gravity was about a sixth of the gravity on Venus, the takeoff here would be a good dress rehearsal for the Venus lift-off. Available space on the Lander was much more cramped than on the Orbiter. Peyton (Pilot), Adam (Copilot), James (Archeologist), Donatella (Linguist) and Penny (Biologist), were all jammed onto one deck.

Adam said, "Christ! We're so close I can smell that stinky onion breath of Peyton's."

Crystin, who was listening on the com system from the Orbiter replied, "Adam. Are you suited-up?"

"Yes?"

"Well there must be something wrong with your air supply. Each suit has an independent delivery system."

"Crystin."

"Yes?"

"It was a god-damned joke."

"Oh? Oh yes, I see. Not very funny in my opinion."

Scott could feel some of the crew's tension slipping away as the com filled with laughter. He let the chuckles continue for a moment and then said, "Okay everybody, let's re-focus. No further non-mission specific comments on the com."

Twenty minutes later the Orbiter was in final countdown. Exactly sixty seconds passed...the astronauts were slammed into their seats as the platform rockets kicked in. A few milliseconds later, the Orbiter's engines ramped up. Then, almost as quickly as it had begun, it was over. They were drifting up to their final Moon orbit. They were on their way!

Chapter 22

TO VENUS

"Coming up on the Moon Orbit Station," Brodie reported, "Deceleration complete."

The Moon Orbit Station was a large, complex jumble of objects floating seemingly impossibly above the Moon. The largest object was the space station itself—a long motionless tube with various docking stations, mechanical arms and solar cell fins protruding from its sides. There were two space shuttles docked at the facility. The crew quarters, with its well-known, "Ferris wheel," which rotated independently from the rest of the complex, was located at one end of the tube. Hovering nearby was another wheel. This was the crew quarters for the Renaissance; it was ready for installation. Beside the wheel, perhaps a few hundred yards away, were the replacement fuel tanks. Not far from the fuel tanks were ten Astronauts with rocket packs, tethered to a special work-platform.

Brodie brought the ship alongside the work-platform and watched as the Astronauts attached it to a point on the ship near the crew quarters section joint. The Astronauts then separated the Renaissance at the joint and the long mechanical arms of the space station moved the crew quarters into place. Finally, the three sections—front ship segment, crew quarters, rear ship segment—were linked together. The entire process took less than nine hours. After that, it was a matter of checking for any problems – air leaks, electrical connections, ventilation systems, and communications. Scott's crew completed the internal checks. It all went very well; the checks, which included testing and verification of all ship functions, took just less than a full twenty-four hour day. During that time, the Lander had docked and the Lander crew assisted with the effort. After all this work was completed, the new rocket fuel tanks were attached and the crew ran through another five hours of final system checks.

Two incredibly quick, uneventful days zipped by. A final parting ceremony, required entirely for the benefit of the media, had been planned. Scott ran through a script that had been carefully written by NASA's Public Relations group. He remembered with amusement all the complaining he had heard from the PR gang as Jack had made them rewrite it over and over again. Just when they thought they were finally done, after the thousandth revision, Jack modified the script one more time and sent it back for updating. The screeching, caterwauling and swearing had been hilarious.

Scott had reached the grand finale of the ceremony and with a slight touch of a virtual button on his control screen, the engines engaged. A precisely calculated burst of energy, just enough to break orbit, shot through the ship causing the massive Space Craft to rattle and rumble as it tore away the Moon's gravitational bonds. Scott let the sound and vibration subside and then said,

"The greatest adventure in human history has begun. We go to meet a new race of beings. We go to prove that we are not alone in the Universe. We carry with us the wonder, the hopes, the dreams and the salutations of twelve billion human souls. We will not fail, we cannot fail, when so many stand beside us."

"Okay everybody, let's run through the hibernation system one last time," said Akemi Matsushita.

The entire crew were standing in the living quarters. Akemi was next to one of the beds. Made of a smooth, gleaming white plastic, they were customized for each individual and were much more comfortable than they looked; the mattress was made of special compartmentalized foam that could be adjusted to apply different air pressure at different times and thus prevent bedsores and back problems. At the head end dangled an octopus of cables with a strange looking connector attached to each one. About halfway down, a thin clear hose with a nasty looking needle protruded from the side of the bed. Once occupied, a clear plastic lid covered the entire sleep structure and to minimize air recycling in the crew quarters, oxygen was then delivered separately to each bed.

They had left moon orbit and were accelerating to cruising speed. In one year, they would arrive at Venus. The length of the trip had been the biggest challenge for NASA. Providing enough food, water and air for a two year round trip was definitely difficult, but those necessities did not pose the greatest problem. The greatest challenge was best phrased by a question, "How do you get twelve Astronauts to Venus and back without them losing their minds during the journey?" Although it sounded silly, the psychological welfare of the crew was a serious concern. There would be very little to do during the trip. Boredom, loneliness and relationship issues born of many months together in a small space all would combine to create a culture of emotional confusion that would germinate disagreements, dissent, dissolution, despair. The hibernation system was the answer to that dilemma.

Hibernation, a curious state of existence and non-existence, had been studied closely over the last twenty years. During hibernation, heart rate and breathing become very slow, the body temperature drops. To the untrained eye, the subject could be mistaken for dead. For humans, the ability to achieve hibernation was not that difficult; the technique had been developed ten years previous and was one hundred percent reliable. The difficulty was preventing muscle atrophy.

In order for the human muscle system to maintain its strength, each muscle has to be exercised. That occurs, albeit at different levels, during the waking state. For human beings the adage, "use it or lose it," is very true when it comes to muscle. Scientists couldn't understand how the animal world did it. After years of study of the bear, the largest mammal capable of hibernation, it was discovered that they maintained their strength by periodically contracting their muscles in a tremor-like, shaking fashion. Finally, after much experimentation, a drug was discovered that when introduced intravenously would cause a level of shivering in the muscles which was sufficient to maintain strength in humans. During hibernation, the Astronauts would be attached to an intravenous drip that would provide the drug; hence the hose with the nasty needle. The drip rate was fine-tuned for each person.

Akemi said, "I've looked over your individual meditation stats; they all look fine. I'm glad to see that everyone has kept to their practice schedule."

To reach the hibernation state, the Astronauts were first trained to meditate. Meditation achieved the level of alpha brain waves required to prepare the subject for the next stage in the hibernation cycle. Strong alpha rhythms are a sign of deep relaxation, so deep in fact that the most primitive parts of the brain, responsible for the body's basic survival, the Hypothalamus and Autonomic Nervous system, are affected. Once the subject, or in this case, the Astronaut, had achieved the correct level of alpha rhythms, a low level electrical pulse was introduced to the brain via conductors surgically implanted in the skull. The pulse maintained the alpha rhythm and in fact drove the alpha waves to an even lower level which then would force the Hypothalamus and Autonomic Nervous system into a state of severe relaxation; causing the body to go into hibernation.

However, even with the assistance of external electrical stimulation, the hibernation state is not perpetual. Each person, depending on his or her own individual makeup or capabilities will rise from hibernation to the normal waking state within one to three months. NASA had studied the Astronauts, via intrusive and non-intrusive tests, to determine their H-Time Constant. The H-Time Constant was the length of time, plus or minus a few days, that they would remain in hibernation. In order to ensure that at least two Astronauts were awake and on-duty at all times during the full extent of the trip, Scott had to review the hibernation time constants of each of them and then develop a schedule that would maintain the on-duty requirement. For the most part, he had a working schedule; however, a couple of times during the trip, an astronaut would have to be artificially awakened to meet the two-person rule. In most cases, the Astronauts would rise from their hibernation state for two to three weeks to perform their shift and then would return to hibernation.

"To draw someone out of hibernation, power off the electrical pulse—the switch is located on the right side of the bed...here." Akemi pointed to a panel next to James. "Then disconnect the electrodes."

"Now this is the important part." Akemi quickly swung her eyes around the room—verifying that everyone was paying attention. "You must swap out the intravenous feed, which currently holds the muscle stimulator mixture, with a special recovery solution. The solution will pull the subject out of hibernation much quicker. For most of you, it will take around an hour to achieve the waking state. You will feel awful for a few hours—very lethargic—and a kind of weird tiredness, sort of like being hung over but without the headaches and...in Adam's case, the puking." She looked over at Adam with a smile on her face, "Have you recovered from the party yet, Adam?"

"Oh very funny! I sacrificed myself for the sake of the team. You'd have all been bored to death if it wasn't for me," he replied. Brodie, who was still feeling a little prickly after the hair-dye affair, gave Adam a hard slap on the back and said,

"I'm soooo sorry for yoooooou!"

Akemi continued, "If you don't install the recovery solution, you will be waiting for days for your hibernating partner to come back to life. So make sure you remember to do it."

With that, Akemi ran through the hibernation roster. Everyone was "heading in" except for Donatella, Heinrich and Scott. Heinrich would observe the Environmental Vegetation for another two weeks and then go into hibernation. Donatella and Scott would spend a month in the first rotation, then others would start popping out of hibernation to take their turn.

An hour later, Scott was back on the control deck. He selected one of the rear outboard cameras, shifted to maximum zoom, then tweaked it ever so slightly to center the view. Already, a day after breaking orbit, the Earth and Moon were shrinking. A year from now he would be looking at a very different scene. He knew that as the Astronauts hurtled through a vast, cold, uncaring universe, cocooned in a tiny bubble of life, they were, in a way never before experienced by humans, truly, utterly alone.

Nothing could help them now.

Chapter 23
CONFIRMATION

We must be crazy trying this! Matt thought as he and Shannon drove to the office. He was scared and for good reason.

After months of discussing, arguing and sometimes fighting, Shannon had finally talked Matt into doing something about Kurt.

At first, Shannon had not believed what Matt was saying. She didn't think Kurt would be able to influence anyone to do something as horrendous as Matt imagined. But there had been a growing feeling amongst a small group of people that the Alien quest wasn't such a good idea. Perhaps these Aliens were dangerous. *We shouldn't go!* The small group was getting bigger, bigger by the day. Fear was spreading, poking its way through communities, towns, cities and countries. It was a small cancer. But cancer can sit quiet, dormant, the victim unaware, and then explode, like a sprinter blowing off the line, through the entire body in an instant. Was it possible that Kurt had found someone like that? Someone who early on had a seed of fear; a seed of fear that Kurt could exploit, could foster, could grow, till it seemed that they had to do the right thing? They had to do what the gutless government wouldn't. They had to help Kurt protect the Planet. Now it appeared to Shannon that it was possible.

At first, they thought that they would reveal what they knew to NASA, but after some reflection Matt realized that his dad, if he thought he was going to be caught, would detonate the fail-safe; thereby destroying the Renaissance and scattering the evidence all over the solar system. After years of watching Kurt in action, Matt was sure that he would know, he would be warned, before NASA could act.

Matt and Shannon had studied the schematics and guessed that Kurt had added a simple command to the engine control software that would cause the liquid fuel mix to be changed. It was a mix that would cause an uncontrolled engine explosion large enough to spread to the fuel tanks themselves. Once that happened it was finito; at least two thirds of the ship would be blown apart. Although Matt was almost sure of their theory, it was still a guess. They had to confirm it and that's why they were driving to the office at one o'clock in the morning.

"Look, maybe tonight is not the best night. Let's wait a couple of days—think it out some more."

"Matt, you've said that for the last two weeks. You're so god-damned predictable. Now's the time. You know it and I know it. Sunday's the quietest night of the week. Nobody is going to be there. And you've got your dad's extra pass-card. We can walk right in."

"Yeah. Okay...that's true. But after that, I still have to get the pass-card back into his car." Another shiver shot through his body. A while back Matt had discovered that his old man kept a second pass-card under the carpet in the trunk right next to where he usually stored his brief case. With much trepidation and with endless prodding from Shannon, Matt had called the Mercedes dealer, told them his dad needed a second key. He had all the details they needed including the special code. Two days later Matt had a key to the car. He had used it to "borrow" the spare office security card.

"All we have to do is dodge the building security. You say they're a bunch of no-minds, so that shouldn't be a problem, right?" questioned Shannon.

"Well.... Ya.... Ummm...."

"Come on MATT!"

"Yes. You're right. I'm.... I'm jus.... I'm scared."

"I know. It's okay to be scared. Don't worry. It's going to be easy. We go into your dad's office; you log into the Renaissance communications link and see if you can find this command. We have all the login details—it will take two seconds. Either it's there or it's not. If it's not then we can go home, have sex and forget about the whole thing. What do you think?" When Matt didn't respond, she looked over at him with a sensual smile and said, "I tell you what, whether or not it's there, we'll go home and have sex. How's that for a deal?" She ran her hand over his crotch for a little further emphasis.

Matt didn't need any more encouragement but he did give it one more try, "How about we skip the first part and just go home and have sex?" he asked with a wry smile.

She reached up and held his hand, "It's going to be okay."

Shannon and Matt were quietly scurrying down the hallway toward Kurt's office. So far so good. They had to wait across the street in the shadows until the security guard started on his walk; Matt had timed the guard's route last week; it took twenty minutes for the guard to reach his dad's floor. Plenty of time for them to get in and out. At least that was what he thought last week when he was safe and sound at home. Now it didn't seem so long. *What if he changes his route? Oh man!* When the guard left his station, they raced across the street into the building and into the express elevator.

They silently approached the office. Matt could see a glow beneath the door. There was a light on in the office! Matt turned to Shannon, "Let's get out of here," he whispered. He was already two strides down the hall when Shannon yarded on his arm.

"No! No! He's probably forgotten to turn the light off."

"He never forgets to turn lights off. The cheap bastard wouldn't want to spend a couple of extra pennies on electricity."

"Go knock on the door. If he answers, just say that you noticed that light was on and make up a story about coming in to pick something up."

"Ummm, umm...."

"Come on! Christ!"

"Yeah.... Okay, but you gotta hide. I don't want him seeing you."

"I'll be over there behind that cubicle."

Matt walked, weak kneed, slowly over to the office door. He looked back to see Shannon—fingers, hair and eyes, peering at him from over the cubicle wall. If it weren't for the fact that he stopped breathing about three minutes ago, he would have laughed.

He knocked quietly on the door. There was no answer. Then he heard some kind of hissing sound from Shannon's direction. He turned his head and saw her violently making a knocking motion with her fist. He tried again, harder this time. No answer. He was getting braver. He knocked firmly. No answer. He pounded on the door for good measure. No answer. He turned to signal Shannon to come over.

There was a face six inches in front of him!

Startled, he let out a yell, which, at the last instant, was choked back to a squeak; simultaneously his electrically charged legs drove him backward with a heavy thunk, into the office door. Shannon's face went in the other direction, with a squeak of her own, tripping over a metal garbage basket at Gina's desk with a resounding clang that seemed to shudder through the entire building. Desperate to steady herself, Shannon reached back and pushed a bunch of papers off Gina's desk. Now there was paper and garbage everywhere on the floor.

"CRAP! CRAP!" Matt screamed-whispered at her as he clutched at his heart. Shannon looked like someone had knocked all the air out of her. They both peered down the hall. It was still quiet. Shannon, her face a blend of fear and determination, turned back to Matt and waved her arm vigorously toward the office. She bent down and started trying to sort out the papers, some for the desk, some for the garbage can.

Matt reached into his pocket, pulled out the access card and waved it at the card-reader. With a click, the door popped open. As Matt hustled over to the desk he thought, *Well I'll be! The cheap bugger did leave a light on. That will put him in a nasty mood in the morning.* He reached over and shut the desk light off—thought better of it and turned it back on again.

He knew exactly which computer terminal to use. His dad had proudly shown him several times the data and voice information he was collecting from the mission. He looked at his watch, *we are running out of time.* He jumped into the chair and dove at the keyboard. In an instant, he was logged-in and surfing his way to the hidden fail-safe command. Out of the corner of his eye, he saw Shannon enter the room. This time she made sure that Matt saw her before she approached the desk. He looked for the command. *Hey! It's not here! Fantastic! I must have been smoking something to think he'd do anything that awful.* He was just about to log-out when he noticed something. He was in the wrong directory. A couple more key strokes and he was there...and so was it. He started to feel sick. With shaking hands, he tapped out a few more commands.

"We're almost out of time. Let's go." said Shannon, urgent-quiet, as she shook his shoulder.

"Just a sec, just a sec.... I want to see something." *How is this software code written?* Shaky or not, his fingers flew over the keyboard. Each time he finished a command he had to wait a few extra seconds. Already the Renaissance was so far away that the time delay was significant. The wait was agony.

"Come on! Come on! We only have four minutes left!" Shannon's voice was starting to rise from a whisper, "We need at least two minutes to make it to the stairs. Come on! What's taking so long?"

"Just wait. I want to see how this works...."

"Jeeze! Forget how it...." A sound! Soft, yet clear! From just down the hallway!

Shannon ran tiptoe to the door, squeezed it open just the tiniest of a crack. With a look of panic, she turned and simultaneously closed the door. The door closed with a solid, resounding, click-thunk. Not loud but perhaps LOUD ENOUGH! Shannon stood frozen—head turned back toward the door, one arm out in front of her, opposite leg thrust forward, near leg delicately trailing on tip-toe. There was another sound, closer now. Shannon bounded gazelle-like over to the desk.

Her face showed scream but her mouth produced a barely intelligible hiss, "Itttssss tooo late! Heeessss comminng!"

Both heads darted around the room. No place to hide!

A click, then the door started to open.

In desperation Shannon shoved Matt under the huge desk and dove after him. Surely, the security guard would just take a look and leave.

No sound. Nothing. Just their half gasping, painful breaths. *He can't possibly hear that from the other side of the room, can he??* As if by telepathy, on exact cue, they both sucked in air and held it. Then, a sound. A carpeted footstep, then another and another. He was coming toward the desk. Shannon pressed up against Matt, pushing him as far as she could under the desk. She looked back and down. Was she completely under it? Suddenly, next to her foot, another foot appeared. It was attached to a security-striped pant leg. Time stretched from a second to a moment to an eternity. Matt could hear his heart pounding. He couldn't hold his breath much longer. His leg was beginning to cramp. His whole body, crammed into the desk, was in agony. Then came a ripple sound as a jacket was moved and reshaped. Then a click and miraculous, comforting darkness descended on the room. Only small slivers of light from the hall poked their way through the cracks in the desk. Finally came the most wonderful sound Matt had ever heard; those same carpeted footsteps that had stopped all time were receding. The world moved forward once again. As the door closed, the air under the desk was sucked into two grateful lungs, then was poured back out. Sound issued from the desk; it was a confused blacksmiths bellows working erratically in and out. Matt felt something wet on his face and body; it was sweat. He was soaked. Shannon crawled out from under the desk. A weak, wobbly Matt followed. Without a word, she quietly walked back to the door; planted her ear against it and froze again—hand up in the air. Abruptly the hand started motioning to Matt to come forward. He slid up beside her and waited. The door opened with its horrible, grating click. Matt cringed as Shannon took a quick peek out the narrow opening.

"He's gone." She whispered as she turned back to Matt.

Then, with ever-increasing volume, "Holy Crap! What a rush!" A quiet, almost uncontrolled, giggle issued from her lips.

Matt stuck his hand over her mouth. "Shut up! Christ! He might just be around the corner!"

Shannon couldn't stop, it was too late, it was coming out—like a barf, there was no stopping it. Matt watched, at first in horror, as her hysterical laughter slipped past his fingers, squirted into the room and perhaps wriggled down the hallway; he watched as the tears started to run, then pour down her face onto the hand that was still hopelessly attempting to halt the muted, melodic, bubbling resonance of happy relief. Matt couldn't take it any longer. Laughter exploded out of his face. They fell to the floor hugging each other—the last of their pent-up, fear-riddled energy escaping with every gurgle of laughter.

They had one more job to do and then it was off to bed...*no, not bed exactly!* Matt thought with satisfaction as they drove back to his dad's house. He could feel a warm, tingling sensation starting up...down below. He looked over at the beautiful, magnificent, incredible...and brave! Shannon. What a Woman! They were holding hands and feeling very smug—still basking in the memory of the adventure. Matt's confidence was at an all time high. They had been patting themselves on the back all the way to Kurt's house. One more small, easy job to do! Matt just had to return his dad's spare security card to the trunk of the car; he'd drive past the house, park around the corner, scoot back through the side gate and wham, bam, thank you ma'am, he'd be done!

As they drove past the house, Matt casually took a look at the car parked in the driveway.

What car??? *Oh my god! Where's the car?* He slammed on the brakes.

"Matt! What the hell are you doing?"

Matt didn't answer, he had swiveled his head backward to an almost impossible degree, looking, praying, for a car that wasn't there.

"Matt! Matt! Wh...."

"The car is GONE! GONE!"

"Oh no! He's left the house!" shouted Shannon.

"YEAH! DAMN!" He banged his hands on the steering wheel, once, twice, thre...*wait a minute*! "Maybe he's parked it in the garage."

"Matt! You took the card out of the car after midnight! Do you think your dad woke up in the middle of the night and said, 'Gee, I think I should park the car in the garage!' He's left! He's gone somewhere!"

"Yeah." With a sinking, sickening sensation Matt said, voice almost at a whisper, "There's only one place he'd go this early on a Monday morning."

Kurt pulled up to the empty office parking lot. He had some European business to take care of then it was off to an early Monday morning meeting. He parked, got out and walked the twenty steps to the building door. He reached into his jacket for the security card. Not in that pocket. What about the right hand pocket? No. Not there. *I forgot the bloody thing again!* He turned, walked back to the car and popped the trunk; Kurt leaned forward, started to reach for the carpet and felt something poke him in the chest. He straightened, his hand reached into his inside breast pocket. *There it is!* In one smooth motion, he shut the trunk, turned and strode back to the building.

Chapter 24

DESCENT

Brodie checked the vehicle velocity. "Approach velocity within normal constraints," he stated in a monotone.

Brodie looked over at Scott, smiled and then with a much more animated voice said, "This is going to be easier than parallel parking on a busy street in New York."

"Just about anything is easier than parallel parking in New York," Scott smiled back.

"Yeah. That's true. I'd forgotten. Amazing what a year in hibernation will do to the memory. That last girlfriend of mine seems like a bad dream now."

"Humm, my memory isn't as bad. I remember you saying that she was a nightmare, not a bad dream."

"That's for sure," Brodie replied somewhat absentmindedly as his fingers tapped a keyboard—he was adjusting some of the orbit parameters. Then as Scott's comments finally sank in, "Hey! Stop that! I don't want any more of that kind of remembering. I'm already getting the shivers."

The smile was replaced by a thoughtful look, then a small smile flipped back on, "Ha-ha! Well I guess that proves it."

"Proves what?"

"A woman can reach out and smother you even when you are millions of miles away." Brodie turned back to the console with a large grin on his face.

"Brodie, I've got a feeling she's very glad you're millions of miles away."

"Are you saying I'm hard to live with?"

"I don't know yet. We've been in hibernation." Scott looked at the flat panel in front of him. It showed a fuzzy, yellow-orange, white ball. *Not much to look at even when you're a lot closer.* He hit the wireless com; everyone wore cordless headsets. "Akemi. Akemi."

"Yes Boss?"

"How's our de-hibernation coming?"

"So far, so good. They all should be moaning and groaning in a couple of hours."

"Okay, excellent. Call me when it's done. I want to have a meeting in the crew quarters as soon as possible."

"Right. Will do."

Three hours later Scott was standing in a room full of groggy Astronauts. "Right, gang. We're here. The ship is just pulling into orbit around Venus. I hope you all slept well."

"I don't think you could call that rotten hibernation sleeping," Peyton growled as he wearily rubbed his face, "It's more like being a frozen meat tray for a year."

"I know that feeling," Scott grinned ruefully as he continued, "I've checked in with Mission Control. There's been no progress with the signal from Venus; it's still transmitting but they haven't been able to decode it."

All eleven astronauts forgot their hibernation related ills and held their breath.

"So, I've received the okay to proceed with landing preparations."

A series of cheers broke out. Akemi high-five'd Penny, Donatella started a little jig, a grinning Brodie took the opportunity to give Adam a somewhat hard punch to the shoulder, but Adam was too busy hooting to notice.

"We will take our time. I want everybody to be fully de-hibernated before I ask for final landing clearance; therefore, the descent is scheduled for one week from today. Any questions?"

"Yes, is the Lander roster still the same?" asked Donatella.

"It is. Peyton will be the pilot, Adam will co-pilot. The specialists are James, you and Penny. I'll be the commander. While I'm away, Brodie is in charge."

Scott looked around the room and asked, "Anything else?" There was no answer, "Okay then, let's start prepping."

As the week flew on, Scott could feel the excitement and strain of the long anticipated descent, at first simmering, then bubbling and finally boiling through the ship. It was an entity to itself, a worrisome thirteenth crew member.

"Hey, Brodie! The grey's coming back. Where's the Hair dye?" Adam smirked.

"Will you bugger-off with the hair jokes! I'm shittin' tired of it!"

"Shittin'? Shittin'? I don't think Shittin' is a word. Use proper English when you're cursing me."

Brodie grabbed Adam by the shirt collar under the chin and pulled him to within an inch of his face and shouted, "I'm...not...kidding... anymore, Asshole!" He reached up, put his great paw on Adam's face, and shoved. On earth the shove would have had caused his head to bend backward a bit, maybe he would have lost his balance but that would have been it; in the Orbiter, weightless, the effect was dramatic. Adam started spinning, backwards—on an unplanned trip to the other side of the Orbiter. He quickly threw his arms and legs out to slow the rotation but still hit the other side with enough force to cause a bruise or two.

"You jerk!" Adam yelled back, then turned and pushed off—head first toward Brodie. Brodie drew back a fist; Adam's head was about to become an out of control asteroid when Scott came through the bulkhead doors, "Hey! Hey! What the hell's going on?"

Brodie lowered his fist, pushed himself out of the way and let Adam bang, arms and head, into the oxygen control panel.

It was Scott's turn to get mad. He dropped his voice and started on Brodie first.

"Have you completely lost your mind? That control panel is critical to our mission to Venus. That's how we load the Lander air tanks. If Adam breaks anything, the trip could be delayed. Besides that, you are going to be in charge up here. If you're going to be in charge, you ***have*** to be in control. Always. Damn it. Maybe I should assign someone else. Should I???"

Brodie responded with an attack of his own, "Why don't you assign me to the Lander team? You shouldn't be going down. It should be me."

"We've had this conversation before. I'm going because quick decisions will have to be made when we meet the Aliens. I need to be there, in their presence, to see what they are like, to see how they react, to see how we react. I can't do that from up here. So DROP IT!" Scott replied.

"I don't want to hear about this again. Understood? Now, let me ask you again, do I need to assign someone else as Orbiter Commander?"

"No, no of course not," Brodie's voice was quietly embarrassed, "You're right. I have more self-control than that. I don't know what I was thinking. I'm sorry—it won't happen again."

Adam had suddenly busied himself with the Oxygen panel that he'd just bounced into, his face a dopey imitation of concentration. Scott rounded on him, "Now, YOU!" he stabbed a finger at him for emphasis, "You are an Astronaut on the most important mission in the history of human space exploration. I expect you to behave like it. No more wise cracks. No more jokes. You will leave everyone alone. Especially Crystin. Don't give me that 'what to you mean?' look. I know you're plotting. I've seen the way you've been watching her; she's getting to you and you've decided to have some fun at her expense. At least you thought you would. Any further trouble from you and you're not going down. We'll just do without a Geologist. I'll then have to explain to mission control why we wasted precious space, air, water and food on you."

"Yes, Boss. Very sorry. Don't worry I'll behave," replied Adam sheepishly.

Scott turned back to Brodie, "Now, how have you made out with the Oxygen transfer to the Lander?" he queried.

"Well, we had some trouble with the mixture. I was just going over it with Adam when we had our.... Ummm...little disagreement," Brodie answered with a deadpan glance over to Adam.

"When will you be finished?"

"A couple of hours."

"Fine. When you're done, call me. I'll go through a final check with you. I don't want to be running out of air when we are down there," Scott paused and stared at each of them. It was a burning, intent, unblinking gaze that could have sizzled their skin at fifty paces. Then he said, in a soft but absolutely clear voice, each word carefully spaced in time, "There is no room for mistakes. A mistake means six people are going to die. Got it?"

"Got it."

James had just taken his seat in the Lander when he looked over at Penny beside him. She was settling in, strapping herself down. They weren't wearing suits. There was no point. If there were a hull breach, they would fry in an instant, no matter what suit they wore. The only suits that could withstand the temperature and pressure of Venus were stored away—there was no room for them here. Penny looked over at James.

"Well, here we go. Are you ready?" Her face couldn't manage the smile that she had tried to put into her voice.

"I'm fine. I'll be okay. You?"

"Yes, I'm ready."

"Good." The tension was worse for the specialists. They didn't have anything to do; there was nothing to distract them on the descent.

Scott, Adam and Peyton were running through final countdown checklists and verifying status with Brodie on the com.

James swiveled to look at Donatella, her normally bubbly self seemed to be caked in concrete.

"Clear for lock-down?" asked Natasha from just outside the Lander hatch.

"Clear," was the reply from Scott.

All three specialists watched, mesmerized, as the hatch began its silent hydraulic closure. Fear and hope were about to be trapped in this oversized diving bell. The mind couldn't help but think back to other catastrophic failures in the space program. How had those poor bastards felt as doom waved hello?

A deep, rich, thunk, almost melodic, reverberated through the ship as the heavy, heavy door shut tight. Eyes roved up, down and around as each of them applied their own unique, personal way of coping with fear.

"I wonder what they will be like?" Donatella asked.

There was a pause. Then from James, "I assume you are referring to the Aliens.... Actually, now that I think of it, I guess we are the Aliens now. We are going to be setting foot on their world, walking on their land." James continued on, not waiting for a reply from Donatella. "I've thought a lot about it. Of course there is no way to know for sure, but to survive the temperature and pressure of Venus they would have to be very stran...well, very different from us."

"Yes.... Yes. They couldn't have blood...as a matter of fact they couldn't be water based at all. They would boil!" Penny's voice grew animated as she shed her fears. "As a biologist, this is an incredible opportunity—to see and study a race that is completely different from us. I hope there will be some way to get samples of skin, organs and tissue."

"I imagine they will want the same from us," James replied thoughtfully.

"Oh! Yes.... I hadn't considered that." A look of concern flashed over Penny's face.

The conversation died as quickly as it had started.

"Okay everybody, we are starting final count down. Sixty seconds from separation." Scott had a quick look around the control room, verifying that they were all locked in their seats.

Sixty seconds ticked away. Ten, nine, eight, seven.... *This won't be bad. Just a bit of a kick then we are on our wa....* A short, sharp sound, like balloons popping, echoed in the Lander. The jolt wasn't bad at all.

Several minutes passed, then came a whoosh and a stronger push. The engines had begun to decelerate the Lander. The Lander would now lose its orbit lock and start to fall toward Venus. There was little for anyone to do; the release and deceleration was precisely timed to drop the Lander within a mile of the target—the location of the radio transmissions. Once they reached the atmosphere, a parachute would eject and the Lander descent would slow. Peyton would use the rockets to fine-tune the Lander's placement and to ensure that the landing velocity was within tolerance.

All they could do was wait.

A slight, almost imperceptible shudder ran through the Lander. Then stillness. Another shudder. A little stronger? Stillness...stillness...quiet... just strained breathing...a shudder, strong enough to rattle a few items... stillness...then a hard BANG! Suddenly, the shudder had become a shaking, rattling, banging pandemonium. Heart rates jumped into the two hundreds. They had entered the Venus atmosphere.

The bouncing and jouncing increased, then died off, then increased, varying unpredictably as they dropped through different layers of the atmosphere. Shrieking, screaming, moaning sounds joined the chorus of rattles, bangs and thunks as the shipped ripped open the atmosphere. It was bad, it was scary, but it was tolerable.

Scott, Peyton and Adam were watching the monitors intently. Checking air pressure, temperature and most importantly, the velocity vector. They had to land within a few miles of the site or the entire mission would be wasted.

Peyton, voice rattling over the mayhem of sound, warned, "Chute deployment in one minute."

They braced for the impact. "Three, Two, One...." Wham! They were driven into their seats, their bodies briefly compressed into blobs of Jell-O, then reformed, human again, as the Lander slowed.

Two minutes passed,

Then doom spoke.

Simple, little, words. "Something's wrong."

"Be a bit more specific, Adam." Scott's voice was calm and cool as if he were lying on a beach getting a good tan.

"We've slowed but not enough!"

"Peyton, check the chute monitor," Scott said.

"It looks fine, it's fully deployed, nothing wron.... Wait! Wait! I see a tear! Yes! Yes! A rip.... It's getting bigger! The chute is disintegrating!"

"Our velocity is increasing!" cried Adam.

Scott looked at a display to his right. "Yes, we are already off course. Wait...wait...."

Ages of time seemed to slip by...then Scott, still composed, "It's getting worse. Peyton, you're going to have to engage the engines. Use the engines to slow the Lander and bring it back on course."

"But we need the fuel to get us back! Back to the Orbiter!"

Scott looked over at Peyton, his face a mask of calm, "One problem at a time. First let's land intact."

The ship was churning its way to the Venus surface, every nut, bolt and screw stressed to its maximum. The sound was incredible—screaming, howling, banging, grating—every noise known to man was being reproduced in that small space. The shaking was so violent that the Astronaut's vision was starting to blur.

"Skinnn temmmmperrrrature at maxxxxximum!" Adam could barely spit the words out without chewing his tongue in half.

"Ennnnngagggging Ennnggines!" Peyton shouted.

A quiet sound slowly grew until it became a roar—swallowing all others. It was the engines, wide open, at full power. Gravity ripped at the Astronauts, crushing them into their seats. Everything was a blur. A communal thought blew through the Astronauts, *How can the ship take this? It's going to be torn to pieces!*

But they were slowing! They were slowing! Another thirty seconds passed before the engines were backed off. The ear-splitting cacophony of sound, the shaking, the rattling was becoming tolerable again.

"I don't want a soft landing! I want you to bang this baby as hard as you think possible into the surface. I want to save every possible drop of fuel!" Scott yelled.

"Roger," replied Peyton.

"Adam, give Peyton continual velocity readings."

"Will do."

"We're still off course. Do you want me to use the engines to redirect the trajectory?" asked Peyton.

"How far off target are we?"

"About five miles."

"Wait.... Let me think.... That's just under the round trip limit of the Rover vehicles. Okay we take a chance; we have to save fuel. Continue on the current course."

"Roger."

The specialists watched helpless as this drama of life and death swirled around them. Penny thought that she had heard someone screaming at one point. Was it her?

"Okay, everybody. As the boss said, I'm going to make a bottom-buster of a landing. Brace yourselves. Landing is in two minutes."

James locked his mind. Refused to think of anything. He waited.

He heard Peyton, “There’s the surface!”

“Surface area is flat. Excellent! Finally, something in our favor! Bring her on in Peyton!” shouted Scott over the noise.

“Okay, twenty seconds folks!”

A huge clang, bang, whump blasted through the ship. They were driven the hardest they had ever been into their seats. Some creaks and groans escaped from the horribly strained vessel; then it was quiet, finally quiet.

It was a short blessing; audible alarms started to complain with their high-pitched shrill voices. Any major alarms? Any leaks? For a heart-stopping moment, they waited while Scott and Peyton checked.

“Minor alarms, nothing life-threatening!” yelled an exuberant Peyton.

“We made it!” Penny shouted.

The room filled with happy, congratulatory human sounds. Donatella was clapping her hands—that wonderful smile back on her face.

As they slowly calmed, a new feeling predominated; it was their bodies finally reporting in, with some aches and pains, but most of all, a strange sensation that they had almost forgotten. It was gravity. It was real gravity, not the simulated gravity of the Renaissance living quarters. Movements weren’t so easy anymore. They were all feeling weak and tired; excitement, fear and now gravity had stolen all their strength.

“Okay, we need to do a damage check,” Scott said, “Peyton, check the alarms. Adam, use the external cameras to survey the exterior of the Lander.”

A couple of minutes later Adam said, “Well, the first thing I can tell you is that three of the ten cameras have failed. It should be okay though; the other cameras can cover the field of view—okay, yeah, two of the six Lander legs are buckled pretty badly. They must have hit solid rock. The rest are driven about eight feet into the soil. That’s why we aren't listing as badly as we should be; by fluke we've managed to balance the broken legs with dug-in ones."

"Good, good, so long as we are reasonably level, I don't care too much about the bottom three quarters of the Lander. It's not coming back with us. What I do care about is the release mechanism for takeoff; is it functional? Can you see any damage at the join between the lower part of the Lander and the escape pod? Can you see that part of the ship, Adam?" Scott asked.

"No, not well enough."

"We'll have to do an external visual inspection once we have settled in."

"Right, what do you have, Peyton?" asked Scott.

"Well some primary and backup systems have failed but in all cases, we have at least one working unit. One Oxygen tank is unavailable and offline—probably a valve is stuck—I suspect we will be able to fix it. We won't need that tank for a while, anyway." Peyton stopped, took a big breath, "Now, I've saved the worst for last."

"What? What?" Penny asked, her voice a bit strained.

"We've lost contact with the Orbiter. The transmitter/receivers, both primary and backup, seem to be functional. I think the problem is either with the cable to the antenna or the antenna itself."

"Okay, that's definitely a problem," said Scott, "The Orbiter crew is going to be very worried. I'll start working on that right away. Now I want the rest of the team to split up and do visual inspections of every inch of the interior of the ship. After that, let's take a rest for a couple of hours; one of us will have to keep watch—I'm volunteering myself for the first shift, that way I can continue to work on the radio. Okay?"

Scott noted that no one asked about the fuel supply; no one wanted to hear the bad news and he wasn't going to offer any info. At least not yet. "Well, Let's go."

James and Donatella inspected the crew quarters in the lower portion of the Lander; the whole area looked like the insides of a WWII submarine. It was dark, grim and very cramped. There were only four beds, stacked in two rows. The isle was so narrow that James had to turn sideways slightly to squeeze down it. There was a small eating area next to the sleeping quarters with just enough room for three. The astronauts would have to eat and sleep in shifts.

James radioed up to Scott, "Peyton did a great job landing this biscuit. You know there's hardly anything wrong in this area. A storage door came loose and some of our wonderfully *good* tasting food escaped. Nevertheless, it's all still...if you could call it such...edible."

"Good to hear that there will be plenty of that dry, tasteless, sawdust to go around. By the way, have you seen Penny and Adam?"

"No, they should be on the deck below us."

"There must be some problem with the wireless antenna on that deck. I can't raise them. Go down and ask one of them to report back to me on the wired intercom. I'll have a look at that antenna after I fix this one."

James half slid, half jumped down the ladder to the next deck. His legs buckled a bit when he hit the floor. He felt so weak. But still, it was great to be back in real gravity.

He rounded a corner to find a very upset Penny by herself in her bio lab. She looked up, teary eyed as James entered, "The lab is wrecked!" she cried. James looked around; there was stuff scattered everywhere.

"What happened?"

"The spectrum analyzer broke loose and slammed into the storage cabinet which then broke open. Half my experiments are ruined!"

"I'm very sorry. Is there anything I can do?"

"No, no, I said the same thing to Adam. He's checking the rest of the deck. I'll cleanup. I need to determine what's been destroyed and what I can still use."

"Fine. I'll find Adam. Scott wants a deck report."

James stepped through a bulkhead into a much larger space than anywhere else on the ship. Compared to the rest of the Lander, it was like walking into the Taj Mahal. He turned to the left and there was Adam, half-stuffed into his Venus suit. James, somewhat surprised, said, “Hey! What are you doing?”

Adam looked up, a happy smile on his face, “Just making sure it didn’t get damaged. It looks fine. I’m starting to get excited! It will be really something to walk on Venus. I want to be the first on the surface. What was that speech? ‘One small step for a man, one giant step for mankind?’ I’ll need one of my own!”

“Adam, you’re right, the first steps will be relayed to earth but it will be Scott making the speeches and taking the first steps.”

“Oh. Yeah, of course,” replied Adam a little disheartened, but then he brightened up, “Well, I’ll be the second guy on the surface. That’s still very, very cool!”

James laughed, “Okay, so far as I’m concerned you can be the second one on the surface. Now, get yourself out of that suit and call Scott with a report.”

Scott gathered status information from the rest of the Lander; it wasn’t too bad. They were in pretty good shape. The worst hit area was the bio lab. That could prove to be dangerous if they couldn’t test for disease. However, right now Penny was still evaluating the situation. They were listing at about a five-degree angle from vertical but that wasn’t enough to be an issue for takeoff or anything else. He had also taken a few moments to scan the surrounding area, just in case there was a “welcoming committee,” but no such luck. Just barren rocks and dust. No sign of life of any kind.

Scott had just found the radio problem—a connector had come loose—when Adam and James entered the control room. Adam walked over to a console and started puttering about. He looked at the external cameras as they scanned the surrounding Venus surface. It was so desolate!

"Hey! Are you sure we're in the right place? There's nothing out there but miles and miles of gravel. I don't see any of those shapes or the antenna tower or any buildings or friggen anything! Oh, man! The mission's screwed! We've landed at the wrong site!"

"Relax!" exclaimed James, "We're at the correct location. Remember, we're five miles from the Radio Transmitter. Also, the shapes that we saw from space are enormous and mostly buried under the soil. All you'd see from here is a slight ridge." James cranked up the camera zoom to maximum and said, "Look to the left a little. See the bump that runs off into the distance? I'm betting that's our square. The antenna tower, well, we never were sure about the antenna tower. We had suspected that it was gone because the signal was so weak."

"Oh yeah. I see."

"Hey you guys. Go get some rest," said Scott, "I'm going to be working your asses off in a few hours and I don't want to hear any complaining that you're tired."

An hour later Scott had just completed his first report to the Orbiter. They were much relieved to hear from him. Now he was working out the schedule. The Lander had two, three-seater Rovers, so if he wished, the entire team could explore the area. But, at least for now, they would travel in pairs and start some basic reconnaissance to look for signs of life and collect samples near the ship. After that—on to the transmitter site!

Chapter 25

THE SITE

James stopped, turned and looked back for Adam. He was loitering behind again, "Adam! Come on! You can't stop and look at every rock on the planet."

They had halted the Rover about a half mile short of the Radio site and were walking the rest of the way. James wanted to be careful—he didn't want the vehicle disturbing any of the soil near the site.

"Sorry. I was distracted again—there's so much to investigate, I don't know where to begin," replied Adam. He picked up his pace in the Venus suit and broke into a lumbering, swaying gait. James waited patiently until Adam waddled up beside him and then said, "There's about a quarter mile to go to the transmitter site."

So far, there was no sign of any kind of buildings or transmitter towers. Except for the edges of the objects—the ridges—maybe a foot high, it was flat as far as the eye could see. Fifteen minutes later, they were at the location of the transmitting signal, or at least, where it was supposed to be.

"Man! There's nothin' here!" exclaimed Adam.

James looked at the transmitter signal level on his heads-up display. It was very strong. He walked a big circle of several hundred yards across and continued to watch the signal strength and direction. It always pointed back toward the center of the circle. James lumbered over to the mid-point and looked down. There was nothing there. Just dust and dirt.

"Come over here and pull the shovel off my pack for me, please," he said.

James took the shovel and started pushing dirt and rock out of the way. Nothing, just more dirt. He looked around the area some more, hoping to see a change in the level of the ground, a depression, anything that might indicate that there was an object buried under the soil. He saw none. He started digging deeper.

A few minutes later, Adam peered into the foot deep hole, "Nothing so far. Bummer."

James glanced over at Adam. He saw something in the soil!

"You think so? What's that beside your foot? Right where I just dumped the last shovel-full...no not there, over by your other foot. That fragment. Pick it up."

Adam brought it over. It was irregular shaped, about two inches on a side, quite thin, maybe a quarter inch thick; it was the same color as the soil. James, with a special heat resistant brush, cleaned the dirt off the object. As he brushed, the color changed to a deep, rich, glossy black.

"Wow! That's not rock!" That's not rock!!" Adam exclaimed, "We've found something! Yahoo!!"

James knew the relief that Adam was feeling. He felt the same. Although there had been no question that some kind of intelligence was transmitting a signal, everyone on the Lander team, if pressed, would have confessed that they had been disappointed not to see any signs of life. After three days of searching around the ship they had not found any evidence—no signs of any kind of structure and nothing in the rock samples at all.

Finally, they had some proof. The object that Adam held in his mechanical hand was uniform in thickness and looked like some kind of plastic. Adam dropped it into a container on the back of James's pack.

"James, pull my shovel off, I want to have a go!"

"Okay, dig over to the right of where I am. That's where the object was found."

Quickly other pieces appeared. They continued to dig. James was about two feet down when he hit what he at first thought was a large rock. As he cleared the soil away, he saw that it was some kind of a flat surface that was too smooth and uniform to be natural. He dug some more in the direction of the strongest radio signal. Then he saw it. A cylinder protruding an inch or two above the flat surface. He turned to Adam, "It's a coax cable! This is it! We found it!"

Adam, encased in his Michelin man bubble suit, stepped back threw his hands in the air and started jumping up and down. Little puffs of dust followed his every move. He looked so silly that James started laughing. Then he realized he was doing the same thing—jumping like a crazy man. He too raised his hands up over his head, and as he happily bounced up and down, James said to Adam, "Do I look as ridiculous as you do?"

"Oh yeah! You've got me beat. You forgot that you still have the shovel in your hand."

An hour later, they were back in the Lander, pulling their suits apart and replacing the seals. The whole team had come down to talk to them. It was smiles all-round.

"Okay, I hate to rain on everyone's parade, but what do we do next? How do we get into the transmitter site? It's under the surface, we haven't found the entrance and no one has come out to say hello," said Peyton.

"Good point. The entrance could be anywhere. There's a lot of dirt out there. We can't dig it all up," replied Donatella.

"Well, if our assumption is correct—that the signal is an invitation, then we should expect either someone will come for us or there will be an obvious entrance very close by," James said.

"Well so far there's no sign that anyone's going to let us in," Scott stated, "So, James, I'd like you to go back out and mark off a dig area. After that we will dig in pairs round the clock."

Two days later Donatella and Penny found it. At first, it was just a fine line in the flat, rough surface. As they scoured away the rock and dirt, a large rectangular shape became visible in the cement-like material. It was fifteen feet wide by thirty feet long with what looked like massive hinges at one end. The whole team had come out to look at it.

"Now that we have a door, how do we get in?"

"How about a gigantic pry bar?"

"Maybe there's a huge key?"

"Perhaps it's like Lord of the Rings: say 'Friend' and enter."

"Why don't we just knock?"

"Alright, enough jokes. James, give me your opinion," Scott said.

"There's got to be some kind of control panel nearby. Let's dig this area out some more."

"I knew it! More digging! I'm getting friggen' tired of it!"

"Well that's too bad, Adam! You and James get the first shift."

"We're running out of time. There's only three days of oxygen remaining," Scott said. He was talking to the team on the Orbiter.

"I take it you want the additional air supply sent down?" asked Brodie.

"Yes. That will give us two more weeks on the surface."

"But what about the chute?" asked Natasha, "It's the same design as the one that failed on the Lander."

"We'll have to chance it. NASA has confirmed that we can't do an in-space redesign. If it fails, we'll be coming back in three days—simple as that."

"There are no other signs of life?"

"No, nothing. I'm almost certain that this location has been abandoned. The entire planet may be abandoned. Who knows?"

"Should I relay your opinion to Mission Control?"

"Yes. Say that we have not encountered any signs of life. Say that I believe the site is abandoned. Tell them that you are going to attempt to deliver the additional two weeks of air."

"Okay and good luck," said Brodie.

"Thanks. Looks like we are going to need it."

Several hours later, Scott received a call from the Orbiter, "Scott, it's Brodie. We're ready to send down the oxygen canisters. The drop zone will be two miles east of you, the other side of the Lander from the transmitter site."

"Right. Everybody is back in the Lander. We're ready."

"Here goes. Release in one minute."

"Scott, the chute has just released. We're tracking it on radar. So far it's on course and slowing as expected," stated Brodie.

Then,

"It's accelerating! Hell! It's accelerating! The chute must have failed. Christ!"

"Is it going to burn up in the atmosphere?" Scott asked.

"I don't think so. The parachute slowed it enough...it's also off course. Damn! I've got bad news for you."

"Bad news? You already gave me the bad news. How much worse could it get?"

"Well...it's heading your way."

"Are you telling me you're going to kill your own crew with those bloody oxygen containers?"

"Yeah...well...it is a possibility. Sorry about that."

"How much time do we have?"

"About a minute and a half."

Scott scrambled for the Lander com, "Everyone get down to the lowest deck as fast a possible!" He dove for the ladder.

A few seconds later, the crew, hunkered down in the depths of the Lander, missed out on a spectacular display as the oxygen canisters, a silver-grey-red streak of light in the hazy sky, smashed into the Venus surface and exploded—exploded a short, tiny, minuscule half mile away. Various bits of Venus rushed to greet the sky, then fanned out and dropped back to the surface at frightening speed. Little puffs of dust and rock sprang up as the fragments dug craters of their own. When the Astronauts left the Lander for a "look see," they found parts of the tanks, rocks and one fairly large sized boulder within fifty yards of the ship. Off in the distance, a new depression in the Venus landscape had appeared, eight feet deep and fifty feet wide.

"Crappy, awful, stinkin' Venus dirt! I'm sick of it!" James calmly listened to Adam's tirade for at least the thousandth time. It didn't bother him. Adam's blithering helped keep James from thinking about...other things. There were only two days left. Then they had to leave, or at least they hoped they would leave; even with every non-essential piece of equipment ripped out of the escape pod, it was going to be close, too close to call. They may have burned just a little too much fuel on the way down. Scott had decided that it would be "all or nothing." No one would be left behind; they either all made it or none of them made it.

James and Adam were standing on the door, taking a break from digging, looking out over the cooked, almost red-hot landscape. It was another day, just like every other day: skies a dull orange-grey; periodic bright flashes of lightening, high in the sky, followed by a low rumble, broke the oppressive monotony of their surroundings. *It sure would be easy doing weather reports here. Record a single statement, "Heavily overcast but no chance of rain," and then just run it over and over again for eternity.*

James's thoughts were interrupted by a particularly vehement outburst from Adam, "We've only got two more days and we've found nothing! We've risked our lives for nothing! Maybe we don't get out, maybe we die here...for nothing! He started swearing and with every expletive, he drove his shovel, point first, into the door. He raised his shovel again and was about to slam it into the door when a subtle vibration touched his suit. Adam stopped his cursing and started turning in a circle, scanning for the source of the tremor. An Earthquake? A Volcano? It was growing. There was a noise, a grinding, scraping noise. It was near them; it seemed to be all around them. Then James saw something on the ground to his right. He looked to see a wisp of dust rise up from a section of door crack. He spun around, as fast as his suit would let him. It was happening all along the crack!

"Get off the door! GET OFF THE DOOR!" he screamed at Adam. They sprang to opposite sides of the entrance. The massive door was pivoting upward on its hinges!

It rose painfully slowly, far too slowly for James. He was considering dropping to his knees to have a peek inside when he heard Adam again, "Yaaaaahoooo! Yaaaahooooo! I did it! I did it!" He looked across the rising, grumbling gateway and saw Adam in another one of his bubble suit dances—open hands wavering high in the air, hopping from one foot to the other, then waddling around in a circle with dust, a dance partner for his feet, rising up around him.

An ecstatic James got on the com to Scott—his voice literally buzzing with excitement and happiness—"We have some good news and some bad news—the good news is that we got the door open—the bad news is that Adam did it and he's not likely to ever shut up about it!"

Adam and James stood silently watching as the door slowly rose above the flat Venus surface. It was as black as black can be in the opening that was expanding before them; the weak, hazy Venusian light had no strength in that dark realm. James couldn't help but think it looked like a mouth opening wide, a mouth without food for perhaps thousands of years and two tasty, definitely plump, morsels standing before it.

Scott had told them to wait, "Don't go in!" he had said. "Wait till we get there," he had said. James was starting to feel that was a very good idea. He looked back toward the Lander and could see the other Rover heading this way, dirt and dust boiling up behind it. They had managed to cram four Astronauts onto the Rover, one of them was sitting, legs jouncing, off the back.

Scott brought the Rover to a short, quick stop—which was a bit of a mistake but understandable given the situation—a nice, thick, cloud of trailing dirt and dust caught up to the Rover and the Astronauts. In a second, James could no longer see any of them. As Adam and James carefully backed away from the dust storm, a figure appeared, then another, then two more, all excitedly waving their hands, trying to sweep the stuff out of the way, trying to get a view of the "miracle." In unison, they all stopped dead. In front of them, at a forty-five degree angle above the surface, hinged at the far end, loomed the thirty-foot door. A long black shadow that just touched the tips of their boots, extended down into the pit of darkness. It wouldn't take much to imagine teeth attached to that gaping maw.

"Not exactly inviting is it?" said Peyton.

"No, but that's where we have to go," replied Scott. He strode forward, stopped at the edge, clicked on his headlamp and peered down, "I see some stairs; they are quite wide and shallow. Boy! The light sure gives up in a hurry! Must be something to do with the material the stairs and walls are made of." He stepped back and turned to the rest of the gang. "Okay, here is what we are going to do. Two of us will make the first descent. The rest stay here. James, I'd like you to go with me, okay?"

"Yes, Boss."

"Good. Peyton, you're in charge up here. We go in for at most a half hour. Let's keep in radio contact every sixty seconds; I'm not sure how well the wireless com is going to work down there. I'm betting it won't last for long... and Penny, scan the horizon periodically. Maybe the door has activated an alarm somewhere and the Aliens are on their way," Scott said.

"If we are not back in forty-five minutes get back to the Lander and radio the Renaissance—don't come after us—I don't want anyone else getting trapped."

Scott turned back to the entrance and started down the stairs, "Right, James, let's see what's down there." James cranked on his light and followed Scott down into the pit.

Adam watched the two of them slowly disappear into the darkness and then made a gulping, swallowing sound followed by a loud, satisfied burp.

Donatella turned to him and said, "That's not funny!"

"Sorry, just trying to lighten the mood. Hey, by the way, did I tell you that I was the one that got the door open? James and I were...."

Scott stopped and shone the light at the walls; they were fifteen feet or so below the surface. The walls were black, totally black, only the smallest amount of light reflected off the vertical surface. He said, "We're going to have to be careful. There's no depth perception. You could easily walk into a wall." He reached out and ran his mechanical hand over the surface, sensing for any roughness. It seemed very, very smooth.

They continued down the stairs, finally reaching bottom after a few minutes.

"How deep do you think we are?" James asked.

"A hundred feet, perhaps a little more, I'd guess."

Scott stretched his hand out and walked toward one of the corridor walls. When he touched it, he reversed course, arm outstretched, went over to the other wall. "The hall is larger now, I think it's about twenty feet wide." He looked upward. There was nothing but blackness. The ceiling could be fifteen feet high or a hundred. There was no way to know. "It's going to be really tough to notice any side entrances or other doors. James, you go to the other side of the hallway, keep one hand on the wall. I'll do the same on the other. That way we'll catch any openings."

As they started down the corridor, James looked over to Scott. Even a short twenty feet away, his light was just barely perceptible.

Twenty-five minutes later, they were back on the surface.

"We lost radio contact with you after five minutes," said Peyton.

"Yes, I know. That's why we came back early," James replied.

"Well? What did you find?" Penny asked.

"Not much. There's a main hall that slowly works its way downward. We traveled along the hall in a straight line for about a quarter mile, then reached some more stairs. At the bottom of those we started down a hallway that spiraled in a continuous downward curve. And then we came upon another straight, flat stretch. At this point, I guess, we were at least three hundred feet below the surface. We never did get to the end of the corridor but we did find several other hallways, off either side of the main corridor."

"What's the temperature like down there?"

"It's cooler but still very hot—around seven hundred and fifty degrees."

"What's next Boss?"

"First, we will go back to the Lander and recondition the vapor rings in the suits. That will give us a full eight hours in the heat. Then I think we need to take some chances. We are running out of time; with only two days to go before we have to leave, we will all have to go down into the corridor. Let's split up into teams of two, one team will search the main corridor, one team takes the first left-hand hall the other takes the first right-hand hall. We will arrange to meet back on the surface after five hours."

Chapter 26

DREAD

Several hours later all six of them were starting down the main corridor.

Adam said, "It sure is weird down here. The light goes nowhere."

"Yeah, it's positively spooky," replied Penny.

Donatella looked back toward the entrance. They were at the bottom of the first set of stairs. She could see a rectangle of light, the eternal haze of Venus, struggling to find its way down to her. Donatella turned and started down the hallway. A minute later, she swung around and looked back again. That rectangle of safety and hope was smaller...much smaller—a slight blotch of light almost at eye level. She lifted her arm and seemingly held the little pocket of light in her hand. Disregarding the danger, she walked slowly backwards and watched it shrink away. Once it was gone Donatella stopped. She was standing on the cusp between dark and light. One step forward was light and life. One step backward was night, endless night and...what? Impulsively, she took a step forward, then another and another.

"Donatella! Where are you?" It was Penny. "Donatella? Come on! You're freaking me out!"

Donatella stopped, then turned toward Penny and the dark. She turned toward the night.

"I'm here. I'm coming."

A few minutes later the team reached the first intersecting hallway.

"Okay, Penny and Donatella, you take the corridor to the right. Adam and Peyton, the corridor on the left is about a hundred and fifty feet further up. In five hours we meet back on the surface. Right?"

"Right."

"Let's go, and good luck."

An hour later, Scott and James had not found anything new—no side entrances, no doors, no rooms—nothing. Their weak lights endlessly grazing the dark, smooth floor and walls provided no diversion from the monotonous search. It was so oppressive.

Then something! Was that a sound? They stopped and listened, turning this way and that, looking for the source of the brief, tantalizing noise. Or perhaps it was their imagination.

They continued on their way.

Darkness.

Endless Darkness.

Nothingness.

Would it ever end?

"Stop."

James stopped.

"I heard something! I'm sure of it!" said Scott, "Listen! Hear it? Hear it?"

James turned; his light was just able to scrape out Scott's murky form.

"No. No, I didn't."

"There! There it is again! Did you hear it? You must have heard it!" Scott's deadpan, calm voice began to waver; a higher pitched bubbling inflection had found a home on his lips. He was speaking with a gurgling, coughing sound.

A thought, yet not a thought, almost a whisper, entered James's mind... *Dread.*

He replied,

"No. No, I didn't."

Dread.

"You must have! You must have!"

Silence.

Dread... Dread... Dread... Dread....

They continued on their way.

Darkness.

Endless Darkness.

Nothingness.

Will it ever end?

Dread!

Dread is here!

"There! YOU MUST HAVE HEARD IT!"

Who said THAT?

James felt a pull on his arm, a light flashed in his eyes. "Are you alright?"

"What?"

"I've been calling to you. You were mumbling and making these strange gurgling noises. Are you alright?"

"I.... I.... don't know.... It's weird.... I think I was dreaming.... I...don't know...." His voice trailed off to a whisper.

Scott looked closely at James's face through the visor and repeated, "Are you alright?"

"Yes.... Yes, I'm okay."

"Can you continue on?"

"Yes, I'm fine. Let's keep going."

They slogged down the hall of darkness. It began to seem to James that they weren't moving at all. They were on a dark silent treadmill...no... not a treadmill, *a....*

Dreadmill!

I feel it! Dread is here!

"Did you hear it?"

NO! NOT AGAIN!

He stumbled on, ignoring the voice. Then he felt a pull on his arm. "James. Stop. I just heard something. Listen."

He stopped and heard it too.

There was a click and then a sound like something being dragged or pulled or pushed over a rough surface. Then a squeak, or was it a creak? Then another click. Then silence.

That series of sounds was somehow familiar to James. What was it? Very familiar. It was on the edge of his subconscious. The sounds kept replaying in his mind.

"I know what that was."

"What?"

"It was the sound of a door sliding open or closed. Somewhere very near."

Dread is here!

"Something could be nearby, just out of sight," James said, his voice raising. "Something that came through the DOOR!" he swung around on his heal, hair on the back of his neck standing tall—a shock of fear ran through his body. He tried looking in all directions at once. There was nothing...nothing.... But...

Dread is here!

"I don't think so. I don't think anyone is here, besides us. But just in case let's try to communicate," Scott switched on his external speaker and called out, "IS ANYONE THERE?"

Silence.

Then,

"IS...IS...ANYONE...ANYONE...THERE...THERE?"

Then,

"IS...IS...ANYONE...ANYONE...THERE...THERE?"

And again.

It was an echo and then an echo of an echo... then echo upon echo upon echo. It reverberated over and over again, not losing any strength. Already in a state of intense anxiety, the power of the resonance struck James like a physical blow. He uttered a soft moan and put his hands up to his helmet in a useless effort to block the assault. Then suddenly...the echo stopped.

Silence. Ears strained for any sound. Silence.

"I don't think I'll do that again."

"Yes, please don't do that again!"

"That was bizarre. There's more to these walls than I thought. Unless I'm mistaken, they changed physical properties. At first, they were a perfect reflector of sound, that's why the echo didn't decrease in volume; then somehow, they changed and absorbed all of the sound. That's why it suddenly stopped," said Scott. "It should be investigated... but not now." He slowly played the light around in a circle, "I don't think anyone is here with us, James."

"Okay.... Yeah.... Possibly.... It's just that I have this feeling. A feeling of some kind of presence."

"Well it's very, very spooky here. That's probably it."

"Of course. That's got to be it."

"Let's proceed."

They took a few more steps forward and then saw a dull light in front of them. With a grunt of surprise, James leapt back.

"Interesting," said Scott. He reached forward; there was a slight metallic sound as his fingers touched a wall. He swung his light to the left and to the right. To the left he saw the tiniest of a reflection. To the right...nothing.

"Well I think I have the solution to this puzzle. I heard two similar, yet distinct sounds. If you are correct James, then I heard one door close and another one open. The wall in front of us is likely a door that was closed just as we approached and the opening to the right was likely a wall. That was the second sound we heard. This is fantastic! I do believe someone or something is trying to control our movements."

"Well what should we do? Continue on or go back?" asked James even though he knew the answer.

"Continue on! We're making progress. I think we are close to meeting our Aliens."

"But why are they being so elusive?"

"I don't know why. But we have no choice. We are almost out of time. We can't be cautious now."

They turned to the right and followed the new corridor. To James's disappointment, it was the same as the previous hallway—dark, dark, dark. They were once again on the treadmill.

James's hand, which was sliding along the smooth, infinite surface, suddenly lost contact with the wall. Scott, from across the way, said, "There's another opening on my side."

"My side too."

"We must be coming into a room."

Dread...! Dread...! Dread...!

DREAD!

DREAD!

James's mind reeled. He started to stagger then regained his balance. A dim light was in front of him! Another to the left! Another to the right!

"Hey! What are you doing here?" That was Adam's voice!

DREAD!

"I was going to ask you the same question," came the reply from Penny.

"We're all here!" said Peyton.

DREAD!

"This can't be an accident," stated Scott. "Did you notice if any doors or walls moved?"

"We thought we heard some kind of door moving, several times," Donatella replied.

DREAD IS HERE!

"We have been brought here for some reason. Can you see anything in the room?" asked Scott.

They started searching the room. Except James. Something all-powerful, all-encompassing and beyond human comprehension had consumed his mind—*DREAD IS HERE!*

"Nothing but crappy black walls!" exclaimed Adam.

Without warning, bright, bright, white light burst from the walls. Their eyes! The light was searing their eyes! The Astronauts squeezed their eyelids tight together but it was no use, the light tore its way through the thin skin as if it were tissue paper. They threw their hands up to their visors to protect their eyes but it was still no use; the massively powerful light was too strong.

As he fought the pain, over the moans and screams, Scott heard that sound again, that familiar sound, just for a moment...but it was enough. He knew!

"The doors are closing! THE DOORS ARE CLOSING! GET OUT! GET OUT!"

Scott, eyelids locked tight, one hand against his visor, the other thrust forward, blindly turned towards where he thought the door was. Stumbling, staggering, he bounced into a wall, scraped himself along the smooth surface, searching for the exit. He could hear the sound again, it was clearer; he was moving in the right direction.

Then he was at the door and there was still a gap. Not much but enough. Scott placed his back against the edge of the opening, pushed both hands against the gradually closing door. Simultaneously, he shouted, "THE DOOR IS HERE! THE DOOR IS CLOS..." But it was too late; he couldn't get his hands out in front of him far enough to slow the door. If he didn't step through now, he would be crushed. Just as the door brushed his chest, just as he was about to be trapped, Scott squeezed through. The door briefly caught the fingers of his trailing left hand, he pulled with all his might—there was a horrible hesitation—just long enough for a feeling of disaster to catch his throat, and then his fingers slipped through. With a soft thump the door closed. Darkness, now a relief, once again descended.

But the Pain! His eyes! His eyes!

He opened them—nothing but blackness. He knew he should see something, his headlamp was still on. Fear rose through him. If he was blind and there was no one else to help him, he'd never make it back to the ship. He tried blinking rapidly, he could feel tears forming, he blinked some more. The pain seemed to be a little less sharp. He waited a few horrible moments, not moving. Then slowly, wonderfully, he began to see the dark reflection of his helmet light on the wall. It was the most beautiful thing he had ever seen. The pain in his eyes was receding. A sigh of relief shot out of him as he leaned rubber legged against the door.

Where was his team? Did they get out? He scanned around the hall but there was no one else there; perhaps they passed through one of the other doors. He opened the com to all channels, "Scott here. Report in."

"Peyton are you there?"

"Donatella...? Penny...?"

"Adam...? James?"

No one was on the com. That wasn't surprising; if they escaped through one of the other doors, he wouldn't hear them; these walls seemed to block all radio communication. The question was—what to do next?

Scott checked the time remaining on the vapor seals; he had five and a half hours before the seals would burn through. He did some quick math—it had taken him two and a half hours, including the trip from the Lander, to get here; therefore, he needed the same amount of time to get back. That left him three hours before he had to leave. He checked the external suit temperature again, it was cooler here—around seven hundred degrees. Would the vapor seals last longer in this temperature? He wasn't sure.

Then,

an awful, frightening, horrible thought surfaced.

Would they let him out?

They controlled all the doors. Perhaps they would lock him in. Trap him! The vapor seals would eventually burn through and he'd cook in his own juices! He thought of leaving immediately, hoping to get out before the doors were closed but the life of the crew was in his hands. He wouldn't leave to save his own skin; he wouldn't leave until he had exhausted every opportunity to save them.

But what to do next? He didn't have many options. How could he find the rest of the crew? Unless new doors were opened, the way back would not get him anywhere. What about going down the corridors the others used? That should get him to the room again. Maybe those doors were open? It would take almost two hours to get to the hallway entrances and then another two hours to walk back to the room. That didn't leave him enough time to get back to the ship.

He leaned up against the door, trying to hear inside. No sound.

He waited.

No sound.

He scratched at the door, trying to push it sideways into the wall. The material was too smooth. He couldn't get a purchase.

He turned on the external speaker and pushed as close to the wall as he could.

"Anyone there? James? Peyton? Penny? Anyone there?"

That awful echo slammed back at him. He could hear nothing but his own voice. Then, once again, without warning...it stopped. He waited and listened.

Nothing!

It was so frustrating! He was helpless! He didn't know if anyone was even alive.

What to do?

What to do?

Then... A CLICK!

A thin line of light in front of him was ripping through the darkness! The door was opening! A gurgling, coughing noise squirmed its way through the narrow crack.

That noise! It was familiar.... What was it?.... It was the same sound he had heard from James when they were walking down the corridor! The strip of light was ever so slowly widening to a band of burning brilliance. Momentarily he turned away. His eyes couldn't adjust to the vicious contrast of blazing white against brutal black. But urgency and desperation swung him back; eyes screaming with pain, he took a step forward then stopped, horrified. A hand, scratched and bloodied was shoved-squeezed through the narrow opening. It was a human hand!

What?

What is that?

How is that possible?

It's seven-hundred degrees down here!

A mangled, bloodied arm, flaps of skin dangling, followed the hand. It was trying to push the door open! The awful gibbering, gurgling sound was growing.

What is going on???

Fear pushed him back a step. The black wall was giving birth to a scene from a horror movie. The door was still opening. Another hand and arm appeared. Then he could make out hair—it's the top of a head! Someone was trying to thrust their head though a four-inch wide space!

Scott leapt forward, grabbed the edge of the door and pulled with all his might. The door continued its grinding, tortured, sluggish motion. Suddenly, the head popped through. *OH NO! IT'S ADAM! NO! NO!* One ear had been half torn off by the door. The skin was pulled away in places from his face. Blood seemed to be gushing from everywhere. Adam was stuck sideways in the door, hands and arms thrusting and wriggling. Suddenly, he turned his mangled head toward Scott and said,

"gguuguglll kikkuk gugulll unnllll"

IT WAS THE NOISE HE HAD HEARD!

The space widened. The thing that was once Adam surged forward, slipped on its own blood, fell to its knees, then jumped up and with incredible strength leapt away from Scott.

It's seven-hundred degrees down here! *IT'S NOT POSSIBLE!*

Instantly a pant leg caught fire. It whooshed upward engulfing the flailing, running body. Scott turned away sickened. As the Adam-thing cooked and sizzled, the horribly inhuman sound continued unabated.

Then, to Scott's relief and horror, it stopped. A flaming carcass lay on the floor twitching and wriggling; impossibly it heaved up, fell back and finally lay still as the flames continued to consume the body.

He swung back to the blinding white slash in the jet black wall—it still wasn't wide enough to allow him passage and it was no longer opening. Scott took hold of the door, braced his foot against the other side and released his fear and anger in a gigantic heave. Rage poured through his body. It overwhelmed all thought, all other emotion. He screamed out, "Agggggggghhhhhh!" But the burning bar of light resisted his insane strength. Scott continued to scream as he ripped at the door. Suddenly he felt a slight movement, heartened, he gave one last tremendous heave, then the door gave way and slid back.

He pushed his way, hands up against the light, into the room. The floors, ceiling and walls all radiated white, pure white. It was so strong! He flung his hands up to his visor, shut his eyes and waited for some relief. Then, eyes open with the smallest of slits, he flashed a look at the room. With white on white on white, he was just able to discern faint, washed out shapes, lying, wriggling, moaning and gibbering on the floor. The pain in his eyes became unbearable. He shut them again, waited and then stabbed another squint-eyed look into the room. He shut them again. Open, Shut, Open, Shut. Open, Shut.

Gradually, he painted an image in his mind. It was a bizarre psychedelic-impressionist painting of an insane asylum in a slaughterhouse.

There were shades of white blended together. There were splashes of deep crimson red. He saw vague, pain riddled outlines—shifting, changing. It was a moving canvass of white horror painted on the backdrop of a groaning, moaning, gurgling, cackling, cacophony of sound. Eyes shut tight, with the music of a madman violating his ears, he mentally placed his team in the room.

Penny was laying on her back about twenty feet in front of him. She had pulled off her headpiece and was nonchalantly tearing at her face with her mechanical hand. Bits of hair, skin, flesh and eyeball were strewn, crimson-white near her. He could see jawbone, exposed, flapping back and forth as she gurgled away—possibly jabbering to a Venusian Grim Reaper patiently waiting to take her. But nothing was on fire...suddenly Scott realized that the temperature in the room had dropped to Earth normal.

Donatella was closer, a little right of center, twelve feet away. She had made more progress with the suit—helmet and top half were off. She was sitting, facing Scott, vacant eyes wide open, blood dripping from a torn lip, hands shaking and twitching. Then a violent shudder shot through her. She arched her body, flung her hands into the air and with a sickening smacking thud drove the back of her head into the floor. Black-red blood splattered in a halo around her smashed skull.

Then Stillness. No movement.

A smear of blood lead Scott to Peyton who was at least thirty feet to the left of him. Completely out of his suit, he looked to be trying to wriggle like a fish, away from Scott over the floor. One leg, broken just below the hip, flopped along at a ninety-degree angle to the rest of him. He was having a detailed discourse with the floor, "chhhk chhhk ggggguug kkkk nnunnnlll nnnnn gggugll gugulll unnllll"

James was the closest to him. He was on his hands and knees ten feet away, suit beside him, unmoving. A groan issued from him, followed by a shake of the head. Then quiet. Then more of that sickening, gurgling, babble. Another shake of the head. A groan. More babble. Over and Over again.

Drawing on the extreme will-power which he had so painstakingly cultivated over the years, Scott shut down all emotion. In a dark, foggy mind-tunnel, he took stock. It was too bright to see his heads-up display but it was obvious that the temperature and pressure in this room was close to Earth normal. He also knew the door was still open and it was seven hundred degrees outside. The air would be heating up in here very quickly. He had to move fast. But what to do? There was only one of him. To save all four was impossible. He had to pick one, help him or her and then, if possible, get him or her to assist with the others. James seemed to be in the best shape. He squeaked open his eyes to have another peek at James. As he did, he witnessed Penny tear away her throat, blood gushing and pulsing like a macabre water fountain. A sour taste filled his mouth as he choked back his stomach contents. He squinted another look at James. James was still in the same position. Physically, he seemed to be intact. Scott felt that the spastic movements and sounds were slowing. Scott shut his eyes and started a careful, blind shuffle over to where he expected James to be. After five steps, he stopped and cracked open his eyes again. James was in front of him, barely a foot away. Scott bent at the knees and the waist and got as close as he could to him. "James! James! It's Scott! Can you hear me?" He waited.

He waited.

He reached out and touched him gently on the shoulder. James was still. "James! James! It's Scott! Can you hear me? Answer me buddy! Come on James!"

"unnnn! unnnn! Yes! I'm ummm kkklkkklk bbbbllllkkk Oh! unnnn my head! Something's in my head!"

"Shut it out! Shut it out James! I need your help! The crew are dying!"

"kkkchchch bbllblb umh umh waaait waait wait, I'mmmm trying!" James started to try to rise, fell back, started again—then wobbled to his feet. He turned to Scott, his face momentarily blank, and then broken words started to bubble out. "unggg whhhh we hhh areee nottttt aaalll-lone alone!"

"Where are they?"

"They aggg they are unnn in my head!" James started to fall but Scott reached out and held him.

"Shut it out! Shut it out!"

"Yessss.... Yes.... I...think I can."

"Adam and Penny are dead. Donatella is in trouble. Can you walk over to her?"

"Yessss," James started to stagger toward her, tripped, stopped and then tried gain. After a few steps he stabilized, walked a few steps more, shuddered, then recovered and continued.

Scott turned toward Peyton, snapped off a quick look and then blind shuffled his way toward him. It took several more iterations to finally reach the fish-like Peyton, swimming belly first in his own blood on the floor.

"Peyton! Peyton! It's Scott! Peyton! Stop!" Scott opened his eyes, got a bearing on the horrible sight below him and reached down to stop him. Suddenly he glimpsed James beside him. With eyes closed, James said, "Scott you can't help him. He's gone."

"What do you mean? He needs help! I have to help him!" cried Scott.

"I can feel him! I can feel him in my head. They have taken him. He is no longer human."

"What? What?"

"He no longer understands English. He has a new language. His mind is gone. It will no longer sustain his body. He is dying."

"We must help him!"

"He is almost dead now. You can do nothing."

"No! NO!" Scott reached again for Peyton. He cursed the suit; he could not touch him. Peyton became still. His breath came with quick hard gasps. Then stopped. One last soft groan then final stillness.

Scott shouted, "NO!"

He turned and reached out with his lumbering mechanical hands towards James. "What about Donatella?"

"She is gone. She is dead."

"What happened? What happened in here??"

"I'm not sure. There was the light. Then it flickered and flashed. Then I can remember nothing. I think I became something else.... It's still here!" James put his hand to his head and grimaced. "Trying to pull me under! I'm slipping! Slipping! Help me! unnn kkkdkddkk ggggllll-glll." James began to puke up garbled, glugging sounds. He staggered again.

"James! Snap out of it! Fight it! You have to get into your suit! I can't do that by myself. You have to help me."

James leaned against Scott, took a deep breath and without a word started back toward his suit. Twenty minutes later, with Scott's help James was back in the suit. It had been a close thing. The heat was burning its way into the room; the temperature had reached one hundred and forty degrees and was beginning to climb quickly.

They started towards the door but James had another attack; he stopped and remained catatonic for ten minutes. Scott was just about to start dragging him when James began moving again. As they left, Scott, unable to stop himself, looked back one more time. The white on white landscape was once again changing—the corpses were beginning to bubble and blacken in the heat.

"I'm slipping! I'm slipping again!"

"Concentrate, James! Concentrate! Hang in there! You can do it! Stay with me, buddy. Stay with me!" Scott tried everything he could to keep James moving. He tried every tone of voice he could think of: soothing, confident, insistent, determined, coercing, angry. Sometimes it worked, sometimes it didn't. They had made progress toward the entrance but it was painfully slow. James kept slipping in and out of sanity. He had not been able to coherently explain what had happened to him; he just kept repeating, "They were in him." Each time he slipped, James would start up that bubbling, gurgling sound again. Scott thought he now knew what that was—it was a human's attempt at some sort of Alien language. How James could have learned an Alien language after a few minutes in that room was beyond Scott. *It just didn't make sense!*

Suddenly, a powerful, frightening sensation struck him—goose bumps leapt to his skin; a shivering, tingling shock zipped down his spine. Scott spun around and stared into the blackness, expecting some sort of horror to be there, poking its monstrous face out of the gloom. But there was nothing.

That sensation, that feeling of being watched, would lie dormant for a time and then, like a cresting wave, break over him and coat him with a frothy sense of fear and horror. Fear struck at him from all directions—was something behind them? Watching them? Chasing them? Would the walls light up and drive him mad? Would the door to the tunnel be open or would they be trapped below the surface? Would they make it back to the Lander before they cooked in their suits or ran out of air?

They stumbled on a few more feet. Then,

"I'm slipping again! It's coming! It's bad this time! Dread is coming! Dread is here! Help! Help me!" James lost his balance and before Scott could stop him, he banged into the wall and slid to the ground.

"James! James! James!"

Scott stood waiting for ten minutes, then fifteen. It was the longest James had been in this state. Scott couldn't wait any longer. He rolled James on his side, pulled off one of the straps attached to the backpack, looped it under one of James's armpits, across his chest, under his back and tied it tight around the arm and shoulder. He took the other end and with a grunt of severe, strained effort, started pulling and dragging the massive suit, with James trapped inside, down the hallway.

Chapter 27

BEGINNING

DREAD!

Dread!

Dread.

As little Lillia leapt ahead of her father, Ranula, she turned to taunt him, "Come Papa you are too slow! I can run much faster than you!" Ranula, laughed as his heart burst with love for this precious being, his one and only, and replied, "I will catch you! I will! I will!" He dove for her feet, carefully landing just out of reach of her in the sweet, wonderful lula grass. A waft of the strong, pungent lula aroma flew up to greet his descent. Nothing could be as magnificent as that smell! Lillia screamed with delight as he swiped and missed her feet. Off she bounded toward the sea. She was perilously close to the water's edge. She looked back at her father, giggled one more time, turned and dove into the deep water. Ranula, now standing, took a run and in an instant was smoothly slicing through the water on the heals of his daughter. She turned, laughed at him once again, her air bubbles gurgling past him, and with a powerful swing of her webbed feet, she spiraled down even farther. They reached the sea bottom at fifty feet. Lillia leveled off and swung around a big boulder covered in plant life swaying to the eternal rhythm of the sea. She ducked under a large school of multicolored minnows, shimmering with red, yellow and blue markings, then rolled on her back, looked towards her father, took a deep breath into her lung-gill and yelled with her water-push membrane, "You are a slow swimmer, too!"

Ranula water-pushed back to her, "I'm going to catch you! I'm close now!" Lillia let fly with another happy scream and flew by a large outcrop of rock with her father right behind her.

Suddenly, a Ripthraw, watching the two happily inattentive Malayians, the people of Venus, playing in its territory, snaked out toward the little one—it's ancient, primitive mind sensing a helpless little morsel.

Ranula, a body length behind his daughter, saw the Ripthraw rising up from the outcrop toward Lillia. He shot forward and down, all pretense gone, right in front of the deadly teeth of the Ripthraw. The Ripthraw, easily distracted, turned and gave chase. Ranula looked back to see Lillia, in the distance, vigorously swimming to the surface. Much, much closer, within inches of his feet, was the thirty-foot eating machine. Ranula waited a few more seconds to be sure that his lovely daughter was well out of harms way, then dove at an incredibly sharp downward angle. The much larger Ripthraw could not follow the turn. By the time it did, the prey was gone.

Moments later Ranula surfaced and was climbing carefully out of the surf. "Papa! Papa! You are safe! Thank you for saving me from the Ripthraw! I take it all back! You are faster than me!" She wrapped her short flipper arms around her hero's soft downy legs and looked up at him with her beautiful face glowing with pride and love.

"Lillia tells me there was some danger, Ranula!" Ranula looked up from his one and only, his sweet one, to see a vision of beauty—his other sweet one—his wife Namia, standing close by. As always, he felt his heart and mind drawn from him as he viewed her sublime beauty one more time. He couldn't explain it, but each time he saw her it was as if it was the very first time. It was the ultimate love—appreciation at its fullest—he felt vast, almost uncontrolled, joy when he was with her and sadness of loss when she left his side. He loved every inch of her—fur soft and slick, the gentle curve of her prominent, absolutely perfect, forehead, her glossy eyes with double lids slightly overlapping in a very sensual way, her body wholesomely plump—still like a maiden's even after giving birth to their beautiful child. The slim, supple finger appendages, all twenty of them, were, at fifteen inches, the perfect length. Legs well shaped, covered in deliciously smooth, short fur—iridescent turquoise-blue in color—and finally

those amazingly perfect webbed feet so capable of swift movement in even rough water, yet delicately formed. Perfect from head to toe! He was so glad she had picked him out of all the hundreds of offered mates!

"Yes! I must say that I am very unhappy, my love!" replied Ranula.

"Why is that, my dear?"

"Well the Dynarts are supposed to keep this area clear of all dangerous species! They have failed in their duty! I must have a talk with Dimra! This is unacceptable!"

"Calm yourself my brave husband! I'm sure it is more difficult than you think to keep these monsters under control. You did your duty and protected our wonderful daughter! I am so proud of you!"

"I know that they have a difficult task. Perhaps I was hasty."

He looked around, the day was still young and it was many hours before rest time. The sun was shining in the lovely blue sky; the plants and animals in the park seemed to be dancing in the warm sunshine. He would not let the incident bother him. He reached out, took both of them in his arms, and said, "Let's have a fun day!" They walked for miles, enjoying the quiet beauty of the park. It wasn't often that they spent much time above the sea.

They were coming to the end of their time. Soon he would have to take his family back home. They walked to the top of a hill that provided an unbroken view of their surroundings. A short distance away, off to the east, was the ocean and home. Ranula experienced the same warm feeling that he always felt when he looked upon the seas that covered nine-tenths of Venus and gave him and his people life. He couldn't help but smile. Directly below and all around them was the park where the many, many colorful plants shimmered and glittered in the light. The caretakers were careful to show off the best the world of air had to offer—after all, the world of air had little left.

He looked off into the distance, beyond the park, and his mood became subdued. He could see the factories, great grey monsters, breathing black smoke and red fire, towering hundreds and sometimes thousands of feet into the sky.

They were all around them. This park, large by venusian standards, was a tiny island in a vast, almost incomprehensible landlocked sea of industry and commerce. Only the air in the park, filtered through the sky bubble that extended almost to the outer atmosphere, was clean.

"Papa! Papa! Why is it so gloomy over there? And there? And there? What are those big buildings? Why do they send smoke into the sky?" asked Lillia.

"This is where all the nice things that we enjoy are made. It makes the air dirty but this park is protected from the pollution. And the Ocean, where we live and eat, is protected. The great wise ones made a decision many thousands of years ago that the ocean would be preserved but the world of air would be used for industry. They believed that making one part of our world dirty and keeping the other clean was a better method than making all the world a dirty place!"

"Oh! I see, Papa!"

"It's time to go home, little one," said Namia.

The happy family turned their backs on the black-grey gloom of the world of air and walked to their transport.

A short while later they came to the air-tube that would carry them back to the city and home. Lillia cried, "Papa! Can we swim home?"

"If we wanted, we could. But it would take several wake-rest periods! The air-tube shuttle will bring us home in a few hours."

"But I am a fast swimmer! You saw today!"

Namia smiled at her little one and said, "Yes, we know you can swim as quickly as a Ripthraw! Papa and I would get tired keeping up with you, but it is best if we take the shuttle."

They descended into the ground and waited their turn for the next private air-tube shuttle. Ranula entered the shuttle and walked to the blank wall opposite the door. He reached out with one of his finger-appendages and lightly touched a spot that he could feel in his mind's eye. Instantly the air-tube control panel lit up. He scrolled through the options with six of his finger-appendages.

Within moments he had entered the destination. The door shut with a smooth swish-click.

A voice issued from a speaker, "Welcome senior geneticist Ranula to Rydal park station Air-tube Shuttle! Please seat yourselves! Departure is in thirty seconds. Enjoy your ride!" Ranula and Namia helped Lillia with her secure straps and then locked themselves in. With only a quick beep to warn of the launch, they were pushed deep into the air cushions as the shuttle shot forward through the tube. In an instant they were at terminal velocity, flashing their way through the air-tube system.

"Lillia! We should have left the land by now. Would you like to look out into the sea?"

"Yes, Papa! Yes!" Lillia squealed with delight. This was her favorite part of the trip, watching the seascape whiz by. Ranula reached up to the control panel and touched the vision pad. The jet-black walls became transparent; the ocean sprang up all around them. They could see fish darting about; in the distance, in the clean, incredibly clear water, they could see large sea plains, mountain ranges and underwater cities dotted about the sea floor. It was so wonderful!

"Look, Mama! Look, Papa! Look at all the Papula farms!" Lillia was standing pressed up against the shuttle looking at the sea floor below them. The loving parents stood and on each side of Lillia they snuggled-close and gazed at the farms that produced the primary staple of the strictly vegetarian Venusians. They could see the blue-black vegetation extending far into the distance.

Ranula looked at his timepiece; it measured the wake-rest intervals as well as the remaining length of the long Venus day or night. He saw that they would be home shortly. He would take his rest period and then he had an important meeting with the Essential Geneticist, the highest-ranking geneticist of the Venusian race. It was a great honor to meet him!

He was still thinking of the meeting, trying to guess its purpose, when he looked up to see his water-world city, sparkling before him. They were home! There it was! He could feel a contented smile spread cross his face. The great translucent air dome, with the many air-locks and air-tubes prickling its surface, shimmered at him. Inside he could see the residential towers rising up from the sea bottom; he could see the small parks, sea pools and swim ways. To his right was a work crew, laboring outside of the dome, repairing one of the air-lock tubes. Nearby was a play area where parents could take their children to practice their swimming skills. It was a familiar, happy place. Even after a short trip, it was good to be home!

"Papa!"

"Yes, Lillia?"

"Why don't we live in the sea? Why do we live in a dome under the sea?"

"I know it seems strange that we, who can breathe in water and air, would build an air city under the water. That is because we want the best of both worlds—the world of air and the world of water. It is easier for us to communicate, to talk, in air. As well, our vehicles move easier in air. There is something called water resistance—you will learn about it when you go to school—it slows vehicles down. It is much easier to move these crafts in air. But we still let the ocean visit us through the great sea chambers, the relaxation pools and the swim-ways. Of course the food farms are nearby on the ocean bottom, so it is not so far for the workers to take the food."

"Mama!"

"Yes, Lillia?"

"Is it rest time yet? I am tired."

"Yes, little one, soon!"

A few moments later or at least it seemed that way to Ranula—the wake period had flown by—Ranula and Namia were sitting in their common room with Lillia peacefully sleeping at the bottom of the special recuperation pool; it was warm, ten feet deep and darkened for relaxation and rest.

"What do you think the Essential Geneticist wants with you, my love?" asked Namia.

"I have asked myself that very question over and over again. I don't know the answer. It is a conundrum! All I know is that there is a special, very secret task that they wish me to perform. It is so secret that only the Essential Geneticist

knows its purpose. Well, I will know after the rest session. For the moment let us put our minds to rest, enjoy calm love, then off to the sleeping pool."

"Yes, my sweet hero of the Ripthraw," with those soft words Namia leaned forward, touched her forehead to Ranula's and drew in his thoughts—felt his love emoting toward her—so, so strong! They sat there, for an eternity, touching at that most intimate of intimate spots, a single entity jointed mind to mind, sharing all the emotions, feelings, sensations—the happiness of the day, the love of each other, the love for their little one, their one and only, their reason for being....

Chapter 28
ESCAPE

"James! James! I need you! I need your help! Answer me! Wake up! WAKE UP!" Scott's voice gradually built up volume until he was yelling as loud as he could. They were in trouble. Using every ounce of his strength, he had dragged James to the tunnel entrance. But his worst nightmare had come true...the door was closed.

He left James at the bottom of the stairs, walked to the top and tried pushing, knocking, banging, anything he could think of to activate the door. Nothing worked. He was exhausted. The fuel cells driving the leg servomotors packed it in twenty minutes ago. He had dragged himself and James the remaining distance on his strength alone; it was a task that many back at NASA would have considered impossible. But now...now he was at his end; despair was draining the last of his energy, draining his life away. The Venusians, or whatever those bastards were, had plugged a spigot into him and were siphoning out the last of his courage and determination. He needed James now or it was over.

"James! Buddy! I need your help! I NEED YOU NOW!"

Silence....

Scott leaned weakly against the wall, his shuddering legs barely able to keep him vertical.

Then, over the gasps of his own shattered breath, he heard a voice, a bored gas station attendant's voice,

"Yes, Scott, How can I help you?"

He looked over at James in amazement. He had not moved. He was still lying on the floor where Scott had left him. Did he hear right? Was he hallucinating?

"James! James! Is that you? Is that YOU?"

"Yes, it's me, Scott."

Scott took the few short, painful steps over to where James was lying. He looked down—James still wasn't moving. His eyes were closed. *I'm hallucinating!*

"James! Say something for me please." He watched his lips, dreading what may not happen.

"What would you like me to say, Scott?" A shudder of relief sagged through Scott's body as he saw James's lips move.

"You're with me! We're in big trouble again, like when we were stuck on the bottom of the sea floor...you remember that?"

"Yes I do, Scott."

"James, why are you not moving?"

"Because...because." A look of pain crossed his face, he swallowed hard. "It is taking all my will power not to fall back." Through the visor Scott could see James's lips violently trembling. "All my power not to fall back to... Dread."

"What is Dread?"

"I don't know, not yet...but I'm beginning to understand."

"Understand what?"

"It's not important now. Scott, I don't have much time. Tell me what you need."

"We are stuck. We're at the exit and the door is shut. I can't get it opened. Now I know why the air pressure dropped to one atmosphere—the

Venusians shut the door, created a sealed tunnel and then vented the pressure off to somewhere. Now I can't get it open!"

"I see, I understand.... Yes.... I know.... I have the solution to this conundrum. Where are we?"

"We are almost at the bottom of the first set of stairs."

"Good. Good. Walk to the stairs until your feet are almost touching the first step. Then go to the wall to your right."

"Okay...okay, I'm there."

"Now, at waist height, at exactly the center of your body, there is a control panel on the wall. You can't see it but it's there. You need to put your finger precisely on the wall at that point."

Scott stretched out his hand; it shook so violently from weakness that he wasn't sure he could place it within six inches of its intended target. He made a stab at the wall. No result. Just a black, useless, wall. His voice, sucked dry of all strength, croaked-whispered, "Nothing happened."

"Then you missed the start-key. Try again."

He tried again, and again, and again...three minutes later, with his whole body shaking and shivering, he struggled to push out a single thought from his lips, "Are you sure this is the correct spot?"

"Yes, I'm sure.... No, not sure. I know. It is there. You have missed the key. It's tiny. It's intended for very small, finger-like appendages. Try again."

Scott placed one hand on the wall to steady himself. He summoned every last ounce of concentration. He stopped his shaking. His sweat soaked body commanded his arm to calmly, steadily, reach out. He touched the wall—it was his last chance, all his strength was gone. The wall remained blank. Scott felt his entire body sag beneath him, he staggered backwards as his balance left him and would have fallen, but then, suddenly, incredibly, light leapt forth to his eyes! Strange characters squiggled and floated in the wall before him!

"I've got it! It's here!"

"Well done. Here is what you need to do...."

Two minutes later, Scott was watching light growing; he heard grinding and screeching as the huge door struggled to open—it was... wonderful! He could feel air whizzing by him as the Venus surface pressure was building and filling the space again.

"Scott, you will have to get me back to the Lander. You will have to do it yourself. I have no strength...and I have to go back.... Go back to my other life...back to...Dread.... I have to understand what happened here...."

"We have a task of great importance for you Ranula!"

Ranula sat at a table across from the Essential Geneticist in a small, quiet room. They were alone.

"You must keep this secret. No one must know. Not even your wife," stated the Essential Geneticist, "Something terrible, something horrible, has happened. We need you to help us."

Ranula walked home. He didn't use the swim way even though it was easier and more convenient. His soul was shattered. His life was in ruins. All he felt was.... Dread.

"My wonderful husband! Welcome home! Did your meeting with the Essential Geneticist go well?"

Ranula did not answer. For a moment he stood still and stared blindly about the room – unexpectedly his head fell to his bosom; he swayed back and forth, struggling for a way to comfort himself, to seal himself from the pain. He could find none.

"My husband! What has happened! What is the matter, my hero?"

Words, briefly held back by a weak emotional dam, poured out of his lips, "Oh my dear, sweet, Namia! Something terrible has happened! I can't tell you what! It is awful! The Essential Geneticist has asked me to try something...but doom is here. There is nothing we can do. It is too late. I cannot say anything more...but the worst...the worst is we can never have quiet love again! I can never share my thoughts and feelings with you again! You cannot know of this tragedy! I have given my word."

"No! No! You cannot say that! You are my life! I must share my life with you through quiet love! Please do not deny me this! I will say nothing about your secret! I promise!"

"I cannot. I have given my word. I will not let you share this horrible tragedy. I will not let you carry this burden. Oh, my sweet one. Oh, my sweet one! My life is ruined! I have lost you!" Ranula's swaying and writhing increased. Namia reached out and held him, tried to stop him, tried to comfort him. It wasn't possible. Can a tree be straightened in a hurricane?

Scott took James's left hand and tugged with his very, very last reserves of strength. As Scott fell to the floor, James slid an inch or two further into the Venus Lander air-lock. While lying flat on his back and with fingers as dead as lead, Scott manipulated his heads-up display and then, after several repeated tries, issued the wireless command to close the door. He listened with grim satisfaction as the air-lock slammed shut and sweet oxygen flooded into the room. They had made it!

But he didn't have the strength to shout or even croak for joy. His carefully rationed water had run out an hour ago. His mouth was dry as a desert. His lips were wrinkled and cracked. His breath sounded like a death rattle. He couldn't move a single limb, appendage, finger or toe—even blinking was a strain. He was a sardine trapped inside a tin can—he just lay there, flat on his back, still breathing the suit-air, trying to build up some amount of strength so that he could remove this damn tortoise-shell from his energy starved, water starved, oxygen starved body. How much air did he have left in his suit? He wasn't sure. Not much he thought.

How ironic if I died here, in the safety of the Lander, unable to find the strength to get my helmet off, thereby smothering while literally inches from fresh air.

Ten minutes later, Scott still wasn't feeling any better or stronger—but he couldn't wait any longer—he attempted to move his right arm; Scott had to reach the one inch diameter emergency switch at his midsection that, when opened, then twisted, and then pushed, would release all his suit-fasteners at once. His armor encased limb shuddered briefly and fell back to the floor. He tried again. It crawled, slowly, incredibly slowly, up his body and halted on his stomach. The tiny, minuscule, insignificant exertion, no more difficult than raising a pint of beer to his lips, caused his heart rate to soar. His lungs, seemingly at the end of a hard sprint, were expanding and contracting at a ferocious, uncontrolled rate. He had to rest for a few moments. Those few moments extended...and extended again...and again. Five minutes passed before he had the strength to start the emergency release procedure. The fuel cells, which were almost completely drained, now only provided power to the life-support systems, so he could no longer operate his mechanical hand in the usual manner; Scott had only limited function via an internal titanium wire that allowed the hand to be turned slightly and the fingers gripped together.

He moved the mechanical hand closer to the switch and positioned the metal thumb such that he could use it to pop the switch cover open. He jabbed at the cover-latch, caught it briefly and lost contact. The cover remained closed. He tried again. No luck. On the third try, it flipped open and the switch, located on a spring-loaded housing, popped out. After another minute of frustrated fumbling he managed to twist the switch and with an angry, weakling swat at the mechanism, he felt the suit-fasteners blow open. Immediately, cool, wonderful, fantastic, *beautiful!* fresh air seeped in through the now open joints. As he lay there, sucking in thin slivers of sweet oxygen, as his mind began to clear, as his strength began to build, he realized how close it had been; he must have been oxygen deprived for some time. He had been only minutes from unconsciousness and death.

His next thought was, *JAMES! What about his air?* He started to wrestle with his suit—still feeble motions, but getting stronger. Scott finally got the helmet off and then worked as quickly as he could to remove the remainder of that awful shell that had almost been his coffin.

He dragged himself over to James and with a couple of quick movements, released the suit-fasteners. James, eyes closed, was still breathing and, in fact looked much better than Scott felt. Scott realized that, as James had not exerted himself over the last hours, he must have had considerably more remaining oxygen than himself.

Scott removed the helmet and then the upper half of the suit, and was just starting on the bottom half when he heard,

"There is a great danger! There is a great danger! Danger! Dread! We must get back to earth!"

He looked down at James. He was breathing normally but his eyes were still shut tight.

A voice, so dry and raspy that Scott hardly recognized it as his own, replied, "What do you mean, James?"

"Contact the Orbiter. We must get back to earth as quickly as possible. I understand. I know why we are here. I understand the invitation. We must stop it."

"Stop what? Stop What? What are you talking about?"

"Destruction. Dread.... Dread is here. The destruction of earth. WE MUST GET BACK!"

"I don't know.... I'll have to contact earth. I'm not sure what to do. It sounds crazy to me. Maybe James has been exposed to some kind of bug. You said they had their suits off—maybe there was an airborne virus of some kind; could be he's gone insane."

"Look Brodie, he's not insane. What he has told me makes sense. There's no bug. There's no virus—I've been exposed to him and I'm fine.

We're coming back up. There's a rendezvous window in ten hours. Then we are heading back. Okay? Warn Earth. Tell them we are coming!"

"Okay, yeah. I'll contact mission control."

"Contact Jack! He can go directly to the President."

"Yeah. Okay...."

"See you soon."

"Yeah...yeah...see you soon."

"Brodie, it's not possible. They are wrong. They are confused. The stress of the situation has overcome them," replied Jack Anderson with careful, calm, certainty. He had to ensure that Brodie, who was millions of miles from Jack's direct control, would feel Jack's confidence. He had to ensure that Brodie would follow orders—his orders.

"But what they said kind of makes sense. It is possible isn't it? Isn't it?" queried Brodie.

"Not to me. No, I don't think so. I've been in contact with a few people—experts in the field—since you told me this strange story five hours ago; they don't think it's possible either."

"What do you want me to do?"

"I'm not sure yet. They are coming back to the Orbiter. That's fine for now. I'll let you know the rest of the plan once I've thought it through some more."

"Ok."

"And one more item."

"Yes?"

"Scott is no longer in charge. You are. And you take your orders directly from me...understood?"

"Yes, understood."

Chapter 29
DESTRUCTION

"God Damn! God Damn!" screamed Kurt as he leapt up from his chair in the office. He whipped off the headphones he was wearing, slammed them on the ground and stomped them to smithereens—all the while a litany of swear words and spittle spewed from his lips.

Matt, who had witnessed some major temper tantrums of his old man's before, had never seen anything like this. *Christ! He's foaming at the mouth!*

"Those bloody idiots on the Orbiter are going to let those virus carrying, nut-balls back on the ship! They're going to bring that shit back with them to Earth! They'll kill us all! Idiots! Morons!"

"I don't know...maybe they're right. It could be true...." Matt's thoughtless mouth stopped dead in its tracks as Kurt shoved his ugly, bulldog face toward him. In an instant it wasn't a face anymore, it was some kind of two dimensional drawing of insanity forcing its way into the third dimension—forcing its way toward Matt. Shocked, he leapt back—sizzling, goose-bump, electric fear shot down his spine and spread throughout his body. He started backing toward the office door as he listened to his dad's ranting, screaming, rage,

"You idiot! You goof! You don't know what you're talking about! Even if they don't have a virus...." He stopped to swallow some of the saliva that had been spitting from his enraged lips. "It doesn't matter if they don't have a virus! If those assholes come back with that story, it could mean the end of everything for me! Ruin! Ruin!" He slammed his fist on the desk and with blood-red eyes bulging out of their dark sockets, yelled, "I won't let that happen!"

He began advancing toward Matt and, reaching for a large, fist-sized paperweight on his desk, said...much quieter, "I'm sick of your back talk." A sudden, gleeful smile latched onto his face. "Time to teach you another lesson, pecker-head."

Matt dove toward the door. He was pulling at the handle when the heavy paperweight struck him in the middle of his upper back. Excruciating pain buckled his knees. Somehow, he kept his feet, dragged the door open, and hobbled through the exit with his father's words chasing him. "There! How'd you like that? You better run! Ha! Gutless bastard! Hahahaha!"

———

"Oh! Matt! Your back! It's so bruised! That monster! That maniac! I hate him! Hate him!" Shannon was simultaneously crying and screaming. "This is it! You've got to get out! Get the hell away from him!"

Matt carefully avoided a direct answer to her demand, instead, he replied, his voice quiet with fear, "He scared the crap out of me—you should have seen his face."

Shannon continued to press him. "Let's go! We've got some money. Let's get out of here. Let's get out of the city—move somewhere else. You've done your bit; you've disabled the fail-safe. The ship can't be destroyed."

"Yes, you're right, the fail-safe is inoperative."

He remembered the night when they went back to the office and shut down the fail-safe. After a frightening half hour with Shannon standing guard at the door, he found a way to prevent his dad from logging into the fail-safe program—the system would only allow a log-in to the fail-safe from a specific IP address, so Matt deleted the IP address and left it empty, consequently preventing a log-in from any remote computer.

"There's nothing he can do, can he?" asked Shannon.

"No, no. I can't even get in now. Without NASA's help, he can't do anything; he'd have to call up NASA and complain that he couldn't blow up their space ship." A triumphant smile briefly crossed his face. "He's lost. We've beat him."

"Good! Then it's time to go."

Matt sat quiet for a moment, then slowly shook his drooping head back and forth, "No. I don't.... I don't think I can."

"Why? Why not?" Shannon's incredulous voice, raised to a shrill pitch, caused a defensive Matt to reply with unthinking emotion. "Because he's my dad! He's not always like this. Sometimes he's okay. He just gets in a bad mood. That's all."

"A bad mood! You've got to be kidding!" Shannon started swearing. "Sometimes I think you're as nuts as that screwed-up jerk of a father of yours."

"Don't say that! Don't! Don't! I'm not crazy!"

Kurt watched as his useless son performed a great impersonation of the hunch back of Notre Dame while escaping from his office. But the satisfied, gloating, snickering happiness that he would have normally felt wasn't there—just an empty void with remnants of rage ricocheting round and round and...it was beginning to build again—he wanted, needed...needed something to destroy—not just destroy, something to mangle, something to hack and chop. He looked at the wrecked headset on the floor and thought, *that's only the beginning! I'm gonna have me some fun!*

He sat down at his desk and dialed into the Renaissance Orbiter.

A wicked, growling grin held steady on his face as he began the login to the fail-safe procedure. His stubby, powerful fingers cautiously stabbed at the keyboard—each stroke intent on mayhem. Kurt selected the final letter of his password, smacked it hard and slid his finger over the enter key. He started to press the key, hesitated, and then stopped as a thought struck him. He wanted to savor the moment, he wanted to feel the power—he'd take his time, finish his login and then one, deliberate, joyful, key-stroke at a time, put an end to those bastards in space. With a quick, smooth movement, he pushed the enter key. As he waited for the radio signal to travel to Venus and then for the Renaissance to reply, he leaned back in the plush leather chair, raised his hands, clasped them together behind his head and put his feet up on his desk.

The same wicked grin was still stuck to his face when he saw the Renaissance response pop-up on the screen. *What?* In a microsecond his smile was gone, his eyes hardened into black, bloodshot marble, his legs dropped to the ground as his head and arms shot forward toward the screen. *What is this?* On the screen he saw three useless words,

Invalid login attempt

What does that mean? He had been very careful with the login, he didn't want to make a mistake and have to painfully re-enter the password and then wait again for the speed-of-light delay. *Could he have made a mistake anyway?* It was very unlikely. He stared at the stupid error message for another minute, trying to understand what might have happened. No solution presented itself. With a sinking, frustrated feeling, he started the login procedure again. This time his smug, relaxed pose was replaced with a tense, unwavering, fingers crushing the edge of the desk, face within inches of the screen, cartoon-image of a human. For those moments, as he waited the hard minutes with breath sucked back, he was an unwitting captive of his computer.

Then, finally,

Invalid login attempt

A great, huge whoosh of air shot out of him, followed by a scream, "BASTARD!"

This time he pounded at the keyboard, all thoughts of "savor the moment" were gone; he just wanted to get past this stupid, piece of garbage statement. He waited, almost forever, then,

Invalid login attempt

Kurt sprang up, held back a scream as his eyes tore around the room—the urge to destroy was overwhelming. He turned to the desk and just as rage hit its peak, reached down and started to pull the desk upward, started to wreck everything on it...when a tiny, smoldering remnant of common sense strained to hold him in check. He lowered the desk and fought his anger...but rage demanded release...he slammed his hand down on the desk as hard as he could, raised his fist again, then hesitated—the pain from his hand provided a distraction, thoughts began to work their way through the cloud—something was wrong. How could that happen? A bug in the program?

His mind churned some more—another conclusion quickly came to him—a more ominous conclusion. Did someone tamper with it? How could that be? He would have heard if NASA had found it. No one else knew except his guy, his guy who wrote the software. He'd have to check on him. Did he have a change of heart? If he did, he was a goner.

Scott looked over at James, still unconscious, strapped into his lift-off chair. They were about fifteen minutes late; there had been a last minute delay—he had to check out an alarm that turned out to be false. Still, the delay wasn't a big deal. It wouldn't affect the rendezvous. Scott shouted, "James! James! Can you hear me?"

"Yes, Scott, I can."

"We're about to takeoff. Can you stay alert?"

"Yes, Yes. It's getting easier. Now that I know...now that I understand. I'll stay here until we are back on the Orbiter."

"Good. Takeoff is in five minutes."

Brodie checked the clock on the display in front of him; they were five minutes from docking. He flipped on his com line and said, "Pascal, contact the Lander and verify their docking status."

Scott was running through the docking procedure when he got a call on the com, "Renaissance Lander! Renaissance Lander! This is Renaissance Orbiter. Please provide status."

Scott quickly fired back with, "This is Renaissance Lander. I was just about to call you. We are four minutes from docking."

Scott heard Pascal reply, "Great. Good. We were starting to wonder. I'll inform B...." Abruptly, in mid-sentence, static filled the com.

"Renaissance Orbiter."

"Renaissance Orbiter. Come in please."

"Orbiter! Are you there? Please come in."

"What's happened?" asked James.

"I was cut off—probably a transmitter failure. I expect Pascal will switch to the backup. We don't need to talk to them in order to dock anyway."

Scott continued to prepare for docking. A short while later he checked his stats; they were three minutes away—time to go to visual. As he turned to the external camera monitor, he heard a sound—a soft, but clear, high pitched ping that sang around the ship's hull.

"What was that? Did you hear it?" Scott queried.

"Yes. Yes, it was faint but it sounded like something hit us. Maybe a very small particle," replied James.

Scott checked for alarms. Everything was fine. Must have been....

Wham! The whole ship shuddered!

Then another collision! Suddenly it seemed that the Lander was in the middle of a hailstorm with an ice boulder or two thrown in for good measure.

"What the hell is happening?" Scott turned to the external camera monitor again and began scrolling through the different camera views. On the rear camera he saw an object, a fleeting, brief image that just barely scraped his retina...it was enough though...enough to rip his heart out of his body. He felt...sickness...sickness...a black sickness, as black as those awful walls on Venus. He kicked over to the front view cameras. He didn't really have to, he already knew what he was going to find. Or perhaps it was better to say what he wasn't going to find....

The Orbiter was gone. They were being struck by pieces of their only salvation, their only way home.

Jack Anderson, head of the Venus NASA program stared at his computer monitor with a blank, absent-minded look on his face. After sometime, *how long? how long? HOW LONG?* an internal clock raised an alarm in Jack's mind. His face screwed itself into an unrecognizable mess, then reformed as a sad caricature of the previously proud Jack. Enormous wrinkles had found a home on his brow; his eyes were beady points of dejection. His plump, round, over-filled face now sagged horribly, dragging bluish lips with it. Bits of white, carefully, cleaned teeth revealed themselves from behind the lolling lower lip. Was that drool at the corner of the dark hole that some might call a mouth?

For the first time in maybe hours, he sucked in a breath. To his surprise, he saw that he had the phone in his hand. *Who am I calling? Who?* Then it came to him. If it was possible, his face drooped lower. He began to punch out the phone number...stalled...went off into the distance... came back, pushed another button, then another...finally an unsteady finger found the last one.

A deep, hard voice answered, "Yes?"

Jack croaked out what he thought might be recognizable words, "It.... It's over. Unnnnnn...it...was the hardest thing I've ever done."

The reply was condescending not consoling. The words came quickly in a matter-of-fact, *I could give a damn,* fashion, "Yeah Jack, I understand. I really do. I know how you feel. You did the right thing and I know that the right thing is often the hardest thing to do. I respect your courage. Remember that you have protected all of humanity—so do not incriminate yourself. Remember that our pathetic government would have never had the guts to do what you did. You made the tough decision, the right decision."

The voice at the end of the line paused and waited for a reply. None came.

He softened his confident, joyful tone a little and then continued, "Don't worry, no one else will ever know—just you and me. Your career is safe. Remember that the Venus tragedy is not your fault. You did your part. That's what the public will think. You'll be okay." He stopped, again listening for a response and again, none came.

All he could hear was Jack's erratic, raspy breath. He tried another tact, "If you wish, I can find you a nice plum position in one of my corporations. What do you think of that?"

The speaker waited one more time for an answer but none came, "Jack? Did you hear me?" Again nothing but raspy and now perhaps groaning, breath. The voice was losing patience—it became aggressive,

"Jack! Snap out of it! This is not a big deal! So what if there are fewer Astronauts in the program. You can always get more."

If Jack had been listening closely he would have heard a quiet, snickering giggle as the voice enjoyed its own little joke, "What do you say Jack? How about VP of "do nothing" in one of my companies and a nice fat salary to go with it?"

Then the voice let a little bit of nasty enter the conversation, "And I'd better hear an answer from you this time, Jack."

Three tired words staggered out of Jack's half-dead mouth, "Yes. Okay...sure."

"Once again, I congratulate you on your courage," with a smug smile Kurt placed his phone back into the cradle.

Chapter 30
REVELATION

Scott scanned the debris. Really, it was a waste of time, the chances that any of the crew were wearing a suit was extremely remote, but he decided to do it anyway. He needed to do it. He needed to keep his mind distracted—distracted from the horrible reality of their situation.

They were trapped.

The Lander was not equipped to make the long journey back to Earth. They didn't have enough air, food or water to even come close to lasting the length of the trip. This merciless piece of metal would be their tomb. He looked at the remnants of the Orbiter; chunks of it were gracefully spinning-twisting-drifting away from the blast area. The parts closest to the explosion were long gone. Some of them had smacked into the Lander as it approached. But Scott and James had been protected by the super-strength of the Lander which had to withstand the massive Venus surface pressure. The Renaissance Orbiter fragments had bounced off it like water droplets off an umbrella. *Probably didn't even hardly scratch it. A coat of paint and it will be just like new. Maybe I can sell it to a Venusian.* Sad, horrified irony sickened his guts—he and James had been saved down on Venus so that they could slowly die of oxygen deprivation in orbit.

The blast must have been huge; he could hardly find any pieces of the Orbiter larger than a few square feet. He had hoped that the first stage of the ship, the first air-lock section, would be intact but it hadn't made it. Scott saw a small part of the nose heading for final destruction in the Venus atmosphere. That was all. There was some good news—so far, he hadn't seen any bodies or parts of bodies. He turned towards James who was still trapped in a partial comatose state, barely functional....

"James, are you conscious?"

"Yes, I am Scott."

"I have some bad news—very bad news."

"Yes?"

Scott worked hard, incredibly hard to keep his voice calm and unemotional, "The Orbiter is destroyed. There's nothing left of it. Everybody is dead and of course, so are we—we're trapped. I figure we've got a week of oxygen left and then that's it."

"I understand. Let me consider...."

Scott waited for James to continue but after some minutes he realized that James had gone somewhere internal again and who knew when he would be back. Scott turned to the monitors, started to scan...but stopped. Rational thought was slowly ebbing away; he sat vaguely listening to the sounds of the ship—the hiss of fans, the hum of the water filtration system, the soft squeal of an unattended alarm—until, like his thoughts they too became meaningless. With his mind blank and sick, Scott could feel determination, his one constant companion over all these years, slipping away—replaced by dejection and resignation. It was the last passenger of a sinking ship—abandoning the Captain, leaving him trapped in an empty shell of sick emotion.

Then, into the void came, "I have an idea. I need some time."

Scott turned to James and said in a hopeless, sarcastic tone, "Well you've got a week of time. Fill your boots. Too bad there's no booze on this hunk of junk. I can't think of a better time to drink myself into oblivion."

"I understand, Scott. It does look bad."

"Bad? Bad? That's an understatement. It's over! We're finished! You know I don't give up. If there was any kind of hope, I'd give'er till the bitter end but this time...we're done."

"I'm not giving up yet Scott."

Scott stared at James in disgust, "How can you possibly think that we have any chance at all? Look at our situation! False hope is worse than no hope at all. What's the point in fooling yourself?"

"I'm not fooling myself. Look Scott, something happened on Venus that has changed me, changed me irrevocably."

"What do you mean by that?"

"I'm no longer entirely human. I'm...I'm...a...," James hesitated as he struggled to find the words, "a multi-being."

"What the hell does that mean?"

"I am a member of the human race, and a Venusian."

"What?"

"I have the sum knowledge of the Venusian society stored away in my brain."

A sudden, despair riddled thought leapt forward—perhaps Brodie was right, perhaps there was something wrong with James.

Scott replied, incredulous, "How is that possible? You only were in that room for a few minutes. It's not possible to transfer that much information in such a short interval—even to a super-computer."

"You're correct. It's not possible. There is another answer. But I don't have time to explain it to you now. We are wasting precious breaths of air. Give me a few moments to review the knowledge that I have been given. They were much more advanced than us—I think there is a solution to our problem."

Scott shook his head in disbelief and said in a patronizing tone, "Okay, fine. I'm in no hurry. It's not as if we're going anywhere. I'll try to contact Mission Control. This transmitter-receiver wasn't intended to radio earth. Unlikely we can reach them, but I'll try."

"I don't think that is a good idea, Scott."

"Why?"

"Have you thought about the explosion?"

"What do you mean?"

"Why did it occur?"

"Who knows, could be a thousand reasons."

"Strange that it should happen just after we contacted Earth about the danger, don't you think?"

"I'm not in the mood for a guessing game! What are you talk...." Suddenly he knew, he understood, Scott stopped, shocked—he let those words drift around in his mind, "No! Are you saying?"

"Yes, I'm saying."

"It is almost done. I will make the final genetic encoding and then they will be ready, your Essential Eminence," Ranula stated.

The Essential Geneticist and Ranula were standing at a large table, looking at ten hairy, ugly bodies—not of this world. They had strangely powerful arms with short claw-like, filthy-dirty, finger appendages—only five on each hand. Their short bowed legs showed five more claw appendages on each foot. There was hair everywhere! And the head, the ugly head! Beady little eyes made smaller by large overshadowing, forehead bumps, folded flaps of skin beside the hearing mechanism, a large thrusting jaw filled with sharp, killer teeth and.... Hair! Hair everywhere! And then! They smelled! What a stench!

Even sedated, they frightened Ranula. They chased him in his dreams. They chased his dreams into nightmare—they ate him—they ate his sweet Lillia—they ate his lovely Namia—they ate his people—they ate his planet. They were at fault for the doom. Not his people!

But it hardly mattered who was at fault now. They had reached the point of no return. It could not be undone. All he felt now was dread. Dread! DREAD! ***DREAD!***

Ranula continued with his statement, "The ten females have been modified. Their offspring will be genetically superior to all others and will supplant this genetic branch. They will have a much greater chance of survival—I have calculated a ninety-nine percent success rate over all other sentient beings on the third planet, Essential Eminence."

"It is good Ranula. I know how hurt you feel but console yourself with this deed that you have performed. We cannot be saved but perhaps, thanks to you, the most talented Geneticist on our planet, this race of beings can be warned." The Essential Geneticist turned away from the monsters on the table in front of him, laid his hand on Ranula's cranium and said, "They will be taken back to their home shortly. Thank you again, Ranula!"

A short time later, the Essential Geneticist connected to the Everlasting Elders, the leaders of their race, and reported, "We are almost complete. A flight is scheduled to return the third planet beings in three rest sequences."

"Thank you Essential Geneticist! The contact site is under construction. It has been decided that our automated machines will monitor the third planet for radio waves. Radio waves will indicate a level of sophistication and capability that will indicate their ability to travel to our home planet and learn of the danger. Once the machines detect the signals from the third planet, we estimate that it will take eighty years more for practical space flight. At that point in time, our radio transmission will begin. After that...well, it will be up to them. May they have the wisdom to prevent our doom," replied the Everlasting.

It is time! We are here! James pulled himself out of hibernation. He glanced over at Scott. Scott looked okay but time would tell—James needed to bring him slowly out of the trance—it would take several hours, only then would he know for sure.

Four hours later, as Scott was beginning to stir, James said, "Scott. Scott. It's James. We are here. We have made, it my friend. How do you feel?"

Scott, who felt like he was both incredibly drunk and horribly hungover, struggled for a moment to find the correct words and then struggled again to engage his mouth, “I...umm...think I’m okay.” He feebly pushed himself up from the makeshift bed into a sitting position, looked down at his hands, turned them over, wriggled his fingers, performed some careful arm curls, stretched his arms over his head and started similar tests on his legs and feet. Satisfied that all the parts were intact and fully functional, Scott finally looked over at James and mumbled, “How are you doing?”

“Oh, I’m fine,” A look of relief crossed his face as he said emphatically, “Boy, am I glad that you are doing so well!”

Scott’s mind was quickly clearing—he immediately noted the sound of relief in James’s voice and was struck by what James had said. He asked, “Why? Why are you glad? I thought you told me that you were one-hundred percent SURE this would work. Glad? Glad? In this case, glad indicates worry. Worry indicates Concern. Concern indicates uncertainty. Uncertainty means NOT SURE!”

“Well, in my enthusiasm, perhaps I overstated the odds a little.”

Scott didn’t try to hide the sarcasm in his voice, “Really? What a surprise. And what were the actual odds?”

“Perhaps a bit less than ninety percent.”

”How much less than ninety percent?”

“Actually, it was closer to fifty percent.”

“Wha???”

James quickly continued, “Anyway, it doesn’t matter! Odds only *predict* an outcome—it’s the outcome that matters and in this case, the outcome is as hoped for—oops!—I mean as predicted.”

“You bastard!” Scott gave him a weak, wry grin. “So where are we?”

“We are half a day away from the Earth Space Station.”

“How long have we been in hibernation?”

James didn’t answer.

“Well? How long?”

“...It took a little longer than I thought....”

"HOW LONG?"

"Eighteen months...." James, who could see a look of shock on Scott's face, hurried on, "After I sent you into hibernation, I recalculated the fuel situation. As you know...because of the...well...the loss of the crew, we didn't need as much fuel to leave the Venus surface, so we could use that additional energy to return to Earth. But I made a mistake with the fuel calculation the first time. There wasn't enough to achieve an acceleration that would get us back in a year and still have remaining fuel to slow the vehicle down. We could have reached Earth in a year but we would have gone right past it. I'm sorry, Scott."

"It's okay. At least we are here." Scott swung his head around the small space that he had slept in for a year and a half and said with a voice much more animated than James expected, "I can't believe we are here! I didn't think you could rig up that hibernation system—without proper tools or the hibernation drug and I was almost certain you were lying your face off about the 'one-hundred percent sure'—I was right about that, at least."

Scott paused for a moment, then, with a quiet, contemplative, slightly embarrassed voice, "James.... I have to tell you.... I have to say.... I lost my faith in you back at Venus. I lost my faith in everything. I thought... well, I thought that you were either insane or were trying to make my death easier by convincing me that we could hibernate without the drug. I'm sorry. I should have had more faith; I should have known that you wouldn't let me down."

"I understand. I didn't have time to explain properly and from your perspective, our fate certainly looked grim. But I really felt that I could find a way to send you into a very deep trance and keep you there for the whole trip. The Venusians had used a similar technique for their space travel but the method they used put them into a much deeper sleep trance. They would use much less air and stay down for the whole trip. Our brains are very similar, so I took a chance."

Scott's sense of humor was back on track, with a wry smile he said, "You mean *we* took a chance."

"If you didn't know you were taking a chance, were you then taking one?"

"Very funny, smart ass! But tell me what happened in that chamber on Venus."

"That was by far the most difficult experience in my entire life," James's eyes became distant, his face, normally so placid and composed, broke into a look of pain, then changed again into something...not quite right...not quite human...something alien. He remained in that condition until a massive shaking shiver took his body; he became James once again, then turned to Scott and said, "It still is the most difficult experience in my life. It's still with me now. I have to be careful not to fall back into that chamber," James shook himself again and continued on, "As you know the whole room lit up. It was intentionally very bright because the Venusians wanted to ensure that the light would penetrate any auto-tinting on our visors, then penetrate our eyelids and then strike the retina. That was very important. You remember—you asked me how I could have had learned the sum knowledge of all Venusian society in such a short time? You said that it was impossible to do such a thing and I said you were correct."

"Yes, I remember. So how did you learn it all?"

"The knowledge was already in me."

"What?"

"It was already in my brain. It's in your brain. It's in every human being's brain."

"No. That's Not Possible."

"Yes, it is. The Venusians genetically implanted it thirty-five thousand years ago."

"You can't store all that knowledge genetically!"

"Yes you can. I am proof. You said yourself that it was impossible for that information to be downloaded in any form in such a short time and you were correct."

"But how? It just doesn't make sense."

"I know it's difficult. But let me give you some interesting facts that might help convince you. Have you heard that scientists—psychologists to be exact—are puzzled that humans appear to only use around twenty percent of the brain's capacity?"

"Yes."

"That's because the rest of the human mind has been locked away, it's a storage area full of Venusian information. The light in the Venusian room flashed at a particular strength and rate that would unlock our minds."

"I still don't believe that you can store such specific information genetically."

"All Venusian children were born with a large amount of genetic knowledge, much more than human children. It had to be unlocked, but it was there already. It was unlocked in a special sequence by the Venusian equivalent of a teacher. The previous generation's knowledge was already in the minds of their children. Think about how much time that would save! Venusian children were productive members of society by the age of six!"

"I don't know...it seems so farfetched."

"Well, think of this...when we are born, we need to have a certain amount of knowledge for basic survival—how to breathe, how to suck at the breast, how to cry. That information is stored genetically. No one taught us how to do it. Did you know that the monarch butterfly has a very specific migration path that it follows every year? It knows how to go to the exact same location, right down to the same tree each and every year."

"That's a learned response. It learns the route."

"You'd be correct except for one very important point—it's not the butterfly that followed the route the first time that returns. It's the children of the original Butterfly that fly it again. How is that possible? There is only one answer, it's genetic knowledge."

"Here's another interesting point for you. Did you ever wonder why it is that humans, the most developed species on earth, are so helpless when born? Many species are fully functional at birth, others are close. For example, a baby Gazelle can run within hours of birth. But in our case, the Venusian geneticist who made the changes made a mistake. He wiped out a portion of the genetic code that provided those capabilities."

"It's just so incredible—so hard to believe."

"I know, but here I am! I am proof!"

"But how did this happen? Why did it happen?"

"The Venusians traveled to earth and took ten female Neanderthals—brought them back to Venus and genetically modified them so that their offspring would have a better chance of survival than any other Neanderthals. They made them stronger and smarter. Did you know that archeologists believe Neanderthals were first on earth but humans, who followed later, dominated? The Neanderthals gradually died off. Now I know why. We humans are the children of those genetically modified Neanderthal women."

"But why do all this? Why would the Venusians do this?"

"Because they wanted to warn us. They wanted to save us from the curse that fell upon them."

"How would they know that it would occur? Maybe it wouldn't happen to us."

"They predicted that any intelligent race would eventually face this problem. The trouble is the technical understanding required to predict and confirm the problem lags behind the problem itself and this disaster has a point of no return factor. Once you reach the point of no return there is nothing you can do to stop it. This is what happened to the Venusians. They developed the complex mathematical structures required to predict the catastrophe after their world had passed the point of no return," said James.

"They had traveled to earth several times and thought that it was likely an intelligent species was in development on our planet. They knew that this meant we would eventually fall victim to their fate if left alone. So they decided to try to warn us."

"Why do it this way? Seems to me it's very complicated and likely to fail."

"Other solutions had an even higher likelihood of failure. How would you do it? Remember at this time, we didn't exist and the Neanderthals were cave dwellers. Let's say they leave some kind of written message. How would they know if it would survive? How would they know if we would ever be able to read it? The message they were trying to leave is incredibly complex. It's not just a warning but also a method of extremely complex mathematical analysis that will allow humans to verify the existence of the impending disaster. Even today, on Earth, we still don't have this level of mathematical competence. Imagine what you would have to leave behind to ensure that we understood these concepts. It would be enormous! It would have to be the equivalent of all of our schooling—from grade one up to a Ph.D. in Math and Physics. Beyond that even. We don't have a Ph.D. level high enough to understand these principles. No—their solution was brilliant in its simplicity. Store the information in the human brain and unlock it when needed."

"So they created the Venus site intentionally to bring us to where they could unlock this knowledge." Scott continued, "But how would they know when we would need this information?"

"They knew that the problem would not manifest itself until after the Industrial Age."

"But how would they know when that was?"

"Simple! They monitored Earth for radio signals. Radio signals would indicate that the industrial age had started. They then estimated how long it would take to develop space travel and programmed their system to start a radio transmission at exactly that time."

"So I have this knowledge buried inside of me. Can I unlock it? I want this. I want to know all about the Venusians. I want the knowledge!"

"Well that's the problem. As a matter of fact, it's more than a problem—it's a disaster. The geneticist that modified the Neanderthals did something he wasn't supposed to."

"What do you mean?"

"He included his thoughts, his dreams, his experiences—his entire life in the genetic code," James stopped as unbidden memories from an alien life wafted over him and then said, with his voice full of emotion, "You see he loved his family so much that he wanted them to live on. He didn't want them to be forgotten. He wanted humans to know what it was like on Venus before doom descended. He wanted humans to know his beautiful wife and daughter and to remember them forever. His mind was clouded. It was clouded with a pervasive feeling of sadness and dread. He did not think or realize what he was doing to the alien race—to human beings. He did not realize that he was cloning his mind into every human being."

James shut his eyes, drew a deep breath and composed himself. Suddenly something strange, frightening, yet exciting began to happen on James's face—the muscles struggled and fought to reshape themselves temporarily into a new form—a shape never before seen on a human—the forehead pushed forward, the chin pulled back, his eyes squeezed into narrow slits—rippling wrinkles began to pile up on his cheekbones. His mouth tightened into a round "O" as a new language briefly bubbled and gurgled. A voice spoke, spitting out coughing, half-human words, "You see Scott, I am now him. My name is Ranula...and I am James. Two personalities coexist in my mind. One of them is from another planet and is of another race of beings."

His face, unable to further maintain the façade, dissolved for a nanosecond into a flaccid, almost formless shape and reemerged once again as James. He continued on as if nothing remarkable had happened.

"It is a horrendous schizophrenia. It destroyed the rest of the crew. It drove them mad. When I look down at my human body, I am repulsed, I am confused, I am frightened. How did I get here? How did I get into this ugly, horrible body? The sounds that you heard from the others and myself were our attempts to speak Venusian with a human voice box. I now know that it's not possible. That's why it sounded so atrocious. I can tell you that the Venusian voice produces a beautiful, wonderful singing sound, spread across a much wider vocal frequency range than ours and is capable of traveling through both air and water," said James.

"When the genetic knowledge is first unlocked, you are overwhelmed by the new personality. You cannot understand what has happened, you become suicidal. That's what happened to Adam, Penny, Peyton and Donatella. They were Venusians in human bodies. It was worse than that; they were Ranula in a human body. Ranula was repulsed and frightened by the Neanderthals. To be found in a very similar body to that of the Neanderthal was more than he could take. This was Ranula's fault. He did it out of love but in doing so, came close to destroying the human race."

"What do you mean? How could he destroy the human race?"

"It would be inadvertent. It would happen because no human being would live to learn the warning of the Venusians." James turned toward Scott, looked directly into his eyes and held them there, "Scott, we are very, very close to the point of no return on Earth. It may already be too late. Regrettably, I don't have enough information to ascertain the current state and that's why I had you try to warn Earth. It would take a year for us to get back and by then it might be too late! Now I fear that our warning was ignored." Still holding Scott's eye, he asked a question that had been trapped in his mind for sixteen months, "Do you know who Brodie told?"

Scott's voice was as flat as flat could be, "Yes. It was Jack Anderson,"

For the first time in an hour, all conversation ceased.

"We are going to have to be careful," said James

"Yes—very careful."

An angry look crossed Scott's face and then calmed, "But first, we get back to Earth. Everybody is going to get a shock. Jack...or whoever blew up the ship won't be prepared for our return and that should be enough to get us on the ground. After that, I don't know. There will be resistance to our warning. Many will be against us—they will try to discredit us."

“Even worse, much worse, some of them will prefer that we and our message didn’t exist at all.”

The conversation ceased again.

“I think we will need to disappear—go into hiding for a while.”

“We are going to need some allies,” said James.

“I was just thinking that myself.”

“Do you have any ideas?” James asked.

“Yes.... I do....”

Jack knelt down, extended his right forefinger and ran it along the name engraved on the weathered gravestone...Emma Anderson. His tears ran indiscriminately down his cheeks and fell onto the soft green grass. When his wife, Emma, had died twenty-one years ago of cervical cancer, it had been his daughter, Cynthia, who comforted him, held his shaking hand at the funeral, told him it was okay, told him that mom’s pain was over, told him that she was in a better place. A little girl of twelve had more composure than he had; she had a power in her that was remarkable.

As she grew, that power grew with her and anyone who met her felt it immediately. It was a quiet confidence that glowed within her, a self assurance that was not ego; it was love—for herself and everyone around her. She was strong, yet compassionate and she listened with an unblinking intensity that caused the speaker to feel that she was looking into their soul.

The pride he felt for his only child was only surpassed by his all-consuming love for her.

When she told him that she had cancer, the very same insidious, aggressive horror that had consumed her mother, all life left him...he died on that day.

The Venus project was underway, critical decisions were required almost hourly but he was so devastated that he couldn’t think, couldn’t make a decision about anything. He didn't trust himself to drive home so he took a cab and spent hours in his house in the dark, sitting in in a chair, crying, unable to even get up and eat. It took him several hours to write up a simple three line resignation email. A knock on the door was all that stopped him from pressing, "send."

Through the door he heard a muffled, "Dad?"

"Dad, open the door."

Jack stood up, wiped away the tears, straightened his shirt, walked to the door, started to cry again, fought it back and opened the door.

"Oh Cynthia, oh...." She reached out and hugged him. He could feel the massive life force against him, the power of her seemed to envelope him and in that instant his pain receded.

"Dad, I'm going to make it. Don't let this destroy you. I'll never give up and neither should you."

They spent the rest of the evening talking—right into the early hours of the morning, reminiscing, joking, laughing. It was one of the best nights of Jack's life. Cynthia's illness was put aside, a distant, black storm on the horizon—only light and happiness was allowed in that room.

A month later Jack heard about a controversial cancer treatment that cost a fortune; more than he could afford, but he enrolled Cynthia in it anyway. He'd never been good with money, had made some bad investments and so, even with a good salary, the house still had a mortgage and the car was leased. He took out another loan on the house but it wasn't going to be enough. He needed more money.

That's when he got a call from someone who said they worked for one of the leading bidders of one of the major Venus contracts—the contract was worth hundreds of millions. They wanted an advantage...and were willing to pay for it. Somehow they knew about his need. By this time Jack was desperate, he had to make another payment for Cynthia's treatment before the end of the week. So he agreed to their request. And so began the decent into hell.

As soon as he received a payment a new demand was made and more money was offered. It was always just enough to make the next cancer treatment payment. He couldn't, he wouldn't, say no and let his daughter die. It went on month after month. Till finally he met Kurt. Kurt wanted even more—access to internal NASA systems, access to programs, access to passwords. Jack balked and then the threats began, money would be withheld. Very quickly Jack agreed.

Then one day came the final step across the threshold of hell.

Kurt called him. "I have one more request...and then your done. We'll give you full payment for your daughter's treatment."

Even over the phone Jack could feel that something wasn't right with Kurt, there was a harsh, almost manic tone to his voice that scared Jack. "What is it?"

"Just a simple little thing. You'd be done in no more than a half hour."

"What?"

There was a pause. It was then that Jack was sure it was bad, very bad.

"I need you to log into a program...a program that's running on a server on the Renaissance."

Jack's voice rose an octave. "What? Why do you want me to do that? What could you possibly have to do with any program on the Renaissance?"

"It's a special program that I had installed on the ship, it's a failsafe. You know..."

"WHAT??? WHAT???" Jack was almost screaming.

"You know what's going on up there, you know that they have a crazy message, an insane message. You know that they've gone nuts. Who knows what disease they picked up on Venus. We can't let them come home."

"NO! NO! I won't do that...never!"

"You know Jack, your daughter is quite beautiful. I've have some pictures of her. I can understand why you love her so much. And I hear that she's making good progress with the treatments. It's a shame she won't make it to the end of them."

"What do you mean?"

"Here you were...all worried that she might die of cancer and instead, surprise, surprise, she has an accident. Maybe that's better anyway. Less suffering, always better to go quick I say."

Spittle flew as Jack screamed the words, "You bastard! You're a monster!"

"Don't worry about what I am. Worry about what's going to happen to your daughter."

He loved Cynthia so much...he'd do anything for her. He couldn't let her die.

The conversation ended a few moments later. Jack felt sick, he started to retch. He grasped the garbage basket by his desk just in time to heave the remains of his lunch into it.

Three months later it was confirmed that Cynthia's cancer was in remission. The price was incalculable, a price that Jack was sure he would pay every waking moment for the rest of his life. A price that others would pay for the rest of their lives...the loved ones of the astronauts that he had killed.

Chapter 31
BACK FROM THE DEAD

"Matt! Matt! You won't believe this!"

Matt looked up from his breakfast at Shannon who was sitting across from him and reading the news, "What?"

"Those Astronauts that your father tried to kill are alive!"

Matt responded angrily, "What? I know he didn't cause that explosion. He couldn't have. I know it!" He stopped as her statement began to sink in, then said, "What? What are you talking about?"

"It's in the news. Two of the Astronauts, the ones that had been on the surface, made it back in the space ship that was used to land on Venus. The paper says it's a miracle. They were in hibernation for a year and a half."

"No way! Are you sure?" Matt leaned over Shannon and scanned the article, just to make sure she wasn't reading some goofy tabloid.

"Yes, I'm sure! What do you think I am? A no-mind?" she glared at him as she continued, "Humm, it says here that they are back on earth but no one seems to know where they are. That's odd. I wonder, is NASA hiding them?"

Matt was back to munching on his toast; with a mouth full of food he said, "Maybe, they grew three heads and NASA doesssn't want ussh to know! Christ! Maybe they are contagioussssh!" Mouth open, Matt spewed toast particles over the table.

"Jesus, Matt! Close your mouth! I hate it when you do that! But... yeah...you could be right there. They might be in quarantine. Yeah.... NASA probably doesn't want the public getting nervous. I wonder what Kurt knows?"

"What do you mean you don't know where they are? How is that possible? You were supposed to take them to quarantine! What? What? I know I didn't say that you were to guard them. I didn't think I had to say it! So they just wandered out of the quarantine area—went for a stroll! And you guys, where were you? Christ! Okay.... Okay.... We have to keep this quiet. This is a major embarrassment. I don't know what I'm going to tell the President. I just hope you can find them before I have to tell him anything." Jack, whose roly-poly face had never fully recovered, rearranged his new wrinkles into an intense frown and slammed down the phone.

"I wish you had contacted me as soon as they got in touch with the space station. They could have been dealt with up there."

"What was I supposed to do? Radio up to the space station and tell them to kill those two? We were stuck! I had to bring them down!"

"Well it's too late now anyway. They're here. You say they've left the quarantine center. That may be a good thing. If I find them before anyone else, they'll disappear forever. It would just be another one of those unsolved mysteries."

"I don't want to know about it. I've done my part. I'm out!"

"Not a chance, Jack. You didn't do your part... or I should say you didn't complete your part. There's two left. I'm counting on you to keep me informed. If someone finds them, your job is to contact me before anyone else. That gives me an opportunity to take care of business. Understood? Jack?"

No answer.

"Jack, you weenie, I'm waiting to hear that you understand."

"I understand." The soft words of commitment hung there, dangling out of Jack's mouth, a reminder that he was a slave, a pawn. Expendable? Perhaps.... Yes.... Most likely.... *I'm trapped! No way out!*

Shannon stepped out into the cold winter night. She looked at her watch, *just after six.* She was a little late; they had been doing some last minute planning for a Green Peace awareness campaign. Shannon tucked her scarf deeper into her jacket and hurried along the quiet, dark street, toward home. She never liked this part—going home in the dark. The Green peace office was located in an isolated section of downtown, amidst warehouse and office buildings that seemed to always empty early. Shannon looked down the street—three long, dark, light-splotched blocks away she could see the hustle and bustle of one of the shopping districts crossing her path—a bright, happy place of shifting shapes and silhouettes—outlines of people striding along, on their way home or going to a restaurant or perhaps completing a little shopping. Cars and trucks flit by—a jumble of ever-changing black, grey and subdued color shapes under great pools of liquid light. That street was her beacon. Her beacon of safety.

She picked up the pace. When she reached the end of the first block, she looked back. She did it every time. *No one there of course!* Shannon turned again toward her beacon, then slowed, breath sucked away. A dark, big shape was coming, half a block distant. *Where did he come from?* Fear struck her, knocked her off stride. *Go forward or back?* She felt stupid being this scared. *Don't be silly, it's just some guy going back to the office. Forgot his briefcase...or something....*

She kept going, eyes leaping back and forth, back and forth, back and forth, between her beacon and the stranger. *Goodness! He's big!* She kept going.

An alley was opening just in front of her to the right. It seemed to her that the giant had picked up speed. It had to be her imagination. She kept going. The alley was beside her now...and so was he. A goliath, cloaked from head to toe—she could hear the swish of the cloth as he swung past her. *Just as I thought, nothing to worr....*

Her feet left the ground! The monster had scooped her up with a massive arm and in one single stride had taken her into the alley. His hand covered her mouth as she attempted to scream, he whispered in her ear, "Don't yell. I won't hurt you. I need your help."

She started swinging all her body parts in every direction. Some of them were trying to hit him, others were trying to get away. A shadow moved nearby—*another one!* Normal sized this time. He was trying to stop her legs from kicking. She applied as much power to her legs as was possible. Nothing happened. She tried to twist. Nothing happened. She tried to scream again. Muffled, muted sound squelched its way past the fingers, dying before it reached the end of the alley. They had her!

"Calm down! Calm down! You will not be hurt! We need your help. Please relax."

The smaller one added, "Calm yourself. We will not hurt you."

Sound was beginning to filter through her panic. She began to regain some self-control. She was caught. She would have to bide her time and wait for a chance. Suddenly she heard the big man say, "We will not hurt you. I'm going to take my hand away from your mouth, don't scream. We just want to talk to you."

Shannon's words followed the hand as it left her mouth, "Will... you...please...put...me...down!"

"I will but don't try to run, you won't get more than a yard."

Shannon peered at both of them, trying to see their faces in the dark alley but it was too dim for her to catch anything other than vague outlines and shifting contours. Quickly she said, "What do you want? You've got some nerve grabbing me like that!"

"We need your help," said the small one.

"You've already said that. I'm getting out of here." She started to turn back to the street and bumped into a very big human wall.

"Not quite yet."

"Have you heard of the Astronauts that returned from Venus?" he asked.

"Yes.... I have. Why?" Shannon looked at the two men again, she still couldn't see their faces in the dim light but suddenly a strange feeling came over her—a fate-filled shudder shocked its way through her body.

"Why'd you pick me?" asked Shannon as they seated themselves in the coffee shop.

"Well, to be honest, you were an easy target. We had watched the office for a few days. You were always the last one to leave. It's a lonely spot—that street at night. Isn't it?" asked Scott.

"Yes, I think from now on I'll have my boyfriend come pick me up."

"A wise idea."

"Why Boston?"

"Pardon?"

"Why did you come to Boston? Why Greenpeace in Boston?"

"We needed some space between us and Florida. We believe that there is an intensive, clandestine search on for us. We also heard that the Greenpeace office in Boston is...well...very militant...and we needed a group that would have the guts to hide a couple of refugees from Venus."

Scott watched Shannon carefully; he studied her face for a reaction: she showed no fear or concern—only interest. He was beginning to think they'd picked the right person.

"Why the hell didn't you just walk into the office and ask for help?"

"We're cautious. Who knows how you or someone else in the office would react to us. Maybe you'd just think we were nuts and call the police."

"I must admit that would be a possibility. Some of us might have thought you were just another batch of weirdos that we see from time to time." Shannon paused, not sure if she should say...and said it anyway, "Do you think that your lives might be in danger?"

With a sudden jerk, James leaned across the table, his face a mask of absolute concentration, and asked, "Why would you say that?"

Scott's eyes left Shannon—he watched James as intently as James was watching Shannon—since the Venus incident, James seemed to know things he shouldn't.

"Well, there's someone I think you should meet." she hesitated, still not sure if it was the right thing to do.

For a few brief seconds only the sounds of clattering of distant cutlery and dishes filled the small booth in the deserted coffee shop.

Then, a flicker of recognition broke across James's face, "Yes.... I agree.... M...Ma...Matt.... Yes, we should meet Matt."

Shannon pulled back stunned, "How? How could you know that?"

"I don't think you are ready for the answer to that question."

"My husband! You must tell me what has happened! You cannot go on like this!" Namia was standing close to Ranula, touching him, soothing him. Her pain was worsened because she did not understand the cause of Ranula's distress. Many rest periods had gone by and she still could not convince Ranula to tell her what this doom was.

"The Everlasting Elders do not want the people to know! I cannot tell you! I have made a promise to the Essential Geneticist!"

"Please! Please! PLEASE! Let me touch you, let us have thoughts together! I must learn of this. I must share your pain, my love! I cannot soothe you if I do

not know what ails you! I will tell no one! You know that I will not do anything to shame you!"

Ranula's resolve, which had withstood the barrage for so long, finally weakened. He said nothing. He reached up took her beautiful head in his hands, leaned forward and touched head to head, thought to thought, feeling to feeling. Namia shuddered, then spasmed as she felt his dread, felt the despair and anguish and recognized their doom. She responded, as all females of their race did, with all-encompassing compassion, her soothing emotion sought his pain, held it, then drew it back into herself, swallowing pain with love. They stood there for much time—Ranula felt Namia's warm life-thought enter him, momentarily rebuilding his scarred, damaged soul. He was happy again, forgetful of events—only the moment mattered, the moment of quiet love—soul to soul—love springing into eternity, it swirled and intertwined...then combined into a unified love for their little one, their one and only, their reason for being.

Days later, Ranula turned slowly around, his eyes following the grim-grey buildings of industry surrounding the park. He hated them. They were a curse! In the foreground, Lillia played and danced in the Lula grass. Namia, as always now, stood close to him,

"My husband! I do not understand! Why cannot the Everlasting Elders fix this doom?"

"It is too late; our science did not predict the curse in time. The residue of our industry has created a layer in the atmosphere that will not allow heat to escape. Our wonderful planet is rapidly heating and there is nothing we can do to stop it."

"How hot will it get?" she asked. Ranula looked down at her, she looked so tired! He could see sad hope painted on her face—perhaps there was a way to survive, maybe it wouldn't be so bad. Eyes glistening, she waited for the answer that she had to hear. The pain! It hurt him so! To see her like this!

"Everything...." He stopped, unable to force the words out, his head dropped to his chest. Finally he took her hands in his and whispered, "Everything...will...

die. No life will exist on this planet. It will be a land of bare rock and dust...our dust...oh!...our dust, my love, will mingle with the dust of every other life. We have destroyed our planet."

She replied, "Then we must leave. Leave this planet!"

"Where would we go? Who would go? There are not enough interplanetary vehicles for everyone."

"The third planet! We could go to the third planet! It is habitable. It is not far! The ships could travel back and forth and eventually take everyone!"

"But Namia.... Namia...." He reached out and touched her face as softly as he could; he looked into her eyes, "There is life there now. Life that would be destroyed by our presence. We cannot destroy life to save ourselves. The Everlasting Elders have debated. Our code has been reaffirmed. We will take no life. Our people have lived by this rule for all the ages. It will not be forfeit now."

Namia hung her head, a slow, almost imperceptible swaying motion, beautiful in its anguish, had started, "Yes, I understand, my sweet love. We cannot.... It is a horror! Our poor Lillia!" she turned and looked into his sad, pained eyes and asked, "When?"

"Oh my dear, dear love! My dear love! My sweet one! I am so sorry! Not long! A few more turns of the planet around our star and the seas will begin to heat, a few more turns and then they will boil. Anything on the land will burn," He cried out, "How could we have done such a thing!" He leaned against Namia and hugged her as hard as he could, "We can hide in tunnels below the surface for some time but who could live that life?"

"What will we do? What of Lillia?"

"I do not know."

As they stood swaying, pain ridden in each other's arms, above them the Venus atmosphere, like Greek gods upon high, looked down at the infinitesimally insignificant figures, on the tiny hill, in the little fortress park—a small, brilliant splotch in endless grey...and already,

air was simmering, air was heating....

Chapter 32
TRAITOR

"Matt! Matt! Wake up! Wake up! Wake up!"

"Whaaa? Hunnnh? Huh? Ummm...what?" Groggy and stunned, Matt dragged himself out of the nether-land that humans call sleep. He gradually became aware of dampness all around him, "I'm sweating like a pig. What time is it?"

"It's two in the morning. You were having that dream again! That noise you make is gross! It's freaky!" Shannon had switched on a lamp on the bedside table that shed a dull yellow-orange glow through the room. Colored in that strange, dim light she looked as though she was a partner to his dream—a beautiful alien siren, sent to tempt him back to a world beyond reality.

"Yeah...oh man." He ran his hands through his gooey, sweat-filled hair. "It was that weird landscape again...strange.... I always feel as if I know it...something was chasing me...my heart was beating so fast. I felt...felt.... Dread."

"Well I wish you'd stop it. It's the second time this week you woke me up."

"Tell me about it. You're not the one who is being chased on some alien world. It's really weird. It just seems so real." He looked at Shannon who was leaning, with breasts dangling, over him. For once, those tantalizing orbs held no attraction—he was still lost in a strange, real, yet unreal world, "I mean, I know that just after you wake up from a dream it sometimes feels real but this...this is really, real! Ummm.... If you know what I mean."

"Well.... I'm not sure...but I'll take your word for it. If it keeps happening maybe you should go see somebody about it."

"A shrink? No way! Nope. I'm not going anywhere near one of those brain-busters. I'm sure it's going to go away...they always do...." He sat up suddenly with a look of concern. "Don't they?"

"Well...yes. I'm sure it will go away. Here, let me see if I can help it along." With a coy smile, she pushed him back down, lay on top of him and kissed his forehead. Matt reached up and put his arms around her. She kissed him on the nose, then the lips, then a little further down.

He stopped her, pulled her back up and kissed her deeply on the mouth—it was an intense loving kiss that was indifferent to sex. Then Matt nibbled-whispered into her ear. "I don't think there are words that can describe how much I love you. I mean I'm just blown away. I just can't get enough of you. I love you! Love you! Love you! Love you! Love you!"

Shannon giggled as she replied, "I think I'm getting your point. But just to be certain, perhaps you could do a little more of that in the other ear, my love." He started over to the other ear, stopped and thoughtfully looked off into the distance.

"What's the matter?"

"I'm not going to meet with those guys."

"Oh, Matt! We've already had this conversation."

"I don't want to get involved. I did what I could, that's it. I'm not doing anything more."

"Matt! Your dad almost killed them. The least you can do is try to help them now. They are on the run. They need help. And you're in the perfect position to help them—your dad has access to tons of info and you have access to his info. If they are correct, the entire world is in danger. Who knows how close we are to the point of no return." She laid her bare breasts on his chest as provocatively as she could, "You said that you loved me...that you would die for me. Didn't you?"

"Yes.... I did."

"Then do this for me. Do this for me if you won't do it for yourself or the rest of the world. Do this for me."

Matt looked into her eyes, beautiful even in the dim light, he loved her so!

"Okay, I will."

"Thank you." As she laid her head on his chest, with his heart thumping happily in her ear, a qualm tickled her mind, a tiny seed of a worry...which was quickly overcome and forgotten by the warmth of Matt's body.

Scott sat at a park bench watching his breath steam away in the cold winter air. He looked over at James. Although James had a lot more control now over his dual personalities, he still periodically slipped away, "You okay there?" he asked.

"Humm? Oh! Yes, fine." James turned back to Scott and smiled, "Or I should say, Yes, Scott I'm still here."

"Just checking."

"No problem, I appreciate the concern," James's head suddenly snapped toward one of the entrances to the park, "They are here."

Scott looked—he couldn't see them, "Where?"

"Nearby," he nodded in the direction that he had been looking, "That way."

Two figures, small in perspective, unrecognizable from that distance, appeared.

"Is that them?"

"Yes."

A quizzical frown strapped itself to Scott's face as he watched James with the intensity of a young boy trying to catch the Magician's trick, he asked, "How? How do you know? How could you know??"

"Wait...be patient."

Scott swiveled back to the two figures, their shapes were larger now, one a man, the other a woman.

"Look! There they are." Shannon lifted her arm and pointed.

"Christ! Don't do that!" Matt roughly pushed her arm down and whipped off bird-like glances in every direction, "Christ! Why don't you just start screaming at them like an Astronaut groupie! That way everybody in the park will see us," a few more bird-glances occurred, "Maybe they're being watched." His pace almost slowed to a stop, "We should get out of here."

Shannon, now a stride ahead, reached back, took hold of his jacket lapel and angrily pulled hard, "Don't you chicken out now! Remember your promise!"

Matt, slightly off-balance, tripped and shot past Shannon on his way to a face-plant. Shannon, whose arm was still attached to Matt's lapel, tried to slow his progress and quickly found herself joining Matt's descent. Self-preservation released her grip on his jacket, but too late. She was heading down. Matt, who had twisted his body upward, was now in an ass down position, coming in for a one-point landing. Shannon was doing a lovely off-balance pirouette, rotating just above him. As Matt's ass was saying hello to the pavement, he saw Shannon's lovely, perfectly shaped rump starting to swallow up his field of view. In almost any other circumstance, he would have been very pleased with the vista but on this occasion, fear predominated. He thrust up a hand to ward her off which probably saved a broken nose but caused further damage to his back and head when he struck the ground. An instant later, Shannon made her own one-point landing on Matt's head. They lay there for a brief, embarrassed, tangled moment. Then Matt, while spewing a constant stream of profanity, started trying to detach Shannon's butt from his face.

"Oh no! Are you alright?" cried Shannon as she rolled herself off of Matt's face.

"No! I'm not alright! The back of my head is killing me and I feel like an idiot!"

Matt's carefully combed and oiled hair, which had been not so carefully rearranged by Shannon's butt now had a punk rock look with spikes and tufts indiscriminately pointing off into the park. The back of his head sported a dried leaf from a nearby bush, some bits of dead grass and oh! A twig!

Expressions of embarrassment, fear and disgust simultaneously cavorting across his face. It was too much for Shannon who was now sitting beside him. Her face started a giggle, halted—it tugged at her lip—halted, twitched, halted...her expression was immobile for a few seconds but suddenly a great peel of laughter blew its way past the struggling face.

"What a spectacle! Well that settles it; I think we are a shoe-in for the Laurel and Hardy spy award." That voice, full of happiness and love, even in the circumstances, settled Matt's emotions—he joined her—smiling, then laughing outright.

From a distance they heard, "Are you okay?"

Matt twisted his sore head toward the sound, "Christ! Here they come."

Shannon, who was now starting to stand, helped pull Matt to his feet and began plucking pieces of the park out of his hair.

"Are you okay?" Scott asked again.

Another giggle squirted out of Shannon, "Yes. Yes, we're fine. Aren't we Matt?"

No answer.

Startled, Shannon glanced over at Matt...he was blankly staring at James. Her eyes flashed over to James—he was returning the stare with an intense, unblinking, pinpoint expression. Some seconds passed and abruptly Matt shook all over—a soft moan escaped from him—he put his right hand up to his forehead and held that pose, frozen like the winter world around him.

With her voice filled with concern, Shannon asked, "Matt! What's the matter?"

Matt remained still.

Shannon's voice gained intensity; she reached over and shook him as she said, "Matt! Matt! What's the matter?"

James interrupted, "He's okay. Just give him a second...."

"What's going on?" Scott queried.

"I think it's time to explain, let's find a place to sit," James said.

They found a picnic bench near the Charles River and sat facing each other—James and Scott on one side, Matt and Shannon on the other.

As they settled, James stared at the water of the river—the weak winter sunshine was bouncing and flickering in his eyes—pieces of sparkling shore ice, wavering with endless shades of translucent white and grey, loosened by the gentle touch of the sun, drifted by. Trees, with bare branches twisted, dangled at the water's edge and waited to see their leaves again in spring. Even in winter, beauty was everywhere. It was the beauty of anticipation, the beauty of expected new life. For thousands and thousands of years the river had seen the eternal cycle of nature....

Eternal?

Eternal?

Ranula rose up...great sadness took him, flowed like the river and overwhelmed—he saw Namia holding little Lillia, alone, protecting her from the intense heat, her grip slowly slipping....

"James. James." Scott reached over and shook his shoulder.

"Sorry, just a minute...just...." He reached up and wiped a tear away from his eye. He buried his hands in his face, a quiet sobbing sound frosted in the air.

"I feel it...feel it...feel it...feel it." So softly did the words issue, that, to Shannon they seemed to rise from the table. She continued to watch James but at her side, there was movement...disturbed, she turned to see Matt—his face etched with sorrow; tears flowing down his face in rivulets. His lips barely moved as he said, "feel it...feel it...." He was holding himself, arms crossed tight over his chest, and swaying in short, pain-filled movements.

"Matt! wh...."

"Leave him. He will be alright in a moment," said James pushing back the tears, "It was my fault, he could feel my strong emotion."

"What?? What are you saying?? How is that possible?" Shannon asked.

James took a moment to composed himself and then said, "That was what I was going to explain...but first let me begin with a question." His eyes swung to Scott and then back to Shannon, "Have you ever heard that we humans appear to have a third eye, undeveloped in the brain, that some people claim gives them psychic powers?"

"Yes, it's a bunch of bunk," replied Scott.

"Actually, it's not," countered James.

He turned to Scott and said, "You know how I said that Ranula altered our prehistoric ancestors genetically? Well the Venusians had a power that was beyond our kind. It's what helped them to develop so quickly; it was a mere ten thousand years from the time that they crawled out of the sea till...their end. They were able to share their thoughts and feelings without words—essentially a form of mind reading but taken to a new level. They discovered that they could connect themselves into a network of minds, all of them working at a single purpose. They became a single powerful brain. They called it a collective."

"Using this method they could solve problems at an astonishing rate. Their technology leaped ahead far faster than did ours. Sadly, it leaped ahead too fast."

"This capability was located in their heads as a bulge to the cranium just above the eyes," his right hand moved upward—fingers delicately caressed a point on his brow, "You could call it a third eye."

Soft, whispered words crawled over the table, "The most intimate method involved touching one forehead against another. The mates of their species would do this to feel every sensation and emotion of their lover." *Oh! Namia!* His right hand moved toward a beautiful, imagined shape locked forever in his mind.

"But they could also, if within a few feet of one another, create a collective of multiple minds. Then at some point in their past, a collective discovered a particular type of material that could transmit thoughts, just like a phone line. They could connect hundreds or thousands of minds together and from that point on, technology increased at an even greater rate. It grew so quickly that it surpassed their natural evolution—they remained part aquatic and part land mammal; they could breath in both air and water and indeed lived in underwater cities," said James.

"The Venusians loved their water world so much that they kept the seas pristine. But in order to maintain their incredibly rapid industrial and technological growth, they abused the land and air. This was their downfall—they let the air pollution build to the point where a greenhouse effect was created—their world would heat uncontrollably until all life would die. Eventually a collective discovered the disaster—but too late. They had passed the point of no return."

"How horrible." said Shannon.

"Are you saying that we have this third eye capability?" asked Scott.

"Yes, but partially developed. When Ranula made those genetic changes, purposefully or not, we were given psychic ability—but normally it's locked away with all the other genetic knowledge. I gained this facility when I entered the light chamber on Venus."

"So you can read my mind?" Shannon asked with concern.

"Oh. No, I can't read your mind as such. I can feel strong emotion and I can pick out very strong, important thoughts—you are in love with Matt, so I could feel his name and I picked up some idea that he could help us—that was all."

"Okay...I see...still it's a very weird feeling—knowing that someone is...well...in your head. I don't like it." She looked over at Matt who was slowly recovering from his episode.

"What happened to Matt?"

"Yeah, what happened to me? What did you do to me? I could feel this incredible sadness; I could feel it coming from you! It was awful."

"I didn't do anything. Your genetic knowledge is somehow unlocked...." He gazed off into space as he thought for a moment, then turned back to Matt, "Or perhaps it's better to say that it's partially unlocked. I don't know why or how. Since I have been back to earth, I have encountered a few people who seemed to be in this state."

"This would explain those people who have claimed to be able to read minds—they had activated—or partially activated their third eye," said Shannon.

"Will I have all the genetic knowledge unlocked?" queried Matt.

"I sincerely hope not."

"Why?"

"There are.... Ummm...some side effects."

"What?? Side effects! What kind of side effects?"

"You may go insane."

"No! Oh! man! I...." Matt's voice was climbing. Scott jumped in,

"I'm sure it won't happen. All these other people that have this... gift...seem to be sane. I think that they haven't completely unlocked. Right James?"

"Yes, of course. Sorry I didn't mean to worry you. Anyway, if anything started to happen, I might be able to help you, now that I know the cause."

"Well I don't want to find out if you can."

"Very understandable."

"What do you need from us?" asked Shannon.

"A powerful computer that I can use to help me compute the status of Earth's atmosphere. As you know, we have been aware of global warming for many, many years now—almost three quarters of a century—there have been countless attempts to significantly reduce greenhouse gas emissions but every time, powerful corporate lobbies step in and either completely block or significantly reduce the initiative. So regardless of our awareness of the problem, the Earth has continued to warm unabated. But the important question is, the real question is, have we passed the point of no return? Can we still stop the warming process or is it too late? To find that answer, I need a very powerful computer."

"Matt, your dad has powerful computers," said Shannon.

"Well, yeah...he's got access to a super computer. But why can't you use a regular computer?"

"I have to accurately simulate the global weather conditions. Until now, no one has come even close to doing this. The math is extremely complex. I also need weather data points from all around the world going back ten years—it's available on the web but it's a huge amount of data. Finally, I need the daily emissions data from vehicles and industrial plants going back ten years—all this information will allow me to project when we would cross the point of no return threshold...that is...if we haven't reached it already."

Shannon turned to Matt and carefully watched his expression as she asked, "You could get James and Scott into your dad's office couldn't you?"

"Yeah.... But it's not safe! You know that!"

"What do you mean, it's not safe?" queried Scott.

"Well...ummm...yeah...." Matt stared off towards the river, his face rippled with varying emotions; fear, disgust, embarrassment all took a turn as he struggled to find words, any words that would lessen the impact of what his father had done. Finally, Shannon said it for him,

"There's something you should know, something very weird...a coincidence...spooky almost...." For the next fifteen minutes Shannon told them about Kurt. "...so you see how strange it is that you should find me, the one person besides Matt who knows Kurt's connection with the Venus project."

Silence descended on the little table in the park; a bird gliding high above saw four lonely shapes, unmoving, perhaps frozen by winter's touch. After a time, Scott, grim as granite, said to no one in particular,

"It's more than strange, it's almost impossible."

"Yet it happened," replied James.

More time passed, then from Scott, "Perhaps we were wrong about Jack."

"Yes, perhaps...." replied James.

"Who's Jack?" asked Shannon.

"Someone at NASA. We thought he might have had something to do with the explosion."

"Look, I still don't know how my da...how Kurt could have done this. I locked him out. There was no way he could get back in. I couldn't get back into the failsafe if I wanted to."

"There could have been another back door that you didn't know about," Scott said.

Matt paused. "True...yeah true...my old man is very thorough, I wouldn't put it past him." A sigh slipped out with his breath. "I never thought of that."

"Well there's no question that we should avoid Matt's dad if at all possible—innocent or not—it's not worth the risk if there is any other alternative. Scott looked over to Shannon, "Does Greenpeace have any high powered computers?"

"No, we don't have the budget for that kind of thing."

"What about MIT? Can we get in there?" asked James

Matt thought for a moment and then replied, "Not without telling them what we are up to. And that would give away your location—it would get out in an instant."

"Okay, not a good idea. Any other possibilities?" said Scott.

"What about buying usage on a super computer?" asked James.

"It's very, very expensive and it will take days to calculate the result—even using a super computer."

"Looks like we are back to Matt's dad."

"Dare we take a chance?"

"We don't seem to have any other choices."

"It's pretty scary."

"Yeah, scary, very scary."

James suddenly perked up, "Hey! I have an idea. What about a remote login? Matt could you get into his office and setup a remote login?

That way we can access his computer from some other location; we don't have to be standing around in his office for hours while I calculate the point of no return."

"Yeah, I can. I don't want to...but I can. If he catches me, we're in big trouble."

"I don't see any other solution."

"Why do I get the feeling I'm using up all my nine lives?" Matt exclaimed.

"Just once more, Matt!" encouraged Shannon.

Matt replied with sarcasm, "Yeah, sure, just once more. Bugger!" He hesitated, clearly looking for some way out...but finally, resigned to his fate, with voice lowered almost to a whisper, he said, "Okay, once more. I'll do it."

Scott looked at his watch; it was coming up on five a.m. He walked over to James who was intently staring at the laptop screen—his face inches away—some characters scrolled up, James leaned even closer, pulled back, then started pounding on the keyboard.

"James."

No answer.

"James."

He waited.

No answer.

Scott gave up calling his name and started phase two—shoulder shaking and, "James... James!... it's time buddy."

"Just a minute...need a little more time...."

"Sorry, James, but the time is up. Remember we don't go beyond five a.m.—we don't want Kurt coming into the office and finding his expensive computer chatting away to itself. Right?"

By now, Scott knew that he had to be very insistent. The first time he did this, he let James talk him into giving him a, 'few more minutes,' and he let himself be conned by, 'just about done, just a sec,' and, 'yup, yup...I'm shutting down...wait...one more thing.' He finally had to physically drag James away from the desk. As it was, they slipped an hour past the cutoff time.

Of course Matt had panicked, "My dad gets in early! Christ! If he sees, we're done! Man! Oh! Man! Maybe I shouldn't go to the office today!"

It took Scott and Shannon another hour to convince Matt that, if Kurt were suspicious, it would look worse if he didn't go. So Matt went to the office but he had been tense and freaked-out all day. Late in the afternoon, Kurt called him into the office to discuss some mundane business issues—afterward Matt had to change his underwear. All in all, it was a bit of a disaster.

Five days later, it was still a struggle to drag James away from the computer but Scott made sure that he always won.

"Time, James.Time." He waited about thirty seconds but received no response at all from James, so Scott started phase three—pulling James up from his seat by his armpits.

"Okay! Okay! I give up! No more physical abuse please!"

"Right, then let me see you logout," Scott leaned over his shoulder and made sure the shut-down command was given. Then, "See. That wasn't so hard."

"But I'm so close! Another hour and I think we would be done. Now we have to wait till one a.m. tonight to finish."

"Sorry, buddy, but that's the way the cookie crumbles. We take no further chances."

"So it's almost done. Fantastic! I gotta tell you...." Matt waved a piece of toast in the air, he took a huge bite and with mouth full said, "it's been scaring the craaappph out of me! Every time my dad callsssh me into the office, I swear I'm go'na die of a heart attaaachhh!" The old breadcrumb volcano had started again. Scott and Shannon pushed away from the table to avoid the spray. Scott looked at Shannon. She just shook her head and gave the universal, "I give up," sign.

"Tonight, after James is done...." To Shannon's relief, the last of the toast disappeared. "I'll delete everything, go into the office and shut down the remote login."

"Sounds like a plan." replied Scott with a toast related smile still stuck to his face. "Well, I'm going to hit the sack. James is already sleeping. I'll see you guys tonight."

It was a great day. Somehow, once again, they had managed to pull another stunt right under the old man's nose. Matt wasn't feeling cocky, just mighty relieved to have escaped with his life one more time. He'd been in the office for about an hour when the phone rang, he didn't recognize the number, was going to ignore it but...curiosity.... "Hello?"

"Is this Matt Dragonovich?"

"Yes it is."

"This is Sheila from the Greenpeace office. We were wondering what happened to Shannon this morning—she didn't come in. Is she sick?"

"...Wha? What?"

"She didn't come in this morning."

"No. That's not possible. She should be at work."

"Mr. Dragonovich I'm at work. She's not here. Trust me."

"Oh. No. Ummm...."

"Obviously you don't know where she is. Should I call the police?"

"What? No! No! Don't!"

"She's missing. The police should be notified."

An uncontrolled shout barked its way over the phone, "No! NO!" Matt's panicked mind was dimly aware that he was sounding very suspicious and weird—he tried to get his voice under control while he looked for an excuse. "Gee.... I'm sorry...just realized...she had an emergency dentist appointment.... Toothache last night.... Damn! I completely forgot. I was supposed to call you. Sorry."

There was a slight pause. Matt held his breath.

"Will she be in tomorrow?"

A sigh of relief almost slipped out of him. "Yes, I think so. I'll get her to call you tomorrow—Bye!"

Matt hung up without waiting to hear the goodbye on the other end. Fear was sizzling away in the pit of his stomach. Did he forget something? Did she tell him that she was going somewhere this morning? He wasn't the best listener in the world but given their current situation, surely he would have remembered if she wasn't going into the office. He shakily punched out the home number on the phone, missed a key, had to redial. It rang four times and then went to voice mail. *Damn!* He hung up and tried again. *Please answer!* Nothing! *Damn! Damn! Damn!* Acid was starting to burn a hole in his gut. *Something is wrong! Wrong!* Matt leapt from his desk and ran out of the office. He fought the urge to sprint towards his dad's office—legs packed full of fear-filled adrenaline reluctantly slowed to a rapid walk. A couple of horribly long minutes later, as he was approaching the office, still fifteen feet away and not slowing his gait one bit, he tried his best to casually say,

"Hi Gina! Is Kurt in?" but the words were loud and desperate. Gina, who had been sifting through some papers looked up startled and replied,

"No, sorry Matt. He's off-site today."

By now he was at her desk—still traveling at a rapid pace and without slowing Matt asked, "Are you sure? He didn't tell me! Are you sure?" He tried to keep his voice level normal but it kept rising in volume. Gina was looking at him like he was off his rocker.

"Yes, I'm sure, Matt."

"I'll just check." He brushed past her desk, bumped into that stupid garbage can and didn't even notice.

"Suit yourself. But he's not there."

He swung the door open, thrust his head in, and looked everywhere—even behind the door. He turned, left the door open and started half running past a very puzzled Gina who was now standing, "See, like I said he's not here." Suddenly, Matt slammed on the brakes,

"Did he say where he was?"

"No."

"Did he leave a phone number?"

"No, just call his cell phone like usual if you want to reach him. Matt! What's the matter?" It was too late, he was halfway down the hall, his mind, seething and churning, was just barely able to direct him to the elevators—he had to go home! He had to find Shannon!

Matt hit the horn and pulled hard on the steering wheel to avoid some goof who was about to cut him off. His car, traveling at a good sixty miles per hour in downtown Boston, swung out into the oncoming lane, forcing another poor bastard to swerve into the far lane to avoid a collision. Matt whipped the wheel back in the other direction and, slightly out of control, just managed to avoid hitting a parked car. *Man! That was close!* Common sense began to prevail. He slowed down. His brain began to engage for the first time since the phone call. *It's just probably a coincidence that the old man is out of the office. Shannon must have gone somewhere and forgot to call the office...or let me know....* He started feeling sick again. He was close to home. She'll be there. *Just his over active imagination!* Matt turned up his street, made a sharp left into the apartment driveway and stamped on the brake pedal. *The security gate remote! Where's the damn remote?* He fumbled around the car wasting precious, fear-filled seconds. Finally, he found it—where it belonged, on the car visor. With a rickety jerk, the gate began its unhurried, leisurely, clattering. He cursed through clenched teeth as it painfully pulled itself open a pathetic inch at a time. Matt began to shout, "*Come on! Come on!*" He pounded on the steering wheel and fought back the urge to slam the Ferrari right through the bloody thing. As soon as he thought that the car would clear the gate, he hit the gas—tires squealed, the radio antenna twanged as it caught the bottom of the gate.

"Shannon! Shannon!"

The front door of the apartment was still banging against the wall as Matt ran down the hallway. He looked in the kitchen. No one there. "Shannon! Shannon! Scott? James? Anyone!" He was screaming now. He turned toward the living room, "Shannon! Shan...." But he couldn't get the word out. He no longer had any breath. Every last air molecule had been pushed out of his lungs—the living room was destroyed. Nothing was intact: the TV had been knocked off the wall, the surround sound system cabinet was smashed, lying on its side, pictures on the walls were hanging sideways—some were on the floor—couches, chairs were upside down, sideways, shoved up against walls, one chair was broken and worst of all...*God! No!* There was blood! A lot of it, some of it pooled, some of it smeared. It was on the floor, on the walls. He ran to the bedrooms, knowing—certain of what he would find.

NO! NO! PLEASE NO!

Matt tried to shout, "Shannon! Shannon!" But only a dry, hoarse whisper touched the air. His whole body trembled as he forced it to peer around the door into their bedroom. It was fine! Nothing out of order and.... No blood! He checked the bathroom, the closet. Everything was okay. His throat finally found its voice; he called out, "Scott? James?" A few strides took him to the spare bedrooms. They were empty too. No bodies. No blood. There was still a chance!

Suddenly legless, Matt dropped to the floor. He sat there drawing in single, sobbing breaths, waiting for some strength to return, waiting for some rational thought to guide him—waiting for some internal, miraculous place in his mind to tell him what to do.

Then,

His phone rang.

His quivering finger pushed at the send button. The voice at the other end started immediately,

"You know you've always been a disappointment to me. I was expecting you to have phoned me by now. I mean how long does it take you to figure something out? What a dumbo!"

"What? You know? You know I'm at the apartment? You've got someone watching?"

"Well...gee...let me think...it's a tough one...of course! Idiot!"

"Is she...is Shannon okay?"

"Yes. Yes she is. And she will remain okay so long as you deliver those two Astronauts."

"Two Astronauts?" Matt half-heartedly tried to play dumb. "What are you talking about?"

"Don't screw with me! Your lady friend is going to start losing body parts if you lie to me one more time!"

"No! Okay! Okay. But I don't know where they are. There's blood everywhere in here. I thought you killed them."

"Yeah, well, we tried...but it turns out, unfortunately, that the blood belongs mostly to the bone-heads that work for me. Those guys are a couple of smart, tough cookies...which I guess explains why they are Astronauts. Anyway, I always have a contingency plan." Kurt was sounding very pleased with himself. "First we picked up your little honey as she left for work, and then had a go at your new friends."

Kurt's voice suddenly hardened into deep psychopathic hatred—killer words with phantom daggers leapt through the phone's speaker at Matt—diving toward his heart, "You traitor! You have no idea of how pissed I am at you. I would have never thought that you had the balls to mess with me." Matt heard him take a quick angry breath, "You've made a big mistake! You pecker-head!"

In an instant Kurt's voice had changed again, back to a happy, gleeful tone. "I don't know what you and your Astronaut buddies have been doing with my computer but you screwed up. You ran it a little too long. I came in and found it crunching away on some weird program. I almost shut it down...but I let it continue to run while I started tracing the remote login. Wow! Was I surprised. It terminated at your place. So I stuck a guy outside the apartment and the next thing you know, he is telling me that the Astronauts that I have been searching so hard for are almost in the palm of my hand. I guess in a strange way, I should thank you for bringing them to me but...I just can't...." Kurt flipped back to pure hatred. "You have no idea how pissed I am at you...you...you bastard, weenie traitor!"

He continued, moderate once again, "You know there is an old oriental curse that goes, 'May you live in interesting times.' Well you and I are living in *very* interesting times. As a matter of fact, I think you might be living in even more interesting times than me...." Abruptly, Matt could hear Kurt's breath, like a firestorm, steaming out of his mouth. "When I get my hands on you, pecker-head, you'll learn a lesson like you've never had before!" Then he was all cheerful again, "Let's get back to the business at hand. You've got four hours to find your buddies and bring them to me. After that, what's her name here is in big trouble."

"Don't you hurt her! Don't you touch her!"

"Well that entirely depends on you. You think you can handle it? You know.... I'm not sure you can."

"Don't hurt her! Please don't hurt her!"

"Well don't start crying on me, prissy pants! Do your job and everything will work out just fine."

"Where? Where are you?"

"Not so fast. You find those guys, then you call me." He hung up.

It was the one and only time in his life that Matt actually wanted to keep his old man on the line. His only link to Shannon was gone. Fear, panic and despair closed in on him. He stood motionless, head hung down, arms flaccid at his side. The phone, in his hand, began a gradual, unknowing slide and landed with a clatter on the hardwood floor. The sound drew his mind out of the mist. He had to find Scott and James. How? Where would they go? Why hadn't they tried to call him? Did they have his cell number? No, no they didn't. He swore a blue streak under his breath. What about the office? He bent down, grabbed the phone and frantically dialed the office number.

"Matt Dragonovich's line, Marcy speaking."

"Marcy! It's Matt! Has anyone tried to contact me in the last hour?"

"Yes, you had several calls; I put them through to your voice mail. There was one creepy sounding guy that kept insisting that he should have your cell phone number—I told him it was not our policy to give that out. He was most insistent but I stuck to the rule. I hope that was alright?"

"Well...it wasn't, but that's okay, you couldn't have known. Did he leave a voicemail?"

"I put him through; I don't know if he left a message."

"Right...ummm...put me through to my voice mail."

He spent an agonizing couple of minutes plowing through all the voice mail prompts and some useless work related messages. Finally, he got to Scott's; "Matt, This is urgent. Four men attacked us at your apartment. If you get this message before ten p.m. tonight, you can find us where we first met. Be very careful. You could be followed. And your phone lines may be tapped."

Mat sat, hidden deep in the shadows of his underground parking, in his Ferrari. While he watched the street through the slats in the gate, the engine quietly rumbled, its harnessed power ready to leap. Matt could see nothing obvious; a few people were walking, striding or sauntering about. All the parked cars within sight were empty and there were no vans that could hide spying eyes. Possibly, Kurt's men were further down the street.

His position provided just enough view in both directions to allow him to assess traffic. Matt waited until all was clear, then activated the gate with his remote control. A half second later, he pushed the clutch in hard, held it, pulled the stick shift out of neutral and rammed it into first gear. Matt drove the gas pedal to the floor and listened to the engine, not yet engaged with the wheels, scream. The anger that had been growing in him found a collaborator in that screaming engine. Raw frustrated hatred—red, red rage poured through his feet into the car. He listened to that violent, powerful sound for a long, time-stopped second and suddenly, without thought, tore his foot away from the clutch—the back tires slipped over the smooth concrete, heating instantly, smoking in frustration, unable to move the enraged beast. Matt's ragged voice joined the screaming chorus of tires and engine, and for a few seconds the garage was smothered with the hating sounds of man and machine. Finally, as the gate reached clearance, Matt, still screaming, still releasing rage that he had never felt before in his life, took his foot off the gas just a little, let the tires sink into the concrete, let them find a purchase. The car shot forward, flew out of the parking lot toward the building on the other side. He was going forty miles an hour when he reached the road—still screaming he yanked on the steering wheel, took the car into a four-wheel, right-hand drift and backed off on the accelerator. As soon as Matt felt the car beginning to change direction, he shoved the gas pedal to the floor. But the Ferrari continued its slide—right toward a parked car; he was going to hit it! In a panic, he released the pedal, corrected his sharp turn, straightened it out slightly and waited a spine tingling split-second until the wheels once again found their grip. Satisfied that he had avoided a disaster, Matt sharpened his turn and punched down hard on the gas pedal. The Ferrari was now on course, ripping down the narrow side street at eighty miles per hour. Matt checked the rear view mirror; sure enough, a car, further down the street, was pulling out with tire smoke billowing. The Ferrari was bearing down on a cross-street at a ferocious pace. He knew this spot very well; it was a one-way street with three lanes open at this time of the day. It should be reasonably quiet, at least one lane should be clear. Matt slammed on the brakes and squealed his way to the intersection. In the brief split second that he had he thought he saw a clear lane —he wasn't sure but he couldn't let the car slow or his advantage was lost—he turned the car hard left up the one way street—in the wrong direction.

Matt had been partially correct—the lane he had pulled into was indeed clear—for about half a block. And there was your typical Bostonian, exceeding the speed limit, flying toward him! The other two lanes were occupied; he had no choice, he had to stay in the lane and play chicken with the now out-of-control, fully braked car screeching toward him. Contrary to all his instincts, he floored the gas pedal, waited till the last possible moment and swung the car into the next lane that was almost, but not quite, clear. His right rear just caught the back end of the car in that lane. With his foot still pushing the gas pedal to the floor, Matt's hands danced one way, then the other, then back, then back again as he fought to control the fish-tailing Ferrari. At last, by some incredible miracle, he brought the car under control.

He had a little space in front of him now. In an instant, the Ferrari was flying down the street at one hundred miles per hour. He didn't look back. He didn't dare take his eyes off the road in front. He needed to utilize every ounce of concentration he had to prevent a disaster, he was watching for cars coming toward him, cars crossing from side streets, cars making left turns, right turns, U-turns. He was frantically trying to anticipate movements a block ahead of him; he was watching for pedestrians and cyclists coming from anywhere and everywhere. Drivers were slamming on the brakes, honking horns, yelling—cars were pulling over, trying to get the hell out of his way—he could see out of the corner of his eye shocked, frightened faces turning, following him. The Ferrari was bounding from one side of the street to other, then back again, then down the middle, then to the right, to the left—he was dodging cars, trucks, bikes, pedestrians. Up ahead a trucker panicked—justifiably—the Ferrari was on a head-on collision course. The driver applied the breaks excessively, causing his thirty-foot trailer to slide sideways along the road. Now the entire street was blocked and it was far too late to stop the hurtling sports car. Matt had only one choice: steer the car under the trailer. Perhaps he could make it and perhaps he couldn't—it didn't matter—the car was at the trailer already. He heard just the slightest sound: a quiet, peaceful swish, as the roof of his car gently brushed the undercarriage of the trailer. Then he was past it, still traveling at a horrendous rate.

A pedestrian, well up ahead of the car, misjudged its speed and stepped out into the road—it was almost the last thing that she ever did. Matt just barely swung the car past her. Had he been able to tear his eyes away from the road, he would have witnessed her dress, trapped by the Ferrari's slip-stream, leap out and touch the car.

Another street came up on his right. He had to wait one dreadful moment for an oncoming truck to pass. The very instant that his car was clear he hung another one of his infamous four-wheel drifts—sliding onto a two way street this time. Unfortunately, his slide left him on the wrong side of the road. Once again, Matt had traffic coming right toward him. There was no time to get back to the proper side of the road. His only choice was the sidewalk. He turned the wheels slightly and let the Ferrari bounce with a great thunk and scrape up onto the concrete. The momentum was just a touch too much—the driver side of the car hit the brick wall of the building and hit it hard enough to cause Matt's head to smack the window—he felt some pain but thankfully the window remained intact. The car bounced off the wall and almost back onto the road, but in that brief, terrifying instant Matt managed to twitch the wheels just enough to keep it on the sidewalk.

The Ferrari didn't get much further down the path when a large, over-filled and long forgotten restaurant garbage can abruptly appeared as a silver smudge in his right-side peripheral vision. Matt didn't even bother to slow the car and he certainly couldn't avoid the container without hitting something worse, so once again he heard that sound—a sound that in the past would have sent shocks of horror though his body but now he was getting quite used to—it was the sound of something damaging his beautiful Ferrari. The garbage can caught the front right side of the car and soared thirty feet into the air, spinning and spewing its putrid contents as it went. The gooey, gunky, garbage fanned out over the street and descended on defenseless bystanders. Matt and the roaring Ferrari left behind a scene of carnage—small, partially decomposed, rancid food bombs were exploding on the sidewalk, on the street, on cars, on trucks—people were running in all directions—screaming with revulsion as they tried to disengage rotted food remnants from their clothes and hair. Some had decided that they no longer needed their own stomach contents and were donating semi-digested food to the cause. Fully decomposed, liquid goo, which had over time settled peacefully to the bottom of the can finally made an appearance, spraying throughout the disaster area. An atrocious smell had now taken the whole block captive—there was no escaping the overpowering, sour scent of puke and decayed food—it set off a whole new round of moans, screams and food regurgitation.

Of course all of this was lost to Matt—he had finally managed to bounce the Ferrari back onto the street and was a block down the road—still dodging cars, bikes and pedestrians. A side street popped up to his left; he slowed and took the corner. He took the next right, then another left. Then finally, at last, with a great sigh of relief, Matt slowed to normal driving speed and checked the rear view mirror. Not surprisingly, there was no sign of the other car. He caught his breath, let his heart rate settle, then picked up his cell phone and made a call,

"Hey asshole, next time you better buy your goons a Ferrari if you want to keep up with me." He didn't wait for an answer. He hung up.

Matt left the badly bruised Ferrari in an hotel parking lot and caught a cab at the lobby. Fifteen minutes later, he was slowly sauntering and strolling through the park—stopping here and there, pretending to be enjoying the view. Each time he checked to see if he had been followed. It was getting close to dusk and so far, he hadn't seen a soul, let alone someone suspicious.

He finished up at the park bench where they had first met. No one was there. He waited, fifteen, twenty, thirty minutes. He was beginning to despair. It was almost dark.

Abruptly a quiet voice said, "It looks safe."

Shocked, Matt jumped a foot off his seat. He shouted, "What! Who's there?" Simultaneously he got to his feet and swung his head and then body in a three hundred and sixty degree pan. No one was there. A tingling shiver rippled down his spine—goose bumps flooded his skin.

Abruptly the same soft voice, seemingly hovering in the air—bodiless—said, "You're not hearing me with your ears but with your mind."

"What? Who said that?" Matt spun around again...and again...and finally saw a movement—out of the twilight shadows, fifty feet away came a body—ghostly grey and dim. Frightened and confused, Matt turned to run....

Another voice, solid and real this time, shouted, "Wait! Wait, Matt! It's us!"

Matt turned back to the apparition and watched as James materialized out of the darkness. James said, quite nonchalantly, "You are improving. That is quite a distance for you to sense my thought."

"Really. Well, how about some warning next time. You scared the crap out of me. Besides...." he was starting to get really angry again, "I don't need some goofy mind-power lesson right now. They have Shannon!"

"Who? Who has Shannon? Who were those people?" asked Scott as he stepped out from behind a nearby tree.

"Kurt's guys! My jerk of a father has Shannon! He's threatening to hurt her if you don't give yourselves up! We've got to do something!" His voice was rising to an angry screech.

"Calm down. Quiet." Scott had another quick look round but no one was in sight.

Matt replied with a spittle-filled whisper, "Well, hell! I'm sorry but I've been a little stressed today! We need a plan! And quick!" Scott was surprised to see a determined, angry look on Matt's face—it was an expression he had never seen before on Matt.

"Where are we supposed to meet him?"

"He didn't say. I'm to call him when I've found you."

"Do you have any weapons? Guns?"

"No, those things scare me...about the best I can do is a large kitchen knife."

Scott grinned, "Unless you're a Ninja in disguise, that's not going to be of much use to us."

"Well? What are we going to do?" asked Matt.

"I have some ideas," stated James.

"Well let's hear'em. Times running out...."

"Kurt here."

"Okay, I've got them. Where do we go?"

"There's a warehouse along the waterfront. In that old derelict area. You know the one—the one I just bought for the new condo development. Very quiet and peaceful, very private—not a soul around, I doubt anyone would even hear a gunshot...and we have a lot of guns...so don't get any ideas. You've got fifteen minutes to get here, after that Shannon starts losing body parts."

"We can't make it there in that time!"

"I don't give a damn. You've got fifteen big ones...I don't want you having time to hatch any plots," Kurt hung up.

"We're in trouble. My car is in a parking lot a good fifteen minutes' walk from here. You guys don't have a car do you?" Matt's frantic eyes leapt between the two faces, hoping for a miracle.

"No. We're going to have to run...." James looked Matt up and down and commented, "You don't look like you're in very good shape."

Matt glanced down at his first class beer gut and said, "What was your first clue?"

Scott said, "James and I will have to help you. Let's go!"

They left at a sprint. Within a minute Matt was dying, his legs we're already feeling soft and rubbery; his lungs had become burning blast furnaces. Abruptly his feet left the ground....

"Good thing you're wearing a leather jacket."

"And a belt."

Scott had a handful of leather; James had the belt at the back of the pants. Matt felt like a complete fool. With alternate feet only touching ground every few strides, he resembled an aging, fat-bellied Peter Pan prancing his way through the city. But he didn't care what he looked like so long as they got to that warehouse on time. Nothing else mattered.

Matt couldn't believe how fast they were going. A couple of minutes later, they were still pounding along but his boxer underwear had become a thong and the pressure on his groin was becoming unbearable.

Matt said, "I've got some strength back, let me go. I think I can make it the rest of the way." He hit the ground at what was, for him, a full sprint. He would have performed a very nice belly-flop if it wasn't for that huge hand of Scott's—without breaking stride it shot out and grasped the back of the collar of his jacket and kept him upright long enough to get his feet going. Matt set off on a lopsided sprint—with one hand slapping and tugging at his butt as he unsuccessfully tried to perform a quick underwear realignment.

A hard, draining, minute later, "Here it is. The parking lot," was all Matt could gasp out. He stopped and both hands shot to his rear. Matt let out a deep, inner sigh of satisfaction as he finally managed to remove the king of all wedgies. Another minute and they were trying to fit three people into a two-seater sports car. James was just barely able to crush himself partially between the seats with his legs contorted around the stick shift and his butt half-on and half-off the passenger seat. Scott and Matt were both jammed up against the doors. It wasn't comfortable but it was manageable.

They flew out of the parking lot—classic Matt at the speedway style. A few close calls later Matt's Ferrari was evenly decorated with damage on both sides of the car.

Suddenly James yelled out, "A pharmacy! Stop!"

Matt cried, "What? We don't have ti...."

"Stop! I have an idea! It will only take a minute to get what I need. Stop!"

Matt was screaming, "We'll be late! Late!"

Scott said, "Calm down, I think I know what James is up to, it's worth taking a chance, a couple of minutes won't matter—Kurt won't do anything if he thinks we're close."

Matt slammed on the breaks and reversed the car. A moment later James and Scott were running across the sidewalk and into the store. Through the window of the pharmacy Matt could see James asking a question to the clerk and then leaping down one isle, while Scott ran down another. Less than a minute later they returned to the counter with arms filled with bottles, packages and cartons. Scott pulled a handful of bills from his pocket, gave them to the astonished clerk and then both of them sprinted out to the waiting car.

Scott was smiling, "Now we have an edge."

"Wha.... What is all this for?" asked Matt.

"No time to explain." Scott began rummaging through the packages, "James, where's the foil pan? And the barbeque lighter?"

Fifteen minutes later Matt's cell phone rang, still concentrating on the final stretch, he tossed it over to Scott,

"Yes?"

"Who's this?"

"One of the guys you tried to kill."

"Well tell the dumb-ass Matt that time's up."

"Wait! Wait! We're almost there! We're in the last block!"

"Yeah? Okay. Yeah, I can hear the car. Park at the back and stay there until I send someone to check you out."

Matt drove the car down an unlit driveway that ran between two of the oldest, most dilapidated buildings he had ever seen. The roof of both buildings had caved-in. The walls seemed to be standing thanks only to the vast vegetation growing up its partially eaten sides. Ivy stalks, as thick as a man's forearm, twisted and turned along the whole length of the building. They were poking in and out of every opening; gaps where siding once proudly stood were now its playground. Good-sized trees that had pushed their way through the pavement many years ago, now laid claim to space that the ivy had not: some were inside the buildings, some were in the walls and some were now the walls. Winter had removed all of summer's vegetation, leaving an intricate, complex pattern of shapes that a photographer would be pleased to call art. Caught in the harsh brilliance of the headlights, it was a strange black and grey graveyard of man's creation. Nature, the alien here, was taking back what was once hers.

Matt swung his rattling, scratched, dented, demolition derby car that only this morning had been a shiny, bright red Ferrari, to the right as he passed the end of the building. The car came to a stop in a pitch-black courtyard bounded by the buildings and the ocean. He had to compliment his dad; it was the perfect location for murder. No one would see or hear them die.

The lights from a parked van flashed on, temporarily blinding them.

Someone shouted, "Out of the car!"

They stepped out and with hands pushed towards the light, they could just make out a sinister silhouette...no two...no...three silhouettes.

"Two hand guns and an Uzi," Scott whispered with his best ventriloquist impersonation to Matt.

"Boss. There's only two in the car."

Suddenly, another silhouette made its appearance. A weird, bulging, powerful shape, a one-of-a-kind outline—there was no mistaking Kurt.

"Where's the other guy?" he yelled across the distance of the parking lot.

"Oh. You mean our insurance policy?" answered Scott.

"Don't get smart with me! How about I just take you all out right now?"

Scott replied, voice quietly steady and unconcerned, "Well that would be pretty friggin' stupid and from what Matt's told me, you don't fit that category. Kill us and our insurance policy goes to the police—you might be able to hide our murders but you won't be able to cover up all that other illegal stuff you've been doing."

"And what illegal 'stuff' are you talking about exactly?"

Suddenly Matt shouted, "All your shell companies you bastard! All those conglomerates that you illegally control!" His voice raised a pitch higher as he shrieked, "Where's Shannon?" His head began to swing from side to side as he strained to see past the car's headlights, "Shannon! Where are you? Shannon! Are you alright?" Matt's very limited self-control was gone; he was already diverting from the plan.

Then Matt saw two stubby, powerful hands clench and unclench as the Kurt silhouette replied with an angry shout of its own, "Shut up! Stop Yelling! Idiot!" Then Kurt's voice dropped its volume—it became almost reasonable, "Shannon is just fine...but not for much longer if your guy doesn't show up. Now, what's this about shell companies? I don't know anything about shell companies. And neither do you, pecker-head."

"You think you're so smart. You think I'm a dumbo. I'm not! I'm not! I know a lot about those fake holding companies of yours. I've got evidence...and now James, our insurance guy...has evidence."

It was Kurt's turn to lose his self-control, "Get away from the car! I'm going to teach you a lesson, you pecker-head!"

Matt, whose heart was now pumping at maximum, remained stock-still—he was unable to move forward or backward. Anger and hatred were perfectly balanced by fear and terror.

Kurt started toward Matt but stopped as Scott moved around the car. He turned to his boys and said, "That big bastard moves one more inch and you can cover the Ferrari in his blood."

"Now come here you traitor. You turd. Time for a lesson!" Kurt's hand was moving to its favorite position, this time though, the normally open mitt had closed to a fist. Kurt began, once again, to advance on Matt.

Finally, fear won over anger—Matt started backing up.

"Come here chicken shit," sneered Kurt.

"NO! Where's Shannon! Where?" Matt demanded, "I want to see her now!"

Kurt didn't reply—he took another stride—Matt took another backward stride. Kurt picked up speed—Matt picked up speed. Kurt tried to cutoff Matt's path—Matt changed direction. They were at an impasse—every step Kurt made, Matt countered with one of his own.

Kurt, aware that chasing his son around a dark parking lot in the middle of the night was a definite loss of dignity, was now in a full rage. He screamed at him, "YOU STOP OR SO HELP ME I'LL KILL YOU NOW!"

Matt countered with a scream of his own, "YOU KILL US AND YOU'RE FINISHED!" Fury like he had felt earlier in the day shot through him—he forgot his fear, stopped, clenched both hands into fists, took a foolish step forward and shouted as loud as he could, "WHERE'S SHANNON, YOU ASSHOLE!!!"

Kurt saw his opportunity and pounced forward. Matt, literally shaking with rage, stood his ground. Kurt was within a few feet of his doomed target when suddenly Matt felt a sensation...one that was not his—one that did not belong in his mind...and yet was there—it was a choking wave of fear and anger mingled with hopeless love....

He knew where she was.

"Get her out of the trunk! You prick! She's smothering!"

Kurt stopped, unable to hide his surprise, stood mute. Then, "Good guess, chicken-shit."

Kurt took several steps back to the car and said to the biggest of his men, "Yank her out of the trunk and don't be too gentle." He turned back to Matt with a sneering smile smothering his face, "You know I've got to hand it to you, you picked yourself some good stuff. Much better looking than I expected. Yeah. That's right. I've known before you shoved your skinny little pecker into her. She must be some kind of slut to hang out with a butt-ugly, jerk-off like you. Is she legally blind? Or just incredibly stupid? Or perhaps blind and stupid?" Kurt chuckled at his own sick joke and looked back at his guys for confirmation that it was indeed funny—wary, sycophant smiles were enough encouragement—he continued with the same theme. "There's got to be something wrong with a girl who would spread for a goof like you."

"MATT! DON'T LISTEN TO HIM!" It was Shannon—Kurt's not so swift guy had taken her gag off. "He's just trying to screw with your mind. He's doing what he's done all your life—put you down so you won't fight back. DON'T LISTEN!"

"Hey, dirt-bag! I didn't tell you to take off the gag. Put it back on!"

As Kurt's guy bent down to pick the cloth off the ground, Shannon, who had managed to undo the poorly tied ropes on her feet, took off. With hands still tied behind her back she launched herself, a human missile, at Kurt. "You bastard!" she screamed.

Kurt, with a look of surprised amusement on his face, stepped slightly to the side, then calmly, almost casually, drilled her in the side of the head with his right fist. A dull, melon-like, smack-thud echoed around the vacant building walls. Shannon fell to the ground, a groan issuing from her already swelling head—her legs were spasmodically digging little tracks in the dirt. With a swift, sadistic movement Kurt lifted a leg—about to stomp her head into the ground.

Scott made a sudden move away from the car—toward Kurt—the gunmen twisted back from the bizarre scene before them, adjusted their aim and started to squeeze....

"NO! NO! Don't hurt her!" Matt cried.

Kurt halted his leg's descent—another one of his sneering smiles was curling its way up his lips. He stood there, on one leg, looking like a bulldog about to whiz and said to Matt, "Say, 'Pretty please.'"

"Please! Please don't hurt her."

Kurt set his foot down, "That's better, but still not what I asked. As usual, you got it wrong. I said, "Say, 'Pretty please.'"

Matt fell to his knees, clasped his hands together as if in prayer and said quietly, "Pretty Please. Dad. Pretty Please. Pretty Please. I'm so sorry. Don't hurt her. Hurt me! It's my fault! Please let her go!"

Scott, helpless, began to feel his self-control slipping. It was one of the most sad, pathetic scenes he had ever witnessed. With each word Matt, hands still clasped together, moved one knee forward, then another, then another—he was crawling toward Kurt.

Scott looked for a way to help him...any way.... He shifted his weight, about to make a suicidal dive for the nearest of Kurt's men. Three guns snapped to attention, their aim tracking his movement. There was no chance. If he moved an inch he was dead.

Matt was now at his father's feet, crying and sobbing like a baby, "Please. Please. Please. Please. Please. PRETTY! PLEASE!"

Abruptly, in a flash of an instant, far faster than Scott could have imagined, the sobbing was transformed to a wicked scream of rage as in one continuous motion Matt got his feet under him and drove with every ounce of strength and weight in his body—drove with every fiber and sinew of his being—drove his cocked arm...into his dad's privates. Matt could hear and feel the soft, unprotected, dangling goods squelch as he turned them into mush.

"That's for Shannon! You Pig! Squeal, you Pig!"

Matt was standing now; ready to kick his old man in the gut when he hit the ground. But incredibly, impossibly, Kurt did not go down. He clutched himself with both hands and started to fall—he bent so far over that his head almost scratched the ground, yet somehow he kept his balance. Not a sound had issued from the contorted figure. Shocked, Matt stood stock still—uncertain of what to do next. Suddenly there came a soft growl—deep, guttural—a horrible, almost inhuman noise. It rumbled louder and louder until it seemed to shake the buildings. Kurt was straightening up! Matt, with fear now blending with rage, took a swing at Kurt's head as hard as he could—and caught him straight on—he could feel his knuckles crushing and breaking on a skull that must have been as thick as a Grizzly's. He took another swing and made direct contact again but Kurt was still rising—still howling and... his fist was pulling back.

There was a quiet pop, almost imperceptible, against Kurt's inhuman noise, and then another, then a little louder crash of a bottle breaking—smoke of some kind was rising up from broken bottles that had smacked into the ground. A second later, a shape dropped from a battered rafter two stories up and landed precisely on the back of Kurt's biggest guy. James, cushioned from the fall by what was now a very broken big boy, sprang up toward his next prey. But the shapes and bodies were beginning to disappear into the smoke. Suddenly, a gunshot rang out, followed by the sickening sound of an Uzi. James looked for Scott, but he was now lost in their diversion of smoke. He took ten steps forward and almost tripped over a body—obviously Scott's first target. He heard more gunshots...he thought he saw a flash just off to his left and immediately felt the fear of someone's desperation. A target was just ahead. A few more steps and a ghostly shadow, grey-black-blurred, began to swirl into shape a few yards off to his left. James increased his pace and with a burst of adrenaline, started a rush toward the back of the now distinct body. Abruptly something clattered under James's foot. The sound provided enough warning. James didn't have to see; he could feel his opponent starting to swing a handgun toward him. He lashed out and caught the arm in mid-swing—he pushed up and swung under the arm—with both hands he pinned the wrist tight...a cruel twist and James had dislocated the arm at the shoulder. A scream of pain sprang into the smoke filled air. He released the dangling damaged arm and swung a fist into the man's head. He hit the ground silent—already unconscious. A split second later, James swung round—looking, feeling for the action. He sensed something brutal, something animalistic ahead and to the left.

As soon as the smoke began to obscure his view, Scott went into action. He sprinted toward Kurt, but was intercepted by one of the other men. A bullet whizzed by Scott's head. The man didn't get another chance. Scott hit him with a pent-up punch that had been intended for Kurt. It was the hardest that Scott had ever hit anyone or anything. He might have killed him—Scott didn't know and didn't care. All he wanted at that moment was Kurt. He swung back toward where he had last seen him and was rewarded with a misty, smoky, stocky silhouette. Scott engaged the deadly shape and immediately found himself struggling with a massively strong opponent.

Kurt and Scott were almost at a stalemate, locked in a slow, silent dance. Pressed tight, each had the other's arms. A gun poked its way out of Kurt's right hand. Bits of dirt and puffs of dust kicked up from feet that were struggling to stay alive. The antagonists moved, almost gracefully, forward, then with a sudden heave slipped back, then rotated in a partial circle. Still clinging tight to each of Kurt's arms, Scott abruptly twisted to one side as Kurt drove his knee upward, attempting what his son had so successfully achieved. The blow glanced off Scott's thigh. Kurt tried again with the other knee. Scott twisted back in the other direction.

Odd music accompanied the dance: grunts and groans, interspersed with great whooshes of breath—violently pushed and sucked in quick, sporadic gasps. Kurt's bulldog, monster face had scrunched itself into a permanent expression of fury and power. As Scott tried to regulate his breathing, his countenance shifted from calm and relaxed, to lips pulled back tight, to bulging, straining cheeks.

The shuffling, gasping, waltz continued for some time. Finally, Kurt, frustrated at the lack of progress, changed his strategy...he focused all his strength and might on his gun arm and started to pull the skyward facing hand, down. A few panting breaths later, the gun was almost down at Kurt's leg. Scott who was much taller than Kurt, to avoid losing his grip, had to bend over so far that he was at a serious disadvantage and was slowly losing his hold on the arm. Suddenly, his hand came away but reconnected before Kurt could pull the arm out of range. Kurt tried to twist his body away from Scott. Scott swung with him. In a surprise move Kurt pulled his arm upward and tried to point the gun at Scott's head. Scott countered by pushing the arm back downwards and outwards. Kurt immediately responded to the pressure by pulling his arm in the same direction as Scott was pushing. Kurt's ploy worked—there was a sudden tearing sound as Scott's hand slipped away with a chunk of Kurt's shirt. The gun was free. Scott tried to re-contact the arm but missed on the first try. The muzzle was turning toward him. He got in as close as he could and in a very temporary effort to keep the gun away, pushed his elbow into Kurt's arm. Simultaneously he stuck his now free hand into Kurt's face—fingers looking for eyes. Kurt, unable to get the gun pointed at Scott, felt his eyes under attack. He let fly a cry as Scott struck gold. Blinded and with a hellish strength born of last-chance fear, Kurt smashed his free arm, with gun still attached, in the general proximity of Scott's head. By incredible luck he scored a direct hit—the butt end of the gun rocked Scott's head back. Scott still hung on to Kurt's face. He took another direct hit. Scott felt dizzy but continued his work on Kurt's eyes. Another hit...and another. Scott felt sick, strangely weak and tired. He knew he was losing. One more dull, almost painless crack against his head and the grip on Kurt's face was gone; Scott waved his hand—wildly searching for the gun. He took one more hit and slipped to the ground, vaguely aware that this was his last moment.

He was on his hands and knees, puking and bleeding—only Kurt's feet remained in his blurred field of vision. Unable to move, he waited for the end....

But something was wrong; he could swear that Kurt's feet had left the ground. Yes. Yes! As a hard blackness swallowed his mind and eyes, as he slipped from consciousness, a darkening image swam briefly before him—those killer feet, held inches from the ground, were kicking back and forth!

James burst into a pocket of clear air. In the middle, with torn shreds of smoky mist swirling around them, he saw Scott and Kurt quietly struggling over a gun that was held in Kurt's right hand. Nearby, Shannon was half sitting—trying to stand; the left side of her face was a mess. Matt was on the other side of the battling bodies, on his knees, head down, blood dripping from a broken nose, one eye bloated—half closed. In the split second that it took to survey the situation, Kurt's hand had come clear and the two bodies swung around until Kurt's back was to James. Immediately James heard a pain-filled yell from Kurt. Then the gun rose and fell in rapid succession. As James leapt forward, his perception began to move in disjointed segments—he saw Scott slip down to his knees...and then onto his hands...blood was pouring from his head. He made no attempt to protect himself. Kurt was bringing the gun down... bringing the gun down...bringing the gun down. Suddenly James could sense and feel, like an electric jolt, crazed neurons firing in Kurt's brain, sending an instruction to the mad-man's trigger finger, sending an angry, psychopathic instruction to kill, to destroy...to obliterate.

Powered by furious neurons of his own, James's hand outraced the electro-chemical reaction that was traveling down Kurt's arm to that horrid finger...and came from behind—contacted the wrist, held it firm, unmoving. Simultaneously, energized by massive adrenalin, he reached around Kurt with his other arm, tucked it under his chin and lifted him by his head off the ground. In an instant—shockingly fast—Kurt gave up on the gun, dropped it and reached with both hands for James's head and face. James, recognizing the tactic, responded just as quickly—he leaned way back and pushed with his legs. As James fell to the ground, Kurt did a slow motion flip in the air and landed on his arms, face, chest and legs behind James. Without a glance in Kurt's direction, James sat up, got his legs under him and thrust toward the gun. He reached and rolled, bringing the gun up in Kurt's direction...but nothing was there, just a lingering swirl of smoke filling a vacant void.

James crouched and waited—his head and gun panned the space in unison. All his senses were tuned for Kurt...but he felt nothing. Kurt was almost certainly gone. As he sat unmoving, just as he was beginning to relax, a shiver shot through him—his close mind-to-mind contact with the man had left James with a psychotic thought-image that he desperately wanted to be rid of—he could see Kurt running through the darkness, wanting to tear and render, wanting to maim, wanting to kill.

"Shannon! Oh! Shannon! Your face! My love! My love!" Matt had stumbled over to Shannon and was helping her to her feet. She was trying to talk but her swollen jaw denied the attempt. Matt, who was bleeding all over himself and her, seemed to be unaware that he was hurt. Scott was still on his hands and knees, barely conscious, staring at puddles of his own blood, struggling to remember who he was.

James knew that precious time was ticking away. He shouted, "We've got to get out of here! Kurt could be bringing more help back any second." He ran to the car under the warehouse. The keys were still in it. James pushed, pulled and piled his bleeding friends into the car and drove off into the safety of darkness.

Chapter 33
FUGITIVES

"Well? What are we going to do?" asked Matt who was sitting on the edge of the dumpy motel bed, with some very unattractive toilet paper sticking out of both his nostrils. They were hiding in a run-down motel, just outside of Boston.

James, oblivious to Matt's question, said, "You need stitches Scott. I can't do much with this." He was standing over Scott holding a blood-stained towel in one hand and looking at his head—shifting matted hair here and there.

Scott replied, "Well that's going to be difficult. I don't think we dare go to a hospital. What about Shannon? How is she doing?"

"She's in the other bedroom sleeping. I don't think her jaw or cheek-bone is broken. She should be okay," stated James.

"My bastard father! I'll kill him!" The horror of that image, his dad punching his beautiful, brave, Shannon and the sight of her writhing on the ground still raged around in his mind.

Scott turned to James and asked, "How are you doing?" He noted some scratches on James's forehead and ear; his shirt was ripped along one arm and his pants had a couple of nasty tears in them but, all in all, he seemed to be in pretty good shape.

James replied, "I'm fine. Just a few scratches—got those when I bailed out of the Ferrari just before the warehouse." A wry smile appeared on those ordinary features, "Next time we try that, let's go a little slower."

Scott grinned back, "I don't ever intend to do that again. By the way, how did you know that you could make a smoke bomb from ingredients at a pharmacy?"

James smiled somewhat sheepishly. "I went through a delinquent phase when I was a boy. I set one of those off in my classroom once."

Scott looked genuinely shocked. "Really? I can't imagine a delinquent James, no matter how young."

"Yes, well...the school Principle straightened me out after that. No more practical jokes."

Scott said, "Good for him. Otherwise I might not have had a savior on Venus."

Quiet descended upon the room; only the irritating sporadic roar and hiss of the highway, just outside their door, broke the silence. Then, after a few more mental images of a dead Kurt at his feet, Matt asked again, "Well? What are we going to do?"

"I think we should go to the Greenpeace office in the morning and see if they can help us," said Scott.

"I agree. We need to get our message out to the public as soon as possible. I didn't get the analysis finished but I now know from the preliminary results that we are close...close to the point of no return. Maybe we have a year. Two at the most. Then it's too late. It will be Venus all over again," James said.

"It's going to be very tough. No one is going to want to believe us. I mean...look at the effect it's going to have. No more gas powered automobiles, no air travel, no trains. It's a disaster. Electricity production will be severely reduced because the coal and oil generators will have to be shut down. Massive unemployment—oil and gas workers, car manufacturing plants, car sales, anything to do with transportation and power will be affected. There will be a domino effect—those that are out of work won't spend money so other businesses will start to go under, creating more unemployment. We're talking about a worldwide depression. No one will want to believe us. There will be denial galore. Even with Greenpeace and every other environmental group on our side I don't think we have a chance," Matt said.

"Matt's right. I thin...."

"I'll show them the proof. The mathematics!" James exclaimed.

Matt snorted out a sarcastic laugh, "Unemployed people don't give a damn about mathematics. All they want, all they care about is money—money to take care of their families, money to buy food, money for a nice car and house, money for the kid's college fund. They are going to deny, deny, deny. They will find any way to justify their jobs—look at those people who build nuclear weapons—weapons that will kill hundreds of thousands. Hell, a nuclear war could possibly destroy everyone, destroy the world, but those workers are, "*Protecting their country.*" When it comes down to it, when it comes to the choice of job or no job, any excuse will do," he said.

"Now, our message is worse; it's not going to affect just one industry—many, many industries will be destroyed, thousands upon thousands of lives will be changed, possibly ruined. The politicians aren't going to want to have anything to do with this. They are going to run and hide. They are going to play the blame game—it will be someone else's fault and someone else's job to fix it—they will stall and stall and stall, they will endlessly debate the problem just like any other troubling issue, right up to the day their pants catch on fire."

Matt swung toward James. "James, you talk about proof, well the only proof that anyone is going to want to see is the proof that protects their job. Truth and proof aren't undeniable, irrefutable, immovable, solid objects like mountains...in times of great stress, truth and proof become fluid; they can be bent, they can be turned and pointed in a new direction, they can be turned in whatever direction is necessary to provide the most wanted solution or excuse. And don't fool yourself, our truth, our proof, will be turned...."

He paused, lost in thought and then quietly, almost to himself, "Yes...yes, possibly turned back to us...somehow it will become our fault—we will be accused of some crime—like trying to cause a stock market crash, trying to profit from others loss. I know my Dad; he'll try something like that."

Once again the conversation stopped. Individual thoughts flew through the room.

Then from Scott, "Yes. You're very right, Matt. .ut we can't give up. We have to find a way. The survival of Earth is at stake." Scott paused for a moment; it was his turn to be pensive. He said, "You raise another good point that I hadn't thought of till now—our proof is in mathematics that only James can understand."

Scott turned to James and asked, "Can anyone understand the theory? Could you teach it to other scientists? You said that it was very advanced. Is it within their capability to understand?"

"Good point...that could be a problem...." James said. "Yes, that's a very good point...." James repeated softly.

James sat on the bed, staring off into the distance.

"I think I've got it. Let me think it through...." James stood up, paced back and forth a couple of times. He turned to Scott and Matt, "I need an hour. I'm going for a walk."

Two hours later James returned with a newspaper in his hand. He tossed it to Scott and said, "Well, I think Greenpeace is out...look at the headline."

Scott stared down at the paper with a sinking feeling in his gut as he read out loud, "INSANE ASTRONAUTS ON THE LOOSE!" Further down he saw, "NASA reports that the two Venus Astronauts have escaped custody. They are considered insane and dangerous and are believed to be traveling with...."

Matt ripped the paper out of Scott's hands, scanned it and then shouted, "No! They've got our pictures on the front Page." He moaned, "Christ. We're dead."

"Looks like Kurt has someone at NASA under his thumb," stated Scott.

"Yes...someone high up...."

"Right."

Matt, reading further, exclaimed, "Listen to this, 'They attacked one of Boston's most prominent businessmen, Kurt Dragonovich and three of his associates. Two of his associates are still in hospital with serious but non-life threatening injuries. It is thought that his son, Matt Dragonovich is one of the gang and that he participated in the attack on his father.'"

"The Bastard! Bastard!!" Fury flashed across Matt's face, which was rapidly replaced by a look of soul-wrenching sadness and loss. He leaned forward, elbows on knees, head in hands and said dejectedly, "What am I going to do?"

"It's not *I*, it's *We*, Matt. We're in this together. We got you in this trouble. We will do everything in our power to get you out of it," Scott said. "Matt...."

"Don't you understand? I'm going to lose Shannon. Shannon is doomed if she stays with me. She has to leave. You don't know my father. He will never give up. He will chase us to the ends of the earth. He will kill us. She has to leave."

"Matt! I saw what Shannon did last night...even if you tell her to leave, she isn't going to do it. I know that. And James and I aren't leaving. You're stuck with us, buddy. And Matt.... We ARE going to win."

"How? How? Kurt has the police, the FBI, NASA and who knows who else after us!"

"We will find a way. Trust me. We will find a way. Promise me... no matter what happens you won't give up, no matter how bad it looks. James taught me this. Even when all seems lost, there is a way. Promise me."

Matt, whose face had slowly transitioned from wretched to resolute, said, "Alright, I promise."

Scott slapped Matt's shoulder and said, "Excellent! Now let's find a way."

"I do have some thoughts on that.... I have a plan...," James said. "I think, no, I'm almost sure...well...ninety-nine percent sure." He paused. "Perhaps a bit less than that...."

Matt, feeling much better, grinned and said, "Come on, tell us your idea. We can't wait all day while you work out the likelihood of success of every step in your plan."

"Okay, here it is...."

Jack Anderson stepped out of the office into bright sunshine. He was leaving early today. After all, there wasn't much to do. Since the Venus disaster, NASA budgets had been paired to the bone. The only project, if it could be called that, was the waste disposal project—someone had finally found a good use for the moon—it was now Earth's official garbage dump for the really nasty stuff—toxic waste and radioactive material. The famous Jack Anderson was now the Garbage Master General in charge of Earth's space garbage. Of course, they didn't call him that; he had a much fancier description—General Manager Space Disposal—but without doubt, Garbage Master General was the most accurate title.

Everyone had been quite surprised by Jack's reaction to the President's suggestion that he head up a project to send an unmanned probe to Venus. It was hoped that the probe could determine what happened... and, of course, that was why he had argued against it. He really wasn't worried—they wouldn't find anything—pieces of the Renaissance were by now spread all over the solar system. He just didn't ever want to think about it again—he didn't want to have his conscience puking up in front of him every day.

He had seriously considered quitting, but that jerk, that turd, that prick, that slimy lowlife murdering bastard, Kurt Dragonovich, had reneged on his promise of a cozy exec job in one of his corporations. Kurt kept stalling—a position was never available and when Jack heard about one, well, it just wasn't a good fit. When Jack pestered Kurt one time too many, he got an earful. "Stop bothering me! You've got a job... leave it at that!" He had finally accepted and settled into his Garbage Master General position—the memory of what he had done, although not faded, was at least shoved far enough down that it took some time to percolate to the surface. He only felt sick and depressed every week or so now. Yes, the Garbage Master General was doing fairly well, taking lots of time off, semi-retired, happy in his work.

But then he got that call from Kurt. They were back. Trust Scott and James to survive. He always had a strange feeling about those two, like they were meant for something special...something important. Certainly they were the toughest, smartest Astronauts that he had ever met and that was really, really saying something. And now, now they were back on earth.

Unfortunately, his conscience came back with them—he was feeling sick and depressed every day. Kurt, the mad puppeteer, was pulling Jack's strings again—do this, do that, say this, say that, lie about this, lie about that. The latest was, "The Astronauts were insane and dangerous." Now the FBI was involved. He was becoming scared as well as sick. Those guys asked difficult questions, and they always looked at you like you were hiding something. Sometimes he thought he was going to crack...go crazy and blurt out what he knew.

But what did he know? He knew what he had done...but wasn't it the right thing to do? It wasn't his fault. Something terrible had happened out there. Something dangerous...dangerous to Earth. He did the right thing. Didn't he? Didn't he? Yes, of course. He did what needed to be done. He saved Earth. But...what? What? What really had happened out there?

On his way to his car, Jack started to walk past an old beat-up van. Head down, deep in thought, deep in guilt, he was only vaguely aware that the sliding side door was fully open. Suddenly a shadow, a very large shadow, stepped from behind the back of the van. Startled, Jack lifted his head. A slack-jawed look of recognition burst onto his face and then he was flying sideways, head first into the open door of the van. He felt a sharp pain in his leg as it caught the lower lip of the door. His elbow cracked into the floor of the van, very quickly followed by his head. Dazed he started to sit up, but something, on top of him... something...a carpet! Suddenly he felt a great weight pressing him down, trapping him—someone was on top of the carpet. He heard a frantic, "Go! Go!" The van jumped forward, bouncing its way out of the parking lot on worn-out springs. Then came the sound he had expected... what he dreaded. "Jack...it's Scott...don't move."

Muffled under a smelly old carpet and pressed cruelly against the hard metal of the van floor, he was bounced around for a good hour—the useless van springs found and amplified every little divot in the road. The constant jostling caused his fear to be replaced by irritation and anger. He was in a very pissy mood when the van finally stopped and he heard the side door slide open. The carpet came off and he started to swear a blue streak at whoever was nearby. He saw Scott and James and two others—a man and a woman. They were the two that Kurt had reported; he recognized their faces from the paper. Scott waited patiently for Jack to catch a breath and then said, "Jack we need to talk to you but first...."

"Jack. It's Kurt."

"Yeah? What?"

"Jack. You're not sounding too friendly. That's no way to talk to an old friend."

"You're no friend of mine."

"Now, now, don't be such a snoot. Here I am trying to help you out, to warn you...."

"Warn me about what?"

"Looks like our enemies are in your territory. The cops have found a stolen van near you. It had James and Scott's fingerprints in it. You better keep an eye out. I don't know why they are down there but I'm sure they're up to no good."

"Yeah." There was a pause and then a noncommittal, "Okay...anything else?"

Kurt didn't reply. Something didn't seem quite right with good old Jack.

Finally Kurt said, "You don't seem too concerned. Why is that? You know they may have suspicions...suspicions about what happened out there...orbiting Venus. Could be they want to talk to you."

"I can't imagine that they would. No...no I don't think so."

"Really?" replied Kurt.

Jack didn't answer.

"Well, keep a look out. Call me if they attempt to contact you," said Kurt.

"Yeah. Sure."

Kurt disconnected, stared at the phone for a moment, got up from his desk, walked over to the windows and stared out at the million-dollar Boston view. He paced along the floor-to-ceiling windows, turned back and paced the other direction. Indifferent to the strikingly beautiful panoramic scene that lay below him he halted, tapped the glass with his fingers and absentmindedly looked up at the elaborately carved oak ceiling. Abruptly he swung around, strode to his desk and made a call, "It's Kurt. Something's wrong, I need you to do a job for me...."

"Mr. President, Jack Anderson is on the line. Says it's urgent."

"Jack Anderson? Urgent? What could be urgent?" The President glanced at his watch, "Okay, I've got a couple of minutes. Put him through."

"Hi Jack, I have very little time. What is urgent?"

"Mr. President, it's about the Venus mission and the missing Astronauts. There is something you should know."

"Let's hear it then."

"I'm sorry but it's something that should be said in person. Can we meet?"

"I have a very busy schedule and I'm not in the habit of just having a meeting for the hell of it. I need to know what we are going to talk about."

"I can't tell you now. It's too important to discuss over the phone. Please Mr. President, you know me, you know I wouldn't waste your time. I need ten minutes. That's all."

The President's secretary poked her head around the door, "Mr. President, your next meeting is ready," The President looked up, distracted, "Yes, Yes one moment."

He spoke back into the phone, "Hell, Jack, I've got no time for this." The President hesitated, something didn't feel right. His mind began to formulate another question for Jack when the secretary tried again, "Mr. President, you have to go."

Pulled in two directions at once, the President made a snap decision, "Okay. I'll meet with you. You get ten minutes—that's it."

It was another awful day in Washington D.C.. The weather had been particularly strange that winter: freezing cold for days on end, then sudden warm spells, then back to the cold. Today was one of the freezing cold days—with a nice strong biting wind thrown in for good measure. Dean Sullivan hated it, standing in the cold, toes and fingers numb, nose an ice cube, waiting for the boss. It was getting dark and turning even colder. He wanted to get this over with. He heard a car drive up behind him but didn't bother to look back. A door opened, then slammed shut; the frozen ground squelched as heavy feet crushed water crystals into oblivion.

"So I was right, they got to Jack somehow. He's in there with them?"

"Yep."

"Where are the rest of the boys?"

"Pete, Burt and Devon are on the other side of the warehouse, out of sight. Henry and Don are behind us to our left. Cameron, Rick and three others are covering the back."

"You've got the best with you this time?"

"Yep, they're all ex-military; Cameron and Burt are ex-Green Beret."

"Good. Excellent." Kurt was beaming with insane happiness, "No messing around this time, no finesse. We rush the building from the front and back. We take no prisoners. No one gets out alive. Right?"

"What about your son?"

"Screw that bastard! Screw that traitor!" Kurt's reply was so vehement that a shocked Dean took a step back.

"Right, gotch ya."

Kurt scanned the area surrounding the building; it was dark and overcast, no moon, no light, no witnesses—the perfect conditions for a murder-fest. Suddenly, his face arranged itself into a look of unforgiving fury and madness, "Okay, let's do it."

Dean pulled out a walkie-talkie and said, "Go."

Bodies, dark and silent, slipped among the shadows, moved towards the building and stopped. A single shape converged on the warehouse door. He seemed to just brush against the entrance and then was gone. A small object remained behind, taped to the door.

A short, sharp explosion briefly froze the courtyard in a burst of light. As the first killer dove through the wrecked door, a second explosion, from the other side of the warehouse, rattled and shook the structure. Kurt's men, pouring in from doors on each side of the building, fingers on triggers, ready to start the massacre, abruptly halted in surprise. The warehouse was empty except for five lone figures standing harmlessly in the center, unmoving, wearing very dark, goggle-like glasses. Kurt leapt forward, raised his gun and screamed, "What are you waiting for? Start shooting! SHOOT!"

Just as Kurt started to squeeze out the first bullet, the room filled with blinding, pulsating light.

"The President will see you now."

"Thank you." Jack rose from his seat and stepped past the secretary. He lifted his briefcase with practiced ease; it was much heavier than it looked.

"Good to see you, Jack!" The President stepped forward, stretched his hand out and warmly shook Jack's. Jack smiled and as he watched the secretary close the door from the corner of his eye, said,

"Good to see you as well Mr. President."

"So what is so urgent that it requires the attention of the President of the United States?"

"Well, Mr. President, I think it's best if I show you," Jack placed the large brief case on the President's desk and opened it toward him. The inner surface of the upper half of the case was made of a jet-black material, so black that no light seemed to reflect from it at all. The lower half was filled with rectangular objects, connected by large, fat wires.

"What's this?"

"This, Mr. President is...Earth's salvation," Jack said as he quickly pressed a thick, pitch-black cloth over his eyes. A split second later the jet-black half of the briefcase transformed into bright, blinding white light. The President shut his eyes, raised one hand up to cover them, slid the other towards the panic button on his desk...but it was too late....

His mind was being torn apart and reconnected.

Fragments of time opened and closed before him. Strange visions floated before the President and then dissipated. Alien resonance—a language from deep within, stirred his soul, comforted and yet frightened him. Awareness of an unknown world shimmered before him. Nothing seemed right, yet nothing was wrong. The President, stunned and groggy, face slack and blank, was struggling to understand.

"Wh.... What? What happened?"

"I'll explain in a moment, Mr. President. First and most important, you must cancel all your remaining appointments for today. My ten minutes are almost up. This is very important. Do you understand Mr. President?"

The President whose defenseless mind was confused, naive and gullible, replied in a monotone voice that no one would have recognized, "Yes...I understand. I will cancel all my remaining appointments for today." Then in a high-pitched timbre, like a child hoping to learn some new secret, "After that will you explain? Please?"

"Yes I will, Mr. President. First, I'd like you to arrange for some of my friends to see you. They will help me explain. Ask security to allow them into the White house. Tell them it is urgent."

"Yes, I will do this."

James, Scott, Matt and Shannon in clean-cut, professional looking suits arrived at the White House security entrance. Shannon, who had shaved off all of her lovely hair, wore a very severe suit and now looked like GI Jane, walked into the security area slightly ahead of the others. Scott and Matt followed Shannon and James took up the rear. Scott had miraculously put on a lot of weight and sported a thick beard. Matt's hair was now short and blonde and his brown eyes were now blue. James, who, through Ranula, had gained much greater control of his facial muscles than the rest of the human race, had changed the shape of his face so that he was virtually unrecognizable. Although they hoped that the President's request to allow them entry would lessen the normally intense security at the White House, they were still very nervous and therefore had asked Jack to meet them in case they had any problem with security.

Shannon was just stepping up to the security desk when Jack arrived.

"Ah! There you are," he called out, a frown on his face. "You're late. The President is almost out of time."

Jack turned to the man at the security desk, "Rick, we have to process these four as quickly as possible. The President needs to see them now."

"Yes, Sir, Mr. Ramsey. Right away."

"Hold it a minute."

Jack turned and inwardly cringed; the speaker, Howard Cheshire, was the head of security, renown as a stickler for detail and a major pain in the butt. Jack thought he got his jollies out of causing as much delay and conflict as possible.

"Howard, we need to get to the President right away. These people are late; they were expected ten minutes ago."

"Really?" Howard pushed past the security guard, took up a paper, scanned it, looked suspiciously at the four of them and said, "Who are they? I don't see anyone on the schedule."

"Last minute change. Very urgent. The President personally called up to the desk."

"Really?" Howard's voice held an almost imperceptible sarcastic tone. He turned back to Jack and stared unblinking at him.

"Really," replied Jack, voice deadpan. He returned Howard's stare, knowing that this was a challenge; if he looked away or looked frightened, they were all sunk.

"We don't have time for this garbage." Matt stepped forward, pushing past Shannon. "This is absolutely urgent, we need to see the President NOW!"

Scott reached out and put his hand on Matt's shoulder. "Now, now, let's not get pushy. We'll come back when it's convenient,"

"No! No! You can't. The President is expecting you." cried Jack, "He really needs to see you now."

Jack turned back to Howard and said, “Howard, you need to let these people through. It’s vitally urgent. National importance.”

“I don’t care how important it is, we follow standard procedure.” Howard turned to one of the armed guards at the gate and said, “I want you to hol....”

Suddenly Howard staggered, put his hand up to his head and groaned. He started to fall. Several of the guards rushed to catch him before he hit the ground.

“Something’s happened to Howard, call an ambulance!” Jack said. He then turned to Rick and said, “I know this is bad timing but we have to see the President now. It’s critical. Please process these people.”

Rick’s eyes looked over to Howard, who was lying on the ground and moaning and said uncertainly, “Well I don’t know....”

“I’ll take responsibility,” said Jack, “Any problems, blame me.”

Rick still looked tentative but, “Okay, sure.” He waved Shannon over to his desk and with Jack standing right beside him, began to look at her ID.

Five minutes later all of them had gone through the security desk. James was the last to go through the x-ray.

As they waited for James to pass through the security x-ray, Jack said in a low, urgent voice, “We need to get to the President as soon as possible. I told him to stay in the bathroom but I’m not sure how long he’ll remain in the confused state. If he comes out of it while we’re away, we might as well go straight to prison.”

“I think we’re safe; no one has come out the confused state that fast,” replied Shannon.

“But still, we shouldn’t take a chance,” said Jack.

“I agree. You three head to the office, I’ll wait for James,” said Scott as he casually looked back to James who got stuck behind someone who had set off the x-ray. Security stopped James from going through the machine while they performed an intense search of the poor offender—he stood with a sour look on his face, shoes and belt in one hand while supporting his sagging pants with the other. Finally James was let through.

As Scott and James hustled down the hall to the President's office, Scott asked, "What happened to that guy back there? I felt something...a burst of emotion."

"I sent a strong thought pattern at him, one that was full of conflicting emotions—hate, love, fear. I expected that this would incapacitate him for some time."

"Well, it worked."

"Yes, it did."

When Shannon, Jack and Matt entered the office, they found a President who was struggling and straining for his sanity. But they weren't surprised; each of them had gone through it. They understood and commiserated. Compassion and kindness left their minds eye and flowed toward him. They knew he would feel it and they knew it would calm him. It would keep him open and receptive to what they had to say.

James and Scott arrived a few minutes later. James looked at Jack and asked, "Everything progressing as usual?"

"Yes, he's in the confused state with no sign of paranoia or psychosis."

"Excellent." James turned to the President. "Mr. President, my name is James McArthur and my name is also Ranula, a long dead Venusian. We have unlocked your mind. You now have the sum knowledge of the Venusian society in your conscious mind. You will feel confused for some time; we are here to help shorten that time and to help you become comfortable with this new...new version of yourself." James halted for a moment while he sensed for anything unusual—but nothing presented itself—the President's confused psychic aura was as he expected. Then he asked, "Do you understand?"

"Y.... Yes."

"I have an important question to ask you...do you know someone named Lillia?"

"La...Lillia?"

"Yes, Lillia."

"No. No. I don't think so...should I?"

"No. You shouldn't." James paused, looked at the President closely, opened his mind, searching for Ranula. He felt nothing. "Look at your hands. Could you describe them for me?"

"What do you mean?"

"How many digits on each hand?"

"Five. Five fingers on each hand."

"How long are your fingers approximately?"

"Three inches."

"Thank you Mr. President." James looked over at Scott and the others and said, "No sign of Ranula. My modified mind-unlocking process has worked again. I am becoming very confident! It has worked for all of you with no repercussions. I now believe that we can apply this to anyone who wishes to be unlocked." He turned back to the patient. "Mr. President, I'm going to take you through a series of exercises intended to help you adjust to the new information available to you...."

The day passed quickly. The President progressed faster than James had expected. He was in much better shape than the rest of them had been at this juncture.

Now, it was time to get to the true purpose. "Mr. President, I'm sorry that we put you in this condition without your consent. We did this because we had no other choice, we...no Earth...Earth needs your help and cooperation. Earth is very close to destruction. Production of any kind of greenhouse gas, anywhere on the planet, must be stopped. The world has maybe a year, perhaps a little more—that's all. Then it will be too late, Earth will follow the fate of Venus. If that happens, if we cross that final, terrible threshold, in a few short years, all life would cease to exist. Mr. President, you now have the knowledge to confirm what I am saying; you can understand the complex mathematics that affirms Earths condition. We need your help."

Something was chasing him...chasing.... Fear struck but within seconds it subsided. He knew what is was and that knowledge calmed him. A moment later Matt's eyes opened and focused on the hotel ceiling while his mind relived the dream. It was the same one that had frightened him horribly ages ago but this time he knew what it meant, this time there was no sickening hang-over effect of fear and confusion. He thrust the covers to the side, swung his feet over the bed and stepped down. As he did he wondered for the thousandth time about Ranula. He had no memories of him except for this dream. But, still, the thought that Ranula was somehow locked away in his mind gave him pause. James was sure that Ranula could not rise up and destroy Matt's mind but still it was weird to think that a psychotic ghost was in him, tickling at his subconscious and sending him the dream. He wondered about Ranula's wife, his child, his world, his life. What had that been like? Only James knew for sure and his words and descriptions just didn't do it justice. A strange impulse took him, much like the urge to jump off a tall cliff without a parachute. What if he could release Ranula? Could he control him like James? Perhaps he could. What would it be like to have those alien thoughts and feelings? It must be an incredible sensation, beyond any that Humans had felt...except James.

Shannon was beginning to stir beside him. He looked over at her and immediately lost his train of thought.

"Okay, let's talk next steps." The President looked at Scott and then the rest of the group, "We're still in danger; no one understands what my interest is in you or why you are occupying so much of my time. It's creating great concern and although most people think that I have enormous power and can overcome anything, I really can't. I need co-operation to achieve almost everything I want to do. I've been asked numerous times what your purpose is and although I've been able to dodge the direct question, if I don't come up with a better answer soon, what power I have will be removed and others will take over," the President paused, lost in thought, "I can't see a solution other than we need more converts—converts within the government—the military, CIA, FBI, Scientists, NASA. People of influence who can help me control public opinion once we announce the truth and we'll have to do that at some point...probably sooner than we would like."

Scott nodded in agreement, "This is very difficult, very difficult. Who do we select next? We can't keep kidnapping people and forcing them to unlock."

"I think we have to trust someone and hope that they will be convinced to go through the procedure of their own will," said James.

"And if they don't? The secret will be out. We'll be sunk. We'll be considered crazy and dealt with in that context—some of us will go to jail for murder and the rest to a sanitarium," said Matt.

"Let's not forget that we have power now—power of thought—mind control beyond anything that the human race has seen before. We can defend ourselves," said Shannon.

"Against the whole world? Not likely," replied Matt.

"What about Kurt and his guys? They're passive now and seem to be genuinely concerned for Earth and the survival of Mankind. Can we trust them to help?"

"I've scanned their minds and can find no aggressive urges at all. I think they can be trusted," said James.

Scott replied, "We need to be cautious. In reality this is an experiment. Other than James, no one has been in this state for more than a few weeks and of course, as we all know, James is special in that Ranula co-exists within his mind. We really don't know what the long term, or even medium term effect will be on any of us. There could be side effects...dangerous ones. We all have great confidence, based on our Venusian knowledge, but who knows...the Venusian's weren't perfect. You just have to look at the current state of Venus to know that. I think we leave Kurt and his boys, exactly where they are now, prisoners in the warehouse."

"Let's go to my most trusted friend, someone I've known since childhood—the Secretary of State, Reg Hardwick," said the President, "I'm sure after I talked to him, he would consent to undergo the mind release."

"I agree, but then what? It's going to take literally forever if we're doing this one person at a time. There are twelve billion people on this planet. We need an overall plan, one which allows us to convert thousands and eventually millions. It's a daunting task," said Scott.

"It's a crazy task. How can we possibly do this?" asked Matt.

"We need people of influence, people that a large portion of the population would believe and trust. And we need enough of them so that it would no longer look like we're just a bunch of kooks, or worse yet, a cult," said Scott.

"How about this? We start with Reg, but at the same time we build a list of those that we think would trust us—we have to rely pretty much on the President for that as he has a lifetime of powerful contacts but Jack can help as well—he has many scientific associates and some political friends."

"I know a few people that I met when I was working for my Dad," Matt hesitated for a moment, "honest ones of course."

"Honest ones? I can't imagine Kurt having many honest acquaintances. How well do you know them?" asked Scott.

"Ah, fairly well I guess."

"Would you call them good friends?"

"Uh...no. I suppose not."

"I think we'll stick with the President's and Jack's contacts."

"Yeah, probably a good idea."

Chapter 34
RUSSIA

Matt shut off the light sequencer and then removed his ultra-darkened, tight fitting glasses. He hated the things, he couldn't see and constantly blundered into objects in the room but he had to use them to avoid the obvious pain and the probable eye damage caused by repeated use of the Mind Release Light Sequencer or the MRLS as it was now being called. But also, even more concerning, James wasn't sure what the effect of a secondary exposure to the sequence pattern would do to their minds. Would it cause a release or perhaps a partial release of Ranula? He was still studying it, reviewing all the Venusian knowledge, looking for some clue, some evidence that would help solve the problem, but really the only way to know for sure was to try it and that wasn't a solution at all—the risk was too high. It could have catastrophic consequences.

He let his mind scan the patient. All seemed as expected, the usual confused state. "Nurse, please take Mr. Raymond to the recovery room."

Three weeks had passed and several hundred people had been released, very influential people, very powerful. As each person was released, they could be counted on to provide further contacts and further opportunities for mind release. The number of participants was growing exponentially; it was no longer a problem of finding the right people, it was now a problem of providing the facilities and staff to support the procedure. They now had two clinics and were planning two more but it was difficult to keep up. Secrecy slowed everything. Only people who had been released could support the procedure and setting up clinics was a challenge as there had to be a believable cover story.

For Matt it was taking too long. He was getting tired of it...bored... bored out of his mind. Doing the same thing over and over again. He wanted something new in his life, something challenging, something exciting.

Initially there had been great concern about what would happen if they didn't have any support in foreign countries when they revealed what they knew—it would be the United States against the rest of the World. Fear and uncertainty could cause conflicts, possibly dreadful conflicts with the super-powers, Russian and China. But they had made some inroads in Canada, Europe, South America and Australia; key officials in a number of countries had been through the mind release and they were bringing new contributions to the cause daily. The real trouble was Russia and China. Relations between those countries and the West were poor, with difficult situations occurring almost daily. Espionage and counter-espionage meant that virtually no one could be trusted. But finally, just two days ago, someone who knew someone, who new someone, had found a possible opportunity in Russia; a person who had power but was favorable to the west and could see an opportunity, albeit for themselves, for advancement. There had been much discussion about it—the possibility of creating a monster was a very scary thought—someone who would use the Venusian knowledge to gain power for themselves and who would work against their goal.

But there appeared to be no other choice. They were running out of time. Too many people were becoming involved. Soon the secret would be inadvertently discovered, the media would get it and that would be that.

So it was decided to meet with Sergei Kozmonov, General Director of Intelligence in the Federation Foreign Intelligence Service (FFIS) which was Russia's equivalent of the CIA and used to be part of the KGB prior to the dissolution of the USSR. Sergei was thought to be a rising star and a possible successor to the President of the Russian Federation. It would be a huge step forward if he agreed to the mind release.

"Who's going to meet him?"

Scott, Matt, Shannon and James were sitting in a private office that they had rented in Washington, near one of the mind release clinics. It was a beautiful day, bright sunshine with a few wisps of clouds. They were on the ground floor; through the blinds James could see silhouetted body shapes passing along the sidewalk.

"Good question, Shannon," Scott replied, "The President wants to keep the government out of it, in case there are repercussions."

"What repercussions?

"Probably something like getting beat-up, shot, killed or just thrown into a lovely Russian prison," said Matt.

Scott laughed, "Well, actually, it's because the US relationship with Russia right now is in a terrible state. The counties have accused each other of spying and a number of diplomats from both sides have been expelled and to make matters worse, China is trying to take advantage of the situation by siding with Russia."

"So he wants us to handle it?" asked James.

"Correct."

Matt's eyes lit up as he said, "I'm in, even if it means danger. Right now, the way I feel, I'd rather be shot than do another day of mind release."

"I don't know who's going yet. There's also something that's just come up, something going on in China...possibly we may need to split up and...." Scott looked directly at Matt, "We still need to maintain momentum at the clinics."

"Oh! I know what that means! You're going to stick me with the clinics, aren't you?" Matt's voice had risen in volume.

"I don't know what I'm going to do yet."

"Oh, yes, you do. You just don't want to piss me off right now; you want a nice happy, compliant Matt, someone to do all the grunt work, the tedious, boring work, the stuff no one else wants to do. You're not fooling me. I've been there before...." His face became tormented. "With my Dad."

Matt stood up. He was so agitated that he was shaking.

"That's not true, Matt, I'm really still thinking about it."

Suddenly Scott felt a strong mental tug and then a violent, dizzying, confusing sensation of disjointed thought patterns that were not his and realized with a shock that Matt was trying to read his mind, something they had all promised not to do to each other. He fought to prevent the violation and for an awful moment it seemed that Matt was inside him.

"Matt! Matt! What are you doing? Stop it!" Shannon stood up and was moving quickly toward him.

Matt's head snapped toward Shannon and with tremendous relief Scott felt the connection break.

"I'm out of here," said Matt. He threw an angry glance at Scott and then turned, strode out of the office, and began to run down the hall.

"Matt! Wait!" Shannon followed him.

Scott watched as they left the room and then said, "That was rough. For a moment I thought I was going to be swallowed by Matt's mind. He's strong. Much stronger than I had thought."

"Agreed. I could feel him and tried to stop it but couldn't." James gave his head a disbelieving shake. "It's a shock, very unexpected,"

Scott said, "I can never tell how he is really feeling. My mind is unable to get a sense of his emotions—since I've been released he's the only one that I've encountered that's like that."

"Yes—the same for me. I can't read his emotions at all. I can send him thoughts—he's the best of us all at reading them and he's good at sending. But I only get what he wants me to get." James became pensive, "He's changed since his mind was released. Before I was able to pick up strong thoughts and emotions, but no longer. There's definitely something different about him, something unique," replied James.

"Something dangerous?"

"Perhaps."

"That's not good. How are we going to watch him? It's likely we're going to have to go to Russia and China at the same time. We'll be split up. And after this episode I don't want him on the trip. We can't afford to have an unstable Matt deep in the heart of Russia or China. He's going to have to stay here."

"It's not going to go over well, as you've seen."

"Yes...I...."

The phone rang, Scott saw the number and said to James, "This might be it...China." He reached for the phone.

Shannon stepped quickly out of the building and looked right and then left for Matt. There he was, walking slowly, head down to the sunlight, about a hundred feet ahead of her. Shannon jogged over to him, reached out and touched him tenderly on the arm.

She was deliberately quiet, "Honey...what happened in there?"

Matt turned to her and looked into those beautiful eyes. Even in his distress, he could feel her love.

"I don't know. It's just...well, lately I've been feeling that I don't count. Scott and James and the others want me to go away, disappear. I get all the crappy jobs, the ones no one else wants."

"But that's not true, Matt."

"Really? Sure seems true to me. I'm doing nothing but mind release. Scott and James and even you have been working with influential people: Engineers, Scientists, Politicians—even the President. Working on strategy—helping to make decisions. Important, exciting stuff."

"But the work that you are doing is as important as any of that. We need people to be released so...."

"So that they can do the fun stuff and leave me with the crap. And what about Jack? He' still involved and he killed the astronauts on the ship."

"Jack is in our prison with your dad and will stay there until his trial. He's helping by providing contacts and that's it."

"It's not right and not fair. It's boring and I feel useless."

"Oh, Matt, I'm sorry you feel that way but having a fit in a meeting isn't going to convince anyone to involve you in anything else. And... and to try to read Scott's mind...to force yourself on him...that was a way over the top. It scared me Matt...it really did."

"Yeah. I know. I feel badly about that."

"You should talk to Scott and apologize."

"I will."

Shannon looked at him carefully, she knew he tended to avoid difficult situations, "Promise?"

"I promise."

"We're going to have to split up," said Scott. They were back in the office, Scott, James and Shannon, "One of us to China. The other two to Russia."

"What about Matt?" asked Shannon.

"He's not coming," Scott looked directly at Shannon and held her eyes, "I'm sorry, but I just can't take a chance. He's apologized and seems very sorry but he's never been the most stable person. I can't take a chance on a meltdown in China or Russia."

Shannon replied with a touch of anger in her voice, "You know he took huge chances for you, risked everything, including his life. He's done everything you've asked him to. Now he wants a favor."

Shannon's tone hardened, "Let's face it...it's not even a favor, that's what he's calling it, but in fact he wants to feel that he's really part of the team. He wants to feel that he is an equal partner. He wants to be treated fairly. He wants excitement. He wants to be challenged."

She lowered her voice, almost to a whisper, "And he's willing to risk his life...again...for you."

She pointed her finger at him and raised her voice, "For you—not for us or for the President or the World."

She angrily jabbed her finger at him again, “It’s for you. You know he looks up to you, you’re his hero. This is such a slap in the face to him.” Tears had begun to well up in her eyes. “Please re-consider.”

There was a long pause in the room as Scott weighed the options—the urge to give in to Shannon’s request was strong. Only the muted sound of the nearby street filtering through the window broke the silence.

“I’m sorry, Shannon. I understand how you feel but I can’t take a chance on something as important as this. Any mistake and perhaps we start a war.”

There was another long pause in the room.

A soft sigh, almost a sob, issued from Shannon, “Yes...yes,” Shannon’s voice was resigned, “poor Matt....”

Matt stood at the window of his hotel and stared out at the world around him. It was a world that was rapidly changing. Massive transformations were on the way. There was no stopping it now. He was sure of that. He heard the sound of a zipper being pulled tight and turned with a sinking feeling in his heart that he hid behind a cheery tone. “All packed?”

“Yes,” said Shannon.

She walked up to him and touched his face. “You alright?”

“Yes. Of course.”

“You’ve taken it pretty well, all considered.”

“Nothing I could do. Scott has made his decision.”

“But still it’s pretty tough.”

“I know but I can take it. I’m mostly worried about you. I don’t want to lose you. You have to be careful. It could be dangerous.”

“You know I’ll be careful.”

“I’ll be thinking of you every minute of the day.”

“I’ll be thinking of you too.” Shannon looked at her watch, “I’ve got to go.”

"I know," Matt said softly, all pretense of cheeriness gone.

Shannon's eyes searched his face; they had been inseparable for months, this was the first real parting since they started dating. She could feel his pain which magnified her own—tears were coming and she knew that she had to control it, she had to be strong.

"I won't be gone long...back in a week." She hugged him, turned abruptly, picked up her suitcase and without looking back walked out the door.

Matt stood staring at the door for some time with a horrible ache in his heart and a fear, a fear not just for her but...for himself as well.

Shannon and Scott stepped off the train at a quiet station in a suburb of Moscow. It was almost midnight. They had been travelling for twenty-four hours and were desperate to get some rest at their hotel. The train station was a small, dingy building that hadn't seen a coat of paint in at least thirty years. One weak bulb illuminated the entrance. Barely visible in the darkness, a trace of mist hovered and slowly swirled.

As they walked out of the station five men approached from the gloom. Scott looked over at Shannon and sent a thought, "Oh, oh. Let me do the talking."

One of them produced some kind of ID; it was meaningless to Shannon and Scott—it could have been a driver's license as far as they knew.

The man said with a strong Russian accent, not as a question but as a statement; "You are Scott Benbow and Shannon Jones."

"Yes, we are."

"Please come with me."

"Wait a minute. We've been travelling for a long time, we need rest—we're going to our Hotel," said Scott.

"No, you're not. You're coming with us. Sergei has told me to bring you." The man smiled at both of them. "You can come with us in handcuffs if you like."

Shannon scanned the five men, one at a time, and with her mind's eye sensed determination—there was no wavering. They were prepared to fight if necessary and a couple of them were hoping for it. They all carried weapons.

Shannon threw a thought at Scott. "We can take them. I'll stun the two on the right with a telepathic blast, you get the other three."

Scott's thought came back forcefully, "No. We'll go with them. No violence."

They walked with the men to a near-by parking lot, empty except for two dark-colored, non-descript cars.

As they approached the cars the leader said, "I'll need your communication devices: phones, watches, tablets. You'll get them back when Sergei says it's okay."

Scott and Shannon got into the back seat of one car, two of the men got in the front and the other three went into the second car. As they left the parking lot, Scott looked back and saw that the other car was following them. Escape, if required, was going to be very difficult.

They passed a few isolated houses near the station and then entered the countryside. Stretches of tall trees, briefly highlighted in stark contrast to their ghostly brothers, lined the road. Scott and Shannon were tossed from side to side as the car flew along the dark, unlit road. Very often the car would cross intentionally over to the other side. Once Shannon gasped as the driver whipped the car back to it's side of the road when oncoming headlights suddenly lit up the interior of their vehicle. The driver looked back at Shannon, grinned and said something in Russian that caused the other guard to laugh.

She tried to note landmarks in case they had to find their way back, but it was hopeless; it was too dark and the vehicle was moving too fast, as well they seemed to make a ridiculous number of turns. Almost certainly it was done on purpose to prevent them from determining where they were. Shannon could feel fear beginning to form and did her best to ignore it.

A half hour later they came to a stop at a large iron gate surrounded by a tall brick wall. In the distance a massive building loomed. The driver pulled out his phone, touched a virtual button and the gate began to open.

They arrived at a large circular parking space with an illuminated fountain in the middle; water cascaded down a pair of dancing nymphs—the pool at the bottom was surrounded by beautifully decorated stone. A green hedge, fifteen feet high, stood on each side of the drive, hiding other areas of the grounds. In front of them rose a magnificent gothic three story mansion with many darkened windows looking down on them. Shannon turned her head to the left and then right; the building seemed to go on forever, walls and windows fading into the mist and darkness. As they stepped out of the car, Shannon saw a curtain move on the second floor and could feel the presence of several people near by. She sent a thought to Scott, "There are guards watching us."

And from Scott, "Yes, I know."

The men from the train station escorted them up polished marble stairs to a massive oak door darkened by hundreds of years of use. The door was covered in strange, almost mystical carvings. One particular image stood out: a man holding a sword in his right hand and a severed head in his left.

They had almost reached the landing; there was one man in front, one at each side and two at the back. No opportunity to run if they had to. A shudder struck Shannon; her fear was returning and she found that she couldn't take her eyes off the horrific image on the door—behind which the man who might determine their fate and possibly the fate of the world, would be found.

The leader touched another button on his phone and the door began to open. Shannon felt her breath involuntarily stop as a golden radiance poured through. She took in the brilliant beauty of the entry hall; patterns of gold frieze were everywhere. The floors were geometrically decorated with the same gorgeous marble as the entrance stairs; huge columns rose almost to the sky; larger than life statues loomed in the shadows; paintings, possibly masterpieces, hung from the walls. She had never seen anything like this in her life. Every nook and cranny cried out for attention. There was so much beauty in the room that her eyes didn't seem able to stay in one spot for more than a few seconds.

Large, paired mahogany doors with gold trim, at least ten feet high, bisected the walls to the left and right. Directly in front was a wide, marbled stairway with carved stone spindles and handrails that fanned out to the second floor.

And descending from those stairs was the handsomest man she had ever seen.

He was so magnificent that if it wasn't for movement, Shannon might have thought he was another decoration of the entry hall. He was about six-foot-two with medium length, slightly curly blond hair containing highlights so intense that his hair shimmered and sparkled. It surrounded his head like a halo and helped to frame a face that literally glowed with self-assured intensity. He had bright blue eyes, a very straight nose and a square jaw that gave a sense of masculine strength and determination. He wore tight, dark, immaculate clothes which purposely exposed a powerful, very fit body. Everything about him exuded confidence and self-control and...it was not a façade; she could feel with her mind's eye a "somebody up there likes me" aura. The sense that he felt that he could do no wrong and was destined for greatness was powerful, palpable.

She scanned his face again; she noticed a thin white scar, his only imperfection, that ran from his right cheekbone, down almost to the crease of his lips. But rather than diminishing his attractiveness, it served to enhance a sense of mystery, strength and masculinity. His lips were full and almost appeared golden in the warm light of the hall. She caught herself imagining what a kiss from those lips would be like. At that exact moment, he swung his eyes to her and...knowingly smiled.

Shocked, Shannon sent a thought to Scott, "This guy is partially unlocked. I can feel it!"

Surprised, Scott involuntarily looked over at Shannon and then sent a thought, "I don't sense that." But at the same time he saw out of the corner of his eye that Sergei had noted Scott's movement and was watching with a strangely curious smile. A touch of fear struck him. If Shannon was right, why didn't he sense anything? *Who was this guy?*

Sergei's eyes never left Shannon as he said with a smile and in perfect English with no discernable accent, "I had heard that you were a beauty but I must say you have exceeded expectations."

She thought, *the same goes for you...and in more ways than one*, but simply replied with a slight smile. "Thank you."

He continued down the stairs, ignored Scott, and held out his hand to Shannon. "I'm Sergei."

She took his hand, immediately felt the emotion of close contact and thought for the first time in her life, *my god, this guy's dangerous. I don't know if I can stay away from him.*

He was running, running faster than he had ever in his life but it was still catching him. He could hear the sound of feet pounding and of heavy, massive breathing, getting closer every second. But he knew what it was, he knew this dream and he knew he had to face his fear.

For the first time ever in the dream sequence...Matt stopped. The pounding feet stopped immediately but the rasping, animal breathing did not. It was still there. Behind him.

In waking, after he had decided to try to actively participate in the dream, he had thought that perhaps if he stopped running the evil would be gone, would dissipate, like mist blown by wind, and there would be empty space when he turned.

But it did not. It was there, he could hear it. Just feet away. Perhaps it could reach out and touch him. His heart raced; he could feel every hair on his back rising. Tingling fear rippled through his body. The urge to run surged...but at the very last second he overcame it. He shook. A sweat took him, ran down his body. He could feel it stinging his eyes and dripping off his nose. He was trying to turn, urging his body to move—to finally face this monster. It felt like he was moving through thick, putrid sludge. His entire body fought his will. Just as he thought he would fail, in a lightning flash, as can only happen in a dream, he was facing the monster. He stepped back, shocked. He had expected Ranula but it was....

Himself.

The image in front of him was pouring with sweat, was shaking. Its loud rattling breath stunk. Its arms hung down low and flaccid and swayed to its heaving breath. Its eyes were bloodshot and beady. Its body hairier than he thought it should be.

"What is this?" He cried out loud. But the sound he heard wasn't English or any other human language, it was a gurgling, clucking, chocking sound. Yet it seemed familiar, almost natural and in a strange way...calming.

That was when he noticed his surroundings. This was not Earth. Far off in his mind he thought with a strange excitement, '*Venus.*' He was on a hill that looked over a deep blue ocean—an incredible resonating color—a deeper hue of blue than anything he had seen on Earth. His eyes clung to the color, a surge of pleasure ran through his body.

The hill was covered in a strange grass, several feet high; bright multi-colored grass which seemed to sway on its own, to some unknown rhythm. To the left he could see tree-like objects but with very thick green trunks and bright orange leaves that danced to his eyes. He felt a sense of beauty that was unlike anything on Earth. His mind sang with happiness.

Then he looked down at his body. It was not Human. He was covered in silky fur. His fingers were long thin, peculiar looking appendages. He began to speak in that strange language again, not sure of what he was saying.

He swung back to the Matt-thing in front of him and unexpectedly laughed. He had no fear of it here. He was safe. He was home.

That was when he woke up.

He sat straight up in bed and calmly said to an empty room, "I'm going to do it."

"There's no need for a hotel. There's plenty of room here," said Sergei, "and I know you have travelled a long way. Stay here and we can talk in the morning."

Scott looked at his watch and replied, somewhat grimly, "It's very late. We'll have to take you up on your offer."

Several servants had appeared and Sergei said to one of them, "Anton, please show them to their rooms."

As they walked down the second floor hall Scott sent a thought to Shannon, "I feel nothing from him...other than huge ego. Do you still think he's partially unlocked?"

"Yes...at least I think so...it's difficult. I'm tired. Tomorrow I'll know better."

"This is your room," said Anton to Shannon.

They entered a large bedroom surrounded by dark wood paneling and covered by an intricately decorated ceiling. A warm fire was blazing in a stone fireplace located some distance in front of the bed. A marbled bathroom was visible through a door to the left. On the right was a large sitting area overlooking the park-like grounds. The four post bed looked incredibly comfortable. Shannon had never felt so tired as she did now; it took all her willpower not to fall into the bed, fully clothed.

She waited for the servants to leave and then performed a careful inspection of the room; looking for surveillance devices, checking window locks, even going to the extent of searching for hidden doors or peep-holes. Shannon knew it was excessive paranoia but she did it anyway. There was a dead bolt on the door that reduced her fear of a break-in while she slept. Satisfied that there were no immediate threats she stripped down to her underwear and sank gratefully into the bed. Within minutes she was asleep.

Suddenly Shannon shot up in her bed—she could have sworn she had heard some kind of gurgling sound in the room. A shiver of fear ran through her body. Then she looked down. She was floating...floating over a strange land...an alien land, beautiful and yet frightening. And she knew something was wrong, horribly wrong. A feeling of dread struck her, so powerful that she almost screamed out loud. That's when she noticed the two small figures below her. One was Matt. The other was an alien with a massive forehead, covered in brilliant fur with long finger appendages. They faced each other, five or six feet apart and the alien was speaking with that same gurgling sound that she had heard. Matt showed no sign of fear. Horrified, Shannon shouted to him, "Matt! Run! Run!"

But Matt did not hear.

Smiling, he walked toward the being and before Shannon could react, he wrapped his arms around it.

The dream began to fade. Shannon struggled to maintain contact. She shouted, "No! No! Matt! Run!"

But it was too late. The dream was ending. She stretched out her arms in a desperate effort to reach him and as she did...Matt merged into the other being. For a brief instant four arms protruded from a single body and then...then...Matt was gone. Only laughter remained.

She shot up in her bed and screamed. She was back in her room. The nightmare had ended. Shannon was vaguely aware of the sound of running feet and then a pounding on the door, followed by a shout from Scott. "Shannon! Are you alright? Shannon!"

The sound shocked her into action; she knew Scott would try to break in the door if she didn't answer. "Scott! I'm coming!"

Shannon unbolted the door and threw it open. "It's Matt! Matt's in trouble! We have to stop him!"

Light burned in from tall windows. Last night's mist was gone, birds sang in the park outside. The dream now seemed exactly what it was, a dream—a horrible nightmare but not reality. Only a small sense of unease remained and it was being rapidly erased by the beautiful setting that surrounded her. Shannon was in the dining room of the mansion. The room was bigger than her entire apartment; the floor was made of ancient oak boards, each of them a foot wide, stained with a golden hue that seemed to sing with the bright sunshine that filled the room. A massive table ran the length of the room, covered in beautifully decorated white linen and silver candelabra. The ceiling towered twenty feet above her and was coated with brilliant paintings: nymphs dancing through glades and forests, deer leaping across streams, birds flying in the distance, flowers bordered fountains with semi-naked women splashing in pools of deep blue. A wood paneled wainscot ran around the walls. Pale blue, understated wallpaper surrounded the room and provided a subtle emphasis to the many paintings that hung there.

Just then Scott entered. He smiled at Shannon and then turned to the steaming food that was sitting on a side table near to the entrance door. After selecting a few items from the various choices he walked over to Shannon and sat down beside her.

"How are you feeling?"

"Much better, thanks. What a horrible dream."

"You were frantic last night. I thought you were going to run right out of the house, all the way home, if necessary. How do you feel about Matt now?"

"Better...much better. But I think I'll still call...."

Shannon suddenly felt a presence and looked to the doorway. Sergei was there. Certainly he was no dream but even in bright daylight he had a magical aura about him—handsome as any hero in a fairly tale. She resisted the urge to stand up and walk over to greet him.

He strode over to the two of them and sat down beside Shannon.

"Good morning. I hope that you slept well," said Sergei.

Shannon glanced over at Scott and said, "Yes, pretty well."

Sergei looked at her intently and held her eye as he asked, "Has everything been to your liking so far?"

Shannon could feel herself blushing, but she did not look away. "Of course...I've...I've never seen such beauty in one place in all my life."

"I'm glad it pleases you."

"How could it not?"

Sergei smiled at both of them and said, "Please come to my library after breakfast. We have lots to talk about and plans to make." He rose to leave.

"You're not going to eat?" Shannon asked.

"I ate two hours ago."

Shannon glanced at a clock near her and said, "You didn't get much sleep."

"Sleep is over-rated. I do very well on four hours," he said and then turned and left the room.

Scott listened to his footsteps fade down the hallway, then looked for any other ears nearby. There were none. He turned back to Shannon and asked, voice lowered, "Well, what do you think? Do you still think he's unlocked?"

Shannon hesitated before answering, "I think so. Yes...yes, there's something there. I sense he knows, well...knows my feelings and...maybe can even read some of my thoughts."

"I don't sense anything. Are you sure?"

"Yes."

"That's really scary."

"Yes."

"How could he hide it from me? If he can do that then he has power far beyond ours," said Scott.

"I know. And how could he have got this way? How was he unlocked? Who unlocked him?"

"I don't know but we have to find out and even more important—determine who side he's on."

"I think it might be his."

"That's what I'm afraid of."

An hour later Scott and Shannon followed another of the many servants that inhabited the house into the library. Thousands of books lined the floor to ceiling mahogany bookshelves; as with the dinning hall, the ceiling was decorated with beautiful murals of subdued pastel forest scenes. Large windows with stained glass sent color throughout the room. Oak and mahogany reading tables were scattered here and there. A large hearth with fire blazing bisected the long wall and, directly in front, at right angles to the wall, were two large sofas facing each other with an elaborately carved coffee table in-between. And there was Sergei, blonde hair caught by the sun, reading some papers in a nondescript folder. As Scott and Shannon entered he looked up and said,

"Please sit down. Let's talk." Sergei waved his hand at the sofa opposite.

Sergei waited for them to sit and then began. "I won't waste time. I know who you are and why you are here. I know that something incredible happened on Venus and I know you have both benefited from it in a very primal way. This information has come to me from only one source. The same source that connected you to me so there are only two people in all of Russia that know about your...about your power... and the threat to Earth. I have worked hard, very hard, to prevent this knowledge from spreading."

Neither Scott or Shannon were surprised even though their contact had never indicated that she knew anything about their purpose and in fact, Shannon wasn't even certain that Sergei's contact knew the true story. It was Sergei. He knew. How he knew Shannon wasn't certain but she suspected it was his mind's eye. Somehow he had been able to detect others that were unlocked and from that read their minds in some way—pulled out snippets of thoughts and emotions and then deduced what was happening. She wondered if he had been in the States very recently where he could have come in contact with someone who had been released. Or perhaps it was whoever unlocked him, perhaps a traitor within their organization? That was a frightening thought—that there was someone working to release people for their own purpose, perhaps to build an army of super-beings who could take control of the world and would oppose their own plans. If this was the case then he was lying about how many people in Russia knew about it. Shannon felt frustrated. It was almost impossible to know the correct answer.

But...there was a way. She had to know for certain if he had been unlocked.

She was vaguely aware that Scott was telling Sergei of their plans, their intention to unlock as many influential people as possible—people who could support their cause and convince others to do likewise. Impulsively, rashly, she extended her mind's eye in an attempt to determine what Sergei was thinking, or at the very least get some sense of his emotions. Now that she had been unlocked, she could detect when someone was lying or sincere; she could feel their emotions: happy, sad, angry, afraid. If she really pushed she could get thoughts, mostly disjointed and broken, but enough to get an understanding of what they were thinking. The average person wouldn't know it was happening but someone who was unlocked...would know. So she was taking a chance. If Sergei was unlocked, he would know what she was doing. She ignored caution. She opened her mind and listened. But there was nothing, no sense of anything, which was extremely odd. She should get something—some base of emotion, some basic sense of his state. She pressed harder, expanded her sense...but still nothing. She tried harder than she ever had before. Nothing.

Shannon forced herself to remain calm. She now knew that he was unlocked. There was no doubt. Only someone who was unlocked could block her like that. And he was massively strong. Much stronger than anyone she had encountered, stronger than James. And she was sure that he would have felt her presence and therefore understood that she knew he was unlocked. Unable to get any sense of emotion from him, she watched his face. Sergei was talking to Scott and showed no expression whatever.

A sense of dread struck her. She had been a fool. What would he do? They were trapped here. The FFIS were ruthless. He could murder them and no one would stop him.

Sergei's eye's glanced her way for just a second and in that moment she felt a foreign presence in her mind and a calming thought came to her, *"It's okay. You are safe here."*

There was a knock at her door. They had left Sergei an hour before and gone back to their rooms. Shannon had been pacing back and forth, uncertain of what to tell Scott about Sergei. She worried that Scott would be angry about what she had done. She didn't want to confess to Scott but she didn't know if she could trust Sergei and she couldn't sense any of his thoughts or emotions so there was no way to confirm anything he said. She wouldn't know if he was lying. She felt helpless.

Shannon walked toward the door and knew it was Scott even before he spoke and she knew something had happened. She could feel his concern and something worse, something she had never felt from him before...fear.

"Shannon, it's me."

Trembling, she opened the door.

Scott stepped in, swung his head back out and checked down the hallway in both directions. No one was present. He closed the door and lowered his voice almost to a whisper,

"I've just had terrible news. James is in prison in Beijing. I must leave immediately. You're going to have to stay here on your own."

"What?" Shannon's voice reflected the fear she sensed in Scott.

"I know it's not good. But I have to leave you. I need to get to James."

"How did you find out? Sergei's taken all our communication devices."

"My minds eye. I felt him calling me."

"What? But he's a thousand miles from here at least."

"I know it seems impossible but I felt him anyway. I communicated with him. Somehow James found a way to reach me. I don't know how. His mind is even stronger than I thought."

"I'll go with you."

"No. We still need to find out about Sergei. You have to stay here."

"No. I can't."

"You must."

Shannon took a step back. She looked away from Scott. A sense of panic hit her. It was one thing to face danger with friends, people she could trust and rely on, people who would help her even if it meant danger to themselves, it was another to face it on her own. She'd be by herself, alone—the nearest help would be a thousand miles away.

Scott stepped forward, held her shoulders in his hands and looked into her eyes.

"You have to do this. I don't say this lightly. I know the risk and I wouldn't ask you to do it if there was any other way. We have to find out about Sergei. We have to find out what his intentions are, how he came to be unlocked, why he seems to have power greater than ours and if there are others like him. We have to know this. It could affect the outcome of everything we are attempting to do. We don't know what is going on in Russia. Possibly a war is eminent. We need to find out what his plans are."

Scott stopped for a moment, hesitated, as if looking for the right words,

"He is clearly attracted to you. That gives you an advantage. Use it to find out what is going on here."

"What? You want me to flirt with him? Fool him into giving away information?" Shannon was becoming angry, "Or would you have me go to bed with him?"

Scott's voice was soft but firm, "I want you to do whatever it takes to get the information we need. We're not playing a game here. The survival of the world is at stake. Offset against that our lives are forfeit. We do whatever it takes, even if it means the loss of our self-respect, our dignity or our lives."

"I'm sorry, Sergei, but my time is up here. I must leave." Scott glanced over at Shannon. "Shannon will stay to discuss our plans with you in detail, work out how you can recruit others and how we will release them."

"You have to go so soon? That's a pity."

"Unfortunately, I have many meetings. Time is running out for us and for Earth. We have to move quickly."

"Well, it's still a pity. I was looking forward to a candid conversation at dinner tonight about what happened on Venus. I'm very curious." Sergei stood and warmly shook Scott's hand. "I will have Anton take you to the train station." He looked to Shannon and said, "I'm sorry but I have urgent business so I cannot speak to you until dinner tonight. I hope you will forgive me." He reached out, took her hand and gently kissed her fingers.

As they left the library Shannon's legs felt weak; she had never been in a situation like this before in her life, not even close: trapped in a house in a far away country, trapped by the head of the FFIS, a man who was likely the most ruthless man in Russia, a man who was apparently interested in her...and...even worse...she in him.

Shannon spent the afternoon wandering the magnificent halls and rooms of the mansion. She was surrounded by beauty but her heart was in turmoil. She felt a strong physical attraction to Sergei and now, after the conversation with Scott, it seemed likely that something was going to happen. Exactly what, Shannon was afraid to contemplate. She did not want to cheat on Matt but circumstances were forcing her in that direction. And to her dismay...it excited her. He was an incredibly handsome man, intelligent, rich, powerful. The attraction was intense, palpable. She stopped in front of a painting that was almost certainly a Rembrandt and used it to distract her mind. After a few minutes other thoughts began to come. Perhaps she could avoid a romantic relationship. She wondered how she could get information without Sergei's help. What about his office in the basement? Could she get in there without Sergei knowing? It seemed very, very unlikely. This guy was FFIS. The head of the FFIS. The security of his office must be extreme. She stepped closer to the picture to see a little more of the detail. Suddenly another thought came—but it was security designed to stop normal human beings, not ones who had the capability to sense and read and, to some extent, manipulate the minds of others. This gave her an advantage, a big advantage—so long as the rest of the people in this building weren't like Sergei, that is. She wasn't sure, but certainly it didn't seem likely that Sergei would allow that to happen. At least not in the lower levels of his organization. Senior people maybe, but so far as Shannon could tell, the only people in the building right now were guards and servants—no one of importance.

She had seen servants and guards using their smart phones to access doors in the building, including Sergei's office. If she could get one of those and knew the code, she could get into the office. After that how could she get into the computers? Almost certainly they were password protected. Shannon's heart sank. There was no way to read Sergei's mind. She had thought that her mood couldn't get any blacker but Shannon suddenly realized that the majority of the documents on the computers would be in Russian. Since the unlocking, her knowledge and intelligence had risen considerably and she could learn languages very quickly—in a matter of weeks—but she didn't have weeks and didn't have access to anything she could use to teach herself the language.

The pressure was getting to her—she suddenly caught herself biting her nails—something she hadn't done since childhood. Homesickness and dejection touched her. She wished she could instantly transport herself out of this house, out of this situation, away from this man, right back to Matt, right back into his loving arms and forget everything that had happened and...was about to happen. Overwhelmed with sadness she covered her face with her hands and began to cry.

Shannon walked down the hallway; she could see the door to the dining hall twenty feet in front of her. Her pace slowed and then stopped. A thousand thoughts had been flying through her mind all afternoon. They reached a climax now and brought her to a halt. She had thought about staying in her room, claiming to be sick. She had thought about escape, waiting till dark and then breaking out of the building. She had searched all the ground floor entrances and windows this afternoon for some method to get away. She had used her mind's eye to look for guards; they were everywhere, unseen, in the building, on the grounds, covering the doors. She wondered what would happen if she were caught trying to steal secrets. Would he put her in some horrible prison? Would he kill her? She had thought about confessing everything to Sergei; begging him to let her go free. She had thought about his strength, his power, his beauty; she thought about being willingly captured in his arms, she thought about caressing him, she thought about kissing him. She wondered how she would get information from him. Sergei didn't get to where he was by being the trusting type. Likely she would give him everything and get nothing in return.

She could not predict tonight's outcome but she did know one thing... something would happen tonight, something that she was powerless to stop. She straightened her dress, pulled her hair to one side, lifted her chin, shut off all the negative thoughts, and strode forward.

Shannon entered the room and saw that Sergei was sitting at the far end of the table but not at it's head. He sat to the right of the head of the table.

Sergei stood up as she entered and a smile of delight leapt to his face. "You look wonderful. It's like heaven itself just stepped into the room."

Shannon was wearing a dress of autumn colours that she knew suited her well. A gentle swirling pattern reminiscent of leaves falling from the sky decorated the cloth. It fell to just below her knee and hugged her body closely; the top was tastefully cut to show just a little of her breasts, not too much to be vulgar but enough to attract attention. She wore a pair of light-brown high heels that matched her dress perfectly and helped to emphasize the shape of her lower legs.

Shannon smiled back and could not help but feel sensual joy at the happiness she saw in his face. He wore his usual dark-toned clothes, blacks and greys, but this time instead of a tight fitting shirt, it was loose and flowing and silky and seemed to ripple around his body as he moved. His pants were similar, tight around the waist and hips but loose along the leg.

She said, "Thank you, you're very kind."

Sergei laughed. "Not kind. Honest."

She laughed back. "You are smooth with your words but I never know if I can trust a flatterer."

Sergei's expression changed immediately; it became somber and sincere. "You can trust me with your life. That is for certain."

For a few seconds they exchanged a powerful, meaningful glance; no words were said. Shannon could feel all the emotions of the day welling up inside her. Tears began to form. To avoid embarrassment she quickly said, "Where should I sit?"

"Oh. Yes. Please sit here. At the head of the table."

"The head of the table? Really?"

"Yes...please."

Shannon sat down. Flames in a huge fireplace crackled behind her. The hall was filled with a soft golden glow from hundreds of candles and was a sharp contrast from the brilliant sunshine that filled this room when she had breakfast that morning. So much had happened in this one single day!

"I feel a bit silly, sitting here in this huge room with just you. The table alone could seat fifty people."

Sergei smiled, "To be precise, it can seat seventy-six. Kings and Queens, Princesses and Princes, royalty of all kinds, diplomats, great artists and athletes, men and women of power, the elite of this planet all have sat here. And you are sitting where some of the greatest people of all time have sat."

Shannon considered his statement for a moment and then said, "I don't feel deserving. This whole trip has been a whirlwind. I have never experienced anything like this in my life and I feel out of place...wrong somehow."

"I understand." Sergei paused and looked at her as if pondering his next words carefully. "I'm very much the same. Let me take you to where I truly feel comfortable. Where I am at home."

He lead her down various hallways, around corners, down several flights of stairs and then back up at least another flight. Shannon was thoroughly lost but she was certain that they were now below ground, in the bowels of the mansion. She said, cheery voice hiding concern,

"Where are you taking me?"

"You'll see. We're almost there."

They rounded one more corner and faced a set of plain steel-grey doors. Fear began to take the place of concern but Shannon said nothing, did nothing. She was at his mercy; there was nothing she could do.

Sergei punched a code into his phone. There was a click as a lock was released; Sergei pulled the door open and held it for Shannon to step through. She stopped in surprise.

They had entered a large room with bare concrete walls and no windows; a plain large desk covered in computer screens was front and center, a narrow bed ran along the wall to the left. To the right was an open door to what was obviously a bathroom. A large armoire stood near the bathroom door. There were no pictures to be seen and certainly no personal effects. The lighting had a slightly greenish tinge and was dull and depressive. This was the antithesis to the rooms above: plain, almost harsh—utilitarian to the extreme.

Sergei could see the shock on Shannon's face and smiled grimly. "Upstairs is just for show. This is where the real work is done and where I'm most comfortable."

They turned right, walked past the desk and toward a door that Shannon had not noticed before because her view had been blocked by a large steel grey file cabinet. Through the door was a kitchen; a table with just enough room to sit four people was in one corner. The kitchen was small, undecorated, but very clean and tidy.

Sergei turned to her and smiled; he seemed more relaxed now, less formal. "I'll cook you dinner. I'm a reasonably good cook. It won't be anything special but it will taste good."

He reached into a cabinet and brought down two plain wine glasses and from the fridge produced a bottle of wine. He said, "It's nothing like what I could have given you upstairs, but I think you'll like it."

He poured the wine and then began to gather food and ingredients for the dinner.

Shannon watched him for a moment and then asked, "So you spend most of your time down here?"

"As much as I can, yes."

"And the bed...in the other room, in the room with your desk. That's where you sleep?"

"Yes."

"Really? Why? You could live like a king upstairs and yet you choose to live like a pauper down here. I don't understand it."

"Because this is where I came from. This reminds me of home. This is how I grew up...as a matter of fact this is a lot nicer than some of the terrible places that I lived in when I was a boy."

"Oh."

He stopped and looked at her. His face was grim as he said, "It's easy for you to think of me as forever wealthy, isn't it? But that's a far, far cry from reality. I was an orphan. I never knew my parents. I grew up in an orphanage. I grew up in a place where love was unheard of. Where a full belly was unheard of. Where beatings and torture were common place. I've seen children starved to death. I've seen children beaten to death. I was beaten many times. Once one of my wounds became badly infected; no one tended me, no one helped me, I almost didn't make it," he said.

"This place brings me back to reality. It reminds me never to be complacent. I know Scott and many others think that I have a huge ego but that is a façade, a façade intended to fool my enemies, to cause them to underestimate me."

Shannon's voice dropped to almost a whisper. "How did you get out? How did you survive?"

"By being meaner, nastier, tougher, smarter than everyone else."

"How terrible. What a horrible life for a child."

A sad smile crossed his face. "Don't feel sorry for me. Look instead at what I have accomplished; look at my success." Then he laughed outright and waved his hands around the room and said, "Besides, look what I have now."

They had just finished eating when Sergei's cell phone buzzed. He looked at it and said, "I'm sorry I have to take this."

He answered the phone in Russian and rose from the table. As he left the room he closed the door, almost completely, but it remained open a crack.

Shannon could faintly hear a one way conversation in Russian, none of which she could understand. She sat for some time, poured another glass of wine, took a few more sips, waited some more but it seemed like the conversation was not coming to an end anytime soon. Bored, she stood up and walked to the door. She opened it, stepped through and stopped, surprised.

Sergei swung in her direction. His eyes met hers and for a moment there was silence. He covered the mouth piece of his phone and then he said, "You weren't supposed to see this." Sergei then said something into the phone in Russian and hung up.

He was standing beside the armoire and it wasn't in it's usual place—it had swung away from the wall and there was a rough opening behind it. The opening was chiseled through solid rock; it was a door of some kind. Sergei had been putting something in that space.

Shannon should have felt the danger but wine had erased caution. She walked toward him and said, "Where does that door lead?"

For a moment Sergei said nothing. A grim look covered his face. Shannon felt sudden fear, fear that she had gone too far, fear that she had taken too much for granted; thoughts of prison and death leapt to her mind.

Suddenly Sergei smiled and stared quizzically at her, as if considering her for the first time. He shook his head in a puzzled fashion.

"What?" asked Shannon.

"Well, I almost told you. And I can't believe that."

"Why?"

"Because I never let down my guard. Not to anyone...ever...at least not till now."

"I'm the General Director of Intelligence in FFIS. I have enemies. Many enemies. They are everywhere. They are even in this house. No one knows this but I am fighting a battle. A battle to free Russia from endless corruption. From dictator after dictator. And I am on my own. I am alone. I am attempting to finish what Mikhail Gorbachev started many, many years ago. I want to give my people freedom. Only my special talent protects me. The talent that you know about. The talent that I let you know about. And you have told Scott. Already I have opened my heart farther than I have ever done and possibly it may cost me my life," he said.

"You asked me where that door leads. It has two destinations. One is my escape route; it travels a quarter mile underground and comes out in a service building. No one knows about it. The people who built it have been dead for hundreds of years," he said quietly.

"But it is also the door to my heart because I would have never told this secret to anyone that I did not love."

He was not looking at her as he said this. He could not bring himself to look at her. Sergei began talking in a low voice, almost to himself, as if he was solving a puzzle. "Something strange happened. Unexpected. When I saw your picture for the first time. I felt something. Something that I had never felt in my life. An attraction, powerful yet uncertain. I couldn't understand it. Yes, you are beautiful but my life has been filled with beautiful women. None have had any affect on me. And here I was feeling something...strange...and it was only a picture," he said.

"Love at first site? Love based on a photo? A figure etched on a page? How was that possible? I couldn't understand it," he said.

"Then I had an epiphany. It was as if a bolt of lightening had struck me. It was my special talent. And yours. That picture connected me to... to you. Somehow I transcended space and felt your presence, felt your soul and knew the beauty that was found there," Sergei said, his voice wavering with emotion.

"Ever since then I have not been able to keep you out of my mind. And trust me, I have tried. There's no room for love in my battle. Or so I thought. Now it's too late. Now I'm trapped." He looked up into her eyes.

"The day you arrived confirmed it. I felt you well before I saw you. I felt the beauty, not the physical beauty, I felt the beauty of the soul. It was so powerful that for a while I couldn't think. I was intoxicated. I struggled to compose myself, even as I walked down the stairs, in sight of your wonderful face." His voice dropped to a whisper,

"Now it's too late. Now I'm trapped. I'm trapped by my love for you."

Shannon watched his face intently as he spoke. She could see puzzlement, fear, sadness, hope, determination, cross it in waves. The sight was as powerful as any emotion or thought that she could have read with her mind's eye. She was not surprised about his statement of love. She had known it for some time and of course had felt something the same herself but...she was still not sure...of sincerity. She could not read his mind. She was not sure about his statement regarding his sensing her from thousands of miles away. It seemed far fetched and exceptional even for Sergei. She would be giving up everything if she opened her heart to him. She would join his side; she would abandon Matt. She had to know for certain,

"I have a question for you."

"Ask anything you wish."

"When we first met, I could feel you, I could sense you. But after that never again. You blocked me. Why?"

"That first night, I was overcome with emotion. I lost my self control. After that I was more careful. My special talent is what has kept me safe all my life. Since I was a child I have been able to sense things about others, mind reading some would call it. Sometimes I could scare people, put thoughts into their minds, make them jump in fright when there was nothing there. I began to use that to my benefit and once I grew up, I used it to benefit my cause. When I discovered that you and Scott and Matt and James had this same ability and knew how to unlock it in others, I felt threatened. I had to find out more—but I also needed to protect myself. If I had not been so overcome by your presence you would not have known."

Shannon said nothing and contemplated his words. They looked at each other; neither one's eyes left the other. Finally, she came to a conclusion.

She said, "You know what I want."

"Yes, I do."

"Then do it."

Shannon opened her mind and extended it toward Sergei and waited....

The shock of his love flooding her mind was intense, incredible, like nothing she had ever felt. She felt his thoughts, his being, his soul...and presiding over everything...his love for her.

Almost unconsciously they both stepped forward, reached up, caressed each other's faces and then leaned forward and touched forehead to forehead.

Morning light was beginning to work it's way through the drapes in one of the bedrooms in the mansion. Sergei sat up and looked at the beautiful woman lying naked beside him. He felt a touch guilty about what he had done...but only a touch. He had accomplished what he had set out to do. She loved him. She was his now.

Matt walked slowly down the darkened street. It was ten pm. The only light came from a single street light mid-block. He was uncertain, nervous. His mind kept flipping back and forth as he considered the risk of what he intended to do. No one knew what would happen. Perhaps nothing. Perhaps insanity. Perhaps anything in between. He had left a note for Shannon, in case the worse was to occur, in case he could not handle Ranula—could not control him and killed himself like the astronaut crew on Venus. It took him a long time to write that note, three days in fact. He'd write some words, throw it out. He'd write some more, chicken out and decide not to go through with the secondary mind release. He must have written it twenty times. Predominant throughout the note was his love for her, how he missed her and how he longed to see her again. He truly, truly hoped she'd never have to read it.

He still wasn't certain if he'd do it. He reached the door of the clinic and hesitated again. Under his breath he cursed himself and said, "Stop being such a chicken. Do something with courage for once." He reached into his pocket, pulled out the keys, opened the door and stepped through.

Something happened then; a switch in his mind clicked over. He became certain of his choice. A slight smile crossed his face. He would do it! Feel what it was like to be an alien, have Ranula's memories, see his planet as it once was—watch the sun set on Venus, swim in it's ocean, smell the air, eat a Venusian meal, speak an alien language. There must be so much to experience and amazingly it was sitting there—in his mind. Ranula was waiting; he could feel it, he knew it.

He opened the door to the mind-release chamber and flicked on the lights. The walls were bright white and so was almost everything else. James had said that the procedure should have as much light intensity as possible. He sat down at his chair, where he had been sitting, seemingly endlessly for the last few weeks, and started the computer that controlled the light sequencer. He logged in and rapidly typed out the commands until he reached the last one. Then he stood up and adjusted the bank of lights so that they directly faced him. He sat back down and stared at the enter key. This was his last chance to change his mind. No going back after this—he would start down a path that could not be halted. He was jumping off a cliff with no sight of the bottom—a base jumper without a parachute. Would he do it? Could he do it? The confidence of a few minutes ago was gone. He began to shake but he placed his finger over the key anyway. It stayed there for several minutes as his numb mind debated the decision, then almost unconsciously he pulled his hand away. Defeated, he pushed the chair away from the computer. He stuck his hand in his hair and pulled in frustration. Suddenly he yelled out, "Screw It!" and lightning quick, struck the enter key.

Matt cringed as the light assaulted his eyes. He had been through it before and it was just as painful as it was the first time. He held his breath as the light sequencer ran through its procedure. He told himself that it wouldn't be long. It would be over soon. His entire body tensed as he waited for something...something unknown.

The sequence stopped. His eyes still blazed with pain but Matt felt nothing different in his mind—there was no sign of Ranula. He didn't know what to expect but he was sure that he should feel different. Disappointment and relief struck him equally. He started to stand. And that's when it happened.

It wasn't significant at first, just a slight feeling of vertigo. He took a step forward and started to lose his balance. He sat back down. The room began to shimmer, glowing bright one moment, dim and dark the next. His head felt fuzzy and he was having trouble thinking, of even understanding where he was. He was too confused to be scared. He was.... He was what? What? WHAT? An insane giggle slipped from his lips. Some drool ran down his chin and dribbled to the floor. The giggle became a laugh. He swiped at his chin with the back of his hand and saw strange fingers. *What was this?* His laughter stopped. His mind could not grasp what he was seeing. There was something wrong. Terribly wrong. What had happened to him? Panic started; his heart rate sored, his breath was rapid—as if he was running a sprint. He tried to stand but his legs seemed wrong somehow; he couldn't coordinate them. They were rubber and weak one moment and too strong the next. His arms were moving on their own, randomly, in weird spasmodic fashion. His head began to twitch. Suddenly it shot up and backward so quickly that he vaguely felt pain in his neck. Someone whispered in his right ear. His head shot in that direction. Then the whisper was next to his left ear. His head whipped in that direction. Suddenly there seemed to be voices all around him, soft, murmuring. He couldn't understand what was said; the language seemed wrong somehow. His left hand shot up to his mouth. He sunk his teeth into his forefinger and began trying to chew. Blood dripped out of his mouth.

"What is this? What is this?" Matt was vaguely aware that he had not asked the question. It was Ranula.

Ranula was conscious. He was alive. He was taking over. Suddenly a massive thought...a feeling came.... DREAD. Matt's body shuddered. He began talking in gurgling sounds. Dimly his mind could feel Ranula trying to understand what had happened to his body. He could sense Ranula's horror; he could feel him screaming. He had stopped biting his finger and was now pounding on his head with his bloody hand. Matt felt nothing. His neck began to twist awkwardly, as if Ranula was trying to do something with Matt's body that wasn't possible. He was losing his sense of self—he could hardly think, he could hardly feel, he could hardly see. The Ranula being was nearly in complete control and was trying to tear itself out of Matt's body. Matt was losing consciousness but his body continued spasmodically squirming and swinging and hitting. He knew he was almost done; his fate had been sealed. Regret faintly tugged at his muddled mind.

Suddenly, like a brilliant beacon of light ripping through the dark, clarity tore open the Ranula-self and at that precious moment Matt thought of Shannon: how much he loved her, how much he wanted to see her one more time. He opened his mind and blasted out a thought—a scream of terror and horror, a cry for help, a final goodbye. The strength of it seemed gigantic, like a supernova event—powerful beyond belief. Then he faded away. His last sense of self was.... Dread.

Scott stepped off the plane in Beijing and sent a thought out in an effort to find James. He had tried several times from greater distances but had got nothing. He didn't know how James had sent him the message from such a large distance when he was with Sergei and Shannon but he certainly wasn't able to do it. His challenge was now to find him. He had tried calling several people back in the States but no one knew anything about James being in jail but they also had not heard from him for some time. Scott was puzzled; normally if an American citizen was arrested in

China, the embassy was informed. Scott had checked with the embassy and they knew nothing. Whoever had him didn't want it known.

Scott walked down the gangway and entered the airport. He found a quiet spot and pulled out his phone. It was a long shot but he'd try calling James's cell number and see if anyone would answer. If they did, perhaps he might be able to get something out of them. He dialed and waited....

Someone answered, "Hello?"

Scott didn't reply right away; the voice sounded like James. It threw him off.

"Hello?"

"James? Is that you???"

"Yes. Scott? Is that you?"

"Yes! What's happened? You're out of prison?"

"Prison? What do you mean?"

"You sent me a thought-message, you said you were in jail and you needed help."

"Wha...what? No I didn't."

Scott suddenly felt sick, his stomach churned.

James continued on. "I don't know what you're talking about Scott. Things have been going well here and in fact, I'm ready to go back to the states."

"No. Oh no." Scott's voice was at a whisper.

"What? What's the matter?"

"I've made a horrible mistake. I've been fooled. Sergei! Bastard! It was Sergei not you."

James said, "What are you talking about? Scott you're not making sense."

Scott didn't hear him, he said, "Shannon! What have I done? What have I done?"

Shannon woke with a start. She shot straight up, her heart pounding. She wasn't in her bed, for a moment she was confused and then the events of last night came flooding back to her. With relief she saw that Sergei was gone. She didn't want to face him. She felt sad. She felt guilty. And most importantly...she felt uncertain. What had seemed clear and unequivocal in the dimness of night, now was murky in morning light. She still loved Matt and nothing would change that. But she also loved Sergei...or did she? She was consumed with sadness, guilt and uncertainty. She was also aware that Sergei was near and could, if he wanted, feel her emotions, read her thoughts. She wished she could block him—like he did to her but she had no idea how to do that or how he did it. What would he think if he knew how she felt now? The trust that she had in him last night was gone. He was powerful—perhaps he could have fooled her with his emotions. What if he was doing the same as Scott had wanted from her? Playing on her emotions to get information, to use her for his benefit? Suddenly she was frightened and the thought that he could invade her mind at any time was now abhorrent.

Did she really love him? Would she leave Matt for him? A desperate thought took her—call Matt, tell him she loved him, confess and ask for his forgiveness. A moment later she was thinking of the incredible experience she had when Sergei opened his mind to her. The feeling of his love, the feeling of his hands on her body, his physical strength, his beauty. Did she really love him?

Did she really love him?

Did she really love him?

She started to dress. She had to get out of the house, away from Sergei, away from his prying mind. She needed to work this out in privacy. She needed to come to a conclusion. Matt or Sergei. A decision had to be made.

A few minutes later Shannon walked through the front door, past the security guard who looked curiously at her but didn't move to block her way. She tested his mind and found that he had been told by Sergei to give her access to the grounds. It seemed that Sergei had anticipated her reaction and perhaps had predicted how she would feel. His absence was to give her space, give her a chance to think. If that were true, it was an act of unconditional love and served to confuse her further and make her choice even more difficult. What did her heart want? Tears were coming. She ran down the stairs and tried to stay in control. If she broke down here it would be back to Sergei in an instant.

She jogged through a break in the hedge that surrounded the driveway, then covered her face and cried. Tears ran down her face in rivulets. She hadn't felt this confused and sad in her entire life. Her knees buckled and she dropped to the ground. She began to sway back and forth, in pain, in self-hatred, in guilt and then....

A powerful blast hit her; a cry in her mind, like nothing she had ever experienced. It was Matt—screaming, crying out for help, crying for her love. For a moment it incapacitated her—it was so strong. And then...it was gone.

She cried out loud, "Matt! Matt!"

Scott was frantically trying to book a flight back to Russia when the scream from Matt hit him. He stopped immediately. Stunned, he said to James, who was beside him, "What was that?"

James did not reply. Scott turned toward him. James looked pale; his eyes were unfocused but his face showed an intensity he'd never seen before. Suddenly James's hand shot out and grasped Scott's forearm and painfully squeezed.

"James! Let go! Let go!"

James, eyes unfocused, stared at Scott—seemingly unable to understand what he had said. Then he shook himself and said frantically, "It's bad. It's Matt. It's Matt. He's released Ranula."

"What? How do you know? How?"

"I could feel Ranula after Matt's scream. Ranula has much greater mind-power. That's why Matt was able to send us this thought, this cry for help. I was trying to listen—to see if I could hear Ranula—I had him for a minute but now he's gone."

Scott wiped sweat from his brow. "Everything's gone sideways."

"We have to get back to Matt."

"Will he survive?"

"I don't know. If it was anyone else, I'd say no. But there's something different about Matt. Just being able to send that thought when he was being consumed by Ranula is something I would have said was impossible. There's a chance he can survive but we have to get to him quickly."

Scott said, "We're going to have to split up."

"Yes. You go to Shannon. I'll take Ranula," said James.

"Is there a danger? From Ranula I mean, or will you find Ranula or... Matt...or whoever, comatose?" asked Scott.

"I don't know. Could Ranula function in Matt's body without destroying it? That's a good question. Possibly. If so, then yes, there could be danger, great danger, to anyone who encounters him."

Scott shook his head and said, "Could things get any worse?"

"Let's hope not—there's only two of us."

Shannon ran at a full sprint back to the house. The guard was so surprised he reached for his gun and attempted to speak to her in broken English. Shannon kept running. He stepped in front of her but she dogged to one side and yelled at him, "Don't touch me!" Then ran past him into the house.

The guard pulled his gun out and was pointing it in her direction when Sergei appeared in the hallway and caught Shannon in his arms. Sergei said something to the guard in Russian and then took Shannon into the library next to the hallway.

"It's Matt! There's something wrong! He needs help! He needs me!"

"Shannon calm down. I know. I heard him also."

"I have to get to him. I..." Shannon stopped as his words became clear. "You heard him?'

"Of course."

Shannon looked at him quizzically. "I don't understand. How could he send a message so far and so strong?"

"The same way I felt you three thousand miles away when I didn't even know you. The same way I can feel people all over the world."

"What? All over the world?"

"Yes."

"My god. I didn't know. How can...."

"How can I do that? I have no idea. But it's difficult. I had to train myself to ignore all those thoughts. I can hear anyone that has some form of my special talent. What you are doing by releasing hundreds of people, soon to be thousands, is causing problems for me. All those thoughts are like a constant buzzing in my mind."

"I didn't know."

"How could you? I hid it from you."

Shannon stared at him. She briefly wondered what else he was hiding but concern for Matt overwhelmed all else. "I have to get back. I have to get to Matt quickly."

"I know. But I don't want you to go. It could be dangerous. I don't want to lose you. Stay here."

"And leave Matt in danger? Maybe leave him to die? I won't do that. I have to go."

Sergei's face hardened, he took her by the arms. "No. I love you. I won't let you go. You will stay here."

"Let me go!" Shannon writhed back and forth in an attempt to get away. Her face was contorted with anger and hatred.

Sergei lessened his grip, sadness and shame contorted his handsome face. He let her go and stepped back. "I'm sorry. I shouldn't have done that. Forgive me."

"You say you love me."

"Yes. More than anything on this earth."

"Then help me!"

"But I'll lose you! After all I have done. I have searched the world for you. I've waited all my life for you."

"You will lose me for certain if you resist me in this. If you hold me prisoner here."

Sergei looked at her. He stared at her unblinking. "You still love Matt."

"Yes."

"And me? Do you love me?"

Shannon hung her head, unable to look him directly in the eye. "I think so. Last night I loved you so much...this morning I wasn't sure. I don't know. I'm confused."

Shannon tipped her head back up and looked at him. She had never seen Sergei look so sad. He stepped forward, hugged her, took her head in both his hands, tilted her up to him and whispered, "Please love me. Please. I need you."

"Then help me. Get me home. Get me to Matt."

Sergei stepped away from her and stared at her intently. Anguish turned to resignation. He looked to the window and quietly said, "Alright."

Shannon ran back to her bedroom. She frantically stuffed her clothes into her suitcase and vainly tried to remember where she put her dress shoes and then thought, *To hell with it.* She zipped the suitcase and started toward the door when Sergei stepped in.

"The jet is booked and is on it's way. We'll meet it at the airport in twenty minutes. They've registered a flight plan direct to Washington."

"Thank-you."

"I'm putting my career on the line. Possibly my life. You know I have enemies, many of them. When they find out that I've booked a high-speed jet for one woman, a woman who is going to the States...it's going to be bad. This may be the end for me."

"I understand. I know what you are doing for me...and for Matt."

A sudden, crazy, thought came to her. She reached out and held his hand. "Come with me. Come with me. The world is changing. If we accomplish what we intend...you can be a leader of a unified world. A new world. A great world."

"And you...will you love me?"

"I.... I don't know. There's too much happening. Help me save Matt first. Get me to Matt."

Fifteen minutes later they were on their way to the airport. Sergei was staring out the window of the car and then remembered something. He turned to Shannon.

"Who is Ranula?"

"What? WHAT? How do you know about him?"

"I felt him with Matt."

Shannon suddenly became light-headed, sick, weak. She reached out to Sergei to steady herself.

"I know what's wrong. Oh Matt! Matt. Why? Why did you do it?" Shannon whispered to herself.

Shannon contacted Scott and after a quick discussion, even though Scott had serious reservations about Sergei, Shannon convinced him to make new plans and get a flight with James to Washington. Thanks to Sergei, Shannon would arrive many hours before James and Scott. However, the sudden appearance of the head of FFIS was going to cause problems. She asked Scott to talk to his contacts and arrange to allow Sergei into the country.

Sergei leaned over Shannon and adjusted the small blanket that covered her while she slept on the plane. He thought about the situation and common to his personality began to think of possible advantages that he might have, how he could gain from this. He was almost certainly done with the FFIS and his country. Already his enemies would know and would be acting. He would be branded a traitor and a warrant would be issued for his arrest. Everything he worked for was gone: the power, the money. But it did not deter him. He had been in many bad situations before. There was always an out. There was always an opportunity. He looked through the window and then back to Shannon. An idea was already coming to him. He expanded his mind and searched for Ranula.

Chapter 35

RANULA

The plane landed with a hard thump and then swayed slightly to one side and then back to the other, all the while the engines roared in Shannon's ears. She never felt good about landing. Takeoff was okay, but that shuddering and swaying and roar of engines always gave her a sense that the pilot, who she imagined as sweating profusely, was desperately trying to keep the plane on the runway and that any second his hand might slip off the steering wheel, control stick, or whatever it was called, and then they'd crash and burst into flames. She couldn't get that thought out of her mind and on every landing she experienced a mini-panic attack.

Shannon let go of Sergei's hand and noticed that she had squeezed it white in some places. She said,

"I don't like landings much."

Sergei smiled as he shook the blood back into his hand and said, "I noticed."

The plane taxied to a special area of the airport, normally reserved for VIP's and dangerous criminals. Sergei wasn't sure which category he fit into. *I guess I'm about to find out.* It really depended on how persuasive Scott had been and how quick his enemies were. He hastily searched for hostile thoughts and found none.

They stepped off the plane and found the day to be slightly cloudy but warmer than normal. The sun was beginning to set—clouds glowed reddish-orange. A sudden memory came flashing to Shannon's mind:

a beautiful sunset walk along a beach with Matt when they were in Boston—they had just begun dating and Matt was all nerves and Shannon had calmed him by taking his hand. Sadness and guilt swam through her, draining her energy and boosting her anxiety for Matt to an extreme level. She didn't know if he was still alive but if he was she was determined to save him, even if it cost her life.

She said with concern in her voice, "How are we going to find Matt? I've checked with everyone I can think of and no one knows where he is."

"I know where he is."

Shannon abruptly stopped walking and looked sternly up at Sergei. "You're full of surprises, Sergei. Just when I think I know you, I discover that I don't."

Sergei didn't need to be a mind-reader to know that she was angry. He ignored it, smiled and said, "I don't want you to take me for granted."

Shannon ignored his poor attempt at playfulness and asked, "How do you know where he is?"

"I found Ranula. Ranula is in control."

Shannon stepped forward, raised her hand and slapped Sergei across the face. "HOW DARE YOU! HOW DARE YOU NOT TELL ME THIS!"

Sergei took a step back and touched where Shannon had struck. Anger briefly crossed his face but quickly changed to gloom, "I didn't think that it would help...for me to tell you. I thought you'd be upset. I was trying to save you pain."

"You let me decide that. If Ranula is alive, Matt is alive. And there is a chance! A chance to save him!"

Shannon turned and strode at a rapid pace away from Sergei. Then she stopped dead in her tracks and turned back to Sergei and pointed an angry finger, "Don't keep secrets from me Sergei. Don't."

Sergei said nothing. They stared at each other for a few moments.

Shannon slowly walked back to him, stopped and then said, "I'm sorry. I shouldn't have hit you. It was wrong...I'm...I'm falling apart. Too much has happened and I'm so worried about Matt...and what I have done...and what I need to do once we've saved Matt. If we can save Matt. It's killing me." Head down she started to cry. Sergei put his arms around her and held her. Shannon wanted to push away but she was spent, she had no strength, she was powerless...and the sobs gained in strength.

"Namia! Namia! Help! I need you! Where are you?" Ranula looked down at his body, at his feet, legs, hands and screamed out again, "Namia! Help! Something is wrong! Help me!" This was not his body. Something was horribly wrong. Nothing felt as it should. All his sensations, sight, hearing, touch, smell, taste, appeared to exist in some other, unbearable, nightmare dimension that twisted and distorted all experience; his skin tingled, his ears rang and buzzed, his vision blurred and shimmered, his tongue felt bloated and numb. Even the air held a disgusting odor; the sweet scent of home had been replaced by acrid, harsh, irritating smells that seemed to have a texture and taste of their own. It occurred to him that he was engulfed in a horrible dream, disguised as reality, one which he had but to pinch himself and it would dissipate, one to laugh at in the brightness of day, one to forget. But no matter what he did, he could not escape, he could not awake. He bit at the disgusting finger things attached to his hand—vaguely he felt pain. He took the hand out of his mouth; it moved strangely, seemingly dissociated from the body and mind that owned it. Strange red liquid ran from the wounds. He screamed again and swung at his head to break the spell—to stop the dream... and missed several times, but finally connected. He hit himself over and over. The nightmare did not dissolve. He felt little pain, much less than he should have. HE MUST BE TRAPPED IN A DREAM! He spun his head in one direction and then the other. What he saw made no sense—a hazy white room with strange devices all around him—they shimmered and blurred so horribly that he shut his eyes tight. And even worse, the sounds he heard terrified him, strange whisperings; some were in his mind, others emanated, ghost-like, from nearby—none made sense. He threw up his hands to block the sound

and felt protuberances where none should have been. He screamed, "WHAT HAS HAPPENED TO ME?" Then—a horror beyond belief—someone else seemed to speak through his mouth; he felt lips and vocal cords move, not of his command—peculiar guttural sounds struck his ears.

Suddenly his stomach heaved. Strange, horrible liquid ejected from his mouth and splattered on his legs and feet and the floor. He screamed in terror. He began to faint, and at that exact moment, a thought roared through his mind and out to the world, one that he could not understand except for the sense of terror that he himself felt. He struggled to maintain consciousness; the room darkened; he lost all sense of balance; there was a pounding in his chest, his mouth hung slack as it attempted to take in massive amounts of air. As he fought to stay conscious, strange thoughts assailed him—whispers in his mind, silent screams of fear. He felt as if some other being had invaded his body and mind—his arms and legs moved on their own volition. He fought. He fought insanity, he fought to retain his sense of self. It was a titanic battle and he was certain that his very life was at stake. He increased his concentration, greater than he had ever done in his life, and began to push the foreign presence from his mind. For a moment, like an ancient door frozen on its hinges, it resisted and then, with a scream of despair, it began to slowly move. He pushed with one final enormous effort and...the presence scattered, mist before the wind, and then ceased to exist entirely. His mind was clear but he was exhausted. He remained unmoving for some time, eyes closed, ignoring the attacks on his senses, recovering his strength.

That was when he remembered...the monsters from the Third Planet—the ones he had modified, his body in this dream looked something like them. There was less hair but the hands were very similar. The arms seemed to be the same length. Cloth covered the rest of the body but he was becoming certain that the dream had placed him in a monster's body. DREAD! DREAD! All strength left him. Ranula fell to the ground where he squirmed and rolled uncontrollably in the muck and goo that had spewed from his mouth and then nothing...blissful nothing as he passed out.

Ranula woke and found himself lying on a hard white floor; a horrible smell filled his nose. At first he couldn't understand what had happened. He started to call for Namia and then stopped. Memory was coming back. Horrible memory. A nightmare so extreme that he could not escape it. He looked at his body. THE NIGHTMARE! He was still trapped! He began tearing at the cloth, praying to find beautiful fur beneath, but his hands and arms wouldn't move properly. They would move too far or not enough, too fast and then too slow. He would try to move his right arm and his left would move. After many attempts he commanded his right hand to pull the cloth off of the left; it spasmodically grabbed at the arm and then gripped. He pulled hard and heard a tearing sound—some of the cloth came away and underneath...horror...hair and skin...horror! Ranula screamed and scraped at the skin on the arm; it came way in patches and the red liquid appeared. This time the pain was worse. He cried out. He was beginning to feel...to feel that...this wasn't a dream...horror! THIS WAS REAL! NO!

His arms and legs flailed in all directions. He thought, 'Oh, Namia, what has happened?' and in that exact moment he remembered her beauty, her touch, the moments of quiet love—the two of them pressed head to head—all his pain and sorrow being drawn from him by her touch, by her love...and with that finally...came stillness—the monster body stopped moving. He lay for a while like that, trying to stop the fear, trying to prevent panic. Then he attempted to sit. It took several tries but eventually he was able to make the monster body push itself up. Ranula looked around the room but it was difficult to focus on anything. It all seemed hazy and wrong—sometimes objects shimmered violently, sometimes they appeared to move on their own accord, sometimes they disappeared entirely. He had no control over his eyes; they would jump from item to item randomly, rarely staying in one spot for more than a few seconds. He'd shut his eyes tight, then open them again—for a short time the scene would stabilize and then deteriorate again. Once he swung his head too quickly—vertigo struck. He put a hand to the floor for support; his stomach heaved.

Ranula waited for all of this to go away, for the dream to dissipate but nothing happened. He waited and waited...but after a time he knew that it wasn't going to dissipate, that somehow he was in a bizarre reality, as horrible as any nightmare, but a reality all the same, a reality that he could not escape.

He fought against the panic that was rising and thought of Namia. His love for her grew and grew and with it came the calm that he felt when they shared quiet love.

Ranula became aware of the whispering that he had heard before. Now he realized what it was; it was the thoughts of hundreds, maybe thousands, of beings nearby. He could not make out the thoughts; they were jumbled, incoherent whisperings that raked at his sanity, but he did sense emotions—alien emotions, fearsome emotions, ones that he could not understand.

He felt pain in his fingers – they ached terribly, his head hurt, his stomach felt awful and...the smell! He had never smelt anything so disgusting in all his life—it seemed to emanate from the stuff that had disgorged from his mouth. He tried to stand to escape the horrible odor but he couldn't make his legs move correctly. With his stomach heaving, Ranula began to crawl away from the stagnant, putrid liquid, but then bumped into some object which shimmered back at him. He cried out in frustration and tried to swat it away. He made contact but it did not move and then he felt sharp pain in his hand. He cried out again and said, "Where am I? Where?" And then called out, "Help! Help me!" No response. He called out again, "Help! Help!" No response.

He sent out a thought, a cry for help. Perhaps the minds he heard would understand. Perhaps someone from his race was nearby, someone...not a monster...someone who would understand what had happened to him and make him better and take him to his sweet Namia, and then it would all be over, he would be back with his wonderful family, and live a happy, fruitful life. He waited for an answer but he felt nothing in his mind except for the continuous, endless whispering. Nothing! WHERE WAS HE? WHAT SHOULD HE DO?

He had pulled himself past the object and came up against a wall. His eyes seemed to make out a door in the distance but he was so tired, he was exhausted. He curled up against the wall and within seconds fell asleep.

For the second time since this horror began, Ranula awoke. This time there was no confusion. He knew that he was trapped in a monster body, in some strange place with strange minds all around him. He knew it was not a dream, not a nightmare. It was real.

His new body still did not respond properly but it seemed that he had somewhat better control and now his eyes could pick out objects; they were still blurry and shimmered from time to time but he didn't feel so irritated when he tried to focus on the items in the room. He was able to stay with them—his eyes didn't dance from object to object.

He tried to stand again. He used the wall as a support and pushed with his legs. He started to topple but was able to use his good hand to steady himself against the wall. Then he was standing! A surge of happiness ran through him. He took one step toward the door but his head swam; he lost his balance and crashed to his hands and knees. Ranula felt more pain. He cried out in frustration and lurched back up. He leaned against the wall. He could feel the monster body breathing rapidly and something he thought might be a heart pounding away in his chest. He waited a moment and then took a step. And then another one, and then one more. He was walking! With his good hand against the wall, he slowly moved toward the door. A moment later he was there. Ranula looked for the keypad that he could use to open it but he saw nothing. He gave a vocal command which should cause the keypad to appear. But nothing happened. He leaned up against the door and pushed. Nothing happened. Then he noticed the strange object that protruded from the door at about hand level. He reached out and tugged. Nothing happened. He pushed. Nothing happened. Suddenly he lost his balance and accidentally pushed the object downward. He heard a click. He tried pushing and then pulling. The door moved! It moved toward him. He stepped cautiously backwards and pulled on the object that was attached to the door. The door moved open. He felt fresh air. He began to feel... almost excited. He stepped through the door and saw sunlight through a window down a long hallway. He started slowly in that direction, still keeping close to the wall, placing one foot carefully in front of the other. Vertigo would periodically throw him off-balance and he'd have to stop, lean up against the wall and wait until it passed. He finally reached the end of the hallway and saw another door to his right. Sunlight streamed through a small window in the door. He had almost escaped the building! Eagerly he reached for the handle on the door and after a few attempts he was able to push it open and step through. He let go of the handle and the door closed behind him.

The strong sunlight hurt his eyes. He raised a hand to block the light and took stock of his situation. The air was different outside of the building; it smelt different. There were many different scents but he could not identify any of them. The sun was warm on his face. It was warm in a different way than on Venus; with no fur to block the light, it seemed harsh and almost burned. He looked in both directions and saw that he was on a street with tall buildings on all sides.

Ranula was trying to decide what to do next when a being stepped around a corner a half block away and started toward him. It was one of the monsters. He immediately turned to go back through the door but he could not get it open. He furiously pulled on it in both directions but could not make it move. Desperate he turned away from the monster and walked as quickly as he could. He staggered as his foot caught a ridge in the pathway—he felt pain shoot through his right leg. Suddenly his leg would not move properly, Ranula was forced to drag it and hop down the road. He looked back and saw that the monster was much closer now. It had long dark hair that curled slightly at the shoulders and seemed to be smaller and slighter than the body that contained him. The beady eyes stared at him and he was suddenly aware of its thoughts—strange jumbled thoughts that he could not understand but he did sense what he took to be anger or possibly fear. He realized that he could not out-pace it and decided to turn and, if necessary, defend himself. He saw a large stick lying on the ground beside him and stooped to pick it up. As he did so, he heard the monster stop and make a sound.

"What are you doing?"

Ranula did not understand what it said but he felt the fear, and thought he could possibly scare it off so he swung the stick in its direction and shouted at the same time.

The being screamed, turned and ran down the street.

He had bought himself time but he knew that it was very likely others would come. He needed a place to hide and food. He had begun to feel pains in his stomach that he thought were a lack of nourishment. How often this monster body needed to feed he did not know but he understood the science of physical and biological mechanics: the amount of energy used to perform a task, the amount of energy available in various foods and most importantly the amount of energy needed to sustain life. He felt that this body was running short on energy and therefore he needed to provide it fuel. Where to get food and what type of food the monster body required he did not know. He also felt thirst and believed that he was in a water-based body, so regular water ingestions would be required.

Ranula saw a side street; it was narrow and darker than the street he was on and instinctively he felt this was a better place to be, so he lurched in that direction. He turned the corner and ventured a little way down the street when he saw a puddle of liquid on the ground. Possibly it was water. It was about an inch deep and covered an area of about six feet around. He approached it, knelt down and put his nose almost in it and sniffed. It smelt similar to water on Venus but there were some hints of chemicals; ones that he did not recognize. He put his tongue into the liquid and tasted. It was water, he was certain. He began to drink.

After a few minutes his thirst was gone but his hunger remained. He stood and smelt something that seemed to be food. It was coming from a large, box-like object further down the alley.

The smell got stronger as he limped toward it. It smelt like food but food that had begun to rot, or perhaps his understanding of what proper food for this body would smell like was wrong. It might be okay. The box had a lid that was open but the sides of it were too high to easily see into. Ranula found an old crate off to the side that he could use to raise his body so he could see in. He stood on the crate and looked down into the box. There was definitely some vegetation and other materials that smelt like food. But he couldn't reach it. He would have to climb into the box to get it. The sides were very sturdy and looked to be some kind of metal. Ranula lifted his good leg, got it over the side and with a push and heave, propelled his body into the box. He landed sideways in food and other items that he could not identify. Some were hard and some were soft. The smell in the container was very bad—as bad as the smell of his stomach contents. He was almost sure that the food was rotting but he resisted the urge to climb out of the box. Ranula searched for food that did not smell as bad as the rest, hoping that he could find a substance that would not make him sick. He began to dig around the bottom of the box. Quickly he found something that seemed to not smell too bad. It was soft and lightly colored and looked like a third of a round ball. He took a bite, the taste was not repulsive. He continued to eat and found other items that seemed okay as well.

He was almost finished when he heard a sound from the street where he had frightened the monster. There was a shrill bell-like sound and then some talking. He cautiously looked over the box and saw the same monster that he had frightened standing by some kind of machine with another monster inside. He could see wheels attached to the machine and knew that it was able to move. He immediately ducked back down into the box. Ranula was sure that the monster inside the machine was some form of protector, much like the Dynarts on Venus. They would look for him.

He heard a sound as the machine began to move. It turned down the alley he was in. Ranula remained still and kept his breathing as quiet as possible. The machine passed his hiding place and did not stop. He could feel the mind of the being in the machine and could sense authority. The thoughts were still impossible to understand but he was beginning to believe that the emotions of these creatures were similar to his people and that with time he would be able to understand them and perhaps communicate mind-to-mind with them. Nevertheless, he did not want to meet any of them now and remained hidden in the box. Periodically he would scavenge for more food and picked the items that smelled the best. His choices so far seemed good as he did not feel sick.

It was getting dark and Ranula was thinking about his options. He did not think that this planet was Venus. It was too different. The sky was different. The air was different. The smells were different. What plants he had seen so far were different. How he got here, in this monster body, he did not know but he had to find out. He had to find a way back to his body, his planet, his family. He was struggling with what to do next when...he felt a presence. A mind. Somewhere far away but strong. Much stronger than any other one he had encountered. He felt that it was attempting to communicate with him!

There was a sense of confidence in that mind. It sent him an emotion of happiness...but...not really happiness. Ranula struggled with it for a moment and then epiphany! It was...peaceful. A feeling of peacefulness! Ranula realized that this entity was trying to tell him to remain calm. Suddenly the mind sent him an image; it was an image of one of the monsters and right after that he heard in his mind a sound, it was "hume...man." Ranula immediately understood. This mind was teaching him language.

At that moment Ranula could not have expressed the incredible sense of joy that he felt...but he only had to send the emotion. And it was reciprocated! Now he had hope. He had found someone who he could communicate with mind-to-mind. Someone who understood. He had hope.

Shannon and Sergei pulled up in a taxi at the location where Sergei said that Matt would be. It was only half a block from the mind-release clinic.

"Where is he?" asked Shannon. She strained to keep calm but her voice shuddered with the range of emotions that she felt; concern, fear, love, desperation, hope.

Sergei who was paying the taxi driver, hesitated for a moment as he scanned for Ranula. He turned toward an alley just across the street from them and pointed.

Shannon jumped out of the cab and started across the street yelling, "Matt! Matt!"

Sergei cursed under his breath, finished paying the driver and leapt after Shannon. He called, "Shannon! Wait!"

Shannon didn't hear him. She stopped in the middle of the road to let a car go by which gave Sergei time to gain back some of the distance that he had lost while paying the taxi driver. He was almost beside her when she started sprinting to the alley. Sergei was right behind her. Shannon rounded the corner of the alley and stopped hard.

Matt stood just down the alley, leaning against a dumpster. He look horrible; there were bruises and scabs on his face. His hair was matted with dirt and food. His nose appeared to be broken. One of his eyes was black. The fingers on his hand were covered in dried blood. His clothes were filthy and even from a distance of twenty feet, he stunk.

Shannon cried out, “Matt! Oh, Matt!” and started toward him.

Ranula who saw this being shouting and moving toward him backed away in fear. His hand lifted, ready to swing at the monster, if it should get too close.

Sergei shouted, “Shannon! Shannon! Stop! That’s not Matt!” Simultaneously he sent a thought to Ranula to calm him.

Shannon did not hear and moved toward Ranula. Ranula backed away. Sergei leapt forward and took Shannon by the hand and said quietly, “Shannon. Stop. Stop. That’s not Matt.”

Shannon turned to Sergei with tears in her eyes. “He’s hurt. I have to go to him...help him.” Shannon started back to Ranula.

Sergei pulled her hand back and said, “Shannon. Stop. You can’t approach him. Ranula is frightened. He will attack you if you get close. Please understand. This is not Matt. I have to calm Ranula so that he will go with us.”

“Tell him that we are here to help him. Tell him I will tend his wounds!” cried Shannon.

Sergei took her by the shoulders and turned her away from Ranula, “Shannon, it’s not that easy, I can’t...at least not exactly. I can only communicate in a very basic manner, send emotions, some very simple words. I haven’t had time to teach him English. I have to calm him first and then see if we can convince him to come with us.”

Shannon looked at Sergei and then at the being that once was Matt. She remembered all the wonderful times she had with him, the long walks, the long talks, their love making, how he kissed her, touched her, worshipped her. She had done this to him. Left him when he needed her most. She had destroyed him! Shannon began to cry in soul-wrenching anguish. Out of the pain, a flash of lightning in a terrible storm; a thought came; her face hardened, and she said, “I know what I can do.”

Tears streaming down her face, she stretched out her hand, palm up, toward Ranula, and a powerful thought, full of emotion, left Shannon. All it said was, "LOVE."

Ranula stopped backing away. He stood rock still. Shannon saw an intensity in those eyes that she had never seen in Matt. Shannon didn't move; she kept her hand out—reaching to Ranula. The two of them remained in that state for several minutes—frozen statues in a dark alley. Then his face changed and shaped itself into an unrecognizable being, an alien being, and slowly lifted it's hand toward Shannon. When that hand reached its peak, a thought flowed back to Shannon, one that she could not mistake, "LOVE."

They walked toward each other, slowly, hands reaching. When their fingers were an inch apart, Ranula stopped. Shannon stopped. Then Ranula touched Shannon's hand. He explored her skin, gently touching here and there. All the while his eyes never moved from Shannon's face. A massive series of thoughts and emotions flowed toward Shannon, most of which she could not understand. But there was one, more powerful than the others, which she believed might be, "Namia."

Scott and James had just arrived in Washington when Scott got a call; it was Shannon.

"We've got Matt...I mean Ranula...." She hesitated. "I guess."

"Where are you?" asked Scott.

"At that hotel, you know...the one that Matt and I stayed at before we left."

"How is he doing?"

"Not good. Matt's body is pretty badly hurt—he's got a couple of infected wounds. And we're having trouble keeping Ranula calm—he's good for a while and then breaks down and becomes frightened and unexpectedly violent; he hit Sergei pretty hard with a chair. And...and we almost didn't get him into the hotel. He had a fit in the lobby. The police were called but I was able to convince them that Matt was having a seizure. He needs to be monitored twenty-four hours a day. We need all the help we can get. How soon can you get here?"

"We're on our way."

An hour later Scott and James arrived at the hotel suite where Sergei and Shannon were staying. Shannon answered the door,

"We need to do this carefully. Introduce you to Ranula I mean," She said. "We don't want to scare him. Stay here in the hallway and we'll bring you in one at a time. Both Sergei and I will send him calming thoughts."

Twenty minutes later James and Scott had been introduced to Ranula. Shannon took Ranula into the bedroom to rest and to tend to his wounds. The rest of them, Scott, Sergei and James, were sitting around the table in the living area.

Scott waited for the bedroom door to close and then said to Sergei with a hard tone to his voice, "It was you who sent me to China on a wild goose chase, wasn't it?"

"Yes."

"Why?"

"Because I wanted Shannon alone with me."

"Why?"

Sergei shrugged his shoulders and said, "You know why."

"Maybe I do and maybe I don't. Why don't you tell me yourself."

Sergei looked at Scott, then James, then back to Scott. He shrugged again. "I love her. I wanted her to get to know me, I wanted her to spend time with me without interference from anyone else...from you."

"Really."

"Yes."

"I'm going to be frank. I don't trust you. I can't sense your mind. I have no idea if you are telling the truth or if you have some other reason for this charade." Scott's expression became piercing. "What is your true purpose?"

Sergei leaned back in his chair and threw his arms out wide. "My purpose? What else could it be but love? I have lost everything for her. By now there will be a warrant for my arrest in Russia. You know what it is like in Russia. Everything is corrupt. The vultures will be swooping in; they'll be after my position, my wealth, my possessions. They will scavenge everything. In a few months it will be like I never existed."

Scott changed his tact. "It's been very hard for Shannon. I can sense that she is torn—you or Matt. She doesn't know what to do."

"It's been very hard for me as well. I have almost nothing left...well... okay, I do have some money in Western Banks and some...well...investments. It's likely the Russian government won't get their hands on it but still compared to what I had, it's a pittance."

Scott said nothing. His eyes never left Sergei's face.

Uncharacteristically, Sergei began to look uncomfortable. "Listen, don't think of me as some kind of monster—some kind of psychopath who has no interest in anyone but himself. I love her. I'll do whatever I can for her. I'm here to help."

"That remains to be seen, Sergei. But I want you to know...my eyes are on you...I'm watching and let's be clear—Do not hurt Shannon. Or I'll come after you."

Sergei said nothing. There was a long intense silence as the two of them stared at each other.

Then James changed the subject.

"What about Matt?"

Scott looked away from Sergei and considered the question. "Can we get him back?" he asked.

"I'm not sure. This is something I never anticipated—someone actually wanting, foolishly, to become Ranula," said James.

"Can we stick him back in the light chamber? Repeat the sequence again and get him back?" asked Scott.

James's reply was firm. "No. It's a one way street."

"I understand that Ranula is released in you but he didn't take over—he didn't overcome you. Why?" Sergei asked.

"I'm not sure why. I've asked myself that a thousand times. Somehow I've been able to keep him locked up. I have his memories but not his personality. Initially he almost overpowered me but...I...." James paused. "I was able to overcome him. That's not a perfect description but there are no adequate words to describe it. In a way he's a prisoner in my mind, unconscious, unaware of existence. But I feel that I must always be on my guard. I must always be strong or he could rise up and that, well... that would be the last of me."

Sergei said, "Can you speak his language?"

"Yes."

Sergei replied, "That is very good news. We can communicate with him immediately. It will help to calm him. Shannon and I really struggled to tell him anything of value. I had started to teach him basic words but now...with you...we'll be able to teach him English much faster. He'll have a great deal of knowledge, perhaps even greater than yours. Perhaps he'll have an innate ability to solve problems that you would not have because, frankly, you're not him. You have his knowledge but let's face it, you're not him. He has a Venusian mind and experience that can't be replicated by just base knowledge. That perspective could be invaluable."

James replied enthusiastically, "That's very true. I hadn't thought of it that way. His contribution could be tremendous."

"And I've sensed that his mind power is gigantic, far greater than ours, even though he's in Matt's body," said Sergei.

"I've sensed that as well—perhaps he could teach us how to improve on our telepathic communication," said James.

"Wait a minute. You're speaking as if Ranula is here to stay. That Matt is doomed. That we can't get him back," Scott said.

Sergei looked at Scott, his face deadpan. "It does appear that way, doesn't it?"

Scott glared at Sergei. "I wasn't talking to you."

He turned to James. "James?"

"Well, I...I need some time. At the moment, I can't think of a way to get him back."

Scott looked at Sergei, his tone was firm, very firm. "You keep this from Shannon. Not a word, not a thought. I know you can keep your thoughts from her, that's for certain." The sarcasm was not lost on Sergei.

Sergei replied, each word carefully chosen, "I suggest...at least for the moment...while you're looking for a way, that you start teaching him English, so he can communicate and so he has an outlet for his fear and stress. He has to learn everything about humans; when to sleep, how to brush his teeth, what a shower is, what is safe to eat, everything—even where to defecate—his pants were disgusting, he just did his business when the urge came...he had no idea."

James spent the next day communicating mind-to-mind with Ranula in the hotel room. He gave him basic lessons in human existence, explaining to him about his body. Ranula asked over and over again about what happened, why he was in a human body, but James had avoided answering. He knew he would have to tell him at some point but to do it now would increase his stress and he wasn't certain how Ranula would react. He wanted to teach him English so Ranula could use his vocal cords to communicate – the human speech organs were not capable of speaking Venusian. And, more importantly, he wanted to buy himself time...time to work out how to get Matt back.

Shannon and Scott were also in the room with James and Ranula. They were reading emails and sending messages to the various groups involved in the mind-release program. The work had not stopped while they had been gone. Progress had been made, although there had been problems; the opening of another clinic had been delayed again. Shannon was trying to schedule a meeting with several of the participants to overcome the issues. Scott was discussing, via text messaging, the current status of Russia; now that Sergei had unofficially defected, they were no longer certain that they could use him to help start the release program.

Sergei still claimed that he could use his contacts to help but Scott did not trust him.

Sergei also wanted to have his mind released. Scott was dead-set against it. Sergei was already incredibly powerful. With his mind released, he could be unstoppable. Who knew what he might be capable of—perhaps he could control minds, put ideas, thoughts, emotions into others that they would believe to be their own. If he could do that, he could cherry-pick the ones he wanted to control: the key leaders, the President of the United States, the Prime Minister of Britain, the head of the IMF, military generals—anyone he thought he needed to achieve his goals. They would be at his bidding. It was a horrible, horrible outcome and one that he would not be able to stop if Sergei developed that level of control after the mind-release. Scott was determined to prevent Sergei from getting the mind-release at any cost.

He was thinking of this when his cell phone buzzed; to his surprise it was the President. He stepped out of the room and answered.

"Hello Mr. President."

"Scott, I understand that Ranula has been released in one of our team—in Matt, in fact. Is that correct?"

Scott paused. This wasn't common knowledge. Only Shannon, James and Sergei knew. "That's correct."

And although Scott knew the answer, he asked anyway, "Who told you?"

"Sergei."

"I thought as much. Mr. President, you can't trust Sergei. He has his own agenda, his own goals and they are not ours."

"Is he correct about Matt?"

"Yes...but...."

"Scott this is an incredible breakthrough, a Venusian here...on Earth. You should have informed me immediately."

"He's not a Venusian. He's Matt. A Human. Ranula has been released but he doesn't belong in that body. He shouldn't be there. We have to get Matt back."

"Scott I understand your concern about Matt but it's too late. Pandora's box has been opened. We now have access to a being from another planet. There's much that can be learned, much more than the mind release can provide. The loss of Matt is a terrible thing but he did it to himself and there is no obvious way to get him back, is there?"

The President stopped talking as if waiting for Scott to speak but there was no reply. "I'll repeat, We have access to a being from another planet, an alien. This is a first of gigantic proportions. As big as our discovery of the Venusian civilization. We can't let this slip by. I want Ranula taken to a special study center where he can be properly observed and interrogated."

There was a pause as Scott mentally cursed Sergei.

"Mr President...please...."

"Scott, I'm not asking you. I'm telling you."

A tone of resignation was clear in Scott's voice, but it was good that the President could not see Scott drive his fist into his own leg in anger as he bit back the answer he wanted to give and instead said, "Yes, Sir."

Scott stepped back into the room and quietly motioned to Shannon. He said,

"I have bad news for you."

"What? "

"Sergei told the President about Matt and Ranula. We have to take him to a special facility."

Shannon stood still. Tears formed in her eyes. She whispered, "No. Why?"

"They want to study Ranula. They want to communicate with him."

"But Matt? What about Matt? Are they going to bring him back?"

"Shannon, I'm sorry. I'm really sorry. Not in the foreseeable future."

She said, voice lowered but full of passion, "We have to save him."

"I know. I won't leave him like this. I promise you. But for the moment we have to comply." He thought for a moment. "We have one thing going for us. They need James. He's the only one who can communicate with Ranula. We can use that to our advantage."

"Sergei did this?"

"Yes."

"Why? Why?"

"It's hard to know for sure...." Scott hesitated, he didn't want to hurt Shannon but to hide the truth would be worse. "I think he's positioning himself with the leadership of the US. By giving up Ranula, he's gaining attention. He's creating contacts. Powerful ones who can help him strengthen his situation in the United States."

"And trap Matt in doing so? I can't believe he would do that. It has to be a mistake. Perhaps he was overheard talking to us about Ranula. Perhaps he didn't know what their reaction would be. He wouldn't do this on purpose. He loves me. He said he would help!"

"Shannon. Listen to me. Don't trust him. He has only one interest... himself. Don't trust him."

Federal agents drove Ranula to a facility outside of Washington, D.C.. Scott, Shannon and James rode with him. Shannon stared miserably out the window as the van travelled along a sunny, winding country road. It was narrow, so narrow that the trees stretched right over the road, creating a wonderful tunnel of green and brown. Periodically Shannon would catch a glimpse of a forest animal: a squirrel, a raccoon, numerous birds of all types—once she thought she saw a deer. It should have been a wonderfully peaceful trip, with the van flitting through sunshine and shadow, in a living tunnel that only mother nature could have created. But instead it had been very difficult—Ranula panicked several times and the government agents threatened to put him in a straight jacket. After a heated discussion, Shannon convinced them that if they restrained him, Ranula would not cooperate with the interrogation team. Shannon felt very sad and stressed. Nothing was going well. Every moment seemed to be a struggle. The camel's back was breaking. She wasn't sure she could take much more.

They reached a straight stretch and the van picked up speed. A moment later the forest opened into extended fields; bright wild flowers swayed amongst golden grass dazzling Shannon's eyes—begging her to join them. She resisted the urge to order the van to stop, throw open the door, run off into the splendor, run and run and never stop, run until she fell dead and left all her troubles behind.

In the distance she could see a large grey building—an ugly monolith tearing open a scene that should have been hanging in the Louvre. The moment she saw it she knew this was their destination. They pulled up to the gates of the compound and Shannon read on a plaque by the gate, "Hauser's Sanatorium for the Criminally Insane – NO TRESPASSING."

She yelled to the driver of the van, "Hey! What's this? Where are we going?"

The driver, fed up with dealing with Ranula and his pain-in-the-ass entourage, twisted his head in her direction and replied with a sick grin, "Here."

"What? You've got to be kidding me! We're not going to a nut house!"

"I have my orders. This is where we're going."

"No we're not." Shannon reached for the door handle and then was stopped by Scott.

"Shannon. Don't fight this. I'm sure they will have him in a segregated area. He'll be safe. If you resist you'll lose access to Ranula."

Ranula suddenly grasped James's arm. Scott and Shannon felt his thoughts fly to James.

"What's he saying?" Shannon asked.

"Just a sec," replied James. "Yes. Yes, he says he feels great anger, many minds angry, sick, confused."

Shannon cried out, "He can't stay here! He'll have a breakdown! He needs quiet. He needs a peaceful place, a place that will help him remain calm."

Scott whispered, "Shannon, we have no choice. If we try to leave we'll have a fight on our hands and these guys are armed. Someone will get hurt."

Shannon said nothing but Scott could feel her fury and saw a scary image in her mind, the guards lying incapacitated on the ground and Shannon walking hand-in-hand with Ranula...away from the Sanatorium. Scott sent a thought to Shannon. "Don't do it. Hundreds of people now have mind control. They will come after you. You can't fight them all."

Sergei stared out the window of the limo as it sped down the quiet country road. He was very satisfied. Everything was going to plan. Just a little more execution was required and he'd have what he wanted. He opened his mind and searched for Ranula. As expected, he was at the Sanatorium. Sergei could feel Shannon as well...near Ranula—angry, afraid. and confused—about him. Sergei smiled to himself; he wasn't worried. He'd fix that when he got there.

As expected, Ranula had been placed in a secure section of the Sanatorium. The room was locked and guarded and contained just a single bed, a small table and two chairs. Everything was bolted to the floor, including the chairs. Off to one side was a door to a small bathroom. The room was lit by a single, bare tungsten bulb. The walls were colored in light grey, the floor a darker grey and the roof white. The bed, chairs and table were the same color of the walls which caused them to seem even smaller than they were. One lone pillow sat at one end of the bed and a neatly folded blanket at the other. There were no other decorations or colors to offset the depressing nature of the scene.

James had been struggling to keep Ranula calm and it didn't help to have Shannon pacing back and forth and periodically sending unintentional, angry thoughts into the room.

"This place is horrible. How could they possibly think this will be conducive to their study of Ranula? It's ridiculous," she said.

James replied, "They are not calling it 'study', they are calling it 'interrogation'. Interrogators don't care about interior decorating, in fact, the worse it is the better they like it."

James immediately regretted the statement as Shannon's reply was vehement. "Those bastards! They had better leave Ranula alone! If they hurt him, they hurt Matt! I'll tear them apart!"

Ranula swung his head in Shannon's direction and started making excited gurgling sounds. He jumped up from the chair and made for the door.

Both James and Shannon reached for him and pulled him back.

"Shannon, you have to relax. You're causing problems," said James,

"I can't help it. We have to get Ranula away from here," she replied.

"I know. But we can't leave. You heard Scott," said James. "Just be patient. Give Scott time to develop a plan."

"Where is he?" Shannon asked. She had been so upset over the last hour that she hadn't noticed Scott had left the room.

"On the phone, I think," James said absentmindedly and then continued with his original thought. "Look Shannon, you have to remain calm or leave the building entirely. Go somewhere that Ranula can't feel you."

"I can't do that. I have to stay here...protect him."

"You're not doing him any good. You're making it worse."

"I'm not leaving!"

James shrugged his shoulders in resignation. "Have it your way."

Scott came back into the room, swearing quietly under his breath. He said, "I have to leave. The President wants me in Washington for meetings. The Russians are screaming about Sergei. They want him back."

Shannon's voice rose to a higher tone. "They won't send him back, will they?"

Scott gave her a hard look. "If it were up to me, they would. That guy has been nothing but trouble since we met him. I swear we'd be a lot better off if he was locked up."

Shannon glared at him but said nothing, knowing it would start another fight between them.

Scott continued, "Anyway, I have to go back to support the President and discuss Ranula further. I'm hoping to convince them to start up a research project to get Matt back."

"That's wonderful! The best news I've heard since I got back to the states!" exclaimed Shannon.

"Shannon, it's not for certain. I have a huge uphill battle to fight. Don't get your hopes up yet," said Scott. "But while I'm in Washington, please restrain yourself. Don't do anything rash or foolish. Consult me on any decisions."

Twenty minutes later, Scott left the Sanatorium's grounds in a taxi. They passed a Limo that turned into the compound. Scott caught a glimpse of a passenger at the back. Sergei. Scott's angry head followed the Limo. For a moment he considered ordering the taxi back but then realized that there would be little gained—he had no control over Sergei; the State Department was ecstatic over the defection and Sergei was the golden boy at the White House—he was the man who found Ranula. *What a joke.* Sergei was a formidable enemy and with Shannon smitten by him, he couldn't even trust his own team. His only chance was to convince the President that he was dangerous—have him locked up until everything settled down and he had Matt back and Ranula erased forever.

Sergei's limo pulled up to the sanatorium door. He sent Shannon a thought message. "I'm here. Meet me at the entrance."

Sergei stood on the landing, at the main door of the building; he had ascended ten steps from the paved driveway. There was a lovely view of the fields and forest in the distance. He stood, back to the door, enjoying the view, very aware that Shannon was approaching...but he didn't turn until he heard her call to him—her tone was hard, angry.

"Sergei, what happened? Why did you tell the President about Ranula? Why?" Shannon waved her hand at the building. "Look what they have done. They've stuck him in a nut-house."

Shannon approached him tentatively and watched his face closely. Sergei knew she was waiting for his reply and because she could not read his mind or emotions was trying to visually ascertain truthfulness.

Sergei reached out and hugged Shannon; she did not return the embrace and kept her hands at her side. Sergei released her, stepped back and said, his face regretful, "I'm so sorry. I didn't think this would happen. I thought it was the best chance we had to get a team of scientists working to return Matt. I see that it has backfired."

Shannon said nothing. Sergei filled the void. "Trust me, I didn't see this coming."

"Really?" Shannon's voice was disbelieving. Her eyes were still watching him intently. He was so handsome, he had a power about him, a destiny, a destiny she desired to share. She wanted so much to believe him but...she had to know the truth.

Sergei returned the stare, unblinking, sincere. "Of course. You have to believe me. I love you...." His eyes glistened. "Love you so much." He hugged her again.

Shannon's body softened in Sergei's arms. She reached up, hugged him back and said softly, almost to herself, "I believe you...yes...believe you."

And for the first time since Russia, she kissed him full on the lips. The kiss continued for many seconds, becoming sensual...exciting...passionate. She caressed his face tenderly and then said in a much stronger voice, "I do believe you. I do."

Sergei scanned the area to see if anyone was observing them. It didn't seem so. Then he said, "Let's go see James and Ranula."

They entered the detainment room and Sergei sent a thought greeting to Ranula. Ranula attempted to smile but succeeded only in a grimace.

James said, "We're making progress, some progress with English, but it's pretty slow now that were in this place. Ranula is very troubled."

"I can tell. I feel it," said Sergei.

Shannon said passionately, "You have to help us get Ranula out of here. He's stressed. He doesn't understand all the sick minds he senses and he keeps trying to leave. He's going to have some kind of a breakdown. Then maybe we'll never get Matt back."

"I'll help. I'll do whatever I can." Sergei hesitated. "But first I think we should have a candid discussion about Ranula." He looked at Ranula and then to James. "How much English does he understand?"

"Not much."

"Enough to understand what we are saying?"

"No. Especially now. He's having a difficult time concentrating with all the disturbed minds distracting him."

Sergei searched the faces of Shannon and James; his expression was deliberately non-committal, "Okay then, he still doesn't know what happened to his family does he? I think it's time he was told."

"Why?" asked James, surprised.

"Once he knows the full story, that his family is dead, Venus is dead, he'll be more cooperative, more willing to help us. Right now he thinks, or rather, hopes...that he can return to his body and return to his family. I have sensed this," said Sergei. "Once he knows this is not possible, he'll be more likely to assist us with Matt."

"Wouldn't he be more likely to want to keep Matt's body? Surely self preservation will overcome our wishes, which will ultimately result in Ranula's death, at least so far as he would know it," James said.

"I don't think so. He is horrified by the body he is in. He hates it. He hates us. He hates Earth. He'll want to go."

Sergei immediately sensed excitement in Shannon,

"Yes. Yes," she said. She turned to James, her voice intense and determined, "You have to tell him. It's our best chance. We have to get Matt back."

"I'm...I'm not so sure. Let me think about it," James replied.

Shannon raised her voice, it was querulous, "Why? What's there to think about? It makes total sense. You should do it now—before the interrogators can interfere. Who knows what restrictions they may put on us."

"We need to talk to Scott first," said James.

Sergei quickly responded, "Scott will want to consult the President. He is very cautious. Too cautious. Shannon is right. If we wait, our access to Ranula will be restricted. Likely we won't be allowed to see him on our own. Someone who has had the mind-release will be supervising and may interfere if they don't like what they are sensing. And the interrogation team is on its way. We only have a few hours and then it will be too late. We need to act, now."

James did not immediately reply. He considered Sergei's statements—there was some validity to what he said. And there was his idea that he had been working on.

"There's something else. There may be a way to release Matt...get him back," James said.

"What?" Shannon's voice climbed an octave higher.

"I've been thinking a lot about it. I'm still not certain. But I believe there may be a way," said James. "Of course you know that by sending strong thoughts, emotions really, you can incapacitate someone; he becomes confused, disoriented. If it's strong enough, they can lose their balance and if it's very strong, they can lose all motor capacity—they are paralyzed for a short time."

"Yes," said Sergei.

"I think I know why that is. The brain is made up of billions and billions of neurons. Some believe as many as one hundred billion. The neurons are the base building blocks of the brain and control all functions of the body: movement, sight, voice, smell, even the autonomic functions like sleep, heart-beat and breathing. And of course, all thought; the very essence of what you consider to be self—your being, your sense of life, the 'I think, therefore I am,' is contained within this incredible network of neurons," stated James.

"But the neurons do not connect directly to each other. They are connected via chemicals or electrical signals at each intersection between the neurons. These intersections are called synapses. In order for information to be transferred from one neuron to the next, chemicals or electrical signals are required to bridge the space between them. I think that when you send very powerful thought waves, especially strong emotions, those chemical and electrical signals are disrupted so communication between neurons is disrupted, thereby causing the effects I just described. I think it might also be possible that with extremely powerful blasts of emotion the chemicals might actually be destroyed—perhaps even neurons would be destroyed," James said.

"So I believe, it's still a theory, but I believe it is just possible...that we can recover Matt if we can find a way to do this to his mind. Disrupt the Ranula neuron communication long enough to give the Matt-self an opportunity to reassert his personality on the neural network."

Shannon asked, "Do you think Matt is aware of anything that is going on now? Is it possible that in some way he is conscious but just not able to communicate?"

"Highly unlikely, no, I think not. I have not sensed any of Matt's personality in my mind-communication with Ranula." James looked from Shannon to Sergei. "Have either of you?"

"None," said Sergei.

"No," said Shannon.

"Then I think we can conclude that the Matt-self is dormant and unaware, which is very good because otherwise I think my method would not work—we'd short-circuit both minds, Ranula and Matt."

"So how do we do this? Disrupt the neurons I mean?" asked Shannon.

"That's the tricky part. How strong does the mind blast have to be? Too little and nothing happens, too much and maybe we kill him. And we don't know the tolerance of the brain; we don't know the threshold between 'nothing happens' and 'death'. That tolerance could be very, very small."

"Kill him? Kill him? You didn't mention that!" cried Shannon.

James replied, "It's a direct conclusion of the theory. The brain is composed of neurons and requires chemicals and electrical signals to properly communicate the needs of the body throughout the mind. Remove the neurons or chemicals or electrical signals for too long and the body dies. It's nasty. Very dangerous. We'll be experimenting with Matt's life."

No one said anything. The only sound in the room came from an occasional soft moan from Ranula.

Shannon began to sob, she said, "We can't let him die...can't let him die."

Sergei tenderly put his hand on her shoulder and said, "All the more reason to tell Ranula the truth about his family and home. Possibly he could help. Possibly he would know how strong a mind blast is required. Or perhaps he would know of another way. I really don't think he will want to remain in Matt's body. I think he will do what he can to help."

More silence.

Shannon could sense that James was weighing the options, reviewing his theory, looking for other possibilities in the Venusian knowledge contained in his brain.

She said, "We don't have time. We have to do it now if we're going to do it at all. The interrogators are coming."

James said, "We have to consult Scott."

Shannon shouted, "Scott! Scott! I don't care what Scott says. I want Matt back. I have to save him. We're almost out of time."

Her voice dropped. "James, I've never asked you for a favor...ever. I'm asking for one now. Please help me save Matt. The government has no intention of helping Matt. They want Ranula. That's all. They don't care about Matt. Once the interrogators are here we've lost our advantage. Please help me!"

James said nothing.

A tear caught Shannon's eye lash for a moment and then ran down her cheek, but her face remained firm, remained determined. "I made a promise to myself...I would save Matt or die trying. If you don't help, I'm going to take Ranula out of here...before they come. I'll fight everyone of them. I'll fight the entire world if necessary. I'm going to save Matt or I'm going to die. There's nothing in between."

Her voice filled with passion. "Please help me."

James hesitated; he stared at the ceiling, then the floor, then back to the ceiling. Finally,

"Alright."

James turned and Shannon could feel strange alien thoughts travel to Ranula.

Ranula stiffened. He sat upright and focused his eyes intently on James.

Thoughts flew back and forth between James and Ranula. The intensity and strength of Ranula's communication began to increase rapidly.

"What's he saying, James?" Shannon asked.

But James did not respond.

"James?"

"James?"

Ranula's thoughts grew even stronger.

"Sergei! Sergei! Something's wrong! Look at James! Something's wrong!"

Sergei did not answer.

James's face was white, ghost white. His lips were squeezed tight and pulled back as if he was fighting back intense pain. His brow was pursed and his forehead had expanded outward. He stared unblinking straight into Ranula's eyes—prey caught in the gaze of a Cobra. It was obvious that a massive mental battle was underway. Why, Shannon did not know, but she knew that James was in trouble. But she did not know what to do—if she broke James's concentration possibly it would be worse for him. Possibly Ranula would kill him in that one moment of distraction.

"Sergei!"

He still did not answer. Shannon turned and saw that he was watching the battle much the way an excited spectator would watch Roman gladiators fighting to the death in the Coliseum.

She yelled at him, "Sergei! Serg...."

An immense mind-scream surged from Ranula. Vaguely Shannon felt herself falling. She struck the floor hard and wondered why she did not feel any pain. Another blast issued from Ranula. Paralyzed, Shannon knew she had to protect herself—she sent a wave of thought and emotion back at Ranula, hoping that it would be enough to block his attack. She could feel that Sergei was doing the same.

James was lying flat on his back on the floor—as if he'd been blown over by a hurricane. He was not moving. Shannon was too busy protecting herself to try to sense his state.

Sergei was doing better. He was still standing but by the look of his face, he was struggling to keep Ranula's attack at bay.

Ranula turned toward Sergei. In an instant Sergei was on the ground. Ranula walked to the door. Shannon was unable to move but could sense that Ranula was sending a thought command to a guard down the hall. A few moments later she could hear a key enter the door lock. The door swung open and then Ranula stunned the guard with another mind-blast. Then she could hear him walking down the hall, simultaneously sending massive mind-screams in front of him. She could sense other bodies falling. Ranula was clearing a path. He was escaping and there was nothing anyone could do to stop him.

Shannon took almost a half hour to recover. Sergei revived much faster but even though she asked him to go after Ranula, he stayed with her and James, refusing to leave until they were able to walk again.

James was not doing well. He had borne the full brunt of the encounter and was dazed and unable to maintain coherent thoughts. His telepathic abilities were severely reduced so Shannon and Sergei couldn't communicate with him while he was paralyzed. Finally he was able to sit up and they helped him into a chair. He said,

"I...told Ranula...his family...dead. Reaction much worse than I expected. Ra...nula said, *"I don't want to live in this body. I don't want to live without Namia, without Lallia. I don't want to live knowing that they are gone, my people are gone, my planet is a wasteland, destroyed by our greed, by our ignorance. Kill me."* He was horribly suicidal. I tried to calm him and convince him that there was another way, return Matt. But he was distraught. So distraught. I don't think he understood what I said. He said he was going to leave...and die. I told him no, no don't but he did not hear. Then he screamed at me, with...his...mind. I've never felt anything like that before. I tried...tried to protect myself but he was too strong, far too strong." He reached out and grasped Sergei's shirt by the shoulder. "You must go after him...stop him. There's very little time. Leave me here."

Shannon stood up and shouted, "We have to go! Now! Now, Sergei!"

Sergei hesitated; it would be very dangerous, incredibly dangerous. He sensed that Ranula had not used his full force on them, that he could quite likely kill them, but he knew that Shannon would go no matter what. He could feel her determination and her fear for Matt. He stood and turned for the door. "Let's go."

They ran past body after body, each one slowly recovering but in no state to help them. Shannon opened her mind to find Ranula. After a moment she found him, at the edge of the forest, running and looking... looking...for some way to die. Shannon groaned and increased her pace to a full sprint.

"Shannon! Slow down. You can't run like this all the way to the forest."

"He's going to kill himself. He's going to kill Matt!"

"You won't make it like this. SLOW DOWN!" Sergei took hold of her arm and almost tackled her. She fought back, tried to escape. He said, as he struggled to catch his breath, "Listen to me! Listen! We can't reach...him quick enough. He has feelings for you. I think it might be Matt somehow, send him thoughts. Send him...send him.... Love."

In her panic Shannon hadn't noticed that they had run some way into the beautiful flower laden fields—the very place that Shannon had felt her own urge to die. She understood then. She understood what Ranula was feeling...his family...his people...his planet. It was what she felt for Matt only a hundred times stronger. Tears flowed in a torrent down her face. She stretched out both hands, palms to the sky, and sent, "*LOVE.*"

Far in the distance, under the arches of the great forest canopy, Ranula stopped. And turned toward Shannon. He could not see her but the power of the message was intense. Tears rolled down his face and he thrust both hands upward to the sky, tipped his head up and sent another mind-scream, "NAMIA! LALLIA!"

"He's stopped moving," Sergei said. "He's waiting."

They jogged toward the forest. Shannon could sense that Ranula was at a tipping point; his emotional state was extremely fragile. One wrong move and it could be disaster. He had the power to overwhelm them, possibly even kill them. And it was going to be much harder—Ranula still couldn't speak much English. They would have to communicate via telepathic emotions and simple spoken words. How she could tell him about Matt, she didn't know. They needed James.

They approached the forest cautiously. Ranula was near. The undergrowth was thick with a multitude of ferns, blackberries, nettles and young trees struggling to survive. They needed a path. It took a moment but then Sergei spied it—a narrow animal track, not wide enough for a person. Shannon saw a bit of cloth caught by a thorn, it looked to be a piece of Ranula's shirt.

"He's this way."

With difficulty they pushed their way along the path, Sergei first. He'd hold back the various branches and vines until Shannon was able to reach or step past them. In their hurry they both acquired some scratches. The bush was so dense that they could only see a few feet in any direction. They stopped every few steps and listened and then opened their minds. Ranula was very close but they were still not certain where he was. A twig snapped to the left. Shannon jumped in surprise and then stopped and held her breath, listening intently and scanning the area for Ranula. A small rabbit appeared, nose twitching, and then turned and ran. Another sound, this time to the right. A bird came into view, hopping from branch to branch in a bush heavily laden with dark-green leaves.

Sergei moved forward, pushed some more growth out of the way and then stopped abruptly. He held up his hand for quiet. Shannon tiptoed forward until she was right behind Sergei. She leaned her head to one side and peered past him. There was an open glade, entirely canopied by the large trees of the forest. Dappled sunlight touched the leaf-littered floor here and there—providing a stark contrast between light and shade—and standing at the far end, haloed by a beam of sunlight, was Ranula. He turned toward them, a burning beacon in the cool twilight of the forest, and said in a halting, cracked voice, unused to human vocal cords, "Stop."

Shannon pushed carefully past Sergei and said, "Ranula, we're here to help. I...I know how you feel."

Sergei whispered, "Shannon he won't understand you."

Shannon turned her head slightly toward Sergei but kept her body facing Ranula, "I know. I just want him to hear my voice. To calm him. I'm going to send...," and a thought left her, 'Love.' She took a step forward. Ranula's face arranged itself into something that Shannon imagined was Venusian sorrow and then she felt intense sadness. Ranula stretched his hand upward to the sky and said, "Veenuus," and then, "Gone." Tears ran down his face.

Shannon took one more step and said, "I know. I'm sorry. So sorry."

"Naaamia...gone," he said.

"Lallia...." Ranula's voice gargled and choked. He screamed out, "Lallia!" and hugged himself and began to sway back and forth.

"Musst...musst...die."

For the first time Shannon noticed a sharp stick, about six inches long, extending from Ranula's hand. He raised it to his neck and began to press it into the jugular area.

Shannon screamed and leapt forward, "NO! NO!"

Ranula took a step back, lowered the stick and sent a gigantic mind-scream of wretchedness at Shannon. She lost her balance as the mental blow flowed through her. Another blast hit her. She fell to her knees. Then another. She fell forward into the dirt of the forest path. Shannon screamed as she felt her mind being torn apart; the neurons of her brain were being stripped of the precious communication chemicals and electrical signals that kept her brain functioning, kept her alive. A huge weight seemed to be crushing her chest and she realized that she had stopped breathing. She knew she was dying. Ranula was killing her.

Sergei ran forward between Ranula and Shannon and yelled, "NO! RANULA! STOP!"

Shannon felt Sergei join the battle. A powerful thought of rage ripped toward Ranula. Ranula's thought-attack on Shannon stopped and transferred to Sergei. Shannon could hear Sergei gasp as he felt the full power of Ranula's mind. Shannon began to breathe again. She pulled in great gasps of air. In a panic, she tried to sit up. Nothing happened. She tried to move her arm. Nothing happened. Her legs. Nothing happened. She tried to call to Sergei. Nothing happened. She was unable to play a part in the drama that was unfolding before her.

Sergei and Ranula stood ten feet apart, frozen, sending huge mind-blasts at each other. It was a stalemate. Neither seemed able to overcome the other. The onslaught raged on for several minutes, then, unexpectedly, as if he were attempting to walk into a hurricane, Sergei, golden hair blazing in a brilliant shaft of light, leaned forward and took a hesitant step toward Ranula. Sergei leaned forward again. Another step. All the while the thought barrage continued. Sergei's face showed the desperate determination of someone who had never lost, who would never give up; his eyes didn't waver, they were locked on Ranula, pinpoints of blue light in a granite face.

Ranula's forehead had expanded to an incredible degree. He was no longer recognizable as a human being. Shannon could feel the massive power emanating from his mind. She couldn't understand how Sergei could face it, how he could resist it.

Sergei took another slow step and then another. Then another. Each step took a little longer. Each step was a little harder. Sergei groaned. The effort was immense. But he didn't stop.

Finally he was inches away from Ranula.

Then, for a brief instant—only a microsecond, Sergei turned his head to Shannon and in that precious moment, one that she would never forget, she felt, "LOVE YOU."

Sergei reached up, grasped the back of Ranula's head and pulled it hard into his forehead. A searing blast of thought, powerful beyond belief, drove itself into Ranula's mind. Neurons that had been connected in alien form, connections that had created the Ranula-self, were destroyed.

Both of them slipped to the ground. Sergei's arm twitched and stretched out toward Shannon. And became still. A soft moan issued from the body that had been overwhelmed by Ranula.

The two men that Shannon loved most in this world lay before her. She tried to reach out to them, she tried to cry out to them. She opened her mind but found nothing, no conscious thought from either of them. She directed her mind to Sergei, searching for life. There was nothing, no breath, no heartbeat. Intense grief struck her. She felt tears run down her face. She tried Matt. For a moment there was nothing. Then...something...just a hint of life...base energy...breath...heart beat. He was still alive! But Shannon could sense that he was on the edge, hanging to life by a finger nail.

She tried to move—her right hand twitched. She tried again. She could hear the gravel in the path rattle as her fingers pulled at the ground. Another moan from Matt. She could sense that his life force was slipping away; the brain communication to his heart and lungs was dying. She still couldn't move her legs but her hands and arms were getting stronger. She tore desperately at the ground, ripping her fingernails, pulling herself along, inch after inch. Now she was able to push herself up on her hands, her back arched and she began to drag her body and legs, one shaking, tenuous arm movement at a time.

She had reached Sergei's body. She did not look at him. She kept her tear-filled eyes on Matt.

There wasn't much time. Matt's heart beat was very irregular. His breathing periodically stopped and then wheezed back and forth. It was a terrible sound and drove Shannon to even greater exertion. Her hands and fingers were bleeding but she felt nothing.

Five more feet. That's all. She began to wriggle like a snake and then...she could touch him.

She caressed his face, "Matt...Matt," she gasped. "Don't die...please don't die. I love you so much."

She did not know what to do. Was there anything she could do?

Suddenly, instinctively, she took Matt's head in her hands and gently pressed her forehead to his. She opened her mind in a way she had never done before and moaned as she felt the essence of Matt—felt his soul deep inside, trapped there...barely in existence.

and then she...

pulled...

Her mind tugged at that soul and began, unknown to her, rebuilding the connections of Matt's brain. She enveloped his soul with her mind and pulled it toward her. As she did she felt something deep inside her rise up and join with Matt. The essence of the two beings intermingled and she experienced an ecstasy of love, far, far beyond human experience.

Matt's heart beat grew stronger, his breathing calmed, his body warmed.

She cried out loud as she heard a whisper in her mind,

"Shannon?"

She said, "Yes, Matt...it's me. I'm here.... And I will never leave you again, that...I...promise. That...I...promise."

Chapter 36

GOODBYE

Shannon, Scott and James stepped out of the hospital into sunshine in Washington D.C.. It had been two days since the battle between Sergei and Ranula. Matt was recovering quickly and was already complaining about the hospital service, the lack of good television, the nurses, the doctors and anything else that came to mind.

There was a park across from the hospital. They carefully crossed the busy street and found a bench in the shade of an old oak tree.

Scott said, "He's doing well. Much better than I would have expected."

"Yes. It's remarkable. I worried that there would be a long recovery. Perhaps he would never fully recover but instead...the same old Matt is back. I think he could leave the hospital tomorrow," said Shannon.

James said, "I have a theory about that...."

"You always do," grinned Scott.

James grinned back but continued anyway, "I think it's you, Shannon."

"What do you mean?"

"I noticed that you spend much time pressed forehead to forehead with Matt. I think each time you do that he gets better."

"I do it because it feels wonderful. I've never felt anything like it before in my life." She became pensive. "Except once before."

"With Sergei."

"Yes, with Sergei."

Tears welled in her eyes. "I never understood him. I never knew what he truly wanted."

Scott said, "I heard the stories of his life, his childhood. It's natural growing up in that environment to protect yourself, to protect your feelings."

"He gave his life for me." Shannon began to cry.

Scott put his arm around Shannon and said softly, "There's one thing that you do know...without question...he loved you very much."

"Well...I guess it's time to say goodbye," said Matt.

"Yes. But not goodbye, 'Au revoir' is better. Until we meet again." replied Scott.

They—James, Scott, Matt and Shannon, were standing in the departures terminal of the Washington D.C. airport. Matt and Shannon were returning to Boston where they were going to start tearing apart Kurt's shell companies, divesting as required by law and working with the environmental agency to shut down greenhouse gas production. Most importantly, they were going to use their new Venusian knowledge and the remainder of Kurt's empire to develop new non-polluting methods of transportation and power production. Oil could no longer be burned as gasoline for vehicles or used for heating or power. All nations on Earth were now participating in the massive project—the senior politicians and scientists of each country, most of whom had angrily resisted the possibility of an environmental disaster, had their Venusian knowledge unlocked and finally understood...they understood the need, they understood the danger, they understood that this was mankind's last chance. They understood that, on a cosmic scale, the ultimate destruction of Earth was just moments away.

Now the world was changing quickly. There were lineups at the clinics that performed the 'mind release' as it was now called. The initial fear of the procedure, the natural fear of the unknown, had been replaced by the fear of being left behind—the unlocked people were so far advanced in science and knowledge that anyone who did not release the Venusian information would become man's equivalent of the Neanderthal. They would not be able to participate in this new era of Mankind.

"Have you heard anything further about my father? What is going to happen to him?" asked Matt of James.

"Well.... It now seems very likely that the Venusians gave us two gifts. The first gift is the gift of life—I'm now sure we will escape the point of no return. The second gift, almost as wonderful as the first, thanks to Ranula, is the gift of peace. You see the Venusians were a non-violent, aggression-free society. There were no wars on Venus; there was almost no hostility of any kind. It was another reason they had progressed so quickly. They focused their science on what was best for their society, for their families, for the individual. They didn't waste effort on destruction and death. Good, useful, productive lives weren't cut short by war and violence," said James.

"Think of what they did...the sacrifice that they made...they could have left Venus and taken our world for their own. It would have meant the destruction of many species that were struggling to make their way on Earth...including humans. They sacrificed their entire race because other life was just as important to them as their own. Human beings would...well...human beings would never do such a thing." James stated.

"How ironic that a peaceful, loving race should be the authors of their own destruction," said Shannon.

James said, "The Universe is a cold, uncaring place. We can never take life for granted. Death and destruction are always just around the corner. The Venusians protected their world of water but took their world of air for granted...and paid the price."

"We have done much worse."

"Yes, we have. You speak of irony. Think of it, a peace loving race dies to save a war mongering, endlessly violent people. And now it appears that they have also given us a way to put an end to war, aggression and hatred. I was able to prevent Ranula's personality from unlocking but for some reason...a miracle beyond measure...the peaceful love and kindness of his race was released throughout our psyche. Matt, your father has not shown any violent tendencies of any kind since he was unlocked in the warehouse that night. He has done nothing but express concern, remorse and regret for what he has done...especially to you. He is sincere. I know he is. I can feel it through my mind's eye. However, our government is not so sure. He is still under restraint and observation, but trust me, they will come around. Soon he will be released and then you will have another gift from Ranula and the Venusians, a true, loving father."

James sat on a bench in a park, in the dark, alone, waiting for the Venus rising. He thought about the incredible journey that he had begun so long ago.

He was one-hundred-and-forty-six years old. He was the oldest living human on Earth. Venusian science had helped extend the average human life span but even with all that, he was exceptional. What had Scott called him? The Extraordinary-Ordinary Man. He smiled at the thought. That was it exactly, he was an ordinary person transformed to the extraordinary by Ranula.

It had always bothered him.... Why had he survived the Ranula syndrome back in that chamber of horrors on Venus? What made him different from the rest? He had a theory but it took a discovery in Africa just last year to confirm it. By chance, another small miracle, like so many others that had happened to him, a young Archeologist found the remains of one of the original Neanderthal women that Ranula had changed. James traced the genetic heritage of that woman, down the line of human ancestors...*to himself.* He was her direct descendant. His mind was as genetically close to the original Ranula blueprint as was possible and it was the purity of his genetic knowledge that had helped him to overcome Ranula's presence. As he had walked down the corridor on Venus, he was already unlocking...his mind's eye was sensing familiarity and had started the process without the use of the pulsating light. The others had not been as pure; genetic aberrations that had been slowly introduced over thousands of years—generation after generation—caused the Ranula personality to completely overcome the human psyche. When they entered that room on Venus, the human in each of them was overwhelmed and consumed by Ranula. But for James, the human and Venusian coexisted. That was what had saved him. And that was why he had lived for so long, because tucked away in the Ranula personality genetic code was a longevity gene. It had been released along with Ranula. Another gift, bitter-sweet, from Ranula.

The world was a very different place now. Violence and wars were gone. Peace was pervasive. The human population was finally in balance with Nature. There had been great advances in Science. Children were born with the Venusian knowledge released. Thankfully, the children inherited the genetic state of their parents—if Ranula was unlocked for the parent, then Ranula was unlocked for the child. There was only one person that the rule truly affected...himself. He could never have children. The direct line from Neanderthal was about to end. But he didn't mind so much. His ancestral line had done their duty. Their task was complete. They had been messengers—carrying a single message, a warning, across time—for thirty-five thousand years.

He missed his comrades, Scott, Matt and Shannon. They had passed on long ago. He missed Scott the most. He had gone on to greatness, the leader of the unified World for twenty years. James had been honored to witness the birth of Scott's great, great, great grandchild last month. Matt and Shannon had lived a very happy and fruitful life and as with

Scott's family, James had kept in touch with the many Dragonoviches that now populated the planet. Kurt had indeed been permanently changed by the unlocking. For his remaining forty-two years, Kurt did everything in his power to be a good father, grandfather and great grandfather. Jack, who had confessed to the murder of the Astronauts, was, like Kurt, after much debate, released from prison. A world full of love and forgiveness doesn't need to punish.

So here he was, one hundred and forty-six years old, sitting in the dark, in a park, waiting for Venus to rise. He knew his time was near. But he had one more task to complete. A task that he had avoided all these years, a task that he had shoved down, stored away, ignored....

He had to say goodbye to his wife and daughter. He had to say goodbye to Namia and Lillia. He had to say goodbye to his Ranula-self.

He knew how that brave family had planned to face their doom. It was the last thought, the last image that Ranula had genetically encoded before sending the Neanderthals back to Earth. It was his farewell to an unknown race that he had saved. It was his farewell to James.

It seemed he just looked away for a moment...but it must have been longer...there it was...Venus, bright and strong...hovering...waiting...

Ranula took Namia's hand, looked into her sad, sad eyes and said, "Are you ready my, love? My sweet one?"

"Yes, my husband. Yes, my hero."

"Then let us go my love."

Namia took Lillia into her arms and hugged her. She turned and faced Ranula. He reached out and embraced the two of them, with little Lillia snuggled tight between. Head to head to head they became one mind, one thought, one love. The door began to open, heat poured through...for a brief moment the three little figures that had become one withstood the onslaught, then the single, sweet, loving shape slipped to the floor, ravaged and consumed.

Sometime later, a small mound of dust and ash was caught by super-heated wind. The particles lifted and swirled around each other, a small whirlwind of life's remnants, reluctant to dissipate, held there, for a short eternity, perhaps by love alone...

and then

was gone.

The End

Dedicated to the Human Race

May we continue forever, beyond the life of our planet, our galaxy, and perhaps, even, beyond the life of our Universe;
handed down,
from old to young,
from generation to generation,
each time infinitesimally stronger,
each time infinitesimally kinder,
each time infinitesimally wiser.

PG Harding.

PG Harding is an electrical engineer. In the 1990s, he began thinking about the striking similarities between Earth and its sister planet, Venus. It sparked a "what if" that echoed through his mind for the next two decades. What if Venus was once like Earth?

The result of this inspiration is Harding's new book, The Messenger Within. He hopes his work will encourage discussion about Earth's current trajectory and concern about rapid global warming.

Made in the USA
Charleston, SC
28 November 2016